Be Seduced . . .

- In "Roses, Red Room 416," a sophisticated boho sistah addicted to an outrageously sensual lover gets an unforgettable lesson . . .

- When a newly married woman decides to say "Good-Bye" forever to her unfaithful ex-boyfriend, she is swept away by a desperate erotic promise—and faces a reckless choice . . .

- Self-sufficient and savvy, the heroine of "Me Between My Own" searches for satisfaction—only to discover that ultimate sexual fulfillment lies unexpectedly close . . .

- In "Undoings in Amsterdam," a young American lesbian hungry for experience tours a place far off the map, where the rules—and cultural differences—are no match for a transforming desire . . .

Black Silk

Black Silk

A Collection of African American Erotica

Edited by

Retha Powers

WARNER BOOKS

An AOL Time Warner Company

This book is a work of fiction. Names, characters, places, and incidents are the product of the author's imagination or are used fictitiously. Any resemblance to actual events, locales, or persons, living or dead, is coincidental.

Copyright © 2002 by Retha Powers

Contributions copyright: "Jalapeño Love" © 2002 by Bil Wright, "Planting" © 2002 by s smith, "Goodbye" © 2002 by Eric Jerome Dickey, "Kiwi" © 2002 by Jacqueline Woodson, "Fucking the Fat Man" © 2002 by Breena Clarke, "One-Night Stand" © 2002 by Bernice L. McFadden, "Venus in Scorpio" © 2002 by TaRessa Stovall, "Roses, Red, Room 416" © 2002 by Lolita Files, "Stores" © 2002 by Reginald Harris, "The Dawn of Our World" © 2002 by Carolyn Ferrell, "Pisces" © 2002 by Anne Atall, "Me Between My Own" © 2002 by Camika Spencer, "Fish Eyes" © 2002 by Kim McLarin, "Undoings in Amsterdam" © 2002 by Janet McDonald, "The Sexiest Seconds" © 2002 by Kiini Ibura Salaam, "Revelation" © 2002 by Elissa G. Perry, "Summer in the City" © 2002 by Margaret Johnson-Hodge, "Beachwear" © 2002 by devorah major, "The Princess and the Cop" © 2002 by Kathleen Morris, "Popsicles, Donuts, and Reefah" © 2002 by Bruce Morrow, "The Blue Globes" © 2002 by Thomas Glave, "A Different Drummer" © 2002 by Cheo Tyehimba, "Maya" © 2002 by Jennifer Jazz, "The Warm and Quiet Storm" © 2002 by Andrew Oyefesobi, "Sausage Boy" © 2002 by Robin Coste Lewis, "If Only" © 2002 by Krystal G. Williams, "In the Rain" © 2002 by Travis Hunter, "She Cums Every Nite . . . " © 2002 by Jacqueline Powell, "Specialgrl Meets Gntlwmn" © 2002 by Darris, "He Makes Love Like a Woman" © 2002 by Carl Weber, "Mojo Lover" © 2002 by Donna Hill.

All rights reserved.

Warner Books, Inc., 1271 Avenue of the Americas, New York, NY 10020

Visit our Web site at www.twbookmark.com.

W An AOL Time Warner Company

Printed in the United States of America

First Printing: February 2002

Library of Congress Cataloging-in-Publication Data
Black silk : a collection of African American erotica / [edited by] Retha Powers.
   p. cm.
ISBN-13: 978-0-446-67691-5
ISBN-10: 0-446-67691-8

   1. Erotic literature, American—African American authors. 2. African Americans—Sexual behavior—Literary collections. I. Powers, Retha.

PS509.E7 B57 2002
813'.60803538'08996073—dc21

2001045601

Book design by Nancy Singer Olaguera

Cover design by Don Puckey/Julie Metz

Cover photo courtesy of Rundu.com

Contents

Contents

Introduction

Flip the historical coin of black sexuality and we're faced with one of two images. One image cast holds the legacy of the beastly images of wanton black women and sex-crazed black men that gave permission to abuse and silence. These oversexualized stereotypes were married to the other side of the coin—Mammy and Uncle Ben. It was largely the effects of the first image that led to an attempt to counteract the sting of shame by concealing these pictures with a portrait that was upright and chaste, leaving us with a pentimento of our sexual inheritance.

We lacked our own holistic images that would embrace all aspects of ourselves and acknowledge the power and beauty of our passion. Fortunately, we were able to look to strong and creative individuals to reclaim the territory of our sexuality. Although the faces on the coin are still present, artistic and popular images of black folks with full and self-defined sexual selves have subversively emerged. Whether in the form of a bawdy song by Bessie Smith, later screen gems like Pam Grier's Coffy and Friday Foster, or D'Angelo's open sexuality, these artists have inspired a primal response. And whatever you may think of Lil' Kim, she is certainly singing a postmodern version of "Ain't Nobody's Business if I Do." Until recently our own spin peeked through mostly in music, television, and film, so this collection captures an exciting direction for black writers.

Black Silk is the language of body to body, a language that is elusive and essential, specific and universal.

Dear reader, put that old coin in your pocket and immerse yourself in stories through which black writers have minted their own erotic currency. *Black Silk* contains thirty-one original stories by women and men who fully embrace eroticism with incredible diversity. The writers herein represent some of today's best, working in a variety of genres from literary to commercial, from romance to magical realism. Some of the stories celebrate the act itself. Other stories turn us on and tell us something else at the same time. In "The Princess and the Cop," a woman is forced to confront her class issues. In Eric Jerome Dickey's "Good-Bye," the many layers of infidelity are unraveled.

The contributors included in *Black Silk* take on the bittersweet nature of eros, as in Bernice L. McFadden's "One-Night Stand" and Bruce Morrow's "Popsicles, Donuts, and Reefah." Other stories invite us to follow their lovers on odysseys. In Janet McDonald's "Undoings in Amsterdam" and Kiini Ibura Salaam's "The Sexiest Seconds," the journeys take place abroad and lead to self-discovery. For others, the distance traveled is psychically farther than the character has ever been, as in Elissa G. Perry's "Revelation."

Proof that the best sex employs innovation is displayed in stories like Breena Clarke's exuberant "Fucking the Fat Man" and in "The Dawn of Our World," Carolyn Ferrell's engrossing multigenerational tale of lust and its costs and lessons. Wicked humor sets the tone in Reginald Harris's "Stores," which makes us look at grocery shopping in a whole new way.

Everything from the extraordinary to the mundane is woven amid these lusty tales. In many stories music makes a cameo or plays an important role: in Clarke's story, Margaret

Johnson-Hodge's "Summer in the City," and Cheo Tyehimba's "A Different Drummer." As for food, it becomes the language of love. As Jacqueline Woodson points out in "Kiwi," her tale of a singer who falls for another woman's hands, "If it wasn't for food, Negroes wouldn't have no idea how to talk about themselves." I hope *Black Silk* will provide readers with erotic enjoyment and carnal food for thought. After all, life begins with the erotic touch, and we are sustained by it.

Retha Powers
New York, 2001

Jalapeño Love

by Bil Wright

Leave Him and Live. That's the full name of our group, but none of the members actually uses the whole thing. Most of us shorten it to *Leave Him*—as in, "Are you going to Leave Him tonight?" or "I'm gettin' ready to go to Leave Him," and we all know what we mean. Osceola Deadrick and Nelda Battey, the founders, started out calling it *L.H.A.F.G.* for *Leave Him and Find God,* but as the group grew, several of us disagreed mightily on who or what God was or wasn't. Like when the nineteen-year-old who'd just graduated from Yale announced at her first meeting, "God came to me in my dorm room and She's a patchwork-colored woman with breasts and testicles," Osceola was so upset she threatened to resign as secretary rather than record what the girl said in the minutes.

So after a while it was decided that the one thing we could all agree on was that no man was gonna leave us wondering whether we'd survive past the sound of his footsteps fading. Actually, in my case, there wasn't any divorce that left me sighing, wringing my hands. No two-week wonder-if-he-will, I'll-be-only-half-the-woman-I-am-if-he-don't affair leaving me weary and ten pounds overweight like more than a few of the members.

Turtle Washington didn't travel fifty miles from my side without calling to say where he was for the fifteen years we were married till he had a stroke behind the wheel of his UPS truck and drove through the window of a Safeway supermarket. I didn't give myself time to wonder whether I'd survive not having my back up against my Turtle at night, his one hand high between my legs, his rough heel scraping against my leg. "Turtle Washington," I used to tell him, "if you wanna keep rubbin' up against me, you'll get up and put some lotion on those old tough heels of yours." He'd chuckle and ease his hand a little higher between my thighs, but he never lotioned those heels. Not in fifteen years.

By the first anniversary of Turtle's death, I tried to leave a few of those memories behind. I moved from Harlem to downtown and a whole other world, where there were fewer colored men to remind me of my Turtle coming around the corner, staring with his tongue between his teeth like he was seeing me for the first time. Or standing in the middle of the sidewalk pretending to check the sports scores in the *Daily News,* knowing I was coming down the block, watching what the sun did when it hit his lips. Or admiring how nobody could hide the muscles in those calves with wool, cotton, or corduroy.

After I moved downtown, the only time I thought I saw him for sure was when a UPS truck would ease up beside me. I'd look up smiling, knowing I was about to hear him call out, "Old Turtle's got a delivery, baby. A Rotina Special." But it never was my Turtle up there in the driver's seat, and eventually Nelda Battey suggested if I joined the group, I might stop listening for him altogether.

I am proud to admit it was me who suggested at a Saturday Night Potluck that we change our name ever so slightly to "Leave Him and Live," and do you know we voted unanimous on it? (By the way, I have started suspecting that a few of the girls who joined recently are in the group 'cause they decided to Leave Her and Live and they don't wanna tell no one, and that's fine with me. But I do hope they come to understand one day that livin' ain't about hidin'. From nobody.)

Some of us come to Leave Him with our insides so dislocated from our last ten years, ten months, or ten days with whomever we been giving that much energy to, that the first meeting is like a baptism—full immersion. I've seen women run the room like they got the Holy Ghost just because they're so grateful to be in a place where they can wonder out loud how they got to shore and have women who almost drowned to welcome them to dry land. How many times have I seen Nelda stand in the middle of the room like the Great Old Ship of Zion and tell a newcomer, "C'mon girl. What you need is a good old-fashioned hold-on-tight-and-cry hug"?

But the dry-land part—that's the trickiest. That's the part that even today when women are the boldest and the most free-mouthed I've ever known 'em to be, some people still believe a woman who's got any dignity won't talk about being hungry.

And Hungry was exactly the neighborhood I was ashamed to admit I'd been living in for at least six months. I'd Seasons Greeting'd myself through Christmas and redecorated my way through New Year's Eve, but by our February first meeting my L.H.A.L. sisters were wondering if they should chip in for a two-hour massage at the Smiling Muscle Spa (male masseur requested), which several members swore had gotten them through a rough patch or two.

I left the meeting armed with a special herb tea Doreen Chrimney said calmed carnal thoughts and an assurance from Egyptia Nelson that the longer I refrained from having sex, the better it would feel when it finally happened. Neither of these made me feel any less foolish about having confided to them,

"I wish I was talking about a relationship, but I'm not. Sure as I still got my wedding band on my finger, I still got Turtle in my heart. But lately there've been nights when I've gone to bed imagining making love with the driver in an empty crosstown bus, with all the lights on, in the middle of Fifth and Sixth Avenues. And in the Sony Cinema 2, behind the screen with the man who sold me my popcorn, while the audience on the other side was watching the movie. You don't know what I'm going through!" Doreen and Egyptia pulled me into a tight circle of three, whispered the Serenity Prayer over me before I left, and promised to call regularly for support.

I was still shaking my head in regret at having told them, knowing full well it would take about an hour before everyone else in the group had heard about my dreams as well. On Ninth Street, hopscotching my way around some dog business, I jumped even wider to avoid tripping on two big cranberry-colored cowboy boots growing out of a tenement stoop. I frowned at the owner to let him know he wasn't making my life any easier.

"Easy now. You're going to wind up in my lap." At a glance, I decided he was Puerto Rican. With a salt-and-pepper mustache curling around an insulting sneer.

"Not in this life." It was my way of cursing at him without getting knocked into the pile of dog crap I was trying to avoid.

"Well, you have a good evening anyway, sweetheart." He sounded like he'd decided to ignore my snarling and bless me. With a Spanish accent.

By the time I got to my apartment, I'd stomped myself into a substantial pout. I boiled some water and made a mug full of Doreen's Higher Plane Tea, throwing a shot of cognac into it. I slammed the refrigerator door so that all the magnets fell off, letting my Xerox of the L.H.A.L. mantra slide to the floor. I stooped to pick it up, staring at a photo of myself glued to the side. Originally, it was a picture of me and Turtle on the Circle Line boat that goes around Manhattan. I'd cut it in half when I joined the group, as a reminder that I had a responsibility to the one of us who hadn't gone through the Safeway window. Above my head was printed in large purple letters, EVERYTHING THAT TRULY GIVES ME PEACE, I CAN FIND IN MYSELF. A MAN ONLY GIVES ME SOMEONE TO SHARE IT WITH. I stuck my finger deep into the mug of hot tea, honey, and cognac, then slowly up the center of my tongue and farther down into the back of my throat. Soon. Let the sharing begin.

It doesn't feel unusual for me to be coming down the street carrying a mug of spiked tea, although I can't remember ever doing it before. What is stifling, though, is my winter coat with the rabbit collar buttoned up around my neck. I know it's the end of July, so I don't know why in hell I have it on in the first place, but I sense I don't have any choice—it's the only thing I own right now, which isn't exactly a calming thought by itself.

What does seem to have a soothing effect is the sound of singing farther down the block. I know I'm getting closer to the singing because it gets louder, but no matter how close I get, I can't seem to understand what language the singing is in. I'm pretty sure it's Spanish, though, and it's a man's voice. When I get right up to him, I know it's Spanish I've been hearing because it's the man in the cranberry cowboy boots from the stoop. As I get closer, I have to blink my eyes because I am so shocked to see the boots are all he has on.

Well, this time I cross to the other side of the

street because I am not at all interested in whatever
he's exposing right there on the stoop. And I know
this has upset me somehow, because if I thought I was
perspiring before, I can feel the coat clinging to me
now, at the small of my back, under my breasts, and in
between my legs. I can feel that the entire outline of
my body is there for all of Ninth Street to see, as
though I have on a wool skin-diving suit, and I'm
damned humiliated and angry at the same time.

I decide to take a quick look back to see if maybe
I haven't made the whole thing up, and sure enough,
there he is—Mr. Puerto Rico, stark naked with his legs
wide open and that damned sneer on his face.
Grinning at me. Like a lunatic.

The next week I avoided Ninth Street. I suppose my dream
embarrassed me so much I was afraid I might run into Mr.
Puerto Rico again and he'd somehow know he'd mattered
enough for me to dream about him. Exposed like that.

Saturday night, though, at our L.H.A.L. meeting, Ainah
Trotter spoke on Staring Down the Obstacles, and as much as
I find Ainah goes a little heavy on the dramatics when she's
giving her Personal Experience Testimony, I found myself picturing Mr. Puerto Rico again and decided I should definitely
take Ninth Street going home. It was silly for me to avoid an
entire block because of a man I was probably never going to
see again. And as it turns out, I was almost right.

When I got to the corner, all the stoops were clear. I let out
a breath that made me realize I'd been holding on to it, and as
I started down the block, I smiled thinking of how Ainah had
finally closed her testimony by telling us to remember, "Just

when you finally have the courage to look at those obstacles close up without flinching"—and I thought of how foolish she looked doing her version of a flinch—like she was about to be struck by a bolt of lightning and bit on the backside by a rabid Doberman at the same time—"very often," she told us, "those same obstacles have shriveled up and disappeared."

At the same time it was occurring to me that I might want to try to remember a few details of what Mr. Puerto Rico had looked like in the dream. I could admit to myself that the dream had not only been abundantly specific but was also not altogether unpleasant, considering the man was a complete stranger to me.

"You're on my block a lot, aren't you?"

I jumped, instinctively clutched my purse up under my breasts with one hand, and reached into my pocket for my open safety pin with the other.

"Man, why are you always trying to catch somebody off guard?"

"Truly, truly I am sorry. If there'd been any way to give you a warning, I would have."

There it was again. And if it wasn't a sneer, it was the best damn imitation of one I'd seen. I marched away from him, calling back, "If I'd had any warning, I'd have gone in the other direction."

"Now you see how you are to me? And I was going to send you a valentine."

Bastard. I'd gone to the meeting early and stayed late trying to ignore the fact that it was Valentine's Day Eve. Egyptia Nelson, who's got to be somewhere around the same age I am, claims she's had her share of valentines and she's content. She says Valentine's Day is for the card companies to get rich on;

it's only one day on the calendar, and if you occupy your time wisely, you won't notice. Well, I think Egyptia is beginning to sound older than I ever want to feel, 'cause when Valentine's Day comes on the fourteenth of February, I notice.

There were lovers giggling in the A&P, nose to nose in the ATM line, holding on to each other in the Chinese laundry, slapping butts coming out of the YMCA, and the couple in front of me hadn't even stopped kissing long enough to answer how many coffees they wanted at Starbucks. The man just held up his hand for two and paid for them with his mouth still glued to the little blonde's he was with.

"I'm going to wish you a Happy Valentine's Day, anyway." Mr. Puerto Rico was right next to me. I thought he might be exaggerating his accent. He was probably used to revving it up, using it on women who were susceptible to having their ears opened a little wider by a foreign tongue.

"Don't you have anything better to do on a Saturday night than run up and down the street harassing women?"

"As a matter of fact, I have a young lady waiting for me now. But when I saw you go by, I could not pass up the opportunity to come out and say, Hello. *Buenas noches, señorita.* Happy Valentine, beautiful lady."

"And you left another woman to come out here to speak to me?" I suddenly realized that I had actually stopped to have a conversation with this man.

He shrugged and pointed behind him. "She won't mind. She has at least another twenty minutes under the dryer."

He was pointing to a small hairdresser's shop that I'd never really noticed before. It had two oversize flowerpots with white birch trees in them on either side of the doorway. The name of the shop was written in turquoise-blue script that I couldn't read from where I was standing.

"And she doesn't know her man is out here in the street trying to hand a silly line to a woman he doesn't even know. In Spanish."

It wasn't as though I hadn't seen it before. But it had definitely been years and then some since I was the woman being run out to. Well, I've never been desperate enough to stand openmouthed while someone was feeding me a line. I turned to go. He hurried alongside me.

"It's true we have never been introduced. But then you have never stopped long enough for an introduction." He held out his hand. "I am Cortez Rojo Picasso Velasquez. And the woman under the dryer is not my lover. She is my seven-thirty appointment."

"Excuse me?"

It wasn't as though I hadn't heard him. I'd heard him as if there'd been no other sound in the streets. Mr. Puerto Rico grinned so that the one part of his body I hadn't paid much attention to, either live or in my dream, opened in front of me like a velvet drape before a wide white movie screen.

"I'm the lady's hairdresser."

And I was trying hard to take it all in. His announcement, his teeth, the full tan lips that framed them, and the mustache with hair thicker than most women's I knew, dark with silver strands, smiling back at me. More silver at the temples and the nape of his neck. The same as me except he wasn't dyeing his 'cause he must've known it was right on schedule and in exactly the right place. This was more information than I'd had to deal with in a very long time.

"You, you work there?"

"I do. She is my last appointment for the night. If you would consider giving me your number I could call you when I am finished here and maybe you would allow me to take you to dinner. That is, if I knew who to ask for when I dialed your number."

Oh, he was smooth. Yes, indeed, he was. Like Wesson Oil in a hot iron skillet. And this is how I sounded.

"Rotina. Rotina Washington. But I can't go. To dinner. Tonight."

And it's not that I could tell you Mr. Velasquez wasn't real easy to look at, because even if my tongue wanted to start, some other part of me would be whispering, *Rotina, you're lyin', lyin', lyin'*.

"Of course. It's the short notice. I'm sorry, Miss Washington. But you inspire the impulsive in me. Whenever you say. You give me the night. I'll make the reservation."

I looked down at the cranberry cowboy boots with the gold tips, trying to figure out how I could buy some time to think about this without making any commitment—but without turning him down flat either.

"Why don't you give me your number? I'll go home and check my datebook and give you a call."

"Ah! Fantastico!" This Mr. Velasquez shouted, like a ten-year-old at Christmas. "Come to the shop and I'll give you my card."

"I'll wait outside." What would it look like with me coming in there like some gullible schoolgirl waiting for the man to give me his autograph?

He ran ahead. I walked slowly behind. Before I even got to the door, he was back outside already waiting for me. I tried not to go right up to the window where I could be seen, but he wouldn't move from the doorway, holding the card out to me and flashing those white Mercedes teeth. I took the card as quickly as I could and mumbled, "Yes, well, you take care," trying to sound as if I was used to doing something I'd never done before in my life.

He called out, "*Hasta muy pronto!*" which could have been something disrespectful except for the way he bowed when he said it. I hurried across the street determined not to look back, which I didn't until I had prayed, *Please God, if you love me, please don't let him still be there.* And even though I always tell myself God's gonna get tired of me testing Him like that one day, He's never failed me yet. Mr. Velasquez had gone back in to his seven-thirty and I was able to stop long enough to get a good look at where he worked. It was small but clean looking, up to date, I suppose. But nothing could have prepared me for what was over the door. In big, turquoise script it said, PICASSO'S SALON DE BELLEZA and next to that was a neon mustache curling over a pair of full lips. I looked at the card and there it was again. Mr. Velasquez was Picasso! And even though I knew he wasn't the real one, I didn't even think Picasso was Puerto Rican! Well, even if it was just Mr. Velasquez being extravagantly ambitious by calling himself Picasso, I thought it was kind of admirable. It meant he had vision. In those cranberry-red cowboy boots with the gold tips. Picasso. I'd dreamed about Picasso. Imagine.

I carried his card around with me for almost a week before I decided what to do. On Friday I called him at his shop.

"I would say to you that I was beginning to give up hope," he told me, "but number one, it sounds like a line from a bad movie, and number two, I wasn't giving up hope because that is not who I am. I can be disappointed, yes, but I was taught by a very determined woman to never give up hope."

I was impressed, but I refused to sound like it. When he asked me to pick a restaurant, though, I was stumped. "Oh,

I'm open," I told him and immediately regretted my choice of words.

"Well, Rotina, I will have to think of a place with enough light for the rest of the room to see how lovely you are, but romantic enough for me to begin to say the things I've been thinking these past five days."

On one hand I thought Mr. Cortez Rojo Picasso Velasquez was coming on like a local train makin' express stops only, but it was also true I had pretty much given up ever hearing anything that even resembled a seductive routine. Turtle's idea of seducing me was calling to say he was gettin' off his shift early and that I should wait up 'cause he wasn't a bit tired.

Mr. Picasso told me he knew the perfect French restaurant, Les Deux Fleurs, and we agreed to meet there at eight-thirty. He wanted to make it earlier, but I decided to go to my L.H.A.L. meeting, if not to share my news, to at least center myself for the evening ahead.

One of the reasons I didn't feel comfortable telling my Sisters about Mr. Picasso was that there was a not-so-unspoken code among the members that part of sexual sanity as an African American woman means restricting your dating to African American men. Egyptia even went so far as to say, "Stick to men who look like you. Don't no man make you crazier than a man who's got it in his mind that every time he enters a black woman, he's conquering Africa." And she got an enthusiastic chorus of "amens" on that one.

At our dinner at Les Deux Fleurs, Mr. Picasso told me ever so patiently that I was a little hasty in deciding he was Puerto Rican. He told me his father was from a small village in Spain and his mother was Haitian. I was feeling too ashamed of my ignorance to say anything but, "Well, that certainly must mean you're good at languages," which I knew was ridiculous as soon as I'd said it. I told him about Turtle as though he was the only family I'd ever had, and maybe for the moment he was the only family I felt it was important to mention.

The romance that Mr. Picasso had promised for the evening was as potent as the wine he ordered, and when common sense told me to choose one over the other, I put my glass down and concentrated on that mouth. I remained sober enough to stop at my apartment door and say, "It was *muy bien, gracias,*" which I learned from the Berlitz paperback I'd picked up at the ShopRite on my corner. Then I reached into my bag and presented him with my business card. I'd sprayed it with White Diamonds and made sure I'd included my home phone in lilac ink, but I'd printed it out so he could definitely read it, which wasn't always the case with my script.

Mr. Picasso called me on Sunday afternoon to say how much he'd enjoyed Saturday night and even slipped in that he'd gotten a good night's sleep, but not before taking a very cold shower. I pictured what I'd only dreamed about standing at half-mast in his shower and giggled after I'd hung up. I'd agreed to meet him Wednesday night for an early supper. He said, "I've got a late appointment at seven-thirty again, but if we met in the neighborhood at, say, five-thirty, I could get back in time. Would you mind? I do so want to see you sooner rather than later."

Of course I didn't mind. Mr. Picasso suggested an Indian restaurant called the Taj Mahal on First Avenue. He brought me a single sunflower with another business card that said, "Picasso would love to run his fingers through your hair. Join me for champagne and a hot-oil massage. Anytime. After business hours." I smiled slyly as he watched me read it. "I'll let you know," I told him, munching poori.

On Saturday night I insisted that we meet a little later so

that I could go to L.H.A.L. I still hadn't gotten up the nerve to tell the girls, but I'd made a decision concerning Picasso and I wanted their blessing, even if they didn't know they were giving it to me. Picasso wanted to take me to Harlem to Sylvia's Soul Food. Sylvia's is a little touristy for my taste right about now, but the corn bread was still good enough for me to ask for another basket, and I did lick my fingers once or twice, wishing there was one more chop hidden under my fried onions.

Once we got back downtown to my apartment, I barely made it out of Picasso's arms. When I'd locked my door behind me, I ran to the window, watching him cross the street and stroll slowly down my block with his hands in his pants pockets, under his coat. I smiled to myself. Maybe he's playing with his change.

I closed the blinds and took off all my clothes. I sat on my couch in just my heels with my legs spread wide. I pretended the couch was the cab we rode down to the village in and Picasso and I were in the backseat. Picasso was on his knees in front of me; I could see his smooth back and his shoulders in the streetlight. But nobody including the driver could see what Picasso was doing to me or see me holding on to his hair with both hands as his head pressed between my thighs on the leather seat, trying to open me wider, wider. And my heels dug in to the floor of the cab and because I wanted to open them even more for him, for me, because we were both so greedy, I lifted my legs onto the top of the front seat and I held on to Picasso's silver curls, telling him, "Yes. Deeper. Deeper." And he's on his knees, hungry, and there's more—yes—more where that came from. Yesss. And my legs are moving—uh—up the partition toward the ceiling of the—oh—cab. Yes—ahh—yes-ye-ye-ye-ye-yesssss.

During the next week I told every member of L.H.A.L. I'm close to about Picasso, except I didn't go into the Haitian-Spanish part. I considered those details saved for a later date or debate, as I realized it might turn out. All the girls acted surprised and pleased for me, which is the only way you can act unless you want people to suspect you're jealous that one of your sisters might be rediscovering parts of her body and mind she's numbed like a dentist so that the cavities can be filled. Now, everybody knows you don't want to go around Novocained all the time. Tongue, teeth, and gums all got their purpose. It's only when you're trying to fix them that you might want to desensitize 'em for a while.

I told my sisters that I'd decided to cook for Cortez Rojo Picasso Velasquez, which they all decided was genius on my part. Cooking is one of my God-given gifts. I'm not too experienced with international cuisine, but a good cook is a good cook in any language, and it occurred to me that if I could pull off a couple of tasty Spanish dishes, I would not only be very proud of my courageous, adventurous self, but it would be the perfect aphrodisiac for an evening at Rotina Washington's with Mr. Cortez Rojo Picasso Velasquez.

There were Spanish markets in my neighborhood, but I decided that putting together a menu on my own was too risky. I tried to think of who might help me, but I'm embarrassed to say that my circle of friends is fairly small and extremely conservative in their eating habits. For most of them, going to a restaurant like the Temple of Thai after a Saturday-night meeting is a walk on the wild side.

I came up with the idea of going to Pacquito's, my local neighborhood Mexican restaurant. I wasn't sure if Mexican was the same as Spanish, but I'd ask, and if I was showing my cultural ignorance, I'd start again at the beginning. I took it as a sign of good luck that Pacquito himself was there, in his white shirt and pants, standing over the stove.

"*Hola!*" I called to him, a word Picasso taught me. Pacquito smiled and nodded. If he remembered me at all, he remembered I'd never been that friendly before. "Mr. Pacquito, could I speak to you for a moment, please? I'm having a small dinner party and I need your advice."

After the first twenty minutes trying to convince me to hire him to cater the evening, complete with homemade flan for dessert, Pacquito finally admitted there was a difference between Spanish dishes and Mexican take-out. But he convinced me they had enough in common that if I listened carefully to him and followed his instructions, I could prepare a relatively simple meal with a Spanish flair that he guaranteed was the place to begin, but would not be where my evening with Picasso would end.

"The secret"—he paused for a moment, I'm sure to give me some drama—"is jalapeños." He smiled very slowly and raised one eyebrow. "You want your evening a little hot? You let him know."

"Well, I'm not sure that's what I had in mind," I lied, "but I'll definitely pick a few up."

Pacquito's advice was to keep my dinner simple. Quesadillas, beans (not too many) and rice topped with guacamole, sour cream, salsa, and finely chopped jalapeños. A small salad on the side with healthy lettuce, avocado, tomatillo sauce, and, again, finely chopped jalapeños. A bottle of Spanish rosé, and I took the easy way out with dessert. Homemade flan from Pacquito's.

I bought a CD of Spanish guitar music called *From Madrid with Love*. It had a photograph of a bullfighter's hat on the floor next to a pair of backless pumps at the foot of a bed, and I knew somebody thought it was a sexy picture, but I swear to you the first thing I thought of was that this bullfighter was wearing some woman's shoes before he'd gone to bed. But I went ahead and bought *From Madrid with Love*. It was the only thing I could be reasonably sure was Spanish for real, besides Picasso.

When I heard the buzzer, I was putting a few more chopped jalapeños in the salsa to liven it up a bit. They were hot enough to make my makeup run, but I knew Picasso was probably used to them. I threw the last few bits into my mouth. My tongue felt like I'd put it over an open flame. What the hell did I do that for?

Not only was I proud of my dinner, I knew I'd created an atmosphere where I could feel comfortable. In L.H.A.L. a woman learns that it's fine to be the seducer, especially if you feel you can be safe should you change your mind. I watched Picasso's butt as he strode across my living room to study my bookcase and I was pretty sure I wouldn't be changing my mind.

We ate dinner practically in silence. Picasso communicated by putting his hand across the table over mine and squeezing it gently, like a promise. Or tucking a bit of jalapeño back into my mouth and leaving his finger between my teeth for a moment as I bit it, gently.

He said he was surprised at my menu, but that he was flattered and it didn't matter whether it was authentic Spanish or not. "The point is," he told me, "you have a generous soul, and that is a gift." I was preparing to be even more generous and hoped that he had a gift.

We were up and dancing to a ballad called "My Spanish Guitar," which Picasso said was one of his favorites. My fingers ran down his spine; then I used both hands to feel the meat of his back on either side. He held on to me, clasping just above my hips. I leaned back so that he had to get a firmer grip. Turning in his arms, I felt Picasso's guitar against my behind.

I reached back and took his hand, leading him to my bedroom. I lit candles, which I'd placed around the room, and checked for both safety and flattering shadows.

"No," I told him as he reached beneath my dress's shoulder straps. "I want to undress you." Picasso looked surprised for a moment, but then he smiled wide and nuzzled my neck with his mustache, traced the same pattern with his open lips. As I unbuttoned his starched white shirt and slipped it back to his shoulders, he was still smiling. Picasso's shirt slid to his elbows and I slid down his body, reaching around his waist. I pulled gently at each sleeve, and his shirt fell onto my bedroom carpet. Picasso's hands were out to the sides. I looked up at him. As I expected, he was more than ready to let me have my way. But he was breathing harder and I could feel his ass muscles tightening under my palms. I pushed my head into his groin and he moaned softly.

I unbuckled him and took his black dress pants and pale blue boxers with their navy blue stars on them down to the top of his boots. When I looked up now, I saw the guitar between me and Picasso's smile. Now I haven't seen that many instruments, but this was certainly one of the finest, from the rich deep color of the wood, to the healthy, muscular shape, to the energy and life it had just waving there above my head. Picasso leaned down slightly and laughed. "*Hola. Hola, señorita.*"

On my knees, I smiled back. "*Hola,* yourself."

He reached to lift me from where I was kneeling, but I had no intention of stopping. I'd never made love like this before, taking the man for myself before I let him touch me. It gave me a feeling I wanted to remember, one I knew I could grow to really enjoy.

I opened my mouth wide and took one of Picasso's balls in, releasing it quickly. I went to the other side. He arched back and groaned. I started up the shaft of his dick with my tongue and stopped at the head. Sitting up quickly, I stared up at him. I was Rotina Washington, Conqueress. I held on to Picasso's dick as I eased up onto my bed and reached into my nightstand drawer. I'd bought Lifestyle Mano Grande Sensitivo. I didn't have that much practice, but we had a special meeting at L.H.A.L. on Good Sex and Living to Tell about It. We practiced on bananas and all the girls teased me on how well I did putting the condom on it with my mouth and then oral-sexing it down.

I was able to tear open the package without letting go of Picasso's dick. With the condom in my mouth, I moved my fingers gently up the shaft and parted the lips. Picasso's entire body tightened like an iron clamp. I was enjoying my Woman in Charge Sex. I placed my finger directly into the eye of the guitar. Picasso's face turned the color of eggplant and I thought, *I'm better at this than I expected. Go easy on him, Rotina. Make it last, girl. Make it last.*

Then Picasso screamed as though I'd bitten the head off his dick and wouldn't let go. "Aaaaaaah!" I released him and rolled backward onto the bed. "What is it? Tell me! What did I do?"

"It's burning! Burning! Aaaeeeeee!"

Picasso ran into the bathroom as quickly as he could, considering his pants were at his knees around the tops of his cowboy boots. He'd stopped screaming openmouthed, but he was grunting now, like he'd been shot. I was right behind him, feeling helpless, confused. What had happened that quickly?

Watching him at the sink throwing water onto his dick, I put my hand up to my mouth, terrified. What? What? Oh, no. No, it couldn't be. Slowly, behind him, as Picasso continued to dance in front of the sink with his dick in it as far as he could get it, I held my fingers over my nose and breathed in my answer. Jalapeño.

Cortez Rojo Picasso Velasquez was experiencing Rotina Washington's Jalapeño Love. It had been a long, hungry time in coming and now my Picasso was trying desperately to cool his dick from the heat of my touch. Oh, Rotina Washington. Jalapeño Love! Who, at Leave Him and Live next Saturday night, would ever believe me?

Almost an hour later Picasso and I lay on my bed eating flan and Breyers Vanilla Nut. I'd made an ice pack with one of my best towels and placed it between Picasso's legs. He'd told me about twenty-five times it wasn't necessary, that he was perfectly comfortable now. He'd even looked down at his crotch and joked, "I'm afraid to tell you, it has seen much worse." But he quickly apologized, realizing I was still too shook up to find it funny and it certainly wasn't my idea of romantic.

Picasso stayed the night. I began to dream as we held each other. I remember rolling over onto my side and thinking for just one moment of pulling Picasso closer behind me and guiding his hand up where I'd missed a hand as I slept. I felt his foot slide up my calf, but I shifted slightly so that he had to move it.

"Sing to me, Picasso," I whispered. And he did. His own funny, lovely version of "My Spanish Guitar."

Planting

by s smith

The collective rays of the September sun bear into her back and shoulders. It is an intense, deep-heat treatment. Slowly her anger at Jack flows out of her, down her brown arms, into her fingers, and into the deeper brown of the earth. On hands and knees she labors, using the small shovel to turn the dirt. The smell of earth is like fresh-cut, raw potatoes. Subtle and sustaining. It is aromatherapy and the sun is the masseuse.

Small beads of sweat, like delicate pinpricks, spring across her forehead and along her top lip. Short breaths softly escape through her slightly parted lips each time she bends, stretches, and digs. With each release of breath goes another angry thought: Jack's words urging her to sell her grandmother's home; Jack's smug assurance playing along the corners of his mouth when he smiles. He is so sure that she will leave this place and live a life of urban bondage.

She develops a comfortable rhythm—bend, stretch, dig—planting bulbs of narcissus, jonquil, and gladiolus. She continues a rhythm developed by her grandmother, continued by her mother, and passed down to her. True, she and Jack do not live at this house and have slowly allowed the four-hour drive to become more burdensome. But knowing that the place was there provided a foundation for her. And she never misses a September planting her bulbs. She remembers the joy on

Grandmother's face as the blooms and fragrance signaled the beginning of spring.

This year she has carefully prepared the soil, just as Grandmother showed her, adding just a touch of vermiculite so that the right amount of moisture would succor the bulbs. So intent on the digging and careful planting, she jumps when she feels a trickle along her side. She laughs as she realizes it is a rivulet of sweat.

Sitting back on her heels, she gently dabs the sweat on her brow by pressing the back of her forearm against her head. This only spreads the sweat, however, since her forearm is also wet. She enjoys the sun massaging her scalp with its filament fingers. She closes her eyes and silently blows out the last bit of tension she is holding. Sweat trickles down her back, slowly, like fingers playing gently along her spine.

A minute turning of the soil draws her eyes toward the damp, cocoa-brown-colored dirt. A pink, questing head lifts from the soil. Eyeless, it waves about before diving into a patch of dirt next to itself. She watches it as her sweat rolls down her back and meanders down her cleavage. Her shirt begins to cling to her as if shrink-wrapped. The worm's body, a rich magenta muscle, smoothly enters the earth. It hardly disturbs the soil, she thinks. She wishes, just for a second, that her efforts at gardening were so graceful.

Bending forward to continue with her planting, she pauses, not wanting to harm the worm or his mates. Funny that she had not considered them before. She sees another pink head rise from the soil, twisting about. She does not know if it is the same worm or a different one. Curious, she gingerly digs with her hands. The grains of dirt scrub her flesh with a gentle roughness. Soon she feels a rolling movement against her palm and freezes. Looking carefully, she lifts the dirt and lets the earth sift through her fingers. Two magenta bodies remain in her palm, coiling and twining together, seeking the soil. Their heads press insistently into her palm. Their bodies turn and stroke her hand.

Fascinated, she watches them contract then expand, moving until they, like the earth, slide through her fingers back into the fresh-turned dirt. What must it feel like, she thinks, to feel the soil all over your body? The worms writhe as if in extended ecstasy. They ride the dirt, rolling and turning endlessly. Their questing heads search and search for the source of their delight and they dive into the dirt with exuberance. In a minute they have sensuously wiggled their way back into the earth.

Sweat trickles from her scalp and rolls down her neck and over her breasts. The fecund smell of soil wafts into her. The sun has climbed higher. The crest of dirt shows dry, tan patches like an ocean shows whitecapped waves. The sweat travels down her stomach. It feels cold against her skin. She licks her lips and tastes salt. She savors its flavor.

Sighing, she takes off her shoes, pushing each heel with her toes so that the shoes fly away from her and thud against an uncultivated patch of ground. Careful to avoid the earth in which the worms have entered, she puts her feet into the cool dirt. She wiggles her toes in the soil, enjoying the rough crunchiness.

The sound of muffled steps causes her to look up, squinting into the sunlight. Jack is just a dark silhouette against the sky. They are frozen for one of those timeless seconds. Jack looking down at her, feet covered in the soil, and she looking up at him, made faceless by the bright sun's light. The quiet in the garden is like the hush of a cathedral. The sound of birds and the buzz of insects seem to intensify the sanctity.

To her surprise, Jack bends and puts down a bucket and a

gardening shovel. In two strides he is sitting opposite from her. He begins to remove his shoes. She watches his hairy knuckles as his caramel-colored fingers loosen each lace. Once freed, the yeasty smell of his feet mingles with the loamy scent of earth. He digs his toes into the soil and leans back, resting the weight of his body on his hands. The black hairs on his toes are in stark contrast to the pale, ginger-colored skin on his feet. His feet, obviously, have been hidden from the sun for some time.

The cooling dirt and the twittering of sparrows carry the weight of words, the need for words, away. Through the dirt, Jack's feet creep toward hers. Their toes touch. Jack's foot rubs the gritty dirt against her instep. Sweat has sealed her blouse tightly against her back, and her skin is suffocating. She pulls the blouse over her head and tosses it away.

Jack's foot continues to massage hers with the rough dirt. He almost smiles as she throws her blouse away. Slowly his foot works its way until it rests on her calf. He looks at her, waiting. Smiling, she leans toward him, as if to kiss, then gently rubs her dirt-covered hands against his cheeks and over his neck. The dirt mixes with his sweat, creating muddy smears over his skin.

"Umph!" he says. Picking up a handful of soil, he sprinkles it over the top of her head, as if it were baptismal water. It tumbles over her face, onto her shoulders, down her chest, sticking to her sweaty skin.

Her response is to lie down and roll in the drying dirt. Over and over, back and forward, until she is dusty and muddy. His laughter cascades over her like sunshine. Her mahogany flesh prickles with warmth. She sits up and leans toward him until her face is resting in his lap. He smells of earth, and she sighs.

Lifting her face, Jack looks into her eyes. He smiles. With both hands filled with soil, he tenderly holds her face in his hands. He kneads the soil into her cheeks. She presses her face into the scratching grains of dirt, eyes closed. Suddenly she falls forward. She catches herself before she falls, palms digging into the dirt where Jack had lately been. Lithely he stands above her, offering her a hand. He leads her to the garden hose, smiling.

The cold water causes her to breathe in quickly. It flows down her scalp and over her body. She begins to shiver in the warm sunlight. Jack steps toward her, awkwardly holding the water hose, pressing it between their two bodies. It bubbles like a fountain under their chins, held in place by his chest and her breasts. With a free hand, Jack unfastens her pants. Wet, they fall heavily around her ankles. Water splashes her in the face as Jack struggles to pull his T-shirt over his head. The water hose gets free and scatters iridescent drops around them. She helps him shimmy out of his pants. His boxers sag with the weight of water. His member, languidly rigid, bobs against the wet cotton.

Picking up the lost hose, Jack turns and sprays her. Sputtering, she lunges at him, but he dances away, the hose again flying and scattering water around the yard.

The sun shines warmly on the flower bulbs. They sit neatly in a tray, waiting to be immersed in dirt, where they may thrive until spring calls their flowers forth. The water from the garden hose flows and creates a small lagoon. From inside the house the sounds of quiet sighs and the patter of water hitting bathroom tiles mingle and add to the occasional chirps of birds and the steady drone of insects.

Good-Bye

by Eric Jerome Dickey

The sun was setting as the last of the golden-brown leaves fell from the trees. A few had refused to change from green to rust colored, even though it was time for a new season. A mahogany leaf caught my attention as it was carried away by the winds, blown out of my sight, beyond reach. I wondered if it had voluntarily fled its haven, or if some force had expelled it. With closed eyes, I imagined where it might finally land as it pirouetted and fell three floors below.

Then there was a knock at my door. My heartbeat quickened, my palms so wet. She was here. I wiped my hands on my jeans, counted to seven, opened the door, and she stood there in the dim lights of the hallway.

Her black hair in a bob with a hundred strands of premature gray adding salt to her cosmopolitan and conservative look. Her dignified, schoolgirl smile actually widened when our eyes met; then it vanished, as if the memory of what had happened between us had returned in full force.

I saw her, and then I was sixteen again, staring at the wonderment of a woman, my hormones out of control, making me realize how much of a man I was, how much I was a primitive who had bowed down to social order, wanting to touch the breasts of a woman, of that woman, to invade her mystery.

She whispered, "Never thought I'd see you again."

Her hands were folded in front of her, as if she wanted me to see the wedding ring on her finger, drawing a thick line.

I asked, "You coming in?"

"You wanted to talk."

"Yeah."

"So talk."

"You promised me that when things slowed down we'd get together, maybe meet at a coffeehouse, get a cup of cappuccino, and talk, see if we could try again—"

"Things changed."

"You married him."

"Yeah. I did what was best for me."

"And I had to read about it in *JET*. Why didn't you tell me?"

She shrugged. My heart was in her hands, small hands that were slowly closing into a fist, and she shrugged like it was no big deal.

She'd been married two weeks. A big diamond was on her finger.

She came in, didn't take her coat off, strong body language that told me this would be a brief encounter, and drifted toward the window.

She said, "It's cold. Don't think it's ever been this cold in Palmdale."

"Yeah. Ice was on the freeway. It's a record low."

Then a moment of silence as she watched the tree outside my window.

She said, "Only one leaf left. That's weird."

"Yeah. Weird."

I moved next to her and we watched that leaf struggle to hold on.

I asked, "Are you happy?"

"On my honeymoon, I was in Maui."

I made a *hmm*ing sound, the tune of jealousy and envy.

She went on: "You ever see the golden sunset in Maui? Ever watch the sun sink into an endless body of clear blue water?"

"No. As far as we ever went was a four-hour ride to Vegas."

"Well, it's life changing. You see it, the colors, the majesty, the hugeness; you feel so small, feel the power, experience the tranquillity, and you know there's a God."

"Sure it's not the mushrooms?"

"Hush." She sighed and her smile turned upside down. "I was in beautiful Maui, a ring on my finger, a man who told me he loved me more than anything, and in that moment, when contentment should've been the blanket that kept me warm, I was chilled by my own restlessness."

We watched the leaf for a little while, afraid to put our eyes on each other.

She whispered, "I need closure."

"That closure have anything to do with me?"

She nodded. "Has everything to do with you."

I nodded and smiled. "Sounds like that old song."

"What song?"

"The one about—are you gonna stay with the man who loves you, or are you going back to the one you're in love with?"

"Do you love me?"

"Yes."

"Unconditionally?"

"Yes."

"Enough to want me to be happy?"

"Yes."

I wanted to hug her. But she kept herself feet away, arms folded, closed off from my world, the world we used to share.

She chuckled. "I think about you, my stomach jumps, my coochie jumps; all kinds of things happen to my body. Today, knowing that I was going to sneak away and see you, well, I went through two pairs of underwear today."

"Is your coochie jumping now?"

She cleared her throat, looked at her watch, sighed again. "This is the only time you'll ever see me. I came here because I want you to respect my marriage."

"Cut the bullshit. You came because you want to see me."

"Stop calling my job. Don't ask my parents about me. Set me free."

"Setting you free will only make me a prisoner."

"Love me like you say you do. Let me go. Please."

All that mattered was what was in this room.

I moved into her space, unfolded her arms, put them around my shoulders, put my hands around her waist, my warm cheek against hers.

She said, "Please, sweetie, don't do this."

The moment our flesh was reunited, I kissed her lips and her tongue eased inside my mouth. She quivered, moved her flesh closer to mine. I closed my eyes, my breathing desperate as I held her so close that I couldn't tell where she ended and I began. My hands traced along her waist, found the snap at the top of her jeans, then the buttons below.

Her hand came down to my hand, and when I thought she was about to push me away, she said, "Let me help."

"No, let me undress you."

"Wait. I have to do something."

She pulled away, shifted foot to foot, sighed, took her wedding ring off.

We paused, stared at each other.

She swallowed, pulled her lips.

So did I.

I pulled up her sweater and touched the small of her back, caressed her face, brought her tongue to mine. My hand pulled her jeans down to her knees, then my fingers went down below.

I said, "Damn, you're wet."

"I know. Believe me, I know."

I massaged the dampness on her black lace panties, touched the outside of her vagina, these fingers tracing along the edges of that place where all men come from and yearn to get back inside, tracing circles, then moving in and out in tune with her craving, playing a melody of lust on that part of her that swells when she's excited.

She said, "Don't wrinkle my clothes, sweetie."

"You've never worried about that before."

"Just don't wrinkle my clothes."

On the living room floor I pulled everything away from her, piece by piece. Put them neatly to the side. Then I kissed her breasts while I loved her with my hand. My fingers moved away and my tongue took their place, wiggling, licking, becoming the flesh that excited her genitals. Her eyes fluttered, breathing heavy, mouth barely parted. Over and over she said yes, yes, yes.

I wanted to love her back to me. I wanted this to change her mind, change her heart, make her forgive me.

She unzipped my jeans, hurried her hand inside, pulled on that hardening flesh.

"Your penis is so beautiful. I love the way it curves to the left."

"If you won't come back to me, come back to it, then."

I swelled with her small hands on me. Her thumb tracing my dampness as it seeped, whispering in a vulnerable tone that she wanted me inside.

I said, "You know what I want first. Go ahead."

Her mouth surrounded my girth, did that while her hand moved me up and down, mouth and hand playing in harmony, creating so much heat inside me. She moved her mouth away but kept using her hand when she raised her head, moved her hair away from her face long enough to look across the room at the clock. Then she put her mouth back on me.

She said, "You have a big dick."

"Compared to whose dick?"

"Hush."

I laid her back on the carpet, and she parted her legs with the grace of a ballerina. Then with a bright smile she moaned, "Inside me. I want you inside me."

I paused, teased. She begged, reached for me, pulled me, put me at the edge of her opening, and the moment I felt the warmth and wetness I glided inside that moist, hidden world she owned.

Her soft wails became music. "Yes, sweetie, yes."

I squinted my eyes and sang the second chorus: "Yes, baby, yes."

Her short nails marked the walls of my tropical skin, leaving hieroglyphics that spoke of her pleasure. She held my ass and moved into me, bucking into me when it started feeling too good.

"Don't stop, sweetie. Don't stop."

Her love was coming down; trembles had taken over her body. Passion had her tongue. I looked in her face, watched her glow and orgasm. When she was done, she got on top of me and did the same, moved up and down, did that intense rise and fall until my face glowed, until I trembled and pulled her to me over and over.

Then we rested side by side, her leg over mine, our sweat mixing. We rediscovered breathing. I could hardly raise a finger. I had to search for the energy to try to talk. I didn't know what to say. She reached over and touched my dick. Held it. Squeezed it. Made it flop side to side.

I panted, "You okay?"

"Yeah." Her voice was distant, barely audible. "Fine."

She kept on flopping my dick, making it smack one leg, then the other.

I asked, "What's on your mind?"

"I'm lying here, on a wet spot, your come draining out of me, so warm and sticky, trying to decide if you're the best lover I ever had."

"Well, am I?"

"If not, you're a runner-up."

"To who?"

"Whom, not who."

"To whom, then?"

She didn't answer. And she didn't stop flopping me. It started to sound like a pendulum, like a clock that was ticking, tocking, ticking, counting down.

She said, "You've never loved me like that before."

"I know."

"Is it because I'm married?"

"Maybe."

"Because you can't have me."

"Maybe."

Silence. She stopped flopping me, rose to her elbows, and again craned her neck, looked toward the clock.

I tell her, "I love you."

"People aren't looking for love. They want financial security, emotional security. They need and want to be desired."

"If you add that up, that's love."

"I guess. The quest for pleasure."

Again, her eyes go to the clock.

She spoke in a whisper. "And trust. Gotta have trust."

I touched her breasts, rubbed the nipples with the tips of my fingers, felt them harden.

I asked, "Where's your husband?"

"Knicks are playing the Lakers. Told him I didn't want to go."

"What? You don't like Kobe?"

"Overrated."

"Shaq?"

"Overpaid."

We laughed. And I wondered if that was the last laugh we would share.

I said, "There should be a black box to relationships."

"What do you mean?"

"Like on an airplane. When it crashes, there's always a black box that can tell you where you went wrong."

"You don't look at a black box until after the crash. Until it's too late. You learn what you should do to keep from crashing the next time, 'cause it's already too late for the flight you were on."

I didn't say anything.

She said, "You're my black box."

Her hand drifted back between my legs, touched that soft and wet, meaty part of me, each motion telling me she would miss what she felt. Her mouth followed her hand, tasted for a while, made me rise; then she kissed me, giving me back that salty flavor. She kissed me and gave it all back.

Then I took my body to hers again. Eased inside wishing I could trap her here forever.

She said, "You've never gone for a second round this fast."

I watched her face; became so excited by the glowing, by her craving. Then, after a few moments, her back arched in both pleasure and torment. I held her hips and eased in and out, did it with an intensity, still watching her the whole time, taking in the details of her face, listening to her sex sounds, all that good moaning telling me that she was falling into the abyss, into the bowels of a sweet sin.

Her hands grabbed my ass, pulled me into her hips. She kissed me over and over, kissed me and told me, "I need you to set me free. Let me be married. Let me be happy."

"You talking to me or my dick?"

"Whichever part will listen to my heart."

Outside, the wind was singing, trees leaning with the rhythm.

She wanted me to go faster, deeper, not to slow down, not to stop. She came hard, howled like the winds. I came harder. She panted. I panted. Panted and kissed until we had control, until the heat started to get cold. Then we rested next to each other, winded, sweaty, restless.

I asked, "What are you thinking?"

"Wondering if you said the same things to her when you fucked her. Did you tell her how good it was? If you made the same silly face you make before you come. If you held her and pushed deep inside her the same way you did me when you were about to come. Wondering how it tasted when she sucked your dick."

"It always goes back to that."

"It's never left that."

"That's why you married him."

"You broke my heart. I was pretty fucked up behind that."

"We can work it out."

"I can trust him. He loves me."

I rubbed my face against her breasts. Her breasts were soft, the nipples as black as my lonely nights of grief. My tongue found its way down her skin, lapping the traces of sweat on her flesh, over her navel. Her legs opened and I licked her for a while. So many sweet sounds escaped her face.

When I slowed, came up for air, I said, "I can make it better."

She shook her head. "Your sex won't heal me. Don't be like every other man and think that you've been born with miracle genitalia."

She pushed my head away and rolled over on her stomach.

I said, "Let me finish."

"No. You're so fucking good at that. Too good at that."

Silence. My eyes went through the darkness, toward the window, tried to find the little brown leaf that was struggling, holding on for life.

She told me, "He's nice. I've never been with a nice guy."

"Ouch. What kind of man am I?"

"Well, I asked for your soul and you gave me your dick. You tell me."

I put my hand on her. She pushed it away.

She stood and spoke with unmistakable pain. "You should have given me what I wanted. Sweetie, you should've given me a lifetime commitment before someone else took your place."

"It's not too late."

"I'm married."

"Get a fucking annulment."

"And do what, end up right where I started?"

"I've changed."

"Bullshit."

She made a long airy sound that, in the same breath, spoke of her regret and told me I was a fool.

Then she gathered her clothes. Put her wedding ring back on. Opened her purse and took out her own soap.

I said, "You brought soap."

She didn't answer. She had her own soap so she would smell the same way, the right way, when she got back home to her ignorant husband. She had planned this. Knew how this would go before she knocked on my door.

"Want me to shower with you?"

"No. I can manage."

"Okay."

"Shower cap?"

"Same place it's always been."

She went toward the bathroom. The door closed. The shower came on. I remained still, the stickiness that we had made drying on my flesh, its scent worming into my pores, nesting in my nose, the taste of her on my tongue, easing into my system, mixing in my blood, setting fire to the insides of my head. I imagined her with her husband. Anger made my teeth clench. My eyes filled with tears.

Five minutes passed. She stepped into the hall, wrapped in a soft blue towel. Her wedding ring was sparkling in the hall lights.

I said, "You still have things over here."

A slight nod telling me that she already knew.

She pulled the paisley shower cap from her head, dropped it into the black trash basket next to the sink. She went through the cabinets and saw that everything was as she had left it months ago. She piled all her toiletries on the counter and carefully packed them into a clear plastic bag. Then she dropped that plastic bag into the trash as well.

She eased into her ripped 501s, put her hand over her breasts, then politely slipped by me into the living room. She found her black bra, folded it, and stuffed it into her back pocket. Then she pulled her pink sorority sweatshirt from under my golden sweatshirt, pulled it firmly, as if it has been trapped but now was rescued from the weight that held it down.

I tried to think of something to say. I couldn't. No arrangement of words had any meaning.

She kept wiping her hands on her butt, rubbing her neck, touching her face, tugging at the belt loops on her jeans, pulling her dignified hair away from her silver earrings.

She did everything but look at me.

Standing in the mirror, she unsuccessfully fought back the tears.

"Eyeliner's running." She smirked. "I've got raccoon eyes."

She walked over to me, took short steps. Then we strolled through the door and began the long journey down the poorly lit, water-stained, green-carpeted hallway. We held hands as we waited for the temperamental elevator that always came when it was ready. When the elevator took too long, I followed her lead down the three flights of shaky stairs. Felt her body sigh as we leaned into the winds and crossed the leaf-littered parking lot.

The leaves danced with our slow pace across the cracked asphalt.

When she got into her car, it started without hesitation. After looking at me for a second, she slipped back out and stood next to me.

"Don't end up alone the rest of your life," she whispered. "Be better to the next girl, okay?"

I nodded. "So, this is it."

"Gonna miss you."

"Maybe sometime in the future we can get together. Maybe we can actually get a cup of cappuccino and talk."

"Nope. All you'll try to do is slip inside and ride my wild side."

"I really do love you. You know that, right?"

"Then let this be the end of it. Let this be our closure. We ended it the way we began it."

First the final hug, then the last kiss. Then I let her go.

And just like that, with water-rimmed eyes, she got in her car and drove away. I prayed for her brake lights to come on, followed by the bright taillights letting me know she'd put it in reverse. She moved forward.

The wrought-iron gate rattled as it slid open, a rusty wail of pain. My eyes were in her rearview mirror, but she never looked back. Her car accelerated, turned left; then she was gone. My throat tightened.

I walked over to the tree. Watched that one stubborn leaf, watched it hold steadfast against God's frigid breath. The winds gradually died. The leaf fell, twirled and pirouetted, landed not too far away. Maybe it wasn't as strong as it pretended.

I whispered, "Good-bye."

Kiwi

by Jacqueline Woodson

Mercy says it's Kiwi's hands that make everyone act so stupid around her. Says Kiwi knows it and you can tell by the way she holds them, press out in front of her like she's praying but the prayer's aim at you, legs spread, elbows on her thighs. It's those hands but it's also those thighs that seem to go on forever, and even those elbows, the way the sleeves of her shirts fall down across them when she's sitting like that. Mercy says the whole package makes you want to holler. Says Kiwi's no joke.

Some days I get all confused, don't know if I want to be her or be with her. I picture us together—two girl-boys, all straight edges and sharp lines. Mercy says she feels some of that about Denzel Washington—especially when he walks on to the screen like he did in *Devil in a Blue Dress*—wearing just an undershirt and those khaki pants. *Denzel's no joke,* Mercy says. *I'd rather have him over anybody. But him and Kiwi got cut from the same bolt of fabric.*

❀

Saturday night we go over there, bring our clothes underneath dry-cleaning bags; Mercy's got her makeup in a case. Kiwi lives on the East Side, Lower East Side, way over near the river where the people walk right up to you and ask what kind of dope you looking for. Mercy tells the first guy that comes up to us she's got someone who'll show him what kind of dope we looking for, he don't watch what he's saying. The boy walks away backwards, holding his stuff and cussing at us. Mercy doesn't play that—been clean for nearly ten years and can't even stand the smell of pot. Me, I get nice every once in a while when the mood hits me or someone's offering something to take the edge off my day. Most days I'm temping for the All Call Agency. They're good about sending me on long-term gigs. Nights, I practice my singing. Once in a while I get a gig with some fellas playing the clubs. I sing "Smoke Gets in Your Eyes," and people sway side to side and nod like they're remembering something from their way past. On a night when I'm feeling brave, I'll do Tina Turner's "Private Dancer." That song makes me sad, though. Makes me think of all the nights I slow-dance naked in front of the mirror, watching my own body move with just the dim light from the living room coming into my bedroom. Sometimes, if the moon's out and coming in through my window, my skin looks goldlike and I find myself running my hands slow over my breasts and down between my legs.

With my eyes closed, I can imagine it's Kiwi's hands, her fingers pushing my thighs apart and moving slowly up inside of me. Then the music stops and I'm back in my own apartment, alone. And if the moon's gone on behind a cloud, my skin doesn't even look goldlike anymore. Loneliness can eat you whole and leave you standing. Some mornings heading to work, I feel a sadness so deep I want to moan. If I have a gig the evening after one of those mirror dances, I usually see tears in my audience's eyes.

I pull my bag of clothes tight to my chest and follow a step behind Mercy. She's tall and broad shouldered, brown and pretty. Says the next person that uses some sort of food to describe her skin coloring is looking to have their head pulled off. Brothers always saying "Hey, Sweet Chocolate" and "Brown Sugar" and "Miss Truffle." Mercy say she can't stand how people don't have any sense about description. Look in the mirror, she says to me one evening. I look. See my same self staring back at me. Big eyes. Hair pulled back into a braid. Nose is just a nose and lips Kiwi once called *juicy* in a way that made my insides dance around. Teeth white and straight and strong—a gift from my mother's family. One dimple when I smile. People always surprised by it. Some say "Oh!" and nod—like they're seeing me for the first time when it creeps into my cheek. It's right below my left eye. My mama had a dimple there and her mama and so on all the way back, I hear. Mercy says, "What color would you call yourself?"

"Brown."

"What kind of brown?"

"Caramel."

"See, that's the problem," Mercy says. "If it wasn't for food, Negroes wouldn't have no idea how to talk about themselves."

Mercy always finds a way to say something to make me laugh; then that dimple comes out and she says Pretty Girl Ray, which makes me smile even more. Ray from Raylene from my father Raylen. My family's from the South—near Anderson, South Carolina. When I was in school there, there were three other Raylenes in my class. One of them was my half sister. When we figured it out, we thought it'd be like that movie *The Parent Trap,* when those twins discover each other after years going without knowing the other existed. But it wasn't like that. The other Raylene had heard my mama was trash and I'd heard the same thing about her mama and after that first day of sitting in the schoolyard eating our lunch together then walking everywhere all hugged up, smiling like we'd won a million dollars, we couldn't stand each other's guts. Didn't go a single day after that first one without getting into a fight. Raylene's mama finally pulled her out of that school. Some evenings I wonder what became of her—the other Raylene Tyler walking through this world.

⚜

By the time we get to Kiwi's building I'm already out of breath, and then there's five flights of stairs to climb on top of everything else. Mercy takes them two at a time because she runs six miles a day and stairs aren't anything to her. I hear her up above me knocking on Kiwi's door; then I hear her and Kiwi talking and laughing and carrying on. By the time I get up to the top Kiwi's standing there, that one-sided smile she has on her face, shaking her head. My stomach gives a little leap up into my throat and I nod hello, trying to breathe through my nose so I don't seem so tired.

"Work out much?" Kiwi says, holding the door open for me. I shrug and smile, stepping past her into her apartment.

"Can't breathe enough to even talk," Kiwi says. She takes the clothes I'm carrying and points me toward the couch.

Kiwi's wearing a suit—black with a black shirt underneath it and patent-leather shoes. She has a bit of eye makeup on— some liner, that's all, and a tiny gold dot of an earring in her nose. Her hair's short and curly. She's put some gel or something in it to make it look wet. Her hair's blacker than anything and she says it's probably gonna stay that way. Says her Indian—straight from India and not some fake Native-American relative—grandmother had jet-black hair till the day she died at ninety-two. Kiwi gives me another half smile, pours me a glass of water and Mercy a Coke, then sits down on the couch.

"This club might not be as tight as Dixie," she says. "I hear it's all right, though. You ready to kick it, Birthday Girl?"

I take a sip of water. "I guess so."

So far all I know about twenty-three is that it's as trifling as twenty-one. Inside, I still feel lost half the time—like the world is happening over there to my left somewhere. I want to be thirty—like Kiwi and Mercy—know where I'm going and all, have a bit of life behind me. In the corner of the living room Kiwi's police officer uniform is draped neatly over the back of a chair. Even though I can't see it, I know there's a badge that says WINCHELL right above the breast pocket. Officer Winchell. Kiwi Winchell. Kiwi catches me staring at her uniform and a slow smile spreads over her face. I look away from her, not smiling but not frowning either.

❧

I met Mercy two years ago on the corner of Seventeenth Street and Fifth Avenue. One morning I was coming from a temp gig and she was going to one. When I stepped out into the street, she pulled me back just as a cab raced by, saying, "Hey Lil' Sister, you too pretty to be killing yourself this early in the morning." We walked a ways together after that, and by the end of the walk we were friends. I'd been in the city for six months then and didn't know many people. Turned out Mercy lived just a few blocks from me. Turned out, too, her family was from Charlotte, and she threw out a couple of names I recognized. Felt like home.

Kiwi came along later. I'd gone over to Mercy's to see if she wanted to walk some. It was August. The city was hot and my small top-floor apartment was hotter. Kiwi was sitting on

Mercy's couch. What I remember was her left hand palm up in the air, those long fingers the first part of her I ever met. Later on I found out she was showing Mercy a cut on her palm, a tiny nick of a thing she'd gotten cutting a bagel. Narrow but deep. Three stitches like tiny black crosses across the pale peach of her hand. Then she turned full toward me, and her eyes caught me hard. Figure none of that day's anything I need to tell Mercy. And Kiwi, figure she must already know.

Mercy's been in love more times than I can count. Men act stupid around her, and in return she pays them some attention every now and then, then gets bone tired of them before they can think of something clever to say. Some evenings, when me and Mercy are just sitting on the fire escape drinking Cokes and watching the city pass beneath us, she starts talking about what she'd like—a good man, a nice home. Maybe a kid or two. I look down at the people moving around on the sidewalk and wonder how many of them got someplace good to be, somebody to love when they get there. Mercy's eyes hollow out and I think she thinks she's never gonna get what she needs. When she gets that look, I tell her—don't get sentimental; the love she's looking for is out there somewhere. She's a good woman, Mercy is.

"What do you want, girl?" Mercy asked me one night.

I shrugged, took a sip of my Coke. Stared down at all the people moving by us. All different colors and loving every which way.

"To sing," I said.

"You do sing already," Mercy said. We were sitting close and she nudged my shoulder with her own. "You sing like a bird, girl."

"To really sing," I said. "From way deep. Hurt people with my singing. Knock them down with it and lift them back up again."

Mercy nodded. "That'd be some singing."

❊

The first time somebody told me I had a voice was when I was ten and singing in my church's choir. Even then I knew I was only about seventy-five percent holy. The rest of me wanted more than Jesus and "This Little Light of Mine." The rest of me wanted to fly. But more than that—even at ten, I wanted to know something, *someone*. And love them deep.

❊

When we get to the club, it's loud and smoky but the music is pumping. All around us brothers and sisters are getting tight at the bar or loose on the floor. Mercy's wearing a long red dress that cuts halfway across her breasts and promises more with a high split up the back. She dances in ahead of us and gets scooped up by a pretty dark-skinned brother in leather pants. He doesn't look anything like Denzel, but Mercy's smile is saying Denzel *who?*

The DJ throws TLC's "Unpretty" on and I am taken right back to my bedroom mirror when I feel Kiwi's hand pulling me onto the dance floor.

"Pretty girl," she whispers, leaning into my ear. The mirror disappears. The loneliness lifts up off of me. Kiwi moves slower than the music and still it's like the music is moving her. No hips to speak of but the place where hips should be is swaying around me and I find my own self moving closer to her, scared of the lead my body's taking over my mind. I know once she and Mercy were close like this, but then Mercy decided she was more into men than women. I know Kiwi was so hurt, they didn't speak for years, and then they were speaking again but it was different, strained sometimes, like ex-lovers but most times like family, like sisters. Different but connected nonetheless, all but choking on their spit when someone brings up them being together once. And then Kiwi fell in love and stayed in love for a long time. Then that love thing ended and Kiwi went back to just being a cop. A different Kiwi. Sadder, Mercy says. Quieter. A Kiwi that was waiting for something. That was a year ago.

I look across the dance floor and see Mercy's got her arms around that brother and her eyes closed, that red dress flashing. And something about the flash of that dress makes me feel brave enough to pull Kiwi into me. She looks surprised, then laughs, presses her hand against my mouth and says, "We got seven years between us, sweet girl. Seven years is seven years." She lets her hand move around to the back of my neck and down into the collar of my shirt—a navy button-down tucked into black pants. A wide black belt with a silver buckle—a birthday gift to myself. My hair is pulled back into one braid so from far away maybe we look like two slender men on the dance floor—Kiwi's the beautiful one.

Kiwi once told me her parents didn't name her for three days. "They wanted to see who I was first," she said. "And they came to realize that I was sweet and sour as their favorite fruit. I don't mind—it's easy to spell and easy to say."

Now, she slips her hand out of my shirt and smiles again. I feel the smile spread over my body.

"I want this," I say, pulling her hand back to my neck. *This is what twenty-three is,* I'm thinking to myself. *It's the year you get brave, girl.*

"Want what?"

"Whatever's all in those seven years."

Then Kiwi's grinning, all the while holding me by my belt, holding tight, pulling me into her. The DJ throws Sade on, singing "Lover's Rock," telling the whole club that we're the ones that she clings to. I take a step closer to Kiwi, move slowly in her arms. Sade's voice brings up a sadness in me, a loneliness so deep, I need to swallow hard to hold it down. Kiwi moves with me, stroking my back and humming. We stay this way long after the song ends.

Fucking the Fat Man

by Breena Clarke

Her legs were soupy with drink. She laughed to herself. She had been laughing to herself much of the night. She had got tickled when he was singing and smirking and joking on the stage. She had thrown her head back and guffawed just like her mama told her never to do. And she was giggling to herself ever since. She giggled again now and her legs collapsed under her. He caught her under the armpits and supported her. Left to herself she would have sunk in a pool at his feet.

She braced herself on him and pulled herself upright. She walked ahead into the vestibule of the building, and her butt swung from right to left. Her dress, a garment of ambiguous design, was made of a material that draped and flowed. It clung only a little across her hips and across her breasts, lightly dancing around her moving body.

Her hair was looking silly now. Tufts that had been caught up behind her ears were standing out from the side of her head. The hair at the edges of her face and at her nape was frizzy from perspiration. She had stopped caring about how her hair looked several hours ago—when she'd gone into the ladies' room and assessed the damage OLD GRANDAD was doing. It didn't matter anymore. She knew they'd reached the point in the evening when they'd both decided to go after "it."

He periodically tugged on her dress to keep it from riding

up on her butt. He seemed concerned for how she appeared. She thought how silly it was that he was trying to keep her in her clothes until he could get her inside the door of his apartment. Soon as he got her inside he'd be pulling and hauling and working to get her out of this same dress. And for her part she was keeping up with the charade. Was she really as toasted as she seemed?

While he fumbled with his keys she fell back against him. She let herself fall and keep falling into the soft flesh of him. He caught her. His arms were everywhere. That's what she liked most about him. His arms were so fleshy. There was a lot of him, period. She could fall back, lose her balance, fall into him, and never hit the ground.

Going through the door of his apartment he pinched her left ass cheek and said, "Sorry, baby, my hand slipped." A laugh exploded out of her lips. He rolled his eyes around in his head to look like a cherub who had gotten his arm caught in a cookie jar. This kept her laughing long after the joke had passed.

With the door closed and locked behind them, he tossed his hat onto a chair. He said, "Let me take your coat, baby." It was in-between weather—late March. The wrap she wore was not exactly a coat, but a jacket. She giggled again and tried to work her arms out of the jacket. He worked at it and was finally able to get her arms free.

"Plant yourself, baby," he said, waving a hand airily toward the divan like he was Mrs. John Jacob Astor.

He ditched his coat in the closet and came around to the front of the couch. He wanted to remove her clothes slowly, but she hurried him along. They fumbled and their fingers became entwined with each other and with the buttons. They yanked one off. The button dropped and rolled under the couch. She laughed to see it roll away and thought immediately after that she'd be cursing herself tomorrow morning when it came time to have that button or go out in the street half naked.

She stood naked before him for a moment—looking at him from up under her eyelids. She batted her lashes seductively in a way that seemed right out of the movies. She teasingly unhooked her bra and came close to him, thrusting her tits in his face. He didn't touch her breasts. He only looked at them like they were twin pools of water and he had crossed the Gobi Desert without a drink. But all he did was look.

He put his hands on her shoulders, turned her away from him, and found her spinal cord. He ran his fingers up and down the interlocking bones in her back like he was playing piano keys. He said he was trying to get a feel for her back. It seemed like he was funning with her—as if his hands didn't know what to do, but were exploring her. He played arpeggios on her. His fingers were like little hammers pummeling her. Her body got to throbbing, her breath came short, and she grunted.

The majority of rounders that a girl meets in the nightspots figure the best way to get any pussy is to get a girl so juiced up she doesn't know her ass from a hole in the wall. But his hands—his fingers were better than alcohol. Of course she was juiced, but she didn't have to be. What his fingers were doing would have been enough.

He told her to lie down on the divan and close her eyes. Then he started to finger her sure enough. He ran his fingers up and down her back and front. He had her thrilling to his touch. She felt herself to be good and oiled and she started singing to the accompaniment he played on her backside and her stomach. He put his fingers in places she didn't know were there. His fingers plunked and thumped on her and caused a whole lot of trembling and moaning.

"You want to get you some delirium tremblin's running up and down your back, don't you, baby!" He whooped and hollered just like he did on the stage. She laughed along with him even though she didn't know what he was talking about.

Most of the men she'd known didn't use their hands for pleasure. They mostly used their paws for wrestling some kind of living or shoving somebody's face into a wall. These men had gotten out of the habit of touching things gently—if they'd ever learned it.

His touches were gentle and because of this they were shocking—surprising. It felt for all the world like he'd gotten under her skin—like he was fingering her from the inside. Because of that she got a little scared. But she wasn't scared enough to want him to stop.

His lovemaking was like the stuff that Grandma an'em called "The Laying On of Hands." It was like what the old people used to do if you had a bad croup or some other internal problem that was beyond them and they couldn't get you to the doctor. "The Laying On of Hands." They'd try it. They'd all put their hands on you and pray and rub on you. Sometimes it would work. His hands were like those old people's hands: firm, authoritative, soothing, and digging down deeply below layers of skin—reaching the areas that needed comfort.

He took his clothes off oh so slowly. She was glad of that. She wanted to get used to the sight of all the flesh. She wanted him, but she was scared she might be scared by his bulk when she first would lay eyes on it. This slow performance increased the excitement, too. She was curious. Everybody was curious to see what was up under there—in there—what he was like under his clothes.

Actually it wasn't as big as the rest of him. It was normal sized, but it seemed much smaller because of the way it was nestled in among so much other meat. It looked sort of small and pitiful and sad all up in there. He'd waggled it and talked in a silly voice. He urged her to pet it and make it feel less forlorn for being lost in among his hair and all. She giggled again while she fingered the thing and it started to growing like Topsy.

After he got completely naked he went and rooted around in the closet by the door. He came out butt first—his huge ass coming out coyly like a virgin—the ass cheeks moving to a swaying, seductive melody that he hummed. She laughed despite feeling like she shouldn't. He was acting so silly! When he turned himself upright to face her he had on a big red-and-orange turban. There he was before her: a great huge man naked except for the turban. It oughtn't have affected her the way it did. She oughtn't have gotten hotter and juicier and wilder between her legs. But she did.

He was the Sheik of Araby! He sat in something like a cross-legged position on the divan, and when he reared back she could see his dick was as hard as granite. The thing was pointed toward the ceiling.

"Impale yourself, baby!" he said.

Giggling again, she did her best to. She lowered herself onto his whacker and sat on his thighs and he hoisted her, pulled her ass cheeks apart, and bounced her up and down while licking her ears, saying funny things, and tickling her.

In the movies the things that make people all hot and bothered are pretty things—pretty-looking people and pretty, fragrant flowers or a moonlit beach, girls with shining eyes. But what really gets the gut bucket and gets the mouth to twisting up in the most ugly twist that feels like died and gone to heaven is—mostly ugly. It's not so pretty as in the movies. It's worms of sweat cascading down the center of the chest and the myriad stinky smells on your fingers that smell better than Chanel No. 5 when you got your thing on. Like Grandma say, "It's not the beauty, it's the booty." It's the funky little, greasy little things that're caught up in the crevices of the skin.

She sniffed her fingertips, changed hands, and smelled the fingers of her right hand. Exquisite! She was driven along by the music and knew she would come soon. The intricacies of his piano fingering were thrilling her—thrilling the insides of her ears. And she translated that thrilling ear pleasure to her fingers and the device between her legs. You don't waste no time explaining it to nobody else if you do it for yourself. The CD got to the end of itself just at the time she got to that end place. She switched off the vibrator after she'd trembled and grunted. It slid to the floor beside the bed. She continued fingering herself gently—calming the furious pleasure. She *umph, umphed* like he would have done—like she knew he would have done. She'd learned herself by listening to his music. It was all there in the way he'd sung his lyrics decades ago. He showed her how to do it. It was what he taught—he was the professor. He gave her the ultimate permission. "Pleasure yourself, baby. Don't wait for nobody else." This was his best advice.

One-Night Stand

by Bernice L. McFadden

It begins beneath the broken sounds of conversation and an old Marvin Gaye song someone is playing for the third time on the jukebox. There's the dull sound of darts hitting the speckled corkboard at the back of the bar and the low hum of the Knicks game on the television above my head.

"What ya having?" the bartender asks and leans forward on the arm with the hula-girl tattoo and the name SHONA below it. He washes me in the gleaming green blue of his eyes, and I smile and respond, "Dewar's on the rocks," as I adjust myself on the round hardness of the stool.

I sip and wait for the right one to come through the door. I watch from the safety of the bar mirror that sits behind the rows of liquor bottles. I watch, sip, and wait.

I am on my second Dewar's by the time the right one walks in. He is tall, lean, and as dark as the winter night that has ushered him in. Our eyes dance and trip over the colorful tops of vodka, cognac, and chablis before finally finding each other in the looking glass. The Knicks score two points above my head and he pulls up a stool beside me.

He nods to the bartender for his usual and blows warm air into the palms of his hand before finally saying hello and then leaning back to snatch a glance at the game and allowing his eyes to drop down to see how much of my behind the stool was unable to hold.

I've already decided to give myself to him even as the Knicks lose the game by two points and someone curses them from somewhere off to my left.

He grins at me over the rim of his glass and then offers his name before he drinks from it. I don't catch it the first time and so I say, "Sorry?"

He leans in close to repeat it and I close my eyes against the heat of his mouth as it singes my earlobe and travels through its corridors. I cross my legs so that my skirt can rise and he can see the thickness of my thigh and know that I am worth having.

He notices and orders another drink. "Another for you?" he offers. I nod my head yes and unbutton the top of my blouse.

For a while there are no more words between us; not that any would matter. His touch is all that I need now because I know his flesh will speak to me and tell me all that I need to know. As if reading my thoughts he lifts my hand and begins to runs his fingers across my palm, marveling at the length of my lifeline while his eyes beg me to undo a second button.

Me, I just smile and think of the length of his cock as it tries to reach out to me from behind the gray wool of his pants.

His name, already spoken twice, is still just a wisp of air in my head. I forget even that when he begins to roll the tips of my fingers between his own until I gasp and pull away.

I could take him right there, right up against the bar, but I don't, I wait.

He smiles a bit before running his tongue across the full

brown of his bottom lip. He says something that I don't hear because I'm concentrating on his hands; they've found my shoulders and the knot of frustration in my neck and I begin to melt beneath the soft, steady kneading of his touch.

I've already decided to give myself to him even though he's still working at trying to get me.

And I still can't recall his name, but it doesn't matter because I've lost myself in his eyelashes, which are long and curled like a woman's, and I'm wondering what it will be like to kiss his eyelids and run my tongue down the center of flesh between his eyes.

There's heat moving out from between my thighs and I've begun to take irregular breaths and my nipples are shamelessly pushing out from beneath the thin silk of my blouse and I chance a glance at his eyes and I know he knows I'm ready for him. He motions for the bartender to bring the bill.

"I'll get that," he says, and touches my hand as I reach for my purse. The bartender moves the white slip of paper across the bar. It's a sensual motion that makes me think of our bodies moving across bedsheets, and I finally give in and undo the second button.

I need to get up and use the rest room, but my panties are so wet that they're hanging nearly down to my knees and that's embarrassing enough, not to mention the sopping sound they're sure to make when I start walking, so I just squeeze my thighs tighter and imagine that he is between them.

We leave, arms linked, and hold each other like longtime lovers as we stand on the corner to hail a cab.

It's exciting, being next to him in the dewy darkness of the taxi. His hand clasps hold of my thigh and moves across it in long strokes that start at my knee and end at the place the elastic of my panties begins.

His pinkie finger curls around the hair there until I grab his face and kiss him hard on the mouth. We don't speak, we just breathe, and then he slips his finger beneath the material and finds the piece of me that is hard and throbbing.

The driver watches us in the rearview mirror as my hands grip the worn leather of the seat and I swallow to keep the groan that's pushing up from my throat.

We go to my place, and I slip the key in the lock and laugh to myself about how at ease I feel at allowing this stranger into my house when I don't even like to let the cable man in.

I drop my pocketbook to the floor and take his coat while he admires the painting that's hanging over my fireplace. I see the strength in his back and the pride in the broadness of his shoulders and I think that I might want this one for more than just one night.

We move to the bedroom. I light a candle and turn the radio to a station that I know will play quiet songs of passion and hope that when I remove my clothes he won't notice the truth about my body. I hope that he is a gentleman and that he will ignore that damned white tag that's screaming MIRACLE BRA SIZE 34B! because I haven't had it long enough to wash that reminder away. I hope that he won't look twice at the way my belly protrudes after I've removed my control-top pantyhose or make a comment about the gray that's begun to invade the black triangle between my legs.

The nearness of him and the alcohol have my head spinning and I try again to remember his name even as we peel our clothes from our bodies and he climbs on top of me and begins kissing my neck and the side of my face.

Our tongues never dance and our lips barely brush because kissing is more intimate to me than sex so I won't allow his tongue in my mouth, but I will allow his dick in my body.

He eases up and I kiss his chest and suck a bit on his nipples. I wrap my arms around him and inhale his cologne. He eases up some more until his heart is beating above my head and his penis is staring me right between the eyes. I know what that means; I laugh out loud then but I don't say: *If I didn't allow your tongue in my mouth do you think I'm going let your dick in?*

"Uh-uh," I say and grab him by his shoulders and usher him back down until we are face-to-face again. He gives me a look that says: *A brother's gotta try.*

His fingers find that wet space between my legs and they move in and out of me like a slow bow over violin strings and I create music for him when my body shivers and explodes.

I watch him as he dons the condom he had plain as day in his wallet behind the fifty he used to pay for our drinks. I check again with my free hand to make sure that it's secure before I let him in.

His strokes are long, slow, and even, letting me know that he's good at what he's doing and doesn't need me to guide him, so I let go of his hips and allow my hands to stroke his face and play with the stubble on his chin.

His breathing quickens and he is whispering words of want in my ear and it's then that I notice the clean space on his finger, the one next to his pinkie.

I dry up somewhere between the fourteenth and fifteenth stroke because there is no love between us to keep me moist. My grip on his shoulders slackens, and my mind and body lose interest.

"What, baby?" he breathes, and then pulls out so he can flip me over and take me from behind.

I flip even though what I really want to do is sit up and say get out, but it may be another six months before I drink Dewar's on the rocks again, so I oblige and I flip.

I think that it is easier for him in this position; he can look down on my ass and the curve of my spine and imagine that I am anyone, even his wife. His strokes are short, fast, and almost violent as he slams into me. He doesn't call my name when he reaches his climax; he just pulls at my hair and grunts.

I don't cum but I do push against him and grind slowly until his groans subside and I know I every drop of his seed has been spent.

He kisses the back of my neck and the small of my back before pulling out of and rolling away from me, letting out a sigh and dropping off to sleep.

I stare at the ceiling and wonder about love.

It's nearing 4 A.M. when he starts fidgeting and begins to slide even farther away from me until he can sit up and start fumbling through the sheets for his boxer shorts.

I still can't remember his name, but it doesn't matter because there is a Mrs. who has the same. I pull the sheets up around my body before flicking on the lamp on the nightstand. I watch him dress and hope that my staring doesn't make him feel too uncomfortable. He slips on his oxfords and straightens the seam in his pants before our eyes meet and he lies, "I'll call you later."

I walk him to the door and he pecks me on my cheek and walks away without looking back once. He doesn't have my number, I don't know his name, so I know later will never come.

Venus in Scorpio

by TaRessa Stovall

There were three messages in a row from Marcus on my answering machine. He'd been calling nonstop for a couple of days, but I hadn't felt like being bothered. It always amazes me how men heat up when you ig 'em. I'd been experimenting with celibacy for the past six months—a definite change of pace for yours truly—because love and/or lust tend to pull me off track, and it was time to return to Nicola's groove.

I rolled my eyes and started to erase Marcus's messages, but something stopped me. Marcus and I had kicked it for a few months back in the day. We'd enjoyed lethal chemistry, genuine affection, and more than a few sensual pleasures. Still, I'd had to cut him loose.

See, Marcus is superlicious phyne. That's his greatest asset and his biggest problem. No matter what part of the male anatomy you prefer, his is state of the art. Chest: broad and rippling. Abs: sculpted for days. Arms: so buff you wanna grab the outsides and be squeezed up inside them, too. Hands: broad based with long, thick fingers. Waist: nipped just enough to accentuate . . . the booty! His is an African masterpiece—the kind that makes your jaw drop and your hands itch to cup it. And thighs: for days! I swear, Marcus's twin pillars are like tree trunks I want to climb all up under, into, and in between.

Plus Marcus has the face to do the body justice: smooth cinnamon-toast skin, long-lashed eyes that crinkle all up when he smiles, twin dimples, lusciously full lips, and pearly whites that make you want to swim laps inside his mouth. Not to mention a voice so hot that even the most innocuous words become a seduction song.

As you can imagine, Marcus gets play 24/7 from every woman with vision correctable to 20/20. And he's quite accustomed to getting his way. Which, in my opinion, makes him a little lazy between the sheets. Don't get me wrong; he's amply endowed and a good-bordering-on-great-lover when he wants to be. Trouble is that, like most men, he get a little complacent when he figures your sweet stuff is a foregone conclusion. He knew the moves and executed them, but it started to feel like a formula, and I need a steady diet of genuine enthusiasm and creative variety in a lover. So after a few months we parted ways, no hard feelings, and would talk—just talk—from time to time. Marcus would always throw out something suggestive, just to see if I'd bite, but until recently I had never been tempted to revisit that sensual playground.

It wasn't about being scratch-my-itch cool-my-heat horny. I've enjoyed my fling with celibacy—it's helped me appreciate the sensual pleasures of everyday life. The sight, scent, and feel of a ripe piece of fruit can get me juicy. The tickle of wind in my ear puckers my nipples into chocolate chips. But the planets were ready for me to make a change.

I don't normally pay much attention to astrology besides occasionally checking my horoscope (Aries) to see whether it's safe to leave the house. Howsomever, my girl, Lisette, is all up into it and keeps me posted.

Years ago she did my chart and said, "Uh-oh! This explains it!"

"What?"

"Your Venus is in Scorpio, child."

"What's that mean?"

"Under normal circumstances, you're hotter than a frying jalapeño. And when the planet Venus actually goes into Scorpio, honey, hush!"

I didn't pay her any mind, but after a few episodes of sexual overdrive, I learned to be alert. When the Goddess of Love and the Scorpion in the sky hook up with my personal planets, I have dreams that bring me to orgasm; then I awaken and need another climax just to get out of bed. The mere sensation of my silk lingerie against my pertinent parts is enough to send me over the edge. Any delectable man I lock eyes with is in danger of becoming dinner and dessert. And if I'm seeing a brothah on the regular, he may have to beg for a break or call 9-1-1.

I'd been feeling "it" for a few days. Sat through a business meeting with my lovebox humming while imagining the different flavors of every man in the room. Went to the grocery store, heard Sade's "Smooth Operator" over the sound system, and ended up cha-cha-ing with the sweet brown-sugar tenderoni stocking the shelves. After our impromptu dance, I gave him a wink and sashayed myself back to my car. Had an e-mail at work from Lisette saying, "Nicola—watch out. Venus went into Scorpio day before yesterday."

So though I hadn't planned to end my celibate streak, there was something about Marcus's voice on my machine and the urges pulsating beneath my heated skin that made me want to seduce him outta that pretty-boy laziness into a sexual connoisseur.

I replayed his latest message. "Nicola, you've been mistreating me. I am lusting for your luscious body and you won't even call me back. What's a brothah gotta do?"

I decided to end his misery. "Marcus?"

"Nicola! To what do I owe the pleasure?"

"You haven't felt the pleasure . . . yet," I purred.

"I'll be right over," he said, his voice thickening with yearning.

"You're not invited."

"Then when will you be here?"

"Not anytime soon."

"Nicola, you're not making sense."

"I'm hungry."

"Well baby, I am too. That's why I'm so happy to hear your voice," he chuckled.

"Meet me at the Silver Palm restaurant, seven o'clock tomorrow evening."

"Why wait till then? I'd be happy to cook up a little somethin' for you at my place right now." I felt his silky growl all the way to my toes.

"You will. But not yet. Silver Palm. Tomorrow. Bring your appetites."

"Mmmmmmmm. I like that."

"I'm sure you do. Now say, 'Good night, Nicola.'"

"Good night, Nicola."

I hung up the phone.

The Silver Palm was classy and sensual, just the right setting for our first encounter. Marcus arrived before me and had the nerve to look like he was gonna fix his lips to fuss when I strode in fifteen minutes late. But when I slid off my coat to reveal the bloodred silk dress that caressed my sassy curves, his jaws relaxed. As his eyes trailed down to my red stiletto "come-do-me-this-minute" mules and my fierce red toenails, his lips rearranged themselves into a lusty smile.

Halfway through our dinner chitchat, I slipped off my

right shoe and walked my toes up the inside of his left pant leg. He looked startled, but I played dumb and rattled on about the latest political gossip. When my toes started circling his growing anticipation, I thought he'd choke on his shrimp Alfredo. I looked innocently into his eyes while sliding my foot up, down, and around, the silk of my stocking creating an enticing wave of friction against the front of his fine wool trousers.

When the waiter asked whether we wanted dessert, I slid my foot back into my mule. "Definitely," I murmured, "but not here, thanks."

Marcus quickly paid for the meal and managed to stand, his hand teasing the curve of my back as we walked to my car. "Your place or mine?" he grinned.

I responded with a long, searing kiss. Our tongues danced until we could barely stand or breathe. His yang called; my yin answered, and though I was so hot my brain was exploding, I managed to pull away.

"Neither. I'm teaching at the community college tomorrow night. Meet me there at six-thirty and don't be a second late." I turned and slid into my car, leaving Marcus with a look of stunned lust on his perfect face. I blew a kiss out the window and raced home, where I masturbated myself to three climaxes before I could get to sleep.

❄

The community college was filling up for evening classes when Marcus rushed into the hallway a few minutes early. "Nicola, what the hell . . . ?" He was out of breath and adorably disheveled.

I grabbed his hand, pulled him into the classroom, and locked the door. "Class begins at seven and my students are very prompt." I wore a black, Mexican-style peasant blouse with no bra, crotchless panties, and a full, fiesta-type skirt that swirled around my gleaming calves. I took a silk scarf from around my waist and gently tied Marcus's wrists together in back of him.

"Here's the assignment, Marcus. Make me hot, make me come, but you can only use your lips, teeth, and tongue. No hands, okay?" I warmed him up with a sizzling kiss. Then he took one of my earlobes between his smooth lips, nibbling and sucking until my breath was ragged and my nipples strained against my blouse. Reading my mind, he tugged down the elastic neckline with his teeth, exposing my aching breasts to the cool air. He slurped at one breast, then the other, until they danced in jealous competition for his hungry mouth.

Sitting on the desk, I wrapped my feet around his waist, pulling him against me. The coarse fabric of his jeans inflamed my restless heat. I unfastened his belt and pants and eased him back onto the floor. Then I gently guided his long, thick muscle into my mouth. "Turn around," he growled, directing me to hover just over his face. As I teased his velvety balls, Marcus's tongue sucked my lower lips until my upper ones quivered. I felt the delicious scrape of newly grown beard on the tender meat of my inner thigh and stifled a moan while his probing tongue sent my hips into a grind.

Meanwhile, I took him deeper into my throat. He seemed to grow longer, harder, wider, and hotter with each greedy gulp. I heard voices from the hallway as students gathered near the door, but concentrated on first teasing the tip of Marcus's magnificent manhood, then devouring as much as I could. I muffled a scream as he coaxed my love button to the boiling point.

We lost control at the same moment: he plunged into my mouth and I shuddered into his. I helped him to a standing position and we licked the juices from each other's mouths and faces.

"Okay," I gasped, untying his wrists and pulling him into the bathroom, where we quickly washed off. "Get yourself together and go out that side door."

"Girl, you'd . . ." I stopped his words with a teasing kiss and nudged him into the hallway.

I relished the smell of pleasure in the air as I strode back and forth in front of my students, explaining the finer points of gourmet restaurant dining. My whole body purred, the breeze beneath my shirt fanning the embers of my nearly sated lust.

Needless to say, it was difficult getting to sleep that night. I wanted Marcus inside of me as much as he wanted to be there, but I was determined to stick to my plan.

A few days later I e-mailed him from work. "Have an urge to go dancing and it's oldies night at the Purple Haze. Can't wait to feel you."

"Can't wait to come," he e-mailed back immediately.

The Purple Haze was the city's mainstay club for all age groups, but on Thursday it belongs to the old-school crowd. Amar, the gorgeous young DJ, musta been schooled by his daddy 'cause he spun those jams like he'd grown up on them.

Marcus looked scrumptious in skin-tight jeans and muscle T. I wore a flirty short dress and my most comfortable dancing shoes.

We danced every dance, from Aretha to Smokey to Marvin, working up a fine glow, but at the first notes of the Dells' "Stay in My Corner" I walked into Marcus's out-stretched arms with a wicked smile. "I don't know how to slow-dance. Can you teach me?" I pouted, and he pulled me close. We whispered the words of the song into each other's ears and started to swerve like teenagers learning what the *p* in *pleasure* was for. Our hands caressed each other's backs, then ventured lower, and we moved into a sho 'nuff grind. Marcus inserted his thigh between my legs and let his hands explore my backfield, my skin rippling with pleasure at his sure touch. The Dells wailed as he marked my throat with long, hungry kisses that were sure to leave marks the next day. I gasped and molded my pelvis to his. "Come here," he moaned, and next thing I knew we were in the DJ booth.

Amar looked up with a slow smile. "How much time left on that tape?" Marcus asked, peeling off a large bill. "Thirty minutes, my man," Amar laughed, pocketing the bill and slipping out of the booth.

We sank down, tearing at each other's clothes. The rough carpet against my skin excited me even more. I lifted one heel onto the edge of the console that held all the DJ equipment. Marcus trailed his lips up the inside of my left thigh, then licked around the outside of my yearning.

"Can you read my lips, baby?" I cooed. "The ones you're licking? I want your mouth on mine and the rest of you inside me, deep inside me, *now!*"

Marcus laughed and nibbled his way up my stomach to play awhile with each breast, pulling at them with his fingers till the nipples moaned against his skin. He suckled them so long and hard that I nearly came from the delicious pressure alone. Then he tickled my steaming cat with his fingers, smiling as I danced on the tips. We sat facing each other, my feet locked behind his proud hips. He teased me with the tip of his shaft and I gently guided him in. He sighed as my heat engulfed him.

We rode the music, his every stroke on the one, my answering thrusts on the downbeat. He laid me gently back on the carpet, slow-grinding as though we were still on the dance floor. The bass reverberated through our bodies as we quaked and grunted with each sweet stroke. I slid my toes around his gorgeous ass, causing it to quiver each time it rose. Our sweat mingled in a cloud of sweet funk and I spread my legs wide, savoring the way his balls teased my pussy. We drank greedily from each other's mouths and he reared back, poised to explode.

"Wait," I said, sliding out from under him and guiding his face between my thighs. "Don't you want a little taste of what you do to me?"

He groaned and dove in, his tongue jetting in and out of me with such power that I thought he was still inside me. My hips circled wantonly as waves of pleasure rose from my toes.

"Okay," I gasped, pushing him back to lick my juices from his throbbing joystick. It danced wildly in the air, searching for my wet embrace. I teased the glistening head until his hips jutted upward, then slowly took his length into my mouth.

"Oooooh it's good, so damned good, Nicola, I'm about to . . ." I pulled my lips away, moved up to kiss his mouth, and mounted him, moving in languid figure eights and squeezing my inner muscles around him until he roared above the music.

From the corner of my eye, I saw that Amar had reentered the booth. I pretended not to notice, but that made me even hotter. I lowered my nipples to Marcus's mouth and he nibbled them into throbbing pleasure points. I heard Amar's breathing quicken as Marcus and I drove each other to new peaks of ecstasy.

Back on the dance floor I trembled against Marcus with aftershocks, while he gently ran his hands up and down my back. We slow-danced to another orgasm, our tongues grooving to their own rhythm in a long, hungry kiss.

When we could finally breathe normally and speak again, I gave him a slow, appreciative once-over. "I must say you've surprised me, Marcus. Are you in heat?"

"Could be," he chuckled. "Or maybe it's just the stars."

"What do you mean?" I asked, fighting to get my brain back into my skull and my clothing back to normal.

"Did I ever tell you my Venus is in Scorpio?" he asked, grinning wickedly and patting the front of his pants with a satisfied flourish. "And it just so happens that there's a matching planetary alignment that swings through every now and then. Now, if you don't know what that means, I'll be happy to break it down for you . . ."

Roses, Red, Room 416

by Lolita Files

I never knew rose petals could hurt.

It was two days later and I still couldn't walk straight. I semi-waddled down the quiet hall of the hotel toward the room where this last disaster had most recently occurred. That I was back again was a miracle within itself. Recovery was not even near being complete.

The door was closed. New York's equivalent of the do-not-disturb sign was hanging on the handle: FUHGETTABOUDIT.

Cassis was in there. I could feel his presence, even through the heavy divider. He was probably lying back, propped up against four ultrafluffy pillows, languishing in the feel of the soft down-filled duvet as it draped haphazardly across his body. His left hand would be gingerly cradling his nut-brown shaft, the fingers deftly working. His right hand would be gingerly cradling the black shaft of the remote. The fingers deftly working.

I stopped just outside the door, listening to the dim hum of the television as channel after channel whizzed past. He was changing the thing with remarkable speed, much too quickly to register images. Which meant the fingers on the remote were truly fast at work. Which meant the fingers on his shaft, in turn, were just as active.

Cassis would be hard for me. So hard, it would hurt. He

would be wincing when I walked in. I already knew. His dick would be a dagger of pain, fat with hot blood that boiled up within it. He would look to me for release, eyes blazing in demand that I let him stab me with the boiled-blood dagger. I hesitated as I stood by the door. Afraid to go in. Couldn't wait to go in.

Le Parker Meridien was a dangerous place. Safe for patrons. Dangerous for me. Undeniably upscale, the hotel was nestled in the heart of Midtown Manhattan, respectably perched on Fifty-sixth Street between Sixth and Seventh. Behind door 416, however, some not-so-upscale or -respectable happenings had been jumping off for quite some time. Four months, to be exact. Amid eighteen-dollar bran muffins and twenty-dollar pots of tea, wicked acts were taking place. Things that made me sink into prayer once they were over. Things for which I was certain I would go straight to hell.

The scandalous was the norm when I entered that place. Same man, same room, same me, always so scared, always so willing once I passed through the portal. My body, soft and willowy, pliable and ready. A lamb rushing into a slaughter-house of pure visceral joy. When I emerged, hours later, destruction. My body a mosaic of bruises artfully dressed as handprints and tooth marks, nipples braised and glazed from the heat of oft-dripped candle wax, wrists slightly achy from the pressure of too-tight fists encircling them, neck sore from acrobatic feats worthy of an XXX porn star. Ass a series of irreverent stings. The corners of my mouth tender from being stretched too wide for too long, eager to display my fellatial prowess.

Despite the initial damage, things were always intact. No skinned flesh that burned when the wind hit it; no breasts that cried out when returned to the confines of a bra. Everything had always been copacetic afterward, save for the need to drape a scarf around my neck or pull my coat tight as I passed through the lobby doors, back out onto the street.

I'd always been able to walk—no, stride—before. Happy with the glow of the *überfuck*. No problems whatsoever. Cassis was big, but big in a good way. Not that kind of big that ripped you apart and made pleasure an unexplorable option. Not that kind of big that men bragged about but women fled. Cassis was the kind of big that filled you up and put just the right amount of pressure on the walls that called out for it. My body shaped itself to him, my love canal a glove that hungrily enveloped his perfect bigness with delicate precision. His dick brought with it no discomfort or hurt. Just an infinite completion that made me helium-heady, giddy like a crack hoe who'd hit the motherlode—a rock so big there was nothing to do but sit and suck and smoke and suck and smoke and suck and smoke until there was nothing left of the rock, nothing left of me. No consciousness, no sense of restraint. A zombielike state where I just kept taking hits until I was swallowed alive by the thrill of sensation.

When Cassis did bring the pain, it wasn't from the beatdown of his dick. It came from the nastily pleasurable feeling of his massive hand, like an open-faced sandwich, coming down hard and wide against the expectant curl of my ass. It was the perfect accompaniment as he thrust deep within me, like an expert cellist in perfect concert with a liquidly smooth pianist. Me, face forward, derriere airborne, on my knees, teeth gritted, eyes closed, moaning desperately into the pillows that smothered me blind. The sounds of the flat-faced blows of his hand ricocheting and snapping around the room like firecrackers as he smacked me harder with each thrust. Those same hands, with me now lying on my back, squeezing and rubbing my thighs roughly, his palms almost burning, as he pushed himself deep, deep, deep inside my wetness. Those hands hurting me, leaving purple splotches and blue stems where palms and fingers had once been, making me writhe in ways that others less indulged might consider abuse.

Cassis was a true artist. A masterful painter whose stroke would make van Gogh cut off more than just an ear. No lie. In fact, van Gogh would have gladly handed over his dick. "Here man, take it. No need for me to try to compete with your skills."

Cassis's hands were the hands of a builder. Cassis's hands were the hands of a murderer. Behind that door, those hands were my source of renewal. Behind that door, his hands were my deconstruction.

Every time we coupled, I was afraid afterward to look at my body in the mirror. Things always appeared worse than they actually were. Thighs blue, back red, face flushed, hair askew. The battle scars of a sexual warrior.

How we'd met had to be one of life's biggest mysteries. A friend of a friend at a party that neither of us could remember. Gravitation to one another without explanation. A conversation with no sentences, no words. Eyes staring. Mine curious, peering, each lash a revelation. Deep pockets beneath his, what had *he* been doing of late? Three hours later, me, impersonating dinner in the hallway. Him, the diner, on his knees, tongue plunged deep inside me. Me, hanging on to his hair, beautiful gentle ropes, delicate locks that were easily shaped into handlebars for me to grasp. The smell of almond oil. My head back, moans evident, his head at work like Woody Woodpecker on a pulp-ripe tree. Hush, hush. Keep it down now. Voices carry. *Fuck* voices. Deep tongue. Ass aflame. Explosions, screams, clit vigor, watchers in the hall. As I looked down at him, he was all wicked smiles, his visage one big smear of my wetness. He let it remain, my juices a mask of honor, rose to his feet, gave me a piercing stare that made me hostage for life. He took my hand and led me back to the party.

Once I'd had the pleasure of that tongue, it was over. Cassis owned me. I was open. Wide. Anytime, anyplace, anywhere. No reason. That tongue was enough.

An hour later, he'd given me dick.

I had a soprano pussy.

It was news to me. I'd always thought it was alto.

※

I stared at Room 416.

Cassis was a Slasher—an actor-*slash*-director-*slash*-screenwriter-*slash*-author—all careers that typically seemed to mean *poor*. But he'd had a fair share of success, having written, directed, and played the lead in an indie film that won critical acclaim at last year's Sundance Film Festival. He'd been given a budget by a major studio and was filming his first wide-distribution flick on location in Brooklyn and Manhattan. No small feat, considering how expensive it was to shoot in New York. He was also at work on his first novel. He had already published—also with much critical acclaim—a collection of short stories filled with tales that were rich with rites of passage. Cassis's advance had been fat. Six figures, high ones, for the short-story collection and novel that was soon to follow. They called him the voice of a new generation. I called him the tongue of my old one.

He spent many days writing in solitude at the Parker Meridien. Expensive, yes, but the movie studio was picking up the check. He did it all under the umbrella of working on his film (preproduction, location scouting, *yada, yada, yada,* so he told the studio). We fucked all upside and downside and inside that hotel room, compliments of the big studio's dollar. Thank you, Warner Brothers. Afternoon fucks and mini bars never felt so damn good.

Me, I was a successful author, too, but none of this was coming out of my pocket. My biggest satisfaction (other than the obvious one, Cassis's sexual skills) was that most authors' faces were not highly recognizable. Almost no one cared what we looked like, unless we were Slashers. Our notoriety lay in the power of the written word. Thus most authors slipped unnoticed in and out of grocery stores, high-end boutiques, movies, Kmarts, Targets, and all manner of dens of iniquity. They knew me here, although our conversations were always kept to a minimum. This would be the forty-fifth time I'd entered this door. Four months was an awfully compressed amount of time to have made forty-five visits to the same hotel. I'd go to the counter, get the card key, and make my way up.

Sometimes I averted my eyes from the clerks at the front desk, in fear that they would recognize me. Thought I was getting the "aren't you—?" look. *No*, I'd be thinking. *Right now I'm someone else.*

Sometimes I took them head-on, flipping ghetto-fab in my posturing of defense. Yeah, I'm fucking. What you think? I'm the hot pussy woman. You wish you were getting what I'm giving upstairs.

Fuhgettaboudit.

Their eyes reading mine. The message clear. Make way. I'm outta here. There's a tongue upstairs with my pussy's name stamped on it.

Sometimes authors were the worst artists of them all.

I still hadn't opened the door to go in. Deep below, my lips were throbbing, pained from the friction of walking, swollen with the betrayal of rose petals.

Two days ago Cassis had introduced something new.

When I had come into the room, I was surprised to find it swimming in a sea of endless roses, red long-stemmed thorned things covering every possible inch of surface space. The floor, the desk, the top of the TV, the bed. The pièce de résistance was the ultimate surface: Cassis, naked, awash in an ocean of red roses, his erection breaking their seamless flow, a stem clasped between the teeth of that wicked smile.

"What is this?" I giggled. "Are you crazy or what?"

No words from him. Just the gentle jerk backward of his head, instructing me to come closer. The subtle rise of his left brow as I came near.

I dropped my bag on the floor, loosened my Plein Sud trenchcoat, let it slip from my shoulders and fall to the floor.

The weather outside was brick. New York City was in the midst of an ugly wet winter. Inside Room 416 everything was hot, steamy, thick with the threat of sex. All I wore was a zebra-striped teddy and an extremely expensive pair of snake-skin boots.

Before Cassis, I had never done this type to thing. Since Cassis, I couldn't imagine how it was that I never did.

I made a move toward the bed. With his left arm Cassis swept away a clearing for me, a slew of roses falling to the floor, some flying across the room. I slid in beside him. He said nothing, just hovered over me sinisterly, as I leaned back into the softness of the pillows.

Each visit with him was a treat, but this rose thing was definitely something different.

"Did you buy these?" I asked, but of course he didn't

answer. My mystery man, with his right hand, removed the rose from between his teeth. He traced it down the center of my forehead, lightly, past my nose, over the swell of my lips, snaking a trail down my neck that barely grazed my skin. The sensation was electric.

His eyes tightly fastened to mine, he slipped the teddy delicately off my shoulders, down my waist, enlisting my assistance with his eyes. I pushed it all the way down, raising my butt so it could pass, letting it linger around my knees. Beneath me, a thorny-stemmed rose punctured my ass. Caught off guard, I was instantly wet. Pain and pleasure were always excellent bedfellows in the presence of Cassis.

He swirled the rose around my nipples, giving each its moment in the sun before encircling it with his succulent mouth. I could feel the blood rush center stage to meet his tongue, my areola engorged in a dance of fire. I breathed in, my eyes closing, as he nibbled hungrily on each of my buds. He rose from his worship, touched my face with his hand so that I would open my eyes. Petal to skin, he began tracing a deeper descent down my body with the rose. When he reached my clit, he stopped, twirling the thing in circular motions around the hood of my already swollen nub. With his left forefinger he pulled it back, exposing my sensitive button to the now bruised surface of the rose petals. As he twirled and stoked, Cassis stared pointedly in my face, willing reaction, willing change.

"That feels really good," I whispered.

Cassis, my owner, my commandant, said nothing. When I parted my lips to say more, he covered them with his own, his tongue plunging and probing deep inside my mouth.

Kissing, to me, is almost as fulfilling an act as fucking. The ultimate high is to be kissed while fucking. Tongues locked, loins locked, all moving with fevered intensity toward common release. It makes me respond like a man. I bust nuts. Gush like waterworks from here to Massapequa. Bed sopping. Body wet from top to bottom. Oh, goodness, nothing feels as good as a double-lipped fuck!

All that was left was for Cassis to put it in. His dick. He already had his mouth on mine. His tongue was thrusting and sucking, pulling and pushing at my own. Below, I was soaked, my hips throwing hints like crazy as I ground them around.

Instead, Cassis twirled the flower. The rose was now rubbing, hard, up and down the sides of my lower lips. The sensation was wild, so keyed up was I by the kissing. The petals were giving off something that made my labia tingle, and, to me, within the confines of this room, all strange sensations, new sensations, were good sensations. I ground harder, pressing my pelvis up against the rose, crushing it between my legs as they scissored shut, Cassis roughly spreading them apart again and rubbing the flower against my now drenched outer lips.

"Fuck me," I declared, mouthing the words around our dueling tongues. Cassis responded by kissing me harder, tossing the sopping rose aside, and beginning afresh as he rubbed a new flower against my pussy.

The tingling intensified, a distant fire aflame deep within the dermis of my cooch.

I worked my hips now, not just out of lust, but in response to an itch, a hunger, born of rose petals, that desperately needed scratching. I reached for him, rock hard amid a bed of thorny stems. I held him in my hand, trying to guide him home. Above me, Cassis still worked his magic upon my mouth. I wanted to come so bad, I could barely breathe. I wanted him in me, deep, hard, I wanted those hands crushing my thighs, I needed my pussy scratched, my labia scratched, the double itch was too much for me to take.

Before I could get him close enough to my pussy to matter, to my own surprise I erupted. Something deep, deep, deep inside of me let go, and then a jarring sensation that rushed in a wave to the outer edges of my walls, filling them with heat, quakes, an ultrastrong spasm, and, finally, release. Cassis still inside of my mouth, I moaned heavily around him. Thrashed against him, collapsed like a bitch.

He released my tongue and pulled away, the victor, smiling above me.

No words, just smiles.

Beneath him, me, frail, quivering, stunned by such immediate release with what wasn't my typically necessary closure: tongue-on-clit or dick-in-pussy.

"Nice," he finally muttered.

My thighs were trembling much too hard for me to try to form words.

❀

The rose-capade had been so exhausting for me that I had fallen immediately asleep. Slept deep, too, for three solid hours, Cassis over at the desk, naked, hard at work on his book.

The pecking sound of fingers on keyboard finally broke my stream of unconsciousness and I rose, groggy, hungry, my bladder full. I stumbled from the bed, toward the bathroom, blindly flipping on the light, finding the toilet, sitting down. As I relaxed to release my bladder, absently rubbing my eyes, I felt a fullness below that seemed unnatural. Tight skin. Puffiness. I stopped rubbing my eyes to take a peek.

My labia were swollen five times their natural size. As the flow of pee made contact with the skin, I let out a squeal so steep that it didn't even seem to come from me.

Soprano. Only this time the singing emanated from my mouth.

From the room, I could hear the deep distant hum of Cassis's familiar chuckle.

※

I stood outside the room now, legs barely able to close, the card key in my hand, poised to open the door. Through the barrier, the sound of changing channels. Still flickering by with lightning speed. Cassis's hand on his joint must be doing the same.

I stood there, staring at the number on the door.

416.

The number of times I'd come in the past month.

416.

The number of times I'd think about him in the course of a day.

416.

The number I would count to, there, outside the door, until Cassis had jerked himself to completion. Then I'd walk away. My lips couldn't take it.

Fuhgettaboudit.

Sometimes, even a pussy needs a chance to heal.

Stores

by Reginald Harris

Fetish: A rite, or cult of fetish worshipers.

I hate to admit to being weird, but shopping makes me horny.

And not just any kind of shopping, either. Going to the mall does nothing for me. But take me to a grocery store, give me one of those silly carts with the mandatory one wobbly wheel to push around, and suddenly I get very hot.

Maybe it's because we shop together, Ricky and me. We usually have to go late at night. Invariably he gets called on to pull an extra shift at the hospital and doesn't get home until after midnight. I could go by myself, and I did at the beginning of our relationship, but that was never any fun. I did *not* enjoy lugging bags to the car, then out of the car, then up the steps to our apartment all by myself. That's what *his* muscles are for. So now I'm content to wait until he gets home, checking the shelves for what we need, drawing up my list, changing clothes a few times until I find just the right ensemble for our late-night foray into comestibles.

Thank God for twenty-four-hour grocery stores! No swerving to avoid some family and their screaming kids. No guys desperately trying not to look like they're a couple shopping together, fresh pasta and imported olive oil in their carts giving them away, or women with cans of dog food and big bags of litter, buying for two, not caring who notices. No single guys cruising, frozen dinners and canned vegetables rattling like pinballs in their baskets. No long lines at the checkout, either; usually just one or two checkers mostly standing around filing their nails. The store is almost empty but for the overnight shelvers, ripping into boxes like it was Christmas, and the two of us.

When Ricky and I first walk into the store I'm fine, focused, I can control myself. But once we hit the fresh produce, walking past the rows of onions and celery, the bulging bags of oranges or grapefruit, it hits me. I'm overcome with emotion. Something about the ordinariness of it all, how dull and everyday it is to buy groceries together, drives me wild. Ricky's receding back, pushing our cart toward the deli section, becomes suddenly the most beautiful sight in all the world.

My list is filled with innuendo: Meat. Juice. Eggs. Milk. Even the wheat creams here. One night someone had dropped a container of yogurt in Dairy, thick globs of lumpy white suspension still quivering on the floor when we turned down the aisle. I nearly fainted dead away.

"Excuse me, but what aisle are the blow jobs in?" I whisper in Ricky's ear. "Stop it," he says, shaking his head.

I want to drag him into the stockroom, lean against a box of thousand-gross muffin mix, and have him fuck me there. In my wildest fantasies we do it in the middle of the store, rutting on the floor in Aisle 11 between oversize bottles of store-brand soda and cheap pretzels, ejaculating into a pool of waxy buildup.

As we wander through the store, checking off items from our list, beads of sweat begin to form on my forehead. I show Ricky the store's weekly sales flyer. "Look, dear—this is a good price for a nice piece of tail, don't ya think?" He stifles a laugh and keeps on walking.

At the display of oils, the sight of so much lubrication makes my knees grow weak: corn, olive, vegetable. In liquid form, in tubs—sticks! Fortunately the rest of the baking equipment calms me down. Besides, to mention nuts and stuffing mix to Ricky would be too obvious. Then we're at the spices and my excitement returns. Parsley and poppy seed, rosemary, cilantro, leaves of bay, all mix in my head like a sexual *herbes de Provence*.

The dreaded snack aisle looms next, cookies and chips reminding me of our couch potato nights glued to the TV. We pass the cereals and baby food. "Syrup?" I say to him, waving a bottle and licking my lips lasciviously. "And they double our coupons." Ricky stares as if I were insane and tosses the bottle into our cart. We head to the arctic wastes of the freezer section.

He prefers looking at the chicken, steaks, and chops alone, ever since the night I went up to him, saying, "Special on hot cock in the meat section," and squeezed his crotch. I still don't know why he got so angry and slapped my hand from him. "Go find the toilet paper," he told me, as I slunk away. Who cares what those stockboys think they saw anyway?

Finally we press on to bread, butter, orange juice, and milk, as if the store itself knows it's almost morning, and wheel our cart to the lone cashier to check out.

By the time we leave the store I can barely breathe. Ricky glances at me, saying nothing. We travel the short distance to our apartment in silence and divide the bags between us for the long trip up three flights of stairs.

Once inside, the bags are strewn across the kitchen floor, and I sigh, girding myself for the next chore of putting everything away. I lean over to take a head of lettuce out of the first bag, and Ricky tips me off balance with his foot. Sprawling to the floor, I turn over quickly to look up at him.

He's grinning broadly now, has stripped off his jacket and shirt, and looms over me in his blazing white T-shirt. He unbuckles his belt and slowly unzips his pants, pulling out a sausage longer and thicker than the kielbasa resting against my elbow in the bag beside me.

"Here, baby," he says, straddling me, placing his hand behind my head. "I know how shopping makes you . . . hungry. I got a special purchase for you. Eat."

And I do.

The Dawn of Our World

by Carolyn Ferrell

Woe unto them that join house to house, that lay field to field till there be no place that they may be placed alone in the midst of the earth,

thought Rhonda Robinson as she sewed the zipper back into her favorite winter dress, the pink-and-black gingham fashioned coyly like an oversize maid's apron. She did not ask herself why those words were on her lips, the Bible drifting gently from cobwebs of melancholy. Tonight was the night for love, a year's worth of passion; and with her eyes closed and her back to the bedroom window, she enjoyed the surface of nettles that moved beneath her skin, traveling her arms and legs and across her womanly triangle in anticipation of the man from Auntsville. His name was Billy Merry, and he came up to Long Island every December twenty-fourth to make love to Rhonda in various positions of joy and exertion. Otherwise there was little mystery: She knew he had once belonged to her grandmother as a pet or fancy piece of furniture, but now that he had become a man, he was all hers.

She moved the heavy-duty needle back and forth through the ancient fabric—this was a dress she'd been sewing up and down since she arrived on Long Island seven years ago, a dress fashioned into either matronly or sexy, but it was the prettiest one she had. In reality, it never mattered what she was wearing. All he ever wanted was her, the softened spread of woman wrapped snugly around him, licking his salt-block body as if she were dying of thirst.

He usually pulled up at her house around six in the evening. He would get out of the car and stand there like a statue, his sharp country eyes taking in the suburban land, thigh meat bulging from too-tight trousers, chin shaven smooth as a spring limb. From the screen door she'd call his name in varying shades: Bill, William, My Heart, My Lover.

She felt proud of him, of his good looks and musk—a man just as pleasing as those Greek heroes she occasionally glanced in Harriet-Ann Hutchinson's social studies textbook, *The Dawn of Our World*. She held the pages at arm's length and pronounced the names with care, all the while measuring her loneliness in the number of times her breasts knocked against her brassiere. She wished to pronounce something beautifully, but to whom? Who in all of Featherstone really cared? The only person who spoke to her was the janitor, and he was nothing more than an annoyance. Mr. Blank: He had that old-timishness about him she so despised in the elderly, the desire to talk about nonsubjects with gusto and then the expectation of appreciation, one extraordinarily shameless. She hated that.

But with Billy. This visit was number seven, the lucky visit. She closed her eyes and held the dress still over her lap. *He would appeareth*. He would cross mountains and nations for her, lift her up like a new bride and carry her toward the couch (the one without slipcovers), breathe in the seams of her dress, tap his hands along her body like a blind man until they reached the zipper and discovered the speckled velvet of her skin. Her arms and belly would be sheathed, as usual, by a last-minute layer of baby powder and Jean Nate. Then the indulgence, the fire of gluttony. Lights flickering on and off, faces creased and then shuttered into nothingness. Afterward, in the remaining ash that was her body, Rhonda would hold his face in her hands and, like a schoolgirl, gaze woefully into his eyes.

They were eyes she recognized all the way back from the fifth grade in the country, Auntsville, North Carolina, where he had been a miserable boy, an undesirable, someone about whom rumors were spread containing words like *pervert* and *bang*. It was said that his first girlfriend was a dog; when Rhonda once passed his house and saw the lone hound tied to the mulberry in the parched red yard, she felt a certain amount of pity and jealousy. *How was it he could put his finger on desire and name it so painstakingly?* Desire was not crystalline; it was murky, unfettered, gargantuan. In the schoolroom, loneliness and foreboding were her sole allies.

Years; and he had grown into a man. Rhonda set the dress down on her bed and (from sheer force of habit) slipped her whole hand between her unpantied legs and tried to relieve herself. His tobacco field cap and armpits entered her mind— all that glorious history, a Greek statue, just like in the book!— and she went to work. Everything down there was wet and swollen, impossible to get through. She stuck her finger as far as it would go. Though she herself was not religious, she now and then stopped her business to ask God why Christmas couldn't come more than once a year.

※

As usual, Billy took the Belt Parkway once he made it to New York. He rather hated Long Island and what he perceived was box living, but then there was nothing much going on in Auntsville this time of year, the supply of women being at a low. He was a man who loved love. He loved sex, touching, bedroom camaraderie, the predominance of false intuition. And since Rhonda offered this and more, he would just have to deal with the squared communities and endless strip malls advertising the baby clothes and automotive parts and Laundromats and cavernous supermarkets offering everything and nothing. At the end of the line she would be waiting for him.

As a child she was so wanting, and now she'd grown into a woman not at all his type: tall, meandering, wistful, always meaning something she could never say. She wore the same dress year after year, thinking it something special. A pitiful girl. An even more pitiful woman. Seven years now he'd made the trip—seven, an unlucky number. Yet here he was, on his way. *Here he was.*

Those being the disadvantages. What was good about traveling to the North was that Rhonda had a house all to herself, unlike the women he knew at home. Not a room, not an apartment in a city project, but a real single-family house with many rooms in which to fuck. No matter it looked like a box, all fenced in by the same Adirondack posts everyone else had, or that by twilight her roof was indistinguishable from the rest of the land. This woman didn't answer to nobody. She didn't have to cook or clean if she didn't feel like it; there were no obligatory greens pots simmering on the stove, no tobacco-stained clothes waiting in wicker baskets. It was so different from Auntsville, with its large dilapidated faux-antebellum homes, wringers, double-wides, televangelists blaring trumpets. There were no memories on Long Island. Here Rhonda and Billy were new and improved; they could make love until the early hours of sun and never worry about angry lovers barging in, or incapacitated relatives. He and Rhonda (a woman normally too alpine for his taste) could sit naked at the table and nibble

chests, breasts, toes, and elbows, ripened bodies instead of the
usual coffee, butter, and grits they had grown up on.

This night, Billy Merry had a plan. He felt stung by ambi-
tion as he drove the highway, thinking of the plan in all its
glory. And this was his plan: that seven years would end
tonight. It was time to learn from the past.

Billy gripped the steering wheel in fury, and relief—even
though the past was a million miles away, and now he was not
just some ignorant boy in the field. He had been deciding what
to do for quite a while.

How funny that all roads eventually lead to Asenath
Fowler!

Rheumy eyes, arms and legs resembling spiderwebs, a
time-worn mouth tasting of cinnamon and juniper bark. Time
to learn.

She was an old woman back when there were hundreds of
beauties in Auntsville, thousands even, lining up to his door.
Nothing more than a scarf of skin, or a heart that beat like an
African drum. Why had he listened to her? Why had he even
trusted her? But then you would have to ask: Why does moss
grow on the north side of trees? Why is the earth at the center
of the universe?

Outside the snow fell in soft pillows of sky around him.
He stared ahead at the highway, whispering to the windshield,
—Rhonda. Rhonda. It is time to learn from the past.

The woman waiting in the house, however, was ignorant
of his ideas. She did not hear his whispers from the Belt
Parkway or see the particular arrangement of clouds in the
night sky. She was sewing, breathing, conceiving, reconceiving,
imagining, reimagining; but ignorant, all the same. She knew
she was in love, but unfortunately could not read the signs
overhead, heavenly signs that admonished her for sewing that

dress again and that informed her that tonight, Billy Merry was planning on leaving her for the woman of his dreams.

❊

She picked up her dress and resumed sewing. If only he were here already. At the door, she would immediately rise out of the doldrums which had all that month whispered to her: Ain't Christmas a family holiday? Ain't you supposed to have some turkey wings, some biscuits in the fry pan? Where your real people? *A man alone is not real people.*

Her thoughts turned to yesterday, the last day of school: the silence of the hallways as the aged janitor glided his sweeper across the floors; Rhonda standing at the school entrance, waiting for the last child to leave the building. When she went back to comb the rooms for leftover children, she noticed the clock in Mr. Wool's classroom, and the *indecent* way it hung over the map of the United States, almost insulting her with its arcane ticking. (What was it trying to tell her?) The janitor had entered the room and surprised her by pushing a potted Christmas cactus in her direction. —Moo moo, he seemed to say to her, only she couldn't understand his country talk. —Moo moo. Moo.

What was the message? Rhonda took the cactus and pulled her coat tightly around her shoulders. The old man had already acted the fool in the yard that afternoon—now what did he want?

As he got ready to open his mouth again, she quickly wished him a Merry Christmas and left the building.

❊

The old man fell into a rusted folding chair by the door and watched as she walked away. During the day she was in his thoughts as he pushed his broom down the school hallway, or as he swept away gum wrappers and coils of lint and hair, or as he poured a scalding bucket over vomit or a lake of urine, or as he locked and unlocked his myriad cabinets. He had seen many a pretty teacher come and go at Featherstone, but had never met anyone as *gainly* as Miss Robinson.

Earlier that day, the last before Christmas vacation, he'd found her during cafeteria and cornered her with babble, a stream of something unfocused and heady, but incredibly lovely (he imagined) to listen to. He suddenly adored the sound of his own voice, so deep and baritone. Mr. Blank talked about children because he knew that women were always impressed by men with feeling. He talked and talked— an amazing baritone! (Why hadn't he noticed it before?) Often he'd lain in bed, chirping wildly like the birds on the suet. It was only on that day before Christmas vacation, however, that he had become aware of his depths.

It was all quite natural. As he spoke, he thought about the way her breasts would taste in his unencumbered mouth, and how he would love to see her in that pink-and-black gingham just to erase (by hand) the seams that had been crudely stitched and opened and restitched together. He was an old man but he still could make a girl scream; it hadn't happened that way in years (or maybe it had never happened, he couldn't be sure), but something in him, a distant memory of prowess, convinced him of the possibilities of lust that has layered over time.

Through a thicket of words, Mr. Blank found himself admitting to Rhonda that though he'd had his share of grief, it was now time to move on. Keep on keeping on, as the young say. In truth, he rarely thought about his former grief: the gang of unloving kids he had raised, his wife, eternally grim. All of them had left him long ago. Now what remained was to push his broom, clean up after the schoolchildren (bless their nasty little hearts), and watch the teachers come and go. Never anyone as *gainly* as her.

Mr. Blank stopped speaking, and suddenly wondered where he was. His memory sometimes played tricks.

Rhonda Robinson was frowning at him, a deep (but possibly ecstatic) frown. The janitor sank to his knees in the cafeteria; everyone turned and looked. He focused on Rhonda Robinson's legs as though they were the first he had ever seen in his life. Round, slightly knobbed, caramel colored, drenched in pantyhose.

—Rhonda, he suddenly said. —Oh. Oh.

—Mr. Blank, please!

He took her hand. —Please hear what I'm saying, he whispered. —*I want to feel you, Miss Robinson, it's this dream I have.* He could not finish his thought, his sentence. Like the birds on the suet.

Rhonda opened her mouth to say something (he knew it would be harsh, but looked forward to it) and then stormed off, leaving the old man floundering in a pool of children's giggles. He rose slowly and planned his next course of action.

෯

The house on Long Island had belonged to her grandmother when she came up north, and then the old woman sold it to Rhonda and went to live in a nursing home called the Plantation. It was just down the road in East Amity, but the granddaughter was never seen visiting.

Billy, too, rarely made inquiries about Asenath when he came up. He never even mentioned her by name—until this night, he believed the past should remain in the past. He knew, however, that treachery was ugly; that it made you as alone as a dog tied to a tree, cooling the body into parched red earth. When he was with Rhonda, and when he was in that sort of mood, he referred to her grandmother as the old woman, the battle-ax, the crazy bitch. They laughed. They rolled on a bed and then onto the floor and then down the hallway and down the stairs past the slipcovered couch. They grew splinters in the dark knots of their bodies, chestnut locks, and undone frizz. Nothing but laughter.

(Why had he been so stupid for so many years? It seemed a veritable lifetime.)

Billy eventually drifted off to a shoulder. He closed his eyes (a reckless thing to do on the Southern State Parkway, especially on Christmas Eve) and he wept. Treachery was akin to death.

In life she had been different from anything he had ever known. Arthritic, camphorate, and yet bold: She wore an old-fashioned floor-length dress and stood in the elbow of the afternoon sun, waving her long apron in the dust. The neck hole of the dress was so large he could see her brown shoulders slip out from time to time. A stark scent of onion and allspice wafted up from the pleats of her skirt; one day he and she were out on the street, just a stone's throw from the school, and he inhaled that skirt. He wanted desperately to touch the old woman but could not believe she wanted the same.

Now disguised as a spirit, or something the old folks liked to believe in, she arrived most inconveniently in his thoughts, slipping into the unheated car, hushing him; he acquiesced. With a hand like a veil she agitated him gently in his privates, forcing him to put his hand up to his left breast right there in the car and start rubbing underneath his faux-silk shirt and bay rum.

—One thing for sure, Billy murmured, —*Women do not grow shoulders like that anymore.*

Minutes later he slackened the grip on his skin, started the engine, and continued the road to Rhonda. She was waiting for him, and like it or not, there was precious little you could deny a woman in wait.

She had waited him for years, ever since the fifth grade when his name was changed from Billy to *Shame-Billy* on account of his impetuous and horrifying need to smear his lips over the backs and fronts of the flat-chested girls in Miss Fauset's classroom. He used his hands like vise grips, crushing crinolines and doily collars, finding the place where the skin salted the tongue. In the cloakroom he trampled the girls as they ran to and from him. The sugar-snap breast buds burst as he tried to pry them off bodies. Screams, hollering: and once a pretty girl who split her head on the sharp wooden molding. Somewhere in his trousers, the shadow of a miniature boy-bulge appeared.

—*Shame! Shame-Billy!* the girls cried, all of them scurrying to the other side of the room, laughing in the terrified pitch of sparrows. Billy Merry usually came to and stood by himself, on the verge of tears, not understanding his feelings or the haze that had overtaken him. The boys in his class—ages ten and eleven and twelve—broke a few of his bones. The girls went home and complained to their mothers that he was possessed by the devil; that witches used him to do their voodoo, to capture people in spells, to work their roots on innocent souls.

He never once, however, approached Rhonda with his lips. She watched and waited in a corner of the classroom, sitting on upturned palms, but nothing happened. Once he accidentally tapped the bottom of her buttocks, and in a flurry she threw herself on top of him, flailing her arms and her breasts, which looked and moved like a woman's breasts. After that spectacle, the girls refused to let her near their circle and the boys threatened to break her bones as well, saying —*You ain't normal, shame-girl!* Miss Fauset expelled Rhonda from school for wanton acts.

His face took to appearing to her in her dreams, in meadows and forests, in the large vegetable garden at her grandmother's house, on swampy clouds that floated to nowhere. Ironing and starching clothes, sewing buttons back on shirts and darning socks; canning pears and peaches and peas and then preparing the pots for supper; squeezing lemons by hand because that was the best way to make lemonade. Pouring the sugar out grain by grain. She would feel his lips on her flat front, stinging her with desire. (Hunger is a potion, as the old folks say.) One time she lapsed into a dream of Billy only to awaken to a brash whipping by her grandmother, who— annoyed by the moans and words her baby used (and so incorrectly!)—smacked the girl's head, and consequently, the boy from it as well.

—There is a right way and a wrong way, Asenath explained to the girl. —Things you are not ready for.

—What is the right way? Rhonda asked.

—Do any of us really know? the grandmother cried, whipping harder.

But later, as her granddaughter whimpered to herself alone, Asenath Fowler found herself standing outside the school building. The children had long since dissipated. She stood dressed in her church clothes, a sprig of camellia hanging above her breasts. She saw Shame-Billy emerge from the building and called him over. —Are you the boy who thinks he is a man? she asked.

Billy did not lift his eyes.

—Well, Asenath said, looking him up and down, —Come here and talk to me. Let me try to put you right.

❧

The clock moved from six to seven to seven-thirty; startling certainty at each slam of a car door, but it was never him. Late, too late. The dress was finished, laid on her bed for the last-minute rush, but then she got up and threw it on hastily, careful with the zipper. She hadn't had a chance to do her hair, but that could be taken care of in a flash—she kept the curling iron hot in the bathroom. In the next room, the exact place where others on North Moss Drive housed children and oversize dressers, Rhonda moved to a small vanity table and began to paint her nails. Coral Mirage, to match her house, her dress, her underwear. As she spread out her fingers she imagined his hands: broad brown, the color of a wheelbarrow full of dirt, hands creased with motor oil that the detergent had not been able to remove. Sun, dirt, motor oil, detergent, musk. Onion, clove, maybe lemon. His face would be, as ever, handsomely unlined, though he spent most of his days in the tobacco.

He was too late. Eight o'clock. Tobacco did not grow in the winter—why wasn't he here yet? Men did not disappear into thin air for no reason.

❧

The snow was blinding; he'd heard the weather report just that afternoon, during which springlike temperatures had foolishly been predicted. Everywhere around him cars lay frozen, stalled, or in damaged heaps. He glanced at his wristwatch, knowing she would be impatient, likely to burst the moment he drove up. He could read her like a clock on the wall.

He had followed Rhonda north after she left seven years ago, but why? He couldn't tell you. Initially she had seemed surprised to see him standing there at her door, so far from Auntsville. She seemed surprised to learn that he had been thinking of her all these years, and giggled girlishly at his lust. She made some offhand remark about him only caring for her old grandma, to which he laughed, and she laughed as well. Silly ideas clouding a girl's head. Now a woman. (Legs, breasts grown into splashing hills, buttocks that could be construed as roomy and tight at the same time.) And yes, she had thought of him, too.

He promised to visit her the very next Christmas, and the one after that. From Auntsville he sent Rhonda parcels of ladies' undergarments, large bottles of inexpensive eau de toilette, long-stemmed matches, occasional dirty magazines, and locks of his curly chestnut hair (a white person's hair, but sexy nonetheless). From there on in, he was awash in her love.

Once in a great while, when he was in that sort of mood, Billy Merry would ask about the old woman. The old battle-ax. Just out of curiosity, of course.

Rhonda would laugh at him. —Why you care about her? She just fine where she is.

Tears forming in both their eyes. And that was the end of that.

※

She'd gotten in the habit of speaking to him every day as he left the school, lying in wait like the Trojan Horse. As he rounded the corner, she would call out, —Where you taking all those kisses, boy?

Long ago. In the garden behind her house, in the tangle of

catbrier, in the shade of a wisteria hung over a rickety scaffold-
ing, the old woman guided the boy's hands around her waist
and explained to him the importance of courting girls instead
of scaring them away. She had heard things about him—no
matter. This was how it was done.

Her voice soft and treacly, her waist as vast as a rainwater
barrel. He found he had to get even closer to encircle the old
woman, closer than was proper, and when he looked up, she
was smiling greedily into his face.

—This is the way. This is the start. You don't want them to
run from you. You want them to want you.

ॐ

Nine o'clock. Normally she would say to herself: *Nothing new
to this; all men are late.* Normally she would admit to herself
that all they really cared about was *some things,* never *other
things.* They never thought about your wishes, your desire to
break free from a thing unseen or unheard.

Rhonda walked past the Chinese partition separating the
vanity from a brass-and-leather wet bar and poured herself a
tumbler of Bristol Cream. She glanced out the window: nothing, only the shapes of two children, girls possibly, dashing
across the yard, knocking over her only potted plant. From the
left corner of the sky, an owl flitted back and forth between two
elderberry trees. The owl, she remembered from her grandmother's day, was sign of trouble. Rhonda held her breath;
there was definitely something wrong with this lateness.

ॐ

Her job at Featherstone Elementary and Middle Schools was
dull, but she loved to look at the children and secretly open
their textbooks as they played and hit on each other. Sasha

Devine, the little mixed girl, carried *Leaves of Grass* around with her everywhere and sometimes recited,

When lilacs last in the dooryard bloom'd. . . . And thought of him I love.

Plain silly. Mozelle Mountain, the other mixed girl (part Indian she claimed), stuck her nose in a book called *Confederate Spies and Soldiers*. Stupid girl, stupid book. Harriet-Ann Hutchinson, a full-blooded colored girl, carried *The Dawn of Our World* in her book bag, but it was clear that the pages had never really been turned. Why hadn't the stupid girl realized the beauty of those Greek men? They were practically edible! Rhonda shook her head in dismay. She knew a few of their names: Homer, Eurydice, Cupid, Rex. She searched her mind for the details, but nothing came up. It was so long ago, and Miss Fauset had thrown her out like a piece of garbage.

After recess was over and the bell summoned the children inside, Rhonda would sit in the sun—no matter how cold or how softly the snow fell—and bask a few minutes before returning to the hallway. This small space of time outdoors in the yard was like home, where oftentimes the stark North Carolina sun had been her only real company. The companion of her secret.

She had seen her grandmother take Shame-Billy into the garden and remove his trousers behind the blackberry thicket. The woman traveled the boy's hand along her breast, stopping at the nipple, encircling the massive dark space there. —You're all mine, the old woman had said.

Rhonda had witnessed this, the boy writhing in pleasure, a brief period of exploration and gasps, after which the pair of them, thick as thieves, stoically marched up to the house and returned to the garden carrying jars of lemonade. Rhonda had seen this. She had seen naked butts, breasts, arms, necks, tongues; braids and curls undone. Then a tall jar of lemonade, sides beading with sweat, the contents sometimes disappearing in one monstrous gulp.

In the yard the janitor would occasionally push his ash can on wheels over in Rhonda's direction. He would stand in the way of her light, darkening her awake, then make a simple joke about the weather or the misdeeds of the children. Sometimes his words contained faint praise.

—Say Miss Rhonda, the janitor would begin. —You looking pretty good there. You looking like you taking care of business. I know. I do the same myself.

(He knew he was the only one who ever talked to her because to his mind the rest of the teachers were uppity and the principal was a fag; that left him as the only person to appreciate the glory of Miss Rhonda Robinson. He was old as the hills and until now did not think anything of removing his teeth from his overall pocket and casually setting them in his head during conversation. The children made fun of him, leaving nasty notes on blackboards for him to read. He shrugged his shoulder: Hadn't his own kids behaved the selfsame way? Hadn't they called him narrow and dirty, all run away from home in bits and pieces—but that was years and years ago, and nowadays he was even having trouble remembering their names, the years in which they had been born, or even the shapes of their heads.)

Mr. Blank approached Miss Robinson on ash-can wheels. —Hey there, Miss Rhonda, he said.

—Hey there, Mr. Blank, Rhonda replied blandly, watching the children scatter around her. —How you?

—Can't complain, he answered. He held his lips tightly over his teeth. —Kids been treating you right?

—Same as ever.

—You ever think of having any of your own, Miss Rhonda? You'd make a fine woman.

(He'd meant to say *mother*. Mr. Blank kicked himself for this mistake.)

Rhonda nodded demurely; she too noticed what he'd said. He wouldn't have said it if he had seen her last Christmas Eve. In fact, his eyes would have popped out of his head if he'd seen the things she and Billy did together. Old man don't know his dick from his thumb. She turned and walked away.

That night, Mr. Blank took his dreams about Rhonda to bed. He was still a young man, if you counted desire as proof.

He folded his withered hands in prayer, just like his wife of long ago had taught him, only now he did not pray to Jesus or to the Lord Most High but to a caramel woman with large knees; he prayed to her loud fruity perfume and its spell over her shoulders; to the daisy shape of her mouth; to the way she did up her hair in two braided buns on the side of her head like women from the old days. He prayed to the volume of her behind as she switched down the hallways, shooing children to class. He prayed to the big words she used, the airs she put on, the way she smiled at the girls, maternal. He prayed to clothes, in particular to the black-and-pink gingham dress, the one that she had obviously *sewn down* to look more matronly, only for him it was obvious that you could let out a seam here and there and be pleasantly surprised. She was the stuff of dreams.

—Lord, let me not want, he prayed, before falling asleep.

⸎

Back in Auntsville, the meetings between the two lovers had been confined to the vegetable garden in the swarm of a late-afternoon sun, ticklish groping and instruction until ritual lemonade. She knew boys his age loved to drink, just as they loved tearing apart insects and running stolen cars and burying them in the field. This one was different, though; he barely touched the jar.

She sat next to him on the porch swing, where he did not think about insects or lemonade but about how he had just embraced her, how they had lain across vines of sugar-snap peas and moaned in unison. He had never heard voices travel at the same time, and found it bewitching. She'd allowed his tongue in her mouth as they sat amid rows of strawberries, a romantic touch. Through her dress, he massaged the womanly triangle between her legs while she dug her fingers into the earth, upsetting the birth of radish, carrot, and white sweet potato. She was not like the others. She did not scream, she did not harm his body or cause a haze to cover his eyes like a cobweb.

He wanted to go on, but she eventually stopped him, the sun hanging like a grapefruit in the sky. Like the other times, they did not make love. He was a child after all, she reasoned. She only wanted him to know what to do when the time came; said she was tired of girls being afraid of what they really wanted—soon he would become teacher. Just think of this as a sort of practice run.

But he did not want to practice forever. He wanted the seasoning of oldness; in his heart he imagined the heat of something undone and unraveling. He took her in his arms on the porch and uttered the words, —I love you.

Strangely, she shunned him.

Love was not for an old woman with things to teach. She demanded he notice her hips, her thighs, the way her breasts did not sag like other old women's. That he should look and dream; that he should measure up to her imagination; that he should not ask for earth when moon and stars danced in front of his nose. That he should not fall in love.

—Look at my granddaughter Rhonda, Asenath had told him then, wiping away his tears. —Rhonda is a person you can love. She is not like me at all.

❦

Late in the afternoon on the last day of school, Mr. Blank had pushed his broom up to the teachers' lounge and watched Rhonda eat her sandwich: fried chicken cutlet on hero bread, two large sweet pickles, a container of vanilla pudding. He moved extra slow, emptying the wastebaskets and clapping the erasers clean, touching the teachers' coats, straightening arms and lapels. She gulped coffee from a thermos and licked her lips like a cat. Mr. Blank checked the wastebaskets again.

He longed to pass Miss Rhonda and touch her on the cheek. To roll his ash can her way and kiss the velvet off her skin. An act of solidarity: He and she were terribly alone here. They were not teachers. They had no children. They withdrew themselves in dreams, he was sure.

Rhonda Robinson wearily glanced at him, then got up to adjust her dress in the mirror.

All he'd really wanted was a taste of Rhonda's hand. A confirmation.

Mr. Blank went outside the lounge and waited until she miraculously appeared; he walked her to the gymnasium. She was supposed to help line up the colored kids to be tested for sickle cell, help stop the little ones from crying at the sight of the needle. Mr. Blank told her he admired such kindness in a person.

—I wouldn't want to know if I was going to die tomorrow, he said. —I always just want to make the most of my days.

—These are little kids, Rhonda replied, annoyed. —They can't make those decisions for themselves.

—Still, he continued, —I wouldn't want to know. I'd want to live my life in the best way possible. Don't you agree, Miss Rhonda?

—Who wouldn't want to live their life in the best way? she snapped, opening the door to the gym. Then added, —You know, you remind me of someone.

—Miss Rhonda! he interrupted, alarmed that he should actually be in her thoughts. This was too much. —There's something I need to tell you in person!

But it was too late. Rhonda had already walked into the throngs of frightened children and once more left Mr. Blank behind.

❧

The snow had simmered to almost nothing once Billy reached the exit to West Amity on the Southern State Parkway. Oddly, a warmth filled the car, a warmth as damp and spongy as spring air. He had to keep his eyes open for the bright pink house. A shame to ruin a perfectly good house with that color, but what was that his business? The girl had something strange and permanent against her grandmother, but don't ask him.

Shame-Billy pulled the car into the driveway; no Rhonda. He waited.

(At their last meeting, when he was fifteen, Asenath had poked her tongue in and out of his ear, sparking his juices into electricity, but again at the word *love*, she recoiled. There was a warning. If he spoke it again, she would take another boy under her wing. If he spoke it again, she would lock the gate to her vegetables—forever. What was the purpose in loving, anyway? He had his whole life ahead of him. And she would be leaving for Long Island sometime soon, to the place where a body could get a regular house, not some old run-down thing.)

He went through the list in his mind. How he decided to call her bluff. How she'd finally left Auntsville for Long Island in what seemed to him to be the middle of the night. How he'd cried. How she had left him with only the scent of cloves and onion on his hands. How he hated the scent of betrayal.

How he took any and every woman who walked by him and ravished them with his new skills. How he broke hearts. The list continued: How he sent letters to a phantom address called the Plantation and when he received no reply, how he humped one girl after the other in vengeance. How he moved about aimlessly until about seven years ago, when, retribution in mind, he left for Long Island, only to have things change.

He'd vigorously sought out Rhonda, but at her door the first time discovered that the years had softened him. Add to that a house to practically call his own and a woman who answered the door, genuinely happy to see him. A loving woman, a receptive woman, one who would do just about anything at the drop of a hat. Did not trouble him with the word *love* but would walk on all fours or lie still as a dead person. Things had a way of metamorphosing, like a worm into a butterfly. A garden of sheer delights.

In the car he sat alone and waited. Seven years would end tonight. In the morning he and Rhonda would go and find her grandmother. Seven years had gone by without so much as a mention of her full name: Asenath Gertrude Fowler—how ungrateful! To Rhonda he had only called her the old woman, the bag of bones, the battle-ax. The crazy bitch. Now his heart shattered at its cruelty.

The lights were on everywhere in the house. Slowly, Billy Merry left the car and walked up the path to the front door.

※

Minutes before that, Rhonda had fallen into the chair in front of the vanity mirror. —Gone, she said to herself, —gone.

There was no answer to her tears, no legend or inscription on the rock-hardness of her memory, no unearthed instruction to forgive and forget—and the fact of that absence only made her cry harder.

※

Sitting on the corner of his bed, ready to spring into action, Mr. Blank was overcome by the faintest aromas of memory and fell backward on the mattress —Lord, give me strength, he mumbled, only the words came out like cattle's lowing. He put his head in his hands. —My children! he cried.

Why was he alone? Why couldn't he remember them? Everything had backfired, all the lessons and whippings and misguided attempts at feeling; sitting in a corner, in a closet, no light, too much light. Year by year they had all left the house, especially the girls, telling him he was incapable of love, warning him to stay far away. The boys learned to disavow his existence.

He wept. Rhonda Robinson would understand things differently. She would applaud his intentions—only just then he was not completely sure Rhonda wasn't one of his own. Hadn't he raised a girl like her, with legs shaped like vines? Hadn't he seen lips like Rhonda's in his house for years? Where?

Hadn't someone screamed at him because he loved too much? Or not enough? Where were they all?

Flat on the bed, he was convinced of the possibilities of life and of death, of sin and forgiveness, the power of lust that had layered, one night superimposing the next, for years and years and years, world without end. Desire had never abandoned him, had never left him or his dreams for dead.

And so, later that night, Mr. Blank found himself at Sixty-six North Moss Drive, in front of Rhonda Robinson's house. At the far end of the cul-de-sac he saw a car slowly edging its way on the road and knew instinctively that the car was moving toward the pink house. He stepped into a hedge of holly and waited.

Somewhere an owl whispered in the branches. A tiny voice scolded, making him tear his hand along the edge of a leaf. The car pulled into the driveway: a man at its helm. The tiny voice scolded again, and he recognized this as the voice of his wife, long gone. She was advising him to remember himself.

—No one can work miracles, she admonished, then faded into the holly in his hand.

࿐

After some time Billy Merry forced open the front door and found Rhonda curled in a ball by the stove. He unpeeled her gently and placed her in a kitchen chair. He asked her what was wrong.

—My grandma, she murmured. —I just got the call. She died tonight at the Plantation.

He winced, but not too visibly. Gone. He lifted the fainted Rhonda upstairs to the bedroom, passing the familiar slipcovered couch and splintered stair railing. Only after he lay her on the bed did she awaken and recall what this evening was supposed to hold.

—I can't do none of that! she shouted, bolting upright.

(She remembered the curl of his hair, the way he resembled a Greek statue: Homer, Oedipus, Cupid!) —*No! none of that now, please!*

Billy gently motioned her to lie down; all that was far from his mind.

After fixing a wet rag on her forehead, he went into the other room and sat at the vanity. Minutes later he got up, fixed himself a drink, and took off his coat. Seven years had ended sooner than he'd imagined.

❦

In the confines of the holly hedge, warm air lifting the night into Bethlehem, Mr. Blank undid his coat, slipped off the tie he had sloppily fastened to his neck, unbuttoned his best work shirt, and exposed his nubbed chest to the air. —If she wants me, she'll have me, he announced to the owl-less tree.

He looked up at what he thought was her window—beyond it, he envisioned a soft canopied bed and a pair of porcelain ballerina slippers atop an oak bureau. Time would pass; an apple cobbler would burn in the oven. Time would pass. He saw a woman squatting over him as if he were a bath of warm mud, moaning in pleasure, rolling her eyes to the back of her head.

He continued undressing, despite the chill and rustle of the hedge. He did not want her to come out and laugh at him. And yet, he could not help sending her this vision.

—What took you so long? his wife whispered from his hand. —This woman's been here forever, seems.

He shivered. He was almost naked.

—You don't need to ask about me, she continued. —Time heals all wounds. Even I forgive you for looking the other way.

—What do that mean? he asked.

—I was your wife, she answered. —I was the chance you had, but you looked the other way, time after time.

—Now is not the place for all that, he snarled.

—It always has a place, she sighed. —I was there forever, too.

֍

So there was no real reason to keep on coming here anymore, now, was there?

Billy looked at Rhonda in the bed and searched her face, her ears, her nape. He did not like the fall of her tears; they sounded like something he hated to hear in people, in women: loss.

What would loving be like after tonight? Asenath was gone. What was the purpose?

Billy poured himself another tumbler of Bristol Cream and walked back to the bed where Rhonda lay whimpering under a flutter of vanilla sheets. On her dress, the zipper had split itself from the fabric, exposing thousands of tiny threads that wiggled in the open like worms, revealing her large smooth back and the soft length of vertebrae; her shoulders.

He pictured the earth of the garden underneath his feet, the pebbles and soil and secret waterways, and, somewhere in the distance, a pot simmering on the stove. A pitcher of undrunk lemonade. Cloves and onions. His name had never really been Shame-Billy. It had always been Bill. William. My Lover.

He stretched himself out next to Rhonda. Downstairs the doorbell rang, but neither of them seemed to hear it. He reached over to her head and began smoothing the undone hair. Then he laid his hand on her neck. —There, there, baby, he said. —I love you.

She turned to face him. Behind her, the night sky full of the perfume of a dying winter.

—Tell me was it enough! she cried, squared to his face, the first time. —Tell me: Will it ever be enough?

The room settled with quiet. He stared back into Rhonda's eyes, searching for the remainder of the evening, for the remainder of his life with this woman, the inevitability of box living combined with the inevitability of love, the mud tracks out of the garden and onto the asphalt, but just then the door-bell rang again and woke him and Rhonda from their dreams.

❦

—*Why am I changing?* Asenath asked herself in bed earlier that evening. The clock had just rung seven.

Christmas Eve—the time of Love and Bounty and Family, only here she was—alone. For days she'd had the taste for gar-den dirt and for sun-streaked skin against her mouth, but her mind had abandoned her, making it impossible to properly sort out people and places. She threw off her blankets; outside there was nothing but an unusually balmy wind. The other women in the Plantation had stopped in her room to say good night, then turned their faces and wept. Someone gloomily asked if she wanted her Bible.

All her life she had dreamed of coming up north and leav-ing behind the beautiful and oppressive sunsets of North Carolina. All her life.

Now, prone in bed, all she could do was yearn for those skies; for heat and large gardens and busy kitchens and run-down houses and long gospel gowns that swept the floor. Back in Auntsville she had done many things—she had known a boy in the rows of her vegetables and herbs. Where was he now? Why had she turned him away? He fit neatly into a box of her design, but where? Here in Long Island her insides had withered to nothing.

And no, she did not want no Bible. Could someone instead please get that box of letters from the bottom of her closet? She'd read them years before, never answering a one. Now was the time.

From the crack in her windowpane, Asenath felt a startling trace of warmth in the air. She thought about Rhonda Robinson, saw her granddaughter scratching furiously at her flat chest, trying to get at something. (All wrong, all wrong. Wake up girl! Let me show you how. Let me come near you.)

She asked aloud, —*Are you still having those dreams?*

Pisces

by Anne Atall

I am Pisces, which to me explains 2 things:
   #1: why I am bisexual
   #2: why I love to fuck in the water

Let me explain.

About #1:

Pisceans are sometimes described as wishy-washy and indecisive, or as flighty and always coming and going. This notion probably comes from the image of the two fish in the sign: Each one swims directly opposite to the other.

A friend of mine once told me that Libras are more likely than other folks to be bisexual. Something about the Scales, and always struggling to remain in perfect balance. Well, I've decided to appropriate the bisexuality argument for my astrological sign, too. One of the fish is pulled toward the boys; the other swims fast and furious toward the girls. There you go: perfect balance dictated by the stars.

About #2:

I adore being in the water. When I was a child, my mother had to pull me by the hair from the ocean on more than one occasion because, despite chattering teeth and pruny fingers and toes, I refused to get out of the water.

I remember tubing down the Delaware River with a boyfriend of mine a few years ago. We went with a bunch of friends from school. A group had scouted out where the van would drop us off; they had a cooler of beer in the bushes nearby. Once the van had taken off and most of the suburban family day-trippers had floated off down the river, we pulled out the cooler and hooked it up between a few of the tubes with some rope.

The sound of the rushing water and the sun warming my neck and shoulders were all I needed for the Craving to kick in, but I suppose the beer also helped to make me lose what few inhibitions I do indeed have. My tube and my boyfriend's tube had drifted behind those of our friends. They paid us no mind as they splashed around and sucked down their beers. I used the rope to pull my tube over to his and climbed onto his lap. I had just planned on a little kissing, but as I bore down on him, and felt the thick, unyielding seam of his jean shorts pressed to my pelvic bone, his erection growing against the fleshy inside of my thigh, his tongue probing the warm, wet recesses of my mouth . . .

Somehow I managed to get my bikini bottoms off and tucked them into the front of my bikini top, under my T-shirt. I thrilled as the cold water splashed against my ass, and dripped from the thick, black hair between my legs, the drops spiraling down the crinkly strands like kids going down one of those corkscrew slides. My vaginal muscles had that quick little spasm that tells me I'm really turned on—it's kind of like the mild tremor before the Big Quake—which sent cold water shooting up my cunt, making my head spin.

He slipped out of his shorts, leaving him completely naked, but that was okay, because he was on the bottom and pretty much out of view.

And then we started going at it.

It was incredible. It's remarkable we didn't drown, actually. Just as I started to come, we hit rapids and the tube nearly flipped over. There was fear in his eyes, but I couldn't really care at that point; my nails dug in to his back as I struggled to hang on to him and the violent shocks traveling out from my center, wave upon wave, vibrating from my vagina to the tips of my fingers and toes.

Once we reached calmer water, I realized that I had lost my bikini bottoms somewhere along the watery way. I had to rip off the bottom half of my T-shirt to wrap around my waist as a makeshift skirt.

❀

When I am depressed, or stressed, or can't get to sleep, the thing I love most is a shower in the dark. The absolute dark that unplugs your ears before it morphs into a soft gray and the eyes take over once again. The sounds of drops hitting the vinyl curtain, slapping the porcelain tub like waves against the sides of a boat, the tiny pool of water forming in my navel—all work to soothe me.

I met a woman once who hated the dark. She told me she always slept with the TV on when she was alone. Once inside my starkly lit bathroom, I unbuttoned her jeans and tried to persuade her that a shower in the dark is one of the best things in the world. She seemed pretty convinced after I bent down to trace the lines of her navel with my tongue. She dropped her pants and laughingly showed me the shimmering wetness in the crotch. She is one of those women who never wear underwear. This has always struck me as slightly dangerous—rebellious, anyway. I couldn't even imagine what *my* underwear must have looked like.

Anyway, this is beside the point.

That shower was where I first lost my "queer virginity." Actually, that needs a little clarification. Women had gone down on me before, but I never really thought of that as lesbian sex; probably because it really irked me in college when girls I knew called themselves "experimenting" but would never in a million years let girl juice get in their mouths.

Anyway.

In the shower that night, in the dark, we kissed and kissed and kissed . . . I remember the heady sensation of feeling like I was losing myself in her mouth . . . drowning, in the water, in the circling of her tongue, in desire. I was delirious with the smells of her and me, at first separate, then mingling, then distinct again. The pattern of my breathing chased after hers; panting, shallow. My tongue traced the paths of her ear, around the outside curve, and then spiraled inward, flicking at the tiny hoop in the piercing as the hot breath from my nostrils steamed inside and caused a shiver. I kissed one breast as I squeezed the other, sucking, letting my teeth graze the hardening nipple . . . My tongue trailed down to her navel . . . I *love* belly buttons, and the way abdomens curve out from their sinkholes . . .

On my knees, I parted her hair with my tongue. She began to sway, and leaned back against the wall. The shower spray hit the side of my face and tickled my eyelashes. The smell was deliciously sharp; she tasted more salty than the Me I had tasted on her lips and my own fingers.

※

And I think of all this now, as I awaken with pruny fingers and wrinkly toes in the arms of the woman who currently holds my attentions and fascinations. Surprised by a thunderstorm, whose pelting raindrops were much too cold for the middle of August, we stripped down as soon as we reached the apartment. I ran a steaming bath and sprinkled the water with eucalyptus leaves and scented oils (I am a woman seduced by powerful smells) while she raided the refrigerator for the strawberries she had been craving all afternoon. When she climbed into the tub with me, it became clear that she hadn't craved the taste. She clamored for the experience. The easy sinking of her hard, sharp teeth into the soft, yielding fruit; the deep, deep red shocked by that sparkling white; the curve of the berry as she curled her tongue around it; the roughness of the seeds stroked by the tip of that playful tongue; the luscious juice dripping down her chin and making a soft splash in the water.

I chose one of the larger berries and trailed it down her neck before taking a bite. The bite uncovered the coldest, wettest part of the fruit, deceptively pink beneath the ripe red of the dry, seeded exterior. I pressed this wetness onto her collarbone and smeared it down her chest, eventually swirling it around her nipple before it disintegrated and I had to lick the mess from her body.

Me Between My Own

by Camika Spencer

It was 1987. It started with a natural need that came from the core of my young being. I was fifteen, taking a look at my pussy for the first time. It felt instinctive after laying in my twin-size bed gripping my forearm between the unyielding clutch of my legs feeling the need to hunch against something solid. A natural need to have something pressed against me. Inside me. As the overwhelming feeling of curiosity called, I jumped from the bed, careful not to wake my mother sleeping in the next room, and locked myself in the bathroom. I grabbed a hand mirror from the cabinet and propped myself on the toilet. At first glance it had the appearance of a piece of candy I once picked from a Valentine's Day sampler. A small ocean of pinkness surrounded by coconut-shell-colored waves of flesh with dark wispy beginnings of pubic hair. I ran my index finger around it, separating the outer lips, feeling the warm smoothness of my vagina. Exploring that intimate part of myself by traveling my finger in it as far as I could, wiggling it around, and withdrawing.

As I sat gap-legged on the toilet, I touched the tip of my clit. Added pressure . . . resigned . . . then again. It felt good so I repeated the activity, stroking my way into a new addiction. I leaned back on the toilet seat, closed my eyes, and exercised my hand more, humping against it with the fervor of a child pup trying to keep up with its mother. Then, without notice or warning, drums began to beat inside me. I opened my eyes and removed my hand, ignoring the pounding heartlike beat surging from my valley. My vision blurred and I saw myself as a young whore as a clear substance glistened my naive jungle and dripped onto the mirror. I jumped up, wiped myself, cleaned the glass, pulled up my panties, and tiptoed back to my room, cowering beneath my sheets, intending never to visit that sacred place again.

Shame engulfed me, as did the voice of my mother. "Keep your legs closed!" she'd said to me the day I got my cycle, three years prior, and every month thereafter sounding like a broken record, and despite her pointed finger preaching, there I sat, legs opened, revealing myself to myself. Disobeying Mama, I lay in my bed shivering with thoughts that I'd left some omen and my mother would find out I had failed at keeping my legs closed and she'd punish me. But I'd borne a fathomless curiosity that day. One that would send me on a journey later in life that would eventually end where it began. Me between my own.

෯

It was March 1999, I was twenty-seven years old, and Reginald and I had fucked for the last time. He was a beautiful, engaging, and intelligent man who was undersexed and deeply submerged in personal problems. I'd indulged my twenty-seven-year-old self in his drama for three years, until he finally admitted to me that I wasn't the one. With a few tears and a lot of curses, I released him. That sneaky spring night (three months after our relationship was over), as we fogged my car windows and called each other's names, I went as he came. I wasn't his after that. I didn't belong anymore. It was a rebound fuck. One of many fucks that came along once I began searching again for that feeling I discovered at fifteen. That *guilty that I hurt her feelings* or *maybe this will bring him back* kind of fuck. It was rushed, hard, and done without any of the conversation that it deserved. With every thrust and moan, I acquiesced. Finding that valuing myself didn't mean saving myself for Mr. Right, but it meant letting Mr. Could-Be-Right know up front who I was, what I wanted, and for him not to add or subtract to it. That would happen from here on out and it would save me a lot of heartache; so I thought. The months went by as I wrote in my journal and Iyanla-Vanzanted my way to answers as to why I was gainfully employed, childless, honest, dependable, attractive, spiritual, and smart *but* single. I wanted a man to call my own. No, let me change that. I wanted a dick to call my own. A dick that represented me to the fullest. A dick with passion, charisma, rapture, and a little adventure. A smart dick. This dick couldn't just be any old dick. Not the kind with children or girlfriend/wife drama. I wanted a dick that complemented my pussy. A single dick that wasn't down for the bullshit that comes with lack of communication or fear of rejection. I wanted a safe dick. A dick with testimonies about how life has dealt some hard blows but one that knew it was always in the best interest to keep getting back up and fighting the good fight. I wanted an honest dick. I wanted a dick that was sensitive enough to call me when it was thinking about me. Ask me how I was doing. Send me a birthday card. Be free enough to do these things because it was a caring dick and not a dick held up by time constraints, marital obligations, sexual frustration, tainted quickies, or the hassles of overbooking booty calls. Simply put, I wanted a personal, liberated fuck friend.

❊

It was August 1999 and his name was Terry. Beautiful. Talented. Single. Smart. "My reflection" was what he'd crowned himself. Terry had a sexiness that vibrated well past his oblique brown eyes and charming smile. It seeped through the way he smoked a cigarette while stroking himself in the middle of a good football game. His sexiness was in his lazy walk. It whispered to me when he danced, and it smiled at me when he called me by my last name. When he sang his favorite tune, it toyed with me and I let it. Me being five months' deep in excessive masturbation, Terry became my new fantasy. He was the air spirit that roamed over my hardened nipples, at night, as I lay in bed fondling my clit, believing that once we finally crossed that threshold there would be no reason for either of us to have alternates on the side. I had let him know up front that I wanted to put him where no man had been before. "Where is that?" he asked like a curious child. "Not to fuck you before I get to know you," I replied. I had become the new breed of female-nigga. Aggressive. Sly. Up front. Personable. Unattached. I made time to make a man feel special without intentions. Terry became special. I told him secrets, gave him gifts, cooked for him, loaned him money, and even told him how unique he was without batting an eyelash or stuttering. I did it all. Sure I cared, but not enough to entertain any premature thoughts or questions. My heart stayed at home. My feelings came first.

Dealing with Reginald had taught me that. Terry and I kicked it hard. We shared intimate nights at posh restaurants, feeding each other and having warm filling talks. Everything we had, we had in common. From sitting up sharing a joint as Chris Rock politically joked his way through thirty minutes on HBO down to the way we slept together, without touching or letting our libidos take over. He found me sensual and told me that he never doubted for a moment, if given the chance, he'd enjoy a roll in the hay with me. He'd even caught me staring at the modest bulge in his pants on several occasions. I was trying to check the merchandise on the sly and had gotten caught. It was unpretentious even though I was oddly embarrassed, but there were days that my mouth watered thinking about wrapping my warm, wet mouth around his hardened cock while watching him enjoy being enjoyed. He laughed about the whole thing. Joked. Nervous laughter sometimes. In the space of five months Terry and I had become close. I respected him. But it wasn't long before shit began to fall apart. I found out that Terry had been involved in a relationship that lasted longer than the Civil War. He'd been involved with the love of his life for seven years and abruptly she ended it. Left him hanging like the nuts he owned. She'd hurt him. He missed her. She moved away, putting states between them. He kept her picture openly posted in his bachelor's pad. I let it affect me. My lusting disappeared. Fantasies became fragmented. The wetness that consumed my panties when I first met him no longer existed. I'd attracted a man with issues, which meant he no longer had the potential to be a personal, liberated, free fuck friend. Unfortunately, I wasn't willing to spend another five months on a brother only to have my hard work crippled. Terry would have to do. We discussed his feelings, and he voiced that he was okay. Told himself that it was over. Convinced himself that life goes on. Preoccupied himself with preoccupied people to keep from dealing with the detachment. Point-blank, I was embarking upon fucking a passionate but hurt brother. I was considering sharing nakedness with covered nakedness. Having fun while losing in the game of sex.

❦

It was November 1999. I'd turned twenty-eight and had put Terry on the back burner. As much as I wanted to have sex with him, I didn't have the strength or the tolerance to look in his eyes and see his fears, reluctance, and want all at once. As I pondered actually crossing the line between the surreal and the substantial, where my sex life was concerned, I ventured to deeper pastures. Not greener. Found sex without the touching. I went cyber. I logged into a chat room as April_22. A shy, rare, and curious cybergirl typing her way around a room full of bisexual females. It was new. It was exciting. My Scorpion passions took me there. Sure that if the right opportunity presented itself, I would taste whatever nectar dripped from the branches of the chat tree. It was after all safe, noncommittal, and a great way to openly explore taboo fantasies at my own discretion.

As soon as I logged on, sisters acknowledged my presence. I followed along, letting them know I'd never slept with a woman but was curious, which validated my attendance. I opened up and found myself engaged in a conversation with a married woman who too was curious, but afraid. She said that her husband knew about her wanting to lie with a woman and had tried to hook her up with a local beautician, but she wanted to do the search and find on her own. She read hopeless. Her words were without the will to really try and get out there to find that person. She wasn't my type (no pun intended). I relayed my own feelings of wanting to have a woman between my legs but to ultimately remain heterosexual. This was purely fantasy for me. A risk. We talked as women do. Supporting. Comforting. Questioning. Reassuring each other that we'd eventually complete our journeys, but it would not be with each other. Then a private message came to me. It butted in. It interrupted. It asked me what I looked like.

The handle (name) attached to the message was Brklyn Brotha. His invasion was as deliberate as it was familiar. I responded giving him my age, height, weight, eye color, and skin tone. He said deep brown-skinned women turned him on and that his dick was hard as he sat thinking about what I felt like. Instantly I was aroused.

He'd captured my attention. We talked and I learned that he was dissatisfied in a premature marriage gone sour. But unlike the sister I'd been chatting with, Brklyn Brotha was happy, energetic, bright, and knew exactly what he wanted. He was looking for pleasure. Sexual satisfaction. What his wife didn't do for him, cyberwomen did. He was open. Uninhibited. Unafraid. Immediately we clicked. Dirty talk. Deep breathing. Touching myself in places he'd ask me to. Sending me his phone number for one hour and fifteen minutes of extreme phone sex. I leaned against the hallway wall with a dripping-wet twat as he told me where he wanted to lick and taste me. His hard New York accent penetrated my ears. Tingled my soul. Took me places. Electrified me. I met his words with sucking sounds and moans. He asked me to taste myself and I did, hating that this was a chance meeting that could only survive inside modem lines, secret log-on names, passwords, and keyboard kisses. As I fell to the floor, spread my legs, and let Brklyn verbally bring me to orgasm, he exploded on the other end of the receiver and then there was silence. We both were exhausted. I felt at ease. Between deep breaths we ended our relationship as we hung up our phones. I walked around the house naked the rest of the day.

❧

It was December 1999. New Year's Eve. The dawn of a new millennium. Things would never be the same after tonight.

Not only for the world, but for me. Terry had called and asked if he could come over. I hadn't talked to him in weeks. He called at eight and was at my place by a quarter of nine. He brought a gift, two blunts, a bottle of wine, and his charming smile. He said that he never made plans to bring in the coming of the millennium and that he hoped to catch me. I'd spent most of the evening at work and knew I'd be too tired and sullen to want to party. I'd come home, taken a long bath, rented some flicks, and planned to be asleep before midnight struck. Until he called.

He came in smiling. "Put some music on," he said as he breezed past me and headed to the kitchen. "Mitchell," he called my last name, "tonight is going to be our night." He placed the gift on the counter and proceeded rambling around.

I watched him pull two wineglasses from my cabinet and place them in the freezer to be chilled. He then lit a joint and held it between his lips as he walked past me and posted two incense sticks in a nearby plant. Serenity. That was the scent of the thick lines of smoke dancing from the sticks. Terry walked up to me and offered the joint. I took it and inhaled deep. Yeah, I needed to be high right about now. The odor from the J was pure and strong. I liked it. I appreciated it. I put five CDs in the changer. Eric Benet, Sarah Vaughan, Stevie Wonder, Erykah Badu, and Maxwell. If nothing else happened tonight, at least we'd be high and singing some good music. We both sat on the floor and talked. I decided to let Terry call whatever shots would be called this evening. The ball was in his court. I was on defense. Third down and long. I remained lithe to his presence. For the next hour and a half we conversed about everything from our careers to who would put out a Grammy Award–winning CD next year. We laughed. Sang. Questioned. Shared. Things felt like they had been when we first met. I was enjoying the moment. Dry panties. No fantasies running concurrently through my brain. No longer caring if we had sex. Terry pulled me to my feet as I downed the last of the wine. The glasses were still in the freezer and probably cracked from the cold by now. My buzz was strong but I was still aware of what was going on. He pulled me close as Stevie Wonder began singing about all being fair in love. It was a mellow tune. Terry shifted me close to his torso and rested his head near mine. He hummed gently near my ears, causing the fuzz on them to tingle. I felt the bulge in his pants jolt and relax. The dry between my legs no longer was.

"Mitchell," he said cozily.

I pulled back and looked into his eyes. They were a hazy shade of cranberry. I said nothing. Looked concerned. Curious.

"I want to make love to you tonight. Before these thousand years are up, I want to make love to you."

I could hear Stevie's voice loud and clear. He was singing to me. Not to us, but to me.

Terry leaned in and kissed me. Softly at first. Gentle. His lips tasted like soft, wine-and-cannabis-flavored pillows. I closed my eyes as he came in for more. Our tongues touched.

The softness of Terry's mouth washed mine. His hands slid up the side of my Victoria's Secret mesh camisole. The fleshy palm of his hands rested against the skin of my back. He rubbed.

Terry pulled back and looked at me one last time. His eyes wanted a lot of things. Some of the things I could no longer just give. They were things I wasn't ready to give. Things he wasn't ready to receive. I placed my hand underneath his stubbled chin and pulled him back to me. He came willingly. His hands massaged my butt and waist. Cupped my breasts.

Raised me and carried me to the kitchen. Placed me on the counter. He unfurled my legs and removed the pajama bottoms I'd borrowed from him back in September. Tasted me through my panties. Listened to me moan. Listened to me whisper his name.

He lifted his shirt and let it fall to the floor, where he then took me. The refrigerator hummed in the silence between CD changes. Terry's tongue watered my breasts. Rained on them. Gave them renewed life. The warmness of his hands sent chills through me. We looked at each other under the kitchen lights. Confirmation. I met his tongue with mine as he positioned himself under me. Eric Benet crooned about using the pain in his heart to set his lover free. Damn. Revelations began to come to me. Was I as free as I thought I was? Could I do this with no strings attached? I slipped my lips around his penis and tasted him, putting my conscience in the backseat. He tasted good. Too good. He moved his hips in rhythm with my motions. He ran his hands through the wildness of my hair. I felt sounds reach his lips but gave them no entrance to the open air around us. He was still afraid. Taking a chance on taking a chance. I couldn't help him. I could no longer help . . . myself. The music faded as we melded on the kitchen floor. I licked Terry up from his navel to his neck and with that, we entwined.

Ten minutes later we were butt naked and in my bed creating our own song. Told Stevie Wonder he was a liar and deemed Eric Benet a coward. The passion between us made our relationship make sense. Terry looked at me just before he entered. The pulse of his dick thumped against my thigh. I smiled. He smiled. Allowed me to put the condom on. He entered. Smooth. Quick. With care. I sighed. Thrusted against him. Created a new rhythm. His body caved around mine.

Sweat formed between our abdomens. Party goers laughed outside in the night. He rose up. Looked at us. Looked at himself inside me. Watched as his stick, covered and strong, moved in and out, solid against the caverns of my vagina. The friction made me tingle inside. The quicker he moved his hips, the better I began to feel. He closed his eyes, lifted his head toward the ceiling, gripped his hands beneath my buttocks, and shifted me closer. The friction sent that electric feeling through me. I squeezed him in. Suffocated his movements. Grooved with him until the power of my climax overwhelmed me. I became the wild woman he thought me to be. The woman he needed. The woman every man needed, sometimes. He called out my name. My first name. Called it like he was falling and needed to be saved. Another strong thrust. Insanity and laughter rose in my chest. He gritted his teeth. I tried to hold my breath. Quick short immediate strokes. I yelled out affirmations.

We rammed each other. Laughed separate laughs. Grunted. Begged each other for forgiveness and climaxed simultaneously. I'd never come with a man. He withdrew and I became disturbed. It'd been too long. He fell on me. Delirious. Panting. Clutching my hair. Breathing against my neck. Too close. His skin invaded my space. I wasn't used to having a warm body against mine after I climaxed. It had been ten months. I had become accustomed to curling up in my own space. Stroking myself into a peaceful slumber. I was used to letting the spirit dwell over me.

"Get up," I said. It was in my throat. Barely audible. Not sure it wanted to be heard. "Terry, get up." This time louder. Stronger.

He didn't stir.

"You have to leave."

He looked up. Eyes barely opened. "What's the matter?"

"I don't know, but you have to leave."

He frowned. Rose without further argument. "Are you okay?"

"No. I'm not okay. I'm sorry but . . . I just need to be alone."

He stroked my pubic hairs. Stared me in the eyes.

"I hope you're not offended. It's not you." I tried to comfort him, but the comfort wasn't in my voice.

"No, I'm fine. I'm happy. If you want me to leave, then I will."

I sat up. Looked around the room. Looked at him. "I think I've been masturbating too long."

He smiled. "You know, it's possible that you have. The way you turned over afterward indicated your lack of human touch."

"I masturbated last night and this morning," I confessed. Smirked. Enjoyed the thought. Ignored his comment. I was in my own world already.

"Tell you what," he said as he cascaded downstairs to get his pants. "Take a break from it. Discipline yourself. Keep your hands from between your legs for as long as possible and when you can't stand it anymore, then call me."

I frowned as I followed him. I was still naked. "This is not something I need you to conquer. I'm happy before and after I masturbate."

"Baby, I understand your plight," he replied. "There's one thing that masturbation can't give you."

I asked, "What's that?"

He walked over. Hugged me. Squeezed tightly. Kissed my cheek. Told me he enjoyed being with me. Stroked my skin. Irritated me.

I felt crowded. Overused. Like I was being put in a straitjacket. I didn't care for being kissed, stroked, or ego-boosted after sex. I wanted to sleep. I wanted to cum and go the hell to sleep without the closeness of someone else. I'd learned to live without the affection. Had been forced through poor selection to live without the affection. I'd learned that the climax is the goal; everything else was like having seventy clowns at one birthday party with four children. It was too much for a casual experience between the sheets.

"It just dawned on me that my fantasy world is what I like about me," I replied. "I can be whatever I want and sex who-ever I want in my mind without having to worry about stamina, performance, snuggling, or even body odor." My revelation brought out a sigh in me. A sigh that made me feel safe. "I like having that without human intrusion."

Terry was fully dressed. He stared at me longingly. I felt sorry for him and for me. Remembered how much I used to want him. How I still do, in my mind. Still would like to place my mouth on his penis every now and then, but no longer wanted him or anyone else inside of me if they couldn't be happy living upstairs on the left side of my brain.

"Don't forget to open your present," he said. "I got it especially for you." He grabbed his keys, hugged me as friends do, and left.

It was a few minutes till midnight. I turned off the lights downstairs and headed up to my room, gift in hand. I sat on my bed. Leaned down and smelled me and Terry on the sheets. Smiled a grateful smile. Missed his voice. I opened the present, awed. In my hands was a framed photo of me and Terry. It was taken when we first met. On the grass watching an Al Jarreau concert. Hugging. Looking like fuck friends. The best of friends. I fell on the bed and rested the picture beside me. Tomorrow I would place it downstairs on my bookshelf for any visitor to see. I lifted my knees and positioned my legs as if

Terry was between them. As if Brklyn Brotha was between them. As if a female was between them. As if Reginald was between them. I fingered my clit and caressed my vagina, sticking my finger in it as far as I could, wiggling it around and withdrawing. Added pressure . . . resigned . . . then again. Felt the wetness ooze from me. I was glistening. I rotated my hips in slow motions against the pressure. Created friction. Party whistles, excited yells, and fireworks went off in the night somewhere outside. A new era had arrived. Like Indiana Jones, I journeyed my ocean of pinkness surrounded by coconut-shell-colored mountains of flesh with dark wispy adult pubic hair. Tasting who I had almost become at fifteen, who I liked being at twenty-seven, without the aid of a hand mirror. Liberated. Disobeying Mama by opening my legs. I was the something solid I'd been hunching to discover. Me between my own.

Fish Eyes

by Kim McLarin

The first time they slept together everything was normal, and afterward Faith laughed at the worries she had nursed. Charlie was only the second white man she had ever dated. The first was in high school: During her senior year she fooled around with a British exchange student out of curiosity and boredom and because he asked and mostly to scandalize Mother. But Faith didn't sleep with that guy. She kissed him a few times and pressed against him in the dark but she never let him run his clammy hands over her breasts and she never, ever thought about touching his penis, although he was nice enough and very funny, with weak green eyes and wild brown hair and lips like thin slivers of raw fish. That's what Faith used to think about when he kissed her: the catfish her mother bought whole and cleaned at the kitchen sink. It was Faith's job to wrap the heads in newspaper and carry them out to the garbage can. She always imagined she could feel those cloudy fish eyes staring at her in reproach.

Charlie's lips were thin, too, but Faith liked them. She liked most things about Charlie, his smile, his slippery blond hair. She liked the way he looked at her, the way his gray eyes ranged over her face. She liked that he played guitar (she had never learned an instrument but always wanted to) and that he spoke French, as she aspired to do, and that he loved Ellison and Hemingway and that he had no interest in football or beer.

Most of all Faith liked the easily discernible fact that Charlie found her both extraordinary and not. She loved that; it drew her to him like a serious piece of mojo working. Charlie thought her beautiful and talented, and appreciated what she had to say about things, unlike Jerry, her last boyfriend, who had been inordinately concerned about the state of her fingernails and the length of her thick and bushy hair. At the same time, Charlie didn't treat her like some of the white people she knew at work, the ones who clapped her on the back and cried genius every time she wrote a sentence in which the noun and verb agreed. Charlie seemed both impressed and unimpressed.

She had met him at a book-signing party in West Philadelphia and been frighteningly riveted. They stalked one another across the floor all night, avoiding eyes, sneaking glances, until finally she saw him toss back his drink and lope her way, his tail twitching to and fro like a hopeful puppy dog.

He asked for a date. Faith hesitated; and when she saw the effect of her hesitation she hesitated some more. Finally she agreed. She gave him her number. He telephoned almost immediately. They took in a movie—she couldn't remember which—then dined at a Thai restaurant on Eighth Street near Chinatown. They talked and laughed so loud and so long Faith forgot to wonder what all the people around them must think. He drove her home to the sounds of John Coltrane, walked her to her door, kissed her gently, promised to call.

When the telephone didn't ring right away she was disappointed but not worried. She knew the game; the trick was to wait, to not seem impatient. Sure enough, four days later Charlie called to ask her out. They took in a Brazilian film at the art museum, then went downstairs for a giddy tango lesson. It was a young, affluent crowd, mostly white, the kind of liberal-thinking people who in five years would sneak guiltily to the suburbs but for now reveled in the madness of city life. Everyone skidded and laughed and mugged on the dance floor to the sensuously thick music, and they grinned at each other and mopped their brows and said out loud what a handsome, tall, muscular couple Faith and Charlie made.

Over the new few weeks Faith came to see that a dating game with a white man was still a dating game. They went out together, talked wittily, laughed sexily, presented one another their best selves. Then they'd ignore one another for a few days to prove they could and then go out again. But she was having fun with Charlie. There was something about him, a smell, a look, that pulled her toward him. At the end of each date she wound up pressing against him in his car, on the sidewalk outside her apartment building, in the bright but empty hallway outside her door. She even let him into the living room once because she couldn't stand it. They ended up on the couch for half an hour, grinding tongues and mouths until her lips were bruised and they both were moist and panting and it was either kick him out or go to bed. She kicked him out.

She always made men wait before sex; not long, just long enough to weed out the worst ones, the players and scorekeepers. Just long enough to keep herself from feeling used when and if they disappeared. She made Charlie wait even longer, checked as she was by meandering midnight thoughts about the forbidden strangeness of sex with a white man. Him and her, skin to skin, naked and warm and glistening; she couldn't quite make the picture work. He would not be physically different, of course. He'd have the same equipment in the same amount in the same places. She did not believe, as her mother did, that white people smelled like wet dogs or were physically deficient "down there" or possessed gelid skin like the dead. It was her gut that hesitated, not her body or her mind.

Besides, Charlie made it clear he was still seeing other women.

"I have plans for this weekend and for most of next week, but maybe we could get together after that?" he said early on, when they seemed to be getting along well.

"Sure, just give me a call," she said nonchalantly. And when he finally did telephone, she was busy, busy, gone. Which of course just made her more desirable. He called again; she was busy. He called again and again until finally she was free.

On their fifth date they went to a James Taylor concert in the park. Sitting on the lawn in the dusky evening light, drinking wine, she felt expansible. She turned to Charlie. "Let me ask you something." The opening act began clearing the stage. All around them people swarmed and stood and called out to friends far away. "Ever dated a black woman before?"

"Nope." Charlie answered as if he had anticipated the question. Then he grinned. "First time."

The stage lights dimmed and a whisper of anticipation swept through the crowd.

"Another question: When we're out together do you think about the fact that I'm black?"

Charlie looked at her. She looked back. Up front, on the darkened stage, James Taylor's voice rang out. "No, of course not," Charlie said. She couldn't tell whether the tremor in his voice was shock or deception. "Do you think about the fact that I'm white?"

"All the time," she said.

Afterward he drove her home and asked if he could come in to use the bathroom. While he was occupied, she rushed around her apartment, picking up stray dishes, hiding clothes, dimming the light. She popped a John Coltrane CD on the stereo and remembered, with horror, the jar of hair grease lurking on the bathroom sink. She imagined Charlie lifting the great green container in bafflement, sniffing it. *What the hell is this? Some kind of exotic sexual lubricant?* Picturing his confused expression, Faith began to laugh. White people weren't that naive. Were they?

He exited the bathroom with a sheepish smile and said yes to the nightcap she offered. They sat on the couch and talked and talked and talked and she had no real sense of what was being said. Her tipsy brain kept focusing attention on his mouth, his lips, the sly red snake of his tongue. He trained his eyes on her, lowered his voice, ran his thumb lightly up and down her arm until she thought she might, like fine crystal, begin to hum.

"Whoa," she said, standing with great effort. "I think we better call it a night."

"Sure." He stood, too, and took her face into his hands. She sighed audibly and leaned into the kiss. She was a sucker for a guy who touched her face. A guy who touched your face was really looking at you—not just clutching a pair of breasts or groping a butt. At least that was the way it felt to Faith.

He ran his hands over her neck and down to her breasts, then followed with his lips. She molded herself against him, felt her heated flesh like kneaded dough to be rolled and pressed and formed into shape. She heard him moan and noticed the music had ended. He moaned again and came back to her lips, pulled one into his mouth. "You're so beautiful," he whispered.

"Mmmm," she said.

They moved into the bedroom, dropping clothes as they went. She felt as verdant and lush as a rain forest and she wanted him, but still part of her held back, watching. She was waiting for a slip. A word. A whispered sentence that would tumble from his mouth and fracture the ground beneath her feet. She waited while he peeled off their clothes and eased them onto the bed. She waited while he circled her nipple with his tongue. She waited while he nibbled and kissed and stroked until, against her will, her hips loosened and her back arched to meet him. She waited while her body danced and Charlie moved on top of her, eyes squeezed so tight the fine blue veins in his eyelids stood out like the spine of a leaf. She waited while he eased himself inside her, while he tensed and moaned, while be began, slowly, to gallop her, while he moved faster and faster, while he cried, "Oh!" and then her name, while he came with a shudder and cry and collapsed onto her breasts, while he panted and reached out his hand to touch her face. She waited. His skin glowed blue white in the light from the security lamp outside her window. She stroked the moistness from his back.

After a few minutes he moved to her side and took her hand for a kiss.

"I'm sorry. I couldn't wait."

"It's okay. I never come on the first time with a guy. It takes me a while."

"Something for me to look forward to."

"To work forward to." She laughed and turned onto her stomach. He leaned over her and kissed her neck.

"I love your skin," he said. He ran his tongue down her back. "It's so smooth. It's like chocolate."

"Chocolate?" She tensed. "What do you mean by that?"

"Just that it's smooth and delicious. Don't you like chocolate?" Charlie tapped her butt and chuckled and lay his lips against her neck. "Did that bother you? What I just said, about the chocolate? I mean, it was a stupid thing to say, it slipped out. I hope I didn't offend you or anything."

Faith pulled him into her arms and kissed his face, then

picked up his hand and kissed it, too. It was, she noticed, the same color on both sides, the color of bread dough. She wrapped her own two-toned hand around his, wrapped her long, sable legs around his pale ones, and thought they looked like a brotherhood poster there on her bed, cobbled together, side by side, ebony and ivory together. Faith thought about saying this to Charlie, but his eyes were closed and so she closed her own and smiled to herself and floated, becalmed.

She had drifted off when she felt Charlie disengaging himself. She opened her eyes to see him rising from the bed.

"I better go home," he said, beginning to dress. "I've got to work early tomorrow."

"Oh yeah. Okay." She had hoped he would stay the night. "Me, too."

Faith put on a robe and walked him to her door.

"I had a great time," he said.

"Me, too."

"Thanks."

Faith laughed. "You don't have to thank me. It's not like I fixed your car or something."

"I just meant for the wonderful evening. I'll call you tomorrow."

After he left she climbed into bed, tired but exultant. She felt as if she had tiptoed her way through a minefield and made it out the other side and now she could sink into her pillows and relax. Her breathing slowed. Her mind wandered off, dancing on snowy white clouds to the sugary beat of a Paul McCartney song.

※

Charlie went to Chicago for ten days. While he was gone he called her twice, and though he seemed distracted both times

Faith thought the calls were themselves a good sign. She left a teasing message on his answering machine on the day he was due back in town, inviting him to dinner. When he returned the call his voice was warm and seductive, as though his ardor had been only temporarily cooled by the Chicago wind.

They ate Italian that night, barely able to choke down their pasta for the tension pulling them across the table toward each other. Afterward, back at her apartment, they kissed and licked and sucked on the couch for half an hour, until Faith pulled away, breathless, and stood up and took Charlie's hand and pulled him toward the bedroom. Charlie winced.

"What's wrong?"

"It's my shoulder. I think I pulled a muscle yesterday at the gym." He stood in the doorway to her bedroom, rubbing his shoulder, his eyes wide in surprise at the pain like a child.

"Poor baby. Here, lie down and let me massage it for you."

Charlie lay on his stomach. Faith straddled his butt and leaned forward to knead his back. He purred under her hands.

"That feels good," he said. Then a moment later, "Would you really like to do something to make me feel better?" His voice sounded hesitant. Faith laughed. They were half naked on her bed. He didn't have to ask.

"Of course," she said leaned down to kiss him. But Charlie swung her onto her back and caught her face in his hands.

"Let me tie you up," Charlie whispered. His normally pale face had flushed pink, but then he leaned down to kiss her hard against her mouth and when he pulled away there was a tiny white circle around his lips from the pressure. Faith thought: White people are always changing colors.

Charlie's voice was thick. "Or you can do it to me. Tie me up and whip me."

For a moment she heard only the inconstant sounds of the apartment dwellers around her, the noise of human beings packed into too small a space: conga music from next door, the nine-year-old upstairs as he thumped across the ceiling like a monster eager to break in. Her mind raced, in search of a reference point, and, finding none, came back to search his face. Charlie lay above her, staring down at her from a great height, as if she had fallen into a well and he did not know what to do. His face struck her as comic and so she giggled. Faith giggled and then she laughed, harder and harder. Her laughter rolled her away from Charlie on the bed.

She noticed Charlie staring across the bed at her, a smile dimming on his face. The longer she laughed the dimmer the smile, until it faded back into his skin.

"Are you okay?" he asked, finally. He had moved to the edge of the bed and sat with his legs drooped over the side, his back to her. He twisted his head around to face her as she settled down.

"Yeah! Yeah!" She gasped for air, trying to calm herself. "Must be the wine!"

"I had no idea I was this funny," Charlie muttered. "I should be a comedian."

"I'm sorry." Faith panted through her chuckles, as if she were giving birth. "It just hit me wrong."

"It wasn't a joke," Charlie said.

"I know." She began to giggle again.

"I was serious."

"I know."

The giggles started; at the same time Charlie lurched across the bed to kiss her, hoping, she could tell, to head off a second round. "I want you," he whispered, but the tickle of his breath on her face was hilarious. It set her off.

"Sorry!" She convulsed with laughter, curling away from him on the bed. He sat up and crossed his arms.

"Can't say I've ever had this reaction before."

"Sorry!"

"Maybe I should leave," he said. She could tell from the pout in his voice he wanted her to stop him, to beg him to stay. But she couldn't stop giggling.

"Maybe you should."

He grabbed his clothes in a huff. "Don't hurt yourself," he said roughly and left the room.

The front door slammed and her giggles died.

※

Faith needed to talk to someone. Under normal circumstances she'd talk to Pauline, but Pauline wasn't crazy about Charlie. To say she hated him would not be too strong a term, though the two had never met. Pauline was deadly opposed to crossing the color line. If she heard about this little incident it would only confirm her feelings. She'd say, "I told you so," then get in a cab and hunt Charlie down. No, Faith couldn't talk to Pauline. And she couldn't talk to her mother, of course, and she couldn't talk to any of her male friends. What she needed was a white girlfriend to ask. A white woman could put Charlie's request into perspective. A white woman could tell her if white guys all went in for this kind of freaky shit.

He wanted to tie her up. And he wanted to be whipped. The idea, the image rolled around her mind all the next day, bumping into things, shattering her concentration, boggling her. She was alternately angry, disgusted, amused. Most of all she was perplexed. No man had ever—ever—asked her before to do such a thing. Why would Charlie ask now? Was there something about him, or something about her? Had she said something, done something to suggest she was into that stuff?

Faith tried to imagine her last boyfriend, Jerry, stretched out on her bed and trussed up like a pig. Jerry was six foot two, substantial, as thick around the middle as a tree. He was a newspaper photographer whose oft-announced goal was to quit his job and open his own studio, to escape from the soul-sucking pressure of working for the man. He pitched himself as a black prince looking for his queen, but he got antsy when he found out Faith made more money than him, and he didn't like her to say too much at parties. He'd even bought her a copy of that book, that "guide to the black woman," that thinly disguised piece of misogynistic crap. As a joke, he said.

She tried to imagine Jerry shackled to her bed like a slave, begging for a little humiliation while she stood over him with a whip. The image made her laugh it was so absurd; Jerry would rather eat bricks than do something like that.

On the other hand, Jerry had his own sexual tics. He was a wonderful lover, slow but not too slow, gentle but not too gentle, and from the beginning he found her turn-on points. But during one of the first few times they made love, just as she was starting to climax, Jerry grabbed a pillow and put it over her face. In her surprise and panic she kneed him in the balls; that was the end of that little party trick.

Jerry also had an annoying way of always referring to his penis as himself, in the third person. "Please take Jerry in your mouth," he'd say as they sat making out on the couch. Or "Jerry's hard. He wants your hand around him." Or "Jerry wants to be inside you, baby, right now." This kind of body-part animation wasn't unusual for guys, she knew, but it irritated her nonetheless. Toward the end, when everything but the sex was bad, she started pointing out that these things were not literally possible, that she could not take Jerry into her mouth, he was too big. She did it just to piss him off. It worked; Jerry took Jerry and left.

But Jerry had never asked her to do something so sick, so humiliating. Nor Charles, nor Garret, nor any other black man she knew. Only Charlie. Only the second white guy she ever let near herself. She knew what she should do. She knew what Pauline would say: Cut him loose. The only problem was she liked him. She liked him a lot.

Still, by the time Charlie called, creaky-voiced and repentant, she had resolved to cut him loose.

"I miss you," he said. "Have dinner with me."

"I don't think so," she said. But she'd forgotten how alluring was the sound of his voice.

"Please. I've been thinking about you nonstop; I can't get you out of my mind."

"How unfortunate for you," she said. But she was weakening.

"Faith," he said. Just her name, just like that. "Faith."

"I don't know."

"At least let me come over and explain," he asked.

She let the silence build for a while, then said, "I guess I can spare a few minutes tonight."

He arrived bearing wine and red roses and a shopping bag that smelled of lemongrass. She stood in her living room, arms folded, face set like a stone.

"Before you say anything, let me talk, okay?" Charlie laid the roses at her feet. "I'm sorry. I apologize. I just got carried away. But if I offended you, I'm sorry. I didn't mean to." He pulled her into his arms, fluttered his lips against her neck. Her knees softened, and she leaned against him. Maybe she'd been too quick to judge. Maybe he hadn't meant anything, after all. "I just got carried away," he said. "When a man's around you he just naturally gets certain thoughts."

The words pierced her heart like a scalpel. *A man just naturally gets certain thoughts.*

He felt the change in her body and looked into her face. "What's wrong?" he asked.

She felt sick. A knot seemed to have formed in her stomach. He was looking at her all wide-eyed and innocence, which only made it worse. She pulled away from him, walked to the other side of the room. "Let me ask you something, Charlie. You ever try to tie up one of your white girlfriends?"

"What?"

"It's a simple question. Did you ever ask a white woman to do what you asked me to do?"

He stared at her as if she were speaking a language he could not understand. "What are you talking about?"

"I'm talking about why you're with me, white boy. I know what you think: black women, dirty sex."

"I do not!"

Faith crossed her arms and smiled, though the tears were pushing up behind her eyes. "Sure, you do. I bet you couldn't wait to tell all your friends you fucked a black girl once and it was so good. Like eating chocolate, right? You could brag about how she tied you up, how she whipped you and beat you, and then how you did the same, how you played Mr. Charlie and the slave girl all night long!"

Charlie's face blanched and then reddened. Clear evidence, she thought, of his guilt. White people were always changing colors on you.

He whispered, "I can't believe you think that."

"Why wouldn't I?" She glared at him for long minutes,

until he dropped his hands and walked to her couch and collapsed here, shoulders drooping and face down. They were silent then, listening to the salsa music drifting under her door.

When Charlie spoke his voice trembled. "I like you. I like you a lot. Maybe, if I examined my reasons closely enough, it might have something to do with . . ." He let the thought trail off, then continued. "I don't know. Okay, is that what you want to hear? I don't know. But I do know that I like you. *I like you.* Isn't that enough?"

He'd brought carrots and lettuce drenched in sweet vinegar from a favorite Vietnamese restaurant and tangy barbecued ribs from the rib joint down the street and noodles and spring rolls from the Thai place they first visited together, and, most surprising, a whole fish, wrapped in aluminum foil, baked with thyme and lemongrass, from where she did not know. After he left, Faith laid it all out on the dining room table, a cultural feast for two. She opened the wine and took a sip. California red. It was good vintage but tasted bitter in her mouth. She spit it out, looked at the food without appetite. The fish stared back with its cold and colorless eye.

Undoings in Amsterdam

by Janet McDonald

The square outside Centraal Station is jammed with bodies. Leaning against wood, sitting on concrete, and lying on grass, eating, smoking, staring. Strangers at a picnic. Their guidebooks tout museums and tulips but they have been carried here by the same current that has brought generations to Amsterdam—drugs and sex. Jesse ambles along with the crowd crossing the canal bridge, past marijuana-breathing coffee shops, brightly lit currency exchange offices, souvenir stands, and eateries that exhale falafel and pizza. In the distance beyond the canal, a red glow. The red-light district of shopping window sex workers.

Just ahead, the "World's Only Sex Museum." She hurries by, tempted and revolted, the edge of the one feeling sharpening the tension of the other. She glances at the sort of people gathered at the entrance. Tourists. Young. Couples. Innocents, she tells herself, not perverts. A museum, after all, not a sex den. She turns back toward the elaborate porn parlor made safe for dishonest tourists by the word *museum*. The tight space houses a chaos of paintings and sculptures, postcards and drawings. The body's pleasured agonies displayed in explicit splendor. Men bent naked over cows, women's mouths on horses, stiletto heels pressed hard against flesh, nipples and foreskin pierced by silver rings, buxom women with skirts raised above their penises, the fluids of humans and animals running together, flowing, forming little pools.

Alien, unwelcome arousal. She shuts herself into a booth. A cushioned bench and an overhead beam. A guilder falls into the coin slot and for three minutes a head moves up and down in a lap. Her hand slips inside her jeans. Another guilder drops. And another. And another. A muffled groan and it's done. She arranges her clothes, sets her face, and steps out into a group of waiting teenagers. "Weird," she says, adopting what she hopes is a believable look of disapproval. The day had darkened; Jesse steps outside into the dusk and immediately swerves to face a nearby postcard stand. She stares absently at the cards, then steps quickly away from the museum. The canals of Amsterdam tremble with reflected houses, streetlamps, buses, people. An overloaded tram rumbles to a stop.

"Leidseplein?" she asks.

The driver answers with a stream of Dutch words. His smile tells her he'll let her know when to get off.

"Leidseplein!" he announces.

Another packed square. People are playing wooden flutes, dancing with arms waving in the air, weaving on bicycles with raised handlebars through tourists. A young woman with long, matted brown hair stops in front of Jesse and picks up a flattened cigarette butt. She stares at it for a long moment, then stashes it in the back pocket of her grimy jeans. As she shuffles away, it drops out of a hole and falls back to the ground. Above the Bulldog Cafe scowls a huge papier-mâché bulldog, a fat joint in its mouth. Inside, stacks of Bulldog coffee mugs, Bulldog caps, and Bulldog T-shirts.

"Excuse me, uh, where can you buy . . . uh, I was told you could buy . . ."

"At the bar," the cashier says without looking up from her magazine, "follow the corridor and turn right." Jesse looks behind her even though what she's doing is legal where she's doing it. Autographed photos of Chuck Norris, Run DMC, and other celebrities hang from the walls. She finds her way into an obscure haze of heavy smoke. At the bar, figures sprinkle hashish and crumble marijuana onto thin strips of paper. Others study floating tea balls. Music smothers conversation. The bartender is handsome, a mane of tangled dreadlocks, green eyes, and a muscled, unpampered body. A dark tank top, GLEASON'S GYM—BROOKLYN, NEW YORK, boastfully tight.

"Hi!" exclaims Jesse, squeezing between two customers onto a bar stool. "I'll have a beer." The bartender sits a thick glass on the counter, foam running onto her fingers. "Thanks. Hey listen, I'm from Brooklyn, too! We are everywhere, aren't we? I can't believe it, my first time in Amsterdam and I meet another Brooklynite. How'd you end up here?" Jesse is relieved to find familiarity in this stranger. Brooklyn bonding.

The bartender's grin becomes outright laughter, her dimples deepening.

"Birth," she says, her obvious accent sending a warm flush into Jesse's face. "I am Dutch. Sint Maarten, Dutch West Indies. Only the shirt's American. A gift. So now it is my turn? How did you end up here? Holiday?"

A teenager straddles the stool next to Jesse, examining a silver ball bobbing in a teacup. He looks up at the bartender, then at Jesse, then at the bartender's shirt, and again at Jesse. Laughter is shaking his body, his head, the cup of marijuana tea, but there is no sound from his mouth. The sight of the boy along with the Bulldogged air and her own embarrassment unleashes Jesse's laughter. Her hands cover her face, her stomach burning as if from sit-ups. At last she composes herself enough to wipe her eyes and clear her throat. The bartender is still chuckling, dabbing up spilled tea near the boy's saucer. He watches the dishrag absorb the precious, pungent liquid and sighs, "Wow. Bummer."

Jesse feels the woman's eyes on her, and heat floods her face and neck. "Whew, sorry, well . . . anyway . . . where were we, oh yes, what I'm doing in Amsterdam, yeah, I'm on vacation, I mean, holiday. Spring break. I've never been to Europe before. All my friends said Amsterdam is heaven, so liberated, that it's legal to buy . . ."

"Of course. See that bearded guy in the corner with the long, purple ponytail?"

"Don't think I could miss him."

"He is Mars. See our price list on the wall behind him? Go there. But come back, Brooklyn."

"Jesse. And you're . . . ?"

"Come back, Jesse." She waves her hand in front of the boy's eyes. "Another tea ball, Loek?"

AFGHAN HASHISH—20 GUILDERS. About fifteen dollars. MOROCCAN HASHISH—25 GUILDERS. Twenty bucks. Jesse reads down to the marijuana, hash brownie, and tea ball prices. The variety of choices is paralyzing. She is not an experienced drug shopper and feels self-conscious under the fixed stare of Mars, looking either at or through her. The easiest choice is alphabetical. Afghan.

The bartender sees Jesse using a spoon to chip off a piece of the rock-hard hashish. "You haven't been smoking before now?"

"Not really. I tried them, I mean some, in high school but didn't really like it, you know . . . felt kinda . . . I don't know, guess I'm a lightweight. But since I'm here . . ."

The bartender demonstrates with a match. "You hold it over the flame like this . . . see how it softens? Now it breaks up more easily for rolling." Her biceps move like fists as she turns her wrists back and forth, singeing the hash. The sleek joint she rolls is as perfect as a cigarette. She puts it whole in her mouth, then pulls it out slowly, wettened. She brings it again to her mouth, holds the match close, and lights it. Then she places it between Jesse's lips. Jesse inhales. They observe each other. Jesse inhales. And again. Her eyes close.

The stool squeaks. She twists. It squeaks. She giggles. Her eyes find Mars. He doesn't bother to look away. She smiles. He watches, expressionless. Someone hums at her back. She twists around, squeaking the stool. No one. She laughs a long time. Swallows hard. Calls out, "Excuse me!"

"Yes, Jess, the very best," answers the bartender, approaching. Her hair writhing rope and her breasts rising and falling in a slowed motion that Jesse feels in her own body. She instructs herself to look elsewhere but is defied. The bartender's face warms to red as she watches Jesse's eyes.

"Was that a poem? Are you a poet? A nameless, beer-pulling, Dutch Rasta poet? Behind the waist-high fortress. I'm so thirsty."

The Dutch woman traces Jesse's jawline with her finger. "You want a tea, little Jess at sea?" She walks off humming, two brimming mugs in each hand, her thick forearms straining.

The tea-drinking boy is passed out on a nearby table of half a dozen slow-blinking smokers handling a water-filled glass pipe. They don't seem to notice him, but Jesse does. She tells the bartender she'll go with ginger ale. "Not feeling too normal, you know what I mean, Poet? Between the ponytailed red planet over there and you vibing me, well, what world am I in? What world is in me?" She takes the soda the bartender offers and gulps it down. It chills her lips. "Being by myself and everything, I don't want to get too carried away."

"I can carry you away," whispers the bartender. Jesse visibly flinches. A second glass of ice and ginger ale is placed in front of her. "On the house."

Jesse inhales more warm, sweet smoke. She is soft focus, intense lightness, effortless concentration. She doesn't see, but feels, this woman exploring her visually, pausing here, lingering there. She redirects her awareness away from the quake in her stomach. A. Afghan. Afghanistan. Where is that? Asia? Africa? Europe? Her thoughts race from continent to continent, in search of Afghanistan. The enveloping sounds slow her to its rhythm. Lyrics in a foreign language. Doesn't matter, she still likes it. She recognizes a song. It's in English. They all are. She has the CD. Is she smoking or breathing? She can no longer tell the difference.

Pressure on her breast. A hand. Men squeeze. Women caress. This is a woman. Jesse opens her eyes onto the bartender's. "I want to touch the sexy Jesse."

Hands warm on her face, lips soft on her mouth, tongues, breath. "I carry you away." Whispered.

Time stalls in the moment, stuck where a woman reaches across a continent for a young stranger, brings her to a pool of heat. Jesse's eyes seek the door. "Maybe I should . . ." She is on the other side of the bar, much too close to the bartender. "Not here, Poet . . ." The wall, soft wood behind her, holds her steady. Held yet falling. "I really shouldn't . . ."

"Oh, but you should. This world you're in, it is the old world. We love freely. Let it carry you away."

Loosening buttons, belt, zipper; losing thought, words; lost in hands searching in thin cloth, in tangled curls, inside . . . finding. The sudden, stunned gasp. Jesse shudders into the curve of the bartender's neck, her legs no longer holding her. Aloft, she is the smoke curling from mouths, the shadow in their lovers' corner, the music blanketing sound. The blank eyes of Mars on them.

Lights flickering white, red, green, blue, the tourist-bright colors of theater marquees and ice cream parlors. Outside noises resonate inside Jesse's head, a din of wheels, words, wind. The blinding streetlamp hums. She is in one place, then another, not going to but suddenly being there, and there, and there, in one place, then the next. Movement without moving. She takes in the thin, night air. Muscle lifts bone and flesh, heart drums blood, lungs pull air. Such relentless effort, constant, unnoticed until moments like this.

Neon arrows point her through the night to DE CLUB—DANCING. Nudging her way into the press of women, she begins to dance, not alone but with herself. Her body, exalted, trances into the pulsating pump of the music, vibrant still from the tremor left by a bartender in a corner. And then someone is there, intruding. Long-lashed onyx eyes, hair falling smoothly to her waist, bare shoulders, brown as Jesse's. She dances in close to Jesse's ear to ask her simple, predictable question. "What's your name?" The deep, smoky voice is accented by England. When it is the woman's turn to name herself, Jesse can't make it out. Something Indian. Jesse has to ask again. Vijaya.

They dance, each watching when she thinks the other isn't. Jesse eyes the Indian's broad shoulders and thrusting hips, her sleeveless cotton sweater, corduroy slacks and boots, all black, all carefully considered. Sweat collects on Jesse's forehead and runs into her eyebrows and down her face. As the music changes they walk to the bar, not touching. The wall clock shows four A.M. They share beer and talk of New Delhi, of New York. From an old woman she buys a rose, hands it to

Jesse. Jesse accepts the cliché. They stroll to the dance floor, emboldened by the promise of each other. Jesse's thigh is between Vijaya's and that is how they stay, pushing against, grinding into, yearning for. The music slows. Vijaya licks sweat from Jesse's neck and Jesse feels down Vijaya's back, then lower. Something more urgent takes the place of their dance. Vijaya's arms wrap around Jesse's neck, she is pushing back and forth against Jesse's groin. They are already lovers.

A faster track comes on but neither dances. They stand, then leave the floor. Vijaya climbs onto a stool and parts her knees. Jesse steps between them. "Can I see you again?" asks Vijaya, pulling Jesse closer.

Jesse feels her partner's desire. "You can see me right now."

"Let's go then, Jesse."

They stumble from a cab in front of Vijaya's apartment, still panting and kissing. Vijaya closes heavy drapes against the rising dawn. Jesse strips immediately, unable to bear even a moment's pause. She stretches out on an immense, unmade bed. There is no talk and no light. Vijaya eases next to her, naked, and moans instantly at the shock of soft skin. In utter darkness Jesse finds and strokes her hair, neck, shoulders, breasts. Vijaya moans, raising her hips to Jesse's hand. Jesse rolls onto her and tongues down to her firm stomach, farther down, curled hairs. Vijaya is breathless, passive, waiting. Jesse tastes everywhere Vijaya is wet, along her neck, below her breasts, inside her elbows, between her legs. "Do me. Please. Now." Jesse does, her tongue deep inside a complete stranger whose fingers, deep in Jesse's hair, hold Jesse's head to her sex, insistent. Vijaya cries out and floods onto Jesse's tongue. She comes, groaning. Jesse comes, untouched. "That was so good," sighs Vijaya, pulling Jesse up to lie on top of her. In an instant, she is snoring. Jesse wraps up in the blanket.

When Jesse awakens Vijaya is already up making coffee for herself and tea for Jesse. The drapes are wide open, and the blaring daylight hurts Jesse's eyes. "Everybody thinks all Indians drink tea but I don't. I like coffee." She moves around busily in a thick bathrobe, takes a couple of phone calls. Her black hair is tied back. Jesse remembers its smell, Vijaya's taste. A current jolts her and Jesse squeezes her legs together beneath the blankets.

She feels lazy and lingers in bed, hoping Vijaya might return. There has been no touch, and its absence feels awkward. "Thanks for having me over," says Jesse, to remind her morning hostess that a few hours earlier they'd been passionate lovers. Vijaya laughs. "Don't thank me! I wanted you. This wasn't a charity case." Jesse blushes into her tea. Nothing more is said about their morning together. She dresses while Vijaya showers. Her clothes smell like stale cigarettes and her mouth is dry. She can only imagine what her uncombed hair looks like. No wonder Vijaya doesn't want . . . They exchange phone numbers and kiss each other's cheeks. Jesse promises Vijaya that she'll be back. She dials Vijaya's number a few times. All that awaits her is a woman's voice speaking Dutch. Jesse isn't even sure it's Vijaya's. Ungenerous.

Jesse waits to feel hurt and angry. But those emotions elude her. In truth, she is fascinated, almost impressed. A woman who takes what she wants and moves on, with neither guilt nor shame, unburdened by any sense at all of debt. Jesse concludes she was wrong. Vijaya was indeed generous, in her honesty. Something to consider.

In her skin and on her tongue Jesse carries back to New York the ways of the Old World, to the consternation of her friends.

"Girl, what are you doing? This is a public place. I'll be

your dance partner but don't get carried away." Carried away. That is exactly what Jesse craves, to fly off, lifted by wind, swept by waves, blown by breath.

"Why shouldn't we, isn't that life's pulse? In Amsterdam, a breathtaking bartender inhaled me right there in . . ."

Mica flinches almost imperceptibly. Jesse notices. She's out to her straight classmate, who claims to be "cool with that." So why does Mica still recoil at details? Hypocrisy or ambivalence?

"Do you see any wooden shoes on this dance floor, because I don't. You aren't in Amsterdam anymore, so get your hands off my . . ."

"All right, all right! But really, Mica, you would not believe how open they are in their so-called Old World. It seems a lot newer than ours."

"Oh, but I would believe how very open they are. So spare me, please."

Weeks have blurred by since Jesse's return to college. She recognizes her body in the mirror but not this feeling, a yearning, new to someone for whom fear shadowed every desire, however muffled. Fear of words, the judgments used to choke off a woman's sexuality, words like *whore* and *promiscuous* and *slut*—or, even worse, *dyke*. Jesse, gay yet untouched by any woman's hand but her own, a lesbian-in-waiting with no queen to serve. But that was before the black Dutch and Indian Brits of Amsterdam, before her discovery of a world made rich by indifference, by people simply not caring what others do or whom they love. Summer, a short sigh away, will take Jesse back there. And again, she will go into details, explore the particulars of her heart.

The Sexiest Seconds

by Kiini Ibura Salaam

Warmth takes over my body. I spread my arms and tilt my chin to the sky. My face breaks into a smile. If I could embrace the sun, I would. Yesterday I wore layers. Yesterday snowflakes stung my cheeks. Seven hundred dollars and twenty hours later, I am here—in this city, in this heat, on this balcony—surrounded by crumbling buildings painted pastel. Clay tile roofs sprout in irregular patches like weeds. Across the street, a fat vendor sits leaning against a tiny table, absentmindedly fondling his produce. Black letters on torn pieces of cardboard advertise onions, peppers, tomatoes, eggs. A vagrant loiters on the corner, begging coins. The vendor yells at him, a string of curses streaming from his mouth. The coffee boy comes speeding down the slender footpath. His flip-flop-shod feet are a blur. My gaze travels up skinny scarred legs to the spread of bare brown chest. One bony hand rests on a mini steering wheel. He navigates pedestrians and potholes with expert flicks of the finger. His thermoses clink and clank. His wheels creak.

"Cafezinho," he cries.

"Caaafffeeeezzziiinnnhhhooo." A hand lifts from an open window. He halts. Resting his foot on his homemade cart, he tosses coffee into a tiny plastic cup. Coins fall into his palm. He drops them into his pocket and, with a quick upturned

155

thumb, is gone. A tiny bundle of brown fur wanders the sidewalk. It bounds and leaps, pouncing after some invisible foe. It pokes its nose into the trash pile, then tumbles off the curb. My body tenses as a bus roars around the bend. Just as I am covering my eyes and turning away, a hand reaches into the street and lifts the kitten by it neck. I sigh in relief, grateful for the thick muscled arm, the rippling chest, the kitten mewing in its cradle of safety.

Crowning the neighborhood is a wide expanse of sky. No clouds, its blueness goes on forever. Voices full of drunken belligerence drift up from the bar on the corner. Somewhere, a radio is blasting. *Pagode* notes bounce in the air. On the street below me, an old man pushes a wheelbarrow full of fruit. He lowers his load and wipes his face with a rag. He shades his eyes with shaking fingers and looks up at me. *Menina*, he calls out, you want some pineapples? "No," I say and wag my finger in the Brazilian way. Bananas, mangoes? I smile at his upturned face. I shake my head and say, *não, não*. I know his tricks well. If I come down for a pineapple, I return to the kitchen with papaya and passion fruit, too. He lifts the handles of the wheelbarrow and continues on. I watch his crooked back drifting down the steep street.

At the corner a mean-faced old woman sits in the shade. She stirs a moist cornmeal mixture with clawed hands. Undaunted by her gruffness, the fruit seller throws a friendly greeting into her lap. She nods and keeps stirring. The fruit man pauses. The woman ignores him. She deftly coaxes bits of mix into round *acaraje* balls with a huge metal spoon. He rifles through his fruit, testing the ripeness of the sugar apples. She flicks the *acaraje* into a big metal bowl of hot oil. The flames flare. The fruit man hands her a chunk of jackfruit. She hesitates. He insists. She takes it with a spare-toothed smile. He goes on down the road. She leans back and pops a piece of fruit into her mouth. Her eyes wander up to the balcony, over my shoulders, and land on my face. She cuts her eyes at me. I feel a quick flush of embarrassment. My lips lift into a smile and I turn away.

A light breeze blows me back into the apartment. Just as I reenter the living room, a lizard falls off the ceiling and plops on top of my suitcase. It sits frozen and disoriented. I wait for it to wander off. It finally slinks to the floor and waddles away. I roll my suitcase down the long hallway. Then I hesitate. A spider scurries across the closed door. My suitcase slips out of my grasp. I nudge the door open with my toe. Delight explodes in my chest. The walls are exactly as I remember them: clumsily painted in glowing layers of yellow and orange. I drag the suitcase to the middle of the room and sit on it. My eyes roam over every crack and corner. A wounded cockroach staggers through the doorway. I jump to my feet. The cat tumbles in after it. It pounces and jumps and bats the roach with its paws. The roach rustles its wings and stumbles. In a gulp, the game is over. The cat has the creature clamped in its jaws. Get out, I say. The cat stares at me, roach legs wiggling in its mouth. Out, I repeat and point to the door. The cat streaks out of the room. I slam the door behind its swishing tail.

The walls beckon me, vibrating with memory. I spread my fingers and approach the timeworn surface. I bend my knees into a squat and press my palms flat against the cool plaster. My fingertips dip into crumbling holes until they find the familiar grooves. There carved beside the socket are three English words, spelled in Portuguese: AI LUV U. Bilingual love. The doorbell rings. My heart drops into my gut. I fall to my knees and push my ear against the door. With stilled breath, I listen. I can hear the cat tearing through the house. I can hear the little girl downstairs screaming at her big sister. Then I hear the sounds I'm searching for. The creaking of hinges. The drag of wood against marble floor. The front door is opening. Laughter rings through the house. I suck my teeth and bang my fist on the floor. The door slams shut. It is a woman's voice. It is not you.

From beneath the door a determined line of ants marches across the floor. I crush a few out of spite. I watch the ants take stock of the death and, briefly, panic. Then, as I am untying my shoelaces, they cut a path around their comrades' corpses and resume their journey. I tug off my boots and crawl beside the insect trail. I follow them all the way across the room until they disappear into a crack in the wall. I free my feet of my socks and wiggle my toes. My jeans are next. Sweat seeps from my pores as I peel the heavy fabric off my sticky skin. I lean over my suitcase and click open the locks. In my underwear, I straddle it and wrestle it open. Tightly rolled bundles of summer clothes burst from inside. I finger through shorts, halter tops, mini skirts, until a small orange-and-red sundress jumps out at me. In seconds, the dress is dripping from my shoulders and I am fanning myself with its hem. I slide my hands to my hips and look around. *I'm here,* I think, *I'm really here.*

Buried at the bottom of my suitcase is a box heavy with gifts. My host rips it open, her eyes wide in anticipation. She hugs the cheese and chocolate to her chest, squeezes the batteries in her fist. She skips into the kitchen for a knife. My eyes leap to the door. Jesse went back to the States, she yells from the kitchen. She returns with a tray of crackers. In the middle of the tray is the new block of cheese, glowing like a golden treasure. We sip mango juice and breathlessly tell tales of life. What we've written, who we've spoken to, who we never want to see again up. Under the table my legs jiggle nervously. The one person missing from her report is you. My heart feels as if it would burst. Are you seeing someone? Are you safe? Are you here? I wonder if she can see the questions beating under my skin. I don't dare say your name. She looks at me, eyes shining, and lapses into silence.

Well, I say, stretching lazily in the chair, I'm going to make my rounds. In the pizza shop they are happy to see me. They think I've grown fat and white. You need sun, they tell me. How is brother, sister, mother, daughter? I ask. The little one is tall now, with long long legs. She smiles shyly and disappears downstairs when I ask her about school. You, I don't mention. Instead I order a nice cold *suco*. I want to ask if you've been in. Have they seen you laughing? Do you look healthy? My meal comes. I fish the pork out of the beans while telling them about the snow. While I eat, they look at photos of my paintings. They ooh and ahh appropriately. After I'm full, they clear the table. I linger at the bar a moment watching the owner swish the cutlery clean. We pass around smiles and gentle glances. Next time you come to town, you stay with us, they say. Of course, I respond, but for now, I'm going to town for ice cream.

I let the weight of gravity pull me down the hill. My eyes greedily drink in all the details. The gleaming eyes of brown children, the short shorts and bare toes, the discarded dolls and mangy dogs, the art spilling out of shops onto sidewalks. And the faces, endless faces of people I don't know, yet whose features I remember. The homeless woman I once saw masturbating in front of the record shop. The painter who walks around in black rags and a metal mask. The shop owner's son who dresses like an American. And me, who am I to them? A rich Americana? Carlos Capoeira's girlfriend? A fool?

When the square comes into view, I freeze. My heart loses

its mind and forgets its rhythm. I take a deep breath and instruct it to beat. I count for it, and concentrate on lifting one foot after the other. Every cell in my body knows I am entering your domain. I may find you on the stairs of the church. You may be sitting, legs splayed, slurping a pineapple Popsicle. What will I do then? What do lovers say after a year apart? How do I break the silence?

I walk past all your favorite hangouts. My breath squeezes from my lungs in spurts. I feel faint as I discover each place vacant. Not only aren't you there, but neither are your friends. No one. Where is everyone hiding? I walk on, past the craft shops and the restaurants. Past the museum, the church, and the bus stop. Past the street vendors and the Baianas posing for tourist photos. I take the elevator down to Cidade Baixa. The road to the market is chaotic. Cars careen around corners, streaming past pedestrians without pause. I scurry across the street with a throng of daring boys. Adrenaline pounds in my ears. The men at the market are selling jewelry today. They approach me, arms dripping with shell necklaces. I smile in their direction, seeing nothing. My eyes are glued to the fountain where you taught me to shamelessly tongue in public.

I approach the capoeira circle and hide behind a pole. If you are there, I want to see you first. I want to be invisible. I want the delicious pleasure of catching you unawares. All the usual players surround the wooden stage. The tall one with cinnamon skin and freckles. The short one with knife-sharp features and an intimidating stare. The skinny one with the rubber bones and dominating smile. But you aren't there. I back away quickly. I'd rather suffer in silence than ask them for information. American Express, they called me last year. This year is none of their business.

I take a seat outside the dirty wharf restaurant. Your voice is humming a capoeira song in my head. I savor the scene: the fishing boats, the blinding glare of the sun, the raspy-voiced gossip rattling behind me, the laughter of children splashing in the sea. We sat at this same table the last time we were here. I told jokes. You laughed with your mouth full of your favorite fish. Today reminds me of that day: clear, blue, impossibly sunny. Come back to me, you'd whispered when I left. I have, I say out loud in English. Where are you?

On a whim, I decide to go to the beach. I get to the bus stop just in time to wave down a speedily approaching bus. The bus screeches to a stop. I hold on to the door and climb into the too-high stairwell. I fish a bill out of my pouch and push through the turnstile. As the ticket taker is counting out my change, a skinny street kid jumps on. He lowers himself to the ground and slides under the turnstile. Ten more little men burst on behind him. Be careful, you told me once, when you saw street kids harassing me for my crackers. I refuse to show fear. Their rough voices and hungry eyes bounce all over the bus. I clasp my pouch in my fist and pretend not to notice them. They can't steal what they can't see. I have no pockets full of jingling change. No food for them to beg from my fingers. Besides, they aren't looking for prey today. They tumble into their seats, talking in husky voices too adult for their frail frames. The last boy clutches a brown bag, waving it in the air before plunging his face into it. Glue sniffers, I think, and a tiny feather of sadness flutters in my throat.

The bus driver presses the gas pedal, and sound explodes from the back of the bus. The plastic seats are drums; the kids beat and beat and beat. A charged rhythm emerges, a crazy samba fills the air. I drape my arms across the seat back in front of me and rest my head in the crook of my elbow. The pounding vibrates through the metal seat frames, into my bones, into my blood, into me. They chant lyrics of love and longing with breathless exuberance. Each voice strains to be louder than the other. Passion is this moment and every moment I have spent in this crooked seaside city. The kids break into laughter before the song ends. The ocean bursts into view. I shut my eyes and the sea embraces me. Tightness seeps out of my body; a sensation of safety slips under my skin. The bus hurtles down the hill, whips around the bend, and jerks to a stop.

The beach is full today. The thin brown girls are wearing colorful bikinis. So are the fat women. So is everyone, wearing their skin as if it were a suit of clothing. I lean on the wall overlooking the beach and peer at the men below. I imagine you among them, ripping through ferocious repetitions of sit-ups, taking your turn at the parallel bars. Oi, a voice behind me calls out. I turn and see a young man I don't know. Aren't you Carlos's girlfriend? he asks. I am, I say. You've cut your hair. Yeah, I smile. A pause rests between us. I am embarrassed to ask. Have you seen him? He's not at the beach today, he says, I don't even know if he's in town. Thanks, I say, and wave good-bye.

I go down on the beach anyway and sit in the sand. I shade my eyes and stare at the sea-lined horizon. I imagine you walking to the water. You touch your hand to the surface and make the sign of the cross over your body. Then you jump in and disappear into the waves. I close my eyes and follow you into the ocean. Behind my lowered eyelids, I see droplets of water covering your face. I feel the waves pushing me against your body. The saltwater taste of our first kiss invades my throat. I remember you whispering and tugging at my bikini bottoms. I was afraid someone would see us, but you taught me not to care who was looking.

My eyes fly open and I look around self-consciously. At the water's edge, two little boys play capoeira. You were once one of those boys, dreaming of being a big man, the best capoeirista Salvador has ever seen. Today, what do you dream of? Are you dreaming of me?

I imagine you sitting next to me in the sand. You're wearing your yellow swimming trunks and grinning. You hand me a coconut. I swallow the cool liquid and sigh as it slides down my throat. You nudge me softly. Do you want to taste my coconut? you ask. Sure, I say. I gasped when the coconut water glided over my tongue. It was perfect. The sweetest I had ever tasted. Take it, it's yours, you said. You placed the perfect coconut in my lap. A gift. As I greedily sipped, you whispered, remember I don't do this for anyone.

I sit with your ghost until the sun sets. Then I stand and brush the sand off my dress. The scent of urine clings to the stone stairs. I climb them without breathing. At the bus stop, a tall apartment building towers over the street. My friend once lived there. She's in Amsterdam now. She's returned home. I have returned here. Not home. Looking for you. Darkness winds through the city. The bus carries me back to Pelourinho. Pelourinho, where the day merchants are closing their shops. Where the night merchants have come with their steel poles and wooden countertops and blenders. They set up their booths and stir up their concoctions as I head home in my dirty dress with sand between my toes.

When I pass by the doorway of a lit shop, I trip and stub my toe on a loose cobblestone. As I am checking my toe for blood, I hear an exclamation of excitement. Then I hear my name. *Hola,* says the shop owner with a wide grin. You came back! Just arrived today, I say. Oh Salvador has been blessed, he whispers and kisses me on both cheeks. He offers me a glass of the local intoxicant: cane liquor, lime juice, and sugar. I refuse. You are too beautiful to say no, he says and disappears into his shop to search for a glass and alcohol and ice.

I hear an eruption of laughter. Without turning I know it is you. A sudden spear of fear rips through my chest. Some survivalist instinct tells me to hide. Slinking behind a panel of paintings, I obey. I peek into the street. Between the divide of door and frame, I can see pieces of you. A flash of white teeth, a brown nipple, one wide foot. You grin and joke with your friends. Doubt sweeps through my body. How much has changed in a year? Can I handle the history you've created in my absence? Do I still want you? Do you still want me?

My body turns on me. Without my permission, my fingers grip the wall. My stomach locks up. My limbs refuse to step into the light. My heart will not be regulated. The shop owner returns, rattling my drink in his hand. I must turn my back to you or reveal the truth to the shop owner: that I am a grown woman, crouched behind a narrow wooden door, terrified of your freckled face, hiding from your laughing eyes. I face the shop owner with a smile, my pretenses firmly in my possession. He comments on something. I nod, pretending to listen. Out the corner of my eye, I see you swagger by. I let out a nervous breath and you disappear. My body collapses against the wall. The shop owner asks after my health. I'm fine, I insist. Maybe a light sunstroke. I just need to get home.

As I walk away from the shop, cramps rip through my stomach. The pain suffocates all sound. I climb the hill with my hands pressing on my belly. Whispering to my aching gut, I will myself home. When I enter the darkness of the apartment, the cramps subside. I shut myself in my room. A gasp of relief escapes my lips; I am safe. Safe? What is safe? Invisibility? Discovery? I cover my face with my hands. Confusion seeps through my fingers. I thought I wanted to see you, but I have seen you and all I want to do is hide. Can we skip this first moment? Can we just be together again? No questions, no fears, just our union, alive again.

I throw my dress onto the bathroom floor and step into the shower. As the cold water draws chill bumps to my skin's surface, I imagine you lying in bed waiting for me. I remember the time you called to say you were doing a work. You made a deal with the *orishas*. No alcohol, no sex. If you gave them seven days of celibacy, they would fix your knee. I asked them to give me you too, you whispered. I smiled. I knew it was a lie, but I hoped it was true. The fervent prayer of a weak heart. I wanted some powerful force to steal away my choices, some mystical god to rob me of my will and bind me to you. If we can't have sex, you'd better stay away from me, I said. For seven days, Mommy? you whispered, I can't. Three days later you were ringing my doorbell. We laughed, but I said I was going to make you keep your promise.

When you put your hands on me, I gave you a canvas, remember? You protested that you couldn't paint. I told you it was a good day to learn. We painted that day. And it rained and rained. We went to bed early and slept deeply. The next morning I saw that you had painted a blue shark and a strangely shaped, rainbow-colored object. This is you, I said, pointing to the shark. This is my heart, I said, pointing to the object. See those things sticking out, that's my protection because you're trying to eat me alive. Oh God, you said, this woman is always running away from me.

I step out of the shower and grab my towel. You are fucked up, I say to my wet reflection. My mirrored eyes look back at me with pity. I once joked that I was going to take you home with me. You looked at me without blinking, no trace of mirth on your face. You don't have the courage, you said. Those words ripped me apart. I dragged my eyes away from your gaze. I tried to hide what you already knew: I was full of love, but empty of conviction. No courage. Pushing the memory away, I dry myself off. I rub oil onto my pale body, muttering about fear and regret and mistakes.

Back in the bedroom, you invade my thoughts again. You are wrapped in my orange sheets, sleeping heavily while ants march around the bed. We didn't last the seven days. On the fifth day, I went to bed early. You stayed up talking to the neighbor. Even in my sleep I was waiting for you. When you came to bed I pulled you toward me. You wrapped your arms around me and kissed my collarbone. I nuzzled against your neck, not ready to leave my sleep behind. Your hands crept over my hips, up my torso, under my tank top. They danced over my breasts, teasing me awake. You only have two more days, I mumbled, are you sure you want to do this? Yes, you whispered. They will be disappointed in you, I said. I know, but you won't, you said and rubbed your fingers across my nipples. I squeezed your thigh between my legs and rolled on top on you. Mommy, you whispered. And we shared breath for the first time in a week.

Our abstinence made this night sweeter than any other. You licked my palms and kissed my wrists. My teeth gripped your neck, your shoulder, your chest. I wanted to go deep. You groaned and gently pushed me off you. Your lips found my back. By the time you reached my waist, I was whimpering. My hips pressed against the mattress. Weight, heat, and moisture gathered between my legs. Your mouth would not stop moving. I could feel you smiling against my skin. Your knees pushed on my inner thighs. I slid them open and welcomed your tongue. Wider, Mommy, you whispered, and I obeyed.

Without argument we left the condom in its wrapper. I inhaled sharply as you guided yourself inside me. We used pressure and counterpressure. Pauses and jerks. Belly rolls and hip rocking. We were inventing new motion. The air beat against us in furious waves. Suddenly I was impatient to see your face. I rolled over and touched your cheek. I remember how your eyes burned as they held me. I remember thinking there was no other place for me. Nowhere on this earth. I pushed you onto your back. Your face was so serious. I planted a moist kiss on your forehead and I placed my feet on both sides of your hips. We locked hands and stared into each other's eyes. You grunted and pushed your jaw against the pillow. I arched away from you and drew closer. We were alone together. Lost in the currents crackling through our pelvises. I erupted into convulsions. You came inside me. I dropped, panting, against your chest.

Minutes later I was sitting on the toilet, grumbling about pregnancy and responsibility. I heard your voice reaching toward me from the bed. You didn't want to stop, did you? you asked knowingly. I lowered my head without answering. The next morning, you patted my belly and said, I hope it grows. I'm lucky it didn't, I say to the empty room and slip on my black dress. My cells know the truth. That night, me forgetting barriers and precautions, your seed shooting into my womb—those seconds were the sexiest of my life. It is a restless secret germinating inside me. You live here in my flesh. When I touch myself, we are together again. No protection, no regret, no hesitation.

Through the veil of memory, I imagine I hear you calling me from the street. I'm already running down the hall when the doorbell rings. Before it rings again, I'm on the balcony. You are there below. Smiling up at me. Clapping, spreading your arms to welcome me. Come up, I yell. Then I run down the stairs. I don't care about cockroaches tonight. Fuck the mosquitoes and the spiders. This moment is ours. We make the most of it in a dark curved stairway with narrow stairs and no light. Your eyes are moist. I believe I am crying. My face aches with joy. We crush each other as if force can convey our feelings. There is nothing to be said. No words. The answers lie in the press of flesh, the meeting of breath.

Revelation

by Elissa G. Perry

Shelley reached for Darla's hand to soothe the wild this woman had sparked in Darla's eyes. Darla recoiled. Spinning her way to the edge of Shelley's orbital, finding the charged attraction of the outside world much more appealing. Fish continued to hug his beer and stare at the jukebox as if it held the key to the night's unfolding. He was consciously oblivious. Choosing blindness over uncertainty he did not look when Darla walked out and Shelley followed. He did not have the answers. He did not yet have the questions.

ॐ

Darla stood with no thought or rather too many to distinguish just one. She had been splayed open by the tip of this woman's tongue. Her entrails were shiny on the edge of the stranger's wit. She had been branded by the handprint—the brief touch on her back—seared by the certain furtive glance. Her glass, drained of liquid, still held chunks of ice. She had not yet learned the superiority of neat.

ॐ

As she moved toward the door, Glenlivet-given confidence strengthened and lengthened her gait. She swung open the door making an entrance to the world and was met with the receding red lights of some classically finned auto. They blended well with the decor of her movie's set.

※

Red-light district. Perception of light. There was sound and motion everywhere jagged and curved. Musicians were examining linear chronology with instruments and random perceptions of distance. There were odd synchopations of jazzical reality. Wild relationships with time and timing. Lightning and burnout were neighbors with slow and methodical but there was no interdependency required for definition. Differing and contradicting realities in the same plane of existence. Corpuscles pulsing—singing constant within random. Pattern within chaos. There was life and for the first time Darla did not feel dead. Darla was on the brink of something new.

※

Darla wished she was her own culture, but she had not been housed in a consistent nutrient-filled media. She had never known if she was leaving or going to or the requisite piece of time for anything. Her nutrient media had been sharp and leaned toward gin. Shelley came out of the door behind her.

※

Darla sighed at the remnants of a high summer dusk reflected in the storefront window across the street. She spun around to face Shelley and her brother. She felt the slight ellipse in her move taking note then ignoring her hint of imbalance.

※

Darla was surprised not to see the tall frame of Fish standing behind his sister. Their mass number was always three. Yet she was still jealous of Fish and Shelley. She herself had never shared spontaneous homophonic utterances with another. When two people share the same tone, rhythm, and time, there are tingles and smiles and hairs stand on end.

✿

At first, Darla wanted to make Fish jealous, but that was a quicksilver thought that slivered down the back of her throat in a hard swallow. She knew that this was not possible. He was what some people called evolved. Darla had subscribed to that theory of evolution in the beginning, finding his defiance of category mysterious. He seemed to be all contradictions perfectly wed—chaos perfectly ordered—a confounding balance in one being. Now two years into marriage, she found faith in anything elusive.

✿

"Dancing. I want to dance."

"Dancing, huh." Shelley drew her shoulders toward her ears putting her hands in her pockets. There were these periods of time where being with Darla and Fish was a little uneasy. Shelley didn't feel danger or fear but it was clear that they were each uncomfortable and sought Shelley for comfort of some sort. There was always that possibility though that the discomfort did not just signal time for one of them to roll over but time to get out of bed and leave the room all together.

"Yes, I want to dance. Forget about the contemplative one."

✿

It was not that Fish didn't love her or that Darla thought that he didn't. This was not a question of love. This was a question of context. Context influences all things and Darla wanted to step out of hers.

❁

"Take me to where the Xs are, Shelley. No Ys, only Xs." Darla opened her wings and began to turn still talking. "Take me to the East Side, Shelley. Take me to the other side." She faced Shelley again laughing, bringing her hands back down her beaded bag trailing light like feathers.

❁

Shelley exhaled and turned back to Moe's. She pushed the door open again, taking in the transition the place had made from jazz café to swinging bar. Fish was looking at her when she found his face. She displayed the universal sign for leaving—a thumb out the door. Fish declined with a wave of his hand, a nod of his head, and a wink from behind a dangling dreadlock.

❁

Shelley shook her head and smiled. "Damn my brother is smooth." This was not unusual, this splitting into two-thirds and one-third. Shelley knew that he was happy there in the midst of sibling madness and mayhem infused with an unspoken order—biological, social, spiritual—forming bonds, covalent, hydrogen, stable unstable—swapping electrons like crazy. He was in his scientific element. He was observer. He was delighted. In his gut this was foreplay. Darla would observe another galaxy. They would report back, each overflowing with material to analyze, ripe for postulating and considering. They would talk and fuck and make four A.M. peanut butter and jelly sandwiches and talk and make love and make music. It had never been discussed. It had never been conscious but still it was his desired path.

❀

Back outside with the impossible blue of the darkening sky reflected in the window behind her, Darla snapped her purse shut and rubbed her lips together freshly marooned. "It's you and me, kid." Shelley retrieved a wad of keys from her pocket and headed toward her car. Darla threaded her arm through Shelley's and with a flip of her neck threw her wild mane of coarse curls over her shoulder.

❀

Shelley walked taller. She was proud to have this beautiful woman on her arm. Although she didn't know it, Darla could stop the heart of any living thing just for being in her presence. But Shelley was not too proud. This woman was not only a friend but also her brother's wife.

❀

"So where are going, Shelley?"

Shelley knew that Darla was on some sort of journey. She also knew that she could only be transportation, not catalyst nor destination.

❀

"Well, my dear, there's dancing at Babel, pool at Pat's, or reminiscing old hags reeking of Miller Genuine Draft at the Inn; take your pick."

"Hmmm." Darla pulled up her dress and rubbed her

thighs considering her options in one of her moments of self-unconsciousness.

"No Inn tonight. Dancing or pool. Oh they're both so sexy but in entirely different ways. The thought of all that techno is ruining my high though . . . pool it is."

❀

Shelley loved old cars and Darla felt at home in the belly of the Maverick as they crossed the river. The low raspy beat of the V-8 engine all around her like a heartbeat in a mother's womb. Darla pulled her simple black dress back down to just above her knees. "Yeah, let's play pool." Satisfied with her decision, Darla turned to look at the scenery. Smokestacks, ghostly and barely discernible, towered over the riverbank.

❀

Darla relaxed on the plane of transition. It was a place of familiar excitement going from one place to somewhere unknown. The seams of highway had been the rhythm. Each place had always been much like the last but there was always that promise of possibility that things would be different.

❀

"How, how, how, how—Boom, boom, boom boom." John Lee Hooker was on the Thursday-night blues hour of college radio. The three stars were back next to the moon again. Darla, Fish, and Shelley she had named them a year before when they were all living at Shelley's. Three stars in the house of the rising sun. Shelley's house had good sunrises and sunsets. Darla felt herself slipping into a melancholic remembrance and slapped her legs to wake herself.

❀

"Are we there yet?" As the words passed through her lips into the humid night air where they seemed to hang before dissipating, she realized that Shelley had been signaling right and was about to make her exit.

Shelley laughed, "Why are you in such a hurry girl? What're you running from? Or are you running to?"

❀

"I just need some movement, honey, some fun." Darla ignored the main body of the question not knowing the answer or not wanting one. Her buzz was wearing thin but she ignored that fact and pretended that sobriety was not steadily creeping up her spine. She changed the radio station until she found Salt-N-Pepa and began to dance in her seat drowning out thought with sound and motion.

❀

"Can I have one of those?" Darla pointed at the pack of cigarettes in Shelley's breast pocket. They both realized that Darla's question could have been interpreted as a request for Shelley's right breast but both were too sober to acknowledge the double meaning and find it funny.

❀

"You gonna smoke it or are you just gonna get it all wet and ruined like you usually do?" Darla retrieved the pack and put one in her mouth. She continued to dance until the parking brake was set in the gravel parking lot.

❀

The broken ground could have posed a problem with Darla's shoes but she strode toward the door like she'd grown up natural out of rocks and broken glass. Shelley increased her stride behind her arriving at the door just in time to open it for Darla.

The air inside was thick with smoke and noise and innuendo. Shelley added their names to the board—Shelley then Darlene under Dino and Pearl and Dusty—then moved toward the bar. Shelley was the only person besides Darla's mother who called Darla, Darlene.

Darla surveyed the women present all wrapped up in whatever was their own revelry except a few. One certain She stood in the opposite corner in a nicely worn denim shirt open over a black tank top and hanging out over black jeans. Something about the way she observed, intrigued Darla.

"Any requests?" Shelley was back from the bar with her club soda and Shelley's Scotch. "Come on help me pick." They headed to the jukebox, Darla taking hurried sips of her drink anxious to melt into her surroundings instead of resting outside waiting for some enzyme to usher her across the invisible membrane.

"Natural Woman" came on as they made their selections. Darla began to sing and move. "Play some more Aretha. And mix it up with some stuff you can dance to," she said between lines.

❀

She sang the words with a conviction that she didn't recognize was a longing to feel, to savor, these symbols and spaces and notes, to roll them around in her gut and be intimate with each nuance behind them and the gaps in between. She shifted her weight enjoying the feeling of her damp thighs rubbing together.

❀

"Play that one"—Darla slowed to a sway briefly and pointed to Mavis Staples—"and that one"—she pointed again, to Dusty Springfield this time. "'Son of a Preacher Man,' that's a good song." Darla was feeling good again. She was not drunk but her words had a new comfort and confidence that was not all her own.

❀

Darla dared a larger sip of Scotch and sucked her teeth as she swallowed. The burn was good. She had started drinking Scotch because she liked the way it made her feel when she tried it with her coworkers at the restaurant where they worked. But more than the feeling she was quickly taking to the flavor, the aroma, the whole process. She took a deep breath, the smooth amber seeming almost in contrast to the bright fluorescents of the jukebox before them. In an instant Darla remembered that she had the cigarette from Shelly in her bag.

❀

"Shelley give me a light. Never mind." In her rush for gratification, Darla had stepped to the bar and grabbed a book of matches, but before she could tear off a singular catalyst, She was there with a light. Darla drew back slightly at the sudden flame before her then leaned in and pushed her hair back all in one perfectly timed motion.

❀

Darla cocked her head to one side. "I thank you kindly." She said it with a smile that would melt granite. She returned a slight smile and nodded in deference to the lady and turned to face the pool table again.

❀

Darla stepped back to the jukebox and bumped Shelley with her hip. Shelley's eyes were still on the evening's soundtrack choices numbered before her, but she knew what had happened. She didn't have to look.

❀

"We got one more song. You want to pick it?" She did not respond to what was happening either. She would keep Darla out of physical danger but the rest was up to her. Darla's path was her own and Shelley could not interfere or encourage. Darla punched in 3507, the number for Hendrix's "Who Knows," and turned around to catch up on the table action.

❀

"Dusty!" a large mama-looking woman called out from the board next to the pool table. There was no obvious response from the melee of conversation and movement that was Pat's place. "Dusty going once! Dusty going—"

"I'm coming, I'm coming." She still had the hint of smile around her lips as she fished quarters out of the pocket of her snug black jeans. She had a slight round in her back and a small bend in her knees as she reached deep into her pocket.

Men's jeans, Darla thought. *Women's jeans don't have pockets that deep.* Darla was taking smaller sips now, wanting to maintain her loose plateau instead of ascending to falling apart.

Darla watched lips and bodies and the two women shook hands and exchanged names. "Bar rules?" Dusty questioned from her squatting position as she retrieved the balls to rack. Pearl nodded.

"Shelley, what are bar rules?"

"The rules you already know, honey. All the rules you need to know, if you ask me."

Darla wanted to know more about the latter part of this trailing-off answer but was more interested in Dusty's game. Dusty was a persistent challenge for Pearl whose friends interrupted the flow of euchre to harass her like they would a sibling. "What was that shot, girlfriend?"

Later Pearl would still be annoyed and her friends would have to say "Aw you know we were just joking." Then tomorrow things would appear to be the same again, but appearances are not everything. Darla brought her focus back to the moment at hand in time to see Dusty polish off the eight-ball with a certain grace that made her existence seem like slow motion.

"Do you want to play first?" Shelley had been off to Darla's side watching the watcher and the watched.

"No you go ahead. You're up first." Darla swallowed hard. She was not ready to move from silent to active participant.

"Shelley!" Dusty was calling out from the board as she wiped her own name off and slide-slapped the chalk from her hands.

"Right here." Shelley had a similar molasses quality. It was not bothersome or too slow but rather the way things were supposed to be it seemed. Darla decided that it was a peace they had with time—like they were actually experiencing life.

❀

Shelley had racked the balls. They shook hands, laughing about something, then Dusty drew back to break. The comfortable precision, the effortless beauty of the execution—the motion, speed, and texture of body, cue, and ball—made Darla draw a breath then sigh as the worn white ball spread its target in multiple trajectories. *Break* seemed such a simple word.

❀

Darla took in the shape and sinew of Dusty's forearm as she chalked the cue stick and watched the five-ball drop into the side pocket. The sun falling off a pre-Galileo earth. Sizing up her next shot, Dusty bent her knees, one hand spread on the ledge of the table the other wrapped around her stick. She wore a thick silver band on the middle finger of her right hand and a watch with a black leather strap on her left wrist. She bent farther and leaned over to shoot. Her ass fit perfectly in her jeans.

❀

Darla wished she herself were wearing jeans so she could feel the seam run roughshod over her clit as she shifted her weight again and again and again. Without thinking she sat on the barstool behind her and crossed her legs.

❀

Dusty sank two more balls before Shelley got a chance to have her way with the table. She put up a fight, but in the end it was Dusty's table again.

Darla squeezed her legs together one more time then peeled her damp legs off the vinyl stool when she thought no one was looking.

"You must be Darlene?" Dusty approached her, just as she stood upright.

❀

"I am. You can call me Darla though but only if you go easy on me." She put out her hand. "I'm still learning. You don't learn if you don't try."

Dusty nodded again as she took Darla's hand in both of hers. "Pleasure, Darla. Would you give me a minute though?"

"Sure." Darla sounded chipper. She hadn't thought about quarters and went to the bar for change. Shelley was talking to the euchre women. Darla wondered what about as she got her quarters and headed back to the table.

❀

Between the backward letters that from the outside spelled PAT'S BAR & NO GRILL on the window next to the door, Darla made out Dusty's outline as she replaced the receiver of the pay phone. Darla was arranging the balls in the triangle when Dusty reentered, her boots sounding purposeful as they came through the door.

❀

"Someone special?" Darla inquired in what she wanted to be perceived as a knowing way.

"Yeah. She's someone special." Dusty had revelation in her voice. "I've got a thirteen-year-old daughter at home. She's got a friend spending the night."

Darla paused, surprised at the answer—envious and awestruck.

❀

This woman's got a daughter. I want one.

This woman is someone's mother. I want one, Darla thought to herself in waves of emotion, no words.

I'd like to live inside your belly make your brain my summer home . . . Darla recalled the words of the performer from earlier in the evening.

❀

"Wow, she's a lucky girl." Darla dropped the eight-ball into place with the slide of the triangle like Shelley had shown her.

"I don't know if she sees it that way, but thank you."

"She will someday." Darla was sure of it.

"Humph." Dusty responded in a quick burst of air that said *I hope you're right.*

"Now break up those balls in that way that you do and let's play." Dusty got three balls in on the break.

❀

"See. Now how did you do that?" Darla made a production out of being impressed and overwhelmed. Tonight had been a night of two large impressions—almost to the point of revelry. Revelry is far too rare.

"It's just geometry." Dusty laughed.

✿

"No, it is not." Darla had heard this line before but had never begged to differ. "It involves speed and weight and a third dimension. It's physics, I tell you. Physics." Darla let the rubber bottom of her cue stick drop to the floor. The exclamation point to her declaration.

✿

"You know you're right." Dusty paused, their eyes conversing in a language foreign to both of them. "But I guess if you think too much about all those things instead of just playing and letting your body flow with the game, it can mess you up."

✿

Onlookers gave up on watching their game and wandered to nether regions. The two players were oblivious. Together they were a country with a culture, a language, a land all their own.

✿

They played and flirted. Dusty covering Darla's back their arms touching for their entire length and Darla allowing herself to be coached. They complimented each other admiring and desiring—enjoying this momentary paralleling of trajectories— each aware that the draw between them was something more than sex and something that they would not unleash. Not in this context. Not yet.

❀

Darla was floating when the game was over. She had forgotten about her Scotch and her sister-in-law hawking from the corner. Dusty put her hand on Darlene's shoulder. "I can't stay out late tonight, but that was the most fun I've had in I don't know when. Thank you." Dusty bore into Darla's sable eyes with her lion ones.

"Me too, Dusty. Thank you." Darla grabbed Dusty's hand.

"Until next time?" Dusty squeezed.

"Until next time." Darla squeezed back then let go.

They did not exchange numbers—that would be too tempting. One of them would give in and a phone call would come too soon.

❀

The ride home had seemed endless and Darla was glad to see Fish at home when she arrived at last. This making peace with time thing would be difficult. He was lovely there in the middle of their futon with his guitar and a notebook. Three different novels and a dictionary were strewn heavily on the otherwise downy surface.

❀

"Hey, pumpkin." He tossed his dreads back from his face. "How was your time? Did you meet anyone? What did you see? Tell me about it." He was full of questions as usual.

"Shhhhhh." Darla kneeled then crawled up his side and on top of him. "Shhhhhh. Let's make a baby."

Summer in the City

by Margaret Johnson-Hodge

Heat.

Not just Manhattan in the middle of August heat, or the strip of asphalt, brick, and cement that was Fourteenth Street heat, that place she had come to when life at home wasn't enough and a one-bedroom walk-up seemed like some gift from a God who understood what she'd needed most at that time of her life.

It wasn't just the unforgiving tiny three-window one bedroom that surrounded Mora. This heat was special, arriving without warning, blossoming like a dragon that'd slept through the ages. It was her soul hungry to connect to that other self, the one she'd misplaced on purpose when her last relationship had failed her miserably.

It was a fire that the circulating fan could not cool, the old-fashioned claw-footed tub full of tepid water could not quench, nor the fresh-from-the-refrigerator Heineken master. And it had been waiting for her the moment she opened her eyes.

Touching herself there could not take it away; the force of the shower massage could not tame it. Candles, cucumbers, the dildo too large to ever belong to a real somebody could not salve it. Mora was in need of other, something beyond herself, outside of hands, devices, and oblongs unattached. She was in

185

need of the one thing she had deemed unneeded that Fourth of July when he had left her waiting there at the South Street Seaport, making her convert the café table like a momma bear, growling at anyone who drew too close.

She had sat there all afternoon, nursing bottles of Evian, trying to keep her straight-from-the-shower hair coiffed against the ocean breeze, the watermelon lip gloss shiny on her lips, the essence of her patchouli oil fresh upon her body because it was how he liked her—kind of raw, kind of wild, kind of natural.

She had abandoned her hair dryer, her curling iron, and her MAC finishing face creme in the name of him. Had abandoned Tiffany perfume for little bottles of body oil sold on the corner of West Eighth and University. She had given up hiphop and alternative rock because he loved jazz too much to even consider it. Waiting patiently that Fourth of July, Mora realized she had become someone other in the name of love.

Mora decided she would not miss him, would return second by second to the self she had been. She would straighten her hair, wear full face every day, and douse her body like a cheap whore. She did not wait around for the phone to ring, did not anticipate finding him loitering around her building, did not hope for an accidental meeting in the subway. She let it all go, coming back to herself like sap falling from a spigot. Not fast, not slow, but steady, in drips. Pieces of herself reclaimed bit by bit.

Now weeks later she found herself, nipples hard, butternut-brown body rosy, uterus swollen, and moisture oozing with a need she had not anticipated. In need of his sweet fingers inside her, deep.

He had been the first man she'd known who mastered the delicate art of finger to clit, the stroking, the pressure, the contact, the absence when she was about to come. He prolonged it, making her twitch, beg, plead. He touched her like he knew her, like she was special, precious, delicate; a garden there for his discovery; a deity greater than he would ever be.

It was a skill she herself could not master, nor could the man two floors up whom she'd attempted it with. It was a gift she found herself longing for.

Mora rolled onto her side, knees drawn, belly tight. Smelled the fragrance of her lower self, trembled deep. Flat on her back she went, the sheet a canopy poofing in the air. Mora swallowed, waited, soft cotton on her skin. It fell upon the top of her thighs, the hard ridges of her breasts, the slope of her belly. Her body arched, tiny movement upward, pulled away, hungry, open, and wet.

She had not planned on him ever claiming her like that, he just a street musician with Cuba flowing through his veins. But his smile had been a promise he delivered with the magic he possessed in his hands.

Street urchin was what she thought that day she'd spotted him half a block away, playing his conga, his ritual, near private, as if he were master drummer in a Bimbe. In her mind's eye Mora saw him clearly, head back, nappy/curly hair six inches too long from his scalp. But it was the music, hands hitting tight skin, that drew her eye. The rhythm carrying her until she was nearly upon him. Mora made her way through the tight cluster of spectators, saw eyes stretched so far up only the whites showed. Sweat on his brow, mouth turned up in a grimace, he was lost and gone away from the gathered crowd.

She could not look away from the passion that encompassed him. Mesmerized, she watched until he had played his final rhythm, the conga's music fading in the air. His eyes opened, found hers, full of secrets, a quick desire. One that filled her and she was willing to share.

"I felt you coming," he would tell her later after a trip to the Cuban coffeehouse, the stroll to Washington Square Park. "Knew you were there before I looked," he said passing her a joint. "I was calling for you, with my music. Knew you would arrive."

She laughed at his nerve but held fast to her first impression, that he was just a street musician with Cuban roots and nappy wild hair. Nothing would come of them. He was just a blip on the screen of her life to be forgotten.

Then he stopped her, just beneath the Washington Square Arch, and leaned against her, his breath hot, spicy, near foul against her ear. When his chest moved against her breast that swelled and throbbed with its own tempestuous beat, she knew how wrong she had been.

When his right hand moved between them and fiddled with the button of her jeans and he slid warm and callused fingers into the band of her thong, she knew. When he touched her there like she never knew she could be touched, her orgasm coming too swift and fast to savor, she was without doubt.

And as the soft glow of dusk filled the late-Saturday-afternoon sky and he drew his damp fingers to his nose and inhaled them, eyes never from hers, Mora understood that she would never see him as a street urchin again.

He had primed her without knowledge, had seduced with mere sight and sound. It was the conga he had played, the eyes closed, strained back; the wild woolly mane, the fire that burned deep inside his dark brown eyes. It was oppression and a need for freedom, words that sang music without request. It was a calling to which she responded, giving her no other reply than *yes*.

Mora was happy to discover he wasn't homeless, had a job and a real roof over his head. She was happy to see that he only wore his hair wild when he was performing on the streets and that other times he wore it greased and brushed back in a little ponytail. She was happy to learn that he was not involved with anyone and hadn't been for a while; that he didn't cheat, saw only one woman at a time, and was what they used to call faithful.

He cooked like his touch, passionate and intense. He read her poetry in Spanish, burned candles and incense. He held fast that the revolution was coming and the sleeping giants would awake. He was a throwback to the early seventies, though neither one of them had been born.

Mora just went on with him awhile, she working at a Barnes and Nobles bookstore, and he, the unemployment office. She did not involve him with her friends and he didn't introduce her to his. Their world was circular, encompassing, a creation of their own.

It had been his idea to meet at the South Street Seaport and take in the Fourth in style. He had to run up to the Bronx to see his family but promised to meet her by noon.

He never showed.

It had been the sitting, the waiting, the vulnerability of being alone that got her thinking. It had been the minutes passing, constant glances at her watch that forced her to review their life. It became the solitude she felt with thousands of people around her. The endless calls on her cell phone to his apartment, and the empty hollow of unanswered rings.

She would go away as he had entered her life, unexpectedly and without forewarning.

That had been her plan and it had worked until now. But the heat of summer had found her and she was missing all that he was. Missed him even as she touched herself, fingers gliding slippery and wet, deep inside of her as she moaned and pushed trying to reach the secret place. She came fast and empty. Caught her breath. Fires still burning in the aftermath, in no rush to go away.

Her want.

Pulsing, ebbing, flowing, even as she maneuvered her way down the crowded strip of Fourteenth Street, discount stores sporting wares off their awnings, vendors setting up their trade. She caught her reflection in a store window. And even in the faint likeness she could see the hint of rose along her cheeks. And she could feel in love with the smooth brown legs, the way the straps of her sandals put her ankles in bondage. She could have stopped traffic with the extra swell in her breast, how the slight breeze played leapfrog with the end of her short floral shirt. In heat now, she was certain a stranger could smell her, primal and raw.

Mora walked, relishing the delicious contact where her thighs touched. Tiny spasms, like sparks of fire, ignited with every step she took. On the edge, want deep, the need to come again pulsed through her as she remembered the feel of callous hands.

Drums.

Faint as the warm breeze, inexact in its location, the sound was there. She looked around her, the heat of the city filling her, a mosaic of sound and color, motion and noise.

Mora searched for the location of the drums as wetness glided into the hollow of her panties, thin cotton unable to contain the dew. The inside of her thighs became a fast motion of skin and stickiness, slippery and sliding as she pressed on.

Drums calling, she answered, feet moving of their own accord. She bypassed Barnes and Noble as if she were not due at work in seven minutes; a gazelle moving across the African plain.

It was his hands, the magic of those fingers she could not resist. It was her heart forgiving and her soul on fire. It was the heat that was August, touching what she deemed untouchable those many weeks ago. Was Oshun and Shango, the ancient gods he had spoken of so reverently.

It was more than makeup, beyond hip-hop and abandonment at the South Street Seaport. It was the Mora who needed, the Mora who wanted, the Mora who welcomed the transgression. She walked, breeze carried and drum ridden, possessed, he a god riding her soul.

"I knew you would come."

But she disallowed his assertiveness, holding fast her ground, legs planted firmly on the hot concrete, the sun a beam of heat upon her head.

"I knew," he repeated, rising from his stool, hoisting the drum inside the duffel bag, the crowd moving off knowing the show was over.

She looked upon the woolly hair, the eyes of burning brown. Settled upon the hands of sweetness. Felt their magic, luscious music upon her soul. She stood watching the man who had her in his power, unable to resist the capture, unable to break free.

"See, even now, you are feeling me . . ."

Yes, she was a puppet on a string. Her whole body pulsed, yearned, hungry for freedom. That release only he could give.

"Tell me no Mora," he teased, the duffel bag hoisted on a strong brown shoulder. "Go ahead and tell me," he whispered as he took up his stool.

But Mora could not speak, could only wait for him to join her, and without words they swiftly moved away.

A comet crashing toward earth, leaving a trail of burning rock and insidious gas, she hurried, platform shoes made clumsy in her quickness, he beside her matching her stride for stride.

They entered her apartment, a hurricane in the making. He closed the door, carefully laying down his conga and stool. She stood there, hard nipples, round beneath the cotton, thighs wide, steamy, damp.

She closed her eyes, parted her lips, waiting for him to touch her. Swaying, she just wanted an end, but he stood his ground, curious and calculating, hesitating; he tasted her need.

He drank deeply from her hunger. Feasted greedily on her want. Was determined to witness just how deep her desire burned before he would take a single step.

Mora swallowed, trembling like an airborne leaf. Whispered "please" soft and low, the simple word painful. He reached out, took the edge of her top, moving it slow up over her chest. Her arms raised, body tingling at the rough cotton, and brief kisses against her skin.

She shook, legs weak, longing for the support but not strong enough to find it. Prisoner, she leaned back her head as he moved woolly hair against her nipples.

The air grew hot, moist, her essence filling the room with its aroma. Back and forward, nappy edges like silk moved.

"So wet," she muttered, a secret she could no longer contain. "Please *Fernando*, please," his name heavy off her tongue.

It drew his fingers, curious, testing. They danced along her belly, the contact making her quiver. Her pelvis lurched toward him, an attempted lasso, but he was a patient lover, rush not a part of his game.

He moved his hand, unhurried in their destination. Mora bit her lip against a moan. She grew dizzy, a new sapling, victim to the wind. Strong arms surrounded her, took her airborne, and laid her on the bed.

Her spine arched as those fingers danced about the waist of her skirt. Soon it was off and so were her panties. Naked and open she became a ripe mango, glistening, longing to be devoured.

"Sweet," he murmured against the hollow of her belly. "So sweet," he said again, his nose inhaling her scent. "My Mora," he whispered against the top of her pubis. "Mora," he uttered against the jet-black curly hairs.

"You sent me away," he accused as his tongue lapped her lower lips, "away," as he drew nectar from soft luscious center. "How could you?" he wanted answering as his tongue delved deep inside of her.

Mora didn't know, had no answer as she came hard, slow, and, in that moment, forever.

Beachwear

by devorah major

"Joceri, you ain't got no couth," Brenda playfully snapped at Joceri, who was sitting on the sand leaning on her knees and undoing her braids, a pile of plastic extensions lying at her ankles and four-inch spurs coming out from the sides of her head. Joceri wore a red-and-orange-flowered swimsuit with a matching sarong that covered her long, scarred legs. She rarely showed her legs, still self-conscious after fifteen years of living with scars that were a result of repeated surgeries that got her legs working again after a car accident that had occurred when she was a teenager. A drunk driver had collided with her father's car, right at the point she had been climbing from the backseat into the front, changing places with her older sister, Krystal, who always got to read the maps and be the navigator. Joceri had been told to wait until they stopped for gas, but she whined and whined until her father finally acquiesced. Krystal climbed back, purposely hitting Joceri's head with her elbow in the transition. Then Joceri was just pulling her second leg through the space between the driver and passenger seats when *blam*, a car plowed into them, crossing the highway without warning. Two months in traction, six months in physical therapy, and scars at her ankles, knees, and one hip and thigh were the result. Yeah, the insurance money bought a nice college education, and a very nice convertible car with a jamming sound system, but Joceri never was comfortable with the burnt umber vines that had become a part of her once smooth, sand-colored legs.

It was a problem because she loved the beach, loved to swim, thoroughly enjoyed the sun forcing her to lie back and melt into the ground. But she almost always was mostly covered, letting only part of her unscathed left leg poke out from a slit in the skirt. Outside the scars, her legs were quite well formed. Long, muscular, thin ankles, with the toes always manicured and painted, as if to distract from the scrawls and engravings just above.

Joceri just laughed as she pulled loose another strand and shook her head free. "I love the rush of blood back to my scalp. All the air."

"Girl, I'm not out here trying to show off my thirty-six double-Ds just to catch some air. I'm trying to get one of these fine cinnamon-chocolate men to give me a sample, and none of them is coming near your outdoor beauty shop." Brenda was a big woman. Not fat, big, generous in all ways, she liked to say. Large hands, large hips, large lips, large heart. She filled every inch and then some of her bright yellow two-piece suit billowing out with curves and dark toast skin. Brenda talked loud, laughed loud, wore makeup from the moment she rolled out of bed to the moment she climbed back in. She was the cheerleader of her set. If you had a problem Brenda could make you forget it, if she couldn't solve it. Which she could rarely do. But even so, you would definitely feel better about things, feel like there was a solution somewhere, even though it wasn't right at hand.

"Brenda, I told you I had to get these out today. You dragged me out here and now you're fussing at me. I told you what I was doing if I came. You said, 'Hell, I guess the beach is a good a place as any. I mean if you don't mind looking all whack in public.'"

"Which I didn't expect you to really do. I thought you'd wait till tomorrow. It's not like you and church have any meaningful relationship, so Sunday would have been just as good."

"Not when I had decided on today. Anyway, why don't you just take your dessert-loving self into the surf and find that fudge brownie, or whatever it is you looking for, and just leave me be since you don't seem willing to help."

"Because the point was to get you out of your funk and to stop mourning the one that slithered away back to his rock and find you something better."

"Oh, so you into procurement now. You want my profile for your agency?"

"You trying my patience, girl. Why don't you just have a little fun? Just relax and let something come by that ain't about *till death do us part*, just about parting some legs and letting some juices flow."

"When I need help with my sex life I'll let you know, Brenda. Till then . . ."

"Girl, I ain't providing you no help. You really don't have the physique that gets my blood pressure up. I'm just saying your skin is looking a little sallow and your shoulders are getting stooped."

"Oh so now I'm old and tired, huh, two steps away from a walker and Shady Pines . . ."

"Ain't nothing like some oiled joints to get you stepping light." Brenda eyed the auburn pile growing around Joceri's ankles. "You could at least put this trash in a bag. Have a little order around you. Show off your legs. You need to get over worrying about those scars. They're not that bad, and anyway they add character. You have nice legs, nice color, no cottage cheese."

"Brenda, are you sure you not trying to move into procurement and sales? I know you own your own business, but I am not a piece of your merchandise."

"Joceri, you have not been out on a date, in, what, two years?"

"I go out dancing almost every week." Brenda rolled her eyes. "Well every month anyway. And I went to the movies last month with that joker you set me up with. William-what's-your-family-crest-Milweed."

"Millman. And I didn't know he was so stuck up he was talking about pedigrees and brand names as if he was a horse breeder or something. I can see how that would have made you trip, but you have to admit, he makes a good living and he was easy on the eyes. Anyway the idea wasn't marriage. But I wasn't talking date like *go out and see a movie,* I meant date . . ." Brenda licked her lips and ran her hands down her thighs, "as in *sweet tropical fruit that you find at an oasis in the middle of a desert and enjoy all night long.*"

"Hey, it wasn't even good conversation," Joceri hissed.

"You see there, girl, you sound like one of those crystal wineglasses shattering all on the floor. As I was saying at the start, I wasn't suggesting him for conversation. Sometimes, you just got to bend and stretch, girl. It's just not normal for a young woman to go without. I mean nature got to be in balance, and you are out of kilter."

"Not everyone is like you, Brenda. Men are more than a good meal."

"So you keep telling me. But I'm thinking it's just one big smorgasbord out there and my job is to keep my plate full and the cook happy."

"Not everyone likes all-you-can-eat."

"Yeah, well, too much fasting will kill you, girl. You ever looked at those pictures of Gandhi? That man did not look healthy. I mean his shoulders could cut through a piece of cotton. That's why he never wore any shirts, tore them all up."

"Brenda, you are crazy. Help me with the ones all the way in the back."

Just then Rene walked up. He worked in the same firm as Joceri, two floors down. He had tried to talk with her more than once. Had been able to get her for a few lunches and one after-dinner drink, but every time he thought they were moving toward something she jumped away like a wild deer running deep into the bush. And every time she pulled away he let her go, never pressing, never complaining, and never going completely away. For a time it seemed to Joceri that he was dating her supervisor, Debbie. Or at least trying to move in that direction. But Brenda said he was just flirting with Debbie so that he could see Joceri and keep himself on her mind. And Joceri had thought about him. She had thought about him a lot.

"Hey, Brenda. You looking bright and vivacious."

"As always," Brenda replied.

And then he turned to Joceri. "And since you are here, my day is now great. It's always a pleasure to see you." Joceri always thought his voice was a bit high for a man. But it was so smooth, silken.

Brenda had not stopped laughing. "I think you're laying it on a bit thick, bro'."

Rene had not stopped smiling at Joceri, whose cheeks were now flushed with red. "Actually, I meant it."

Joceri smiled back. "Thank you, then." She was squinting into the sun and saw Rene as a tall, sculpted, dark shadow. No details in his face, just round eyes shining out of a dark saucer. Brenda had been right, though: He did look like he worked out. His arms were buff, and his abdomen, while not fully hard, showed definition and lines. Thankfully his swimsuit was loose and hung almost to his knees. Joceri's mind had jumped to wondering and she didn't really didn't want to know more than she needed to about size, dimensions, shape.

Rene kept smiling broadly, his white teeth shining out of his mouth, flashing a little bit of gold from the back. "Jake and Ted are down the way. You ladies want to come over and share a couple of brews, have some food, maybe toss around the volleyball? Joceri, didn't you tell me you were on a team in high school?"

Brenda and Joceri burst out responses at the same time: Brenda with, "Sounds great," and Joceri with, "I'm fine here, thank you. As you can see I've got most of the back, and a whole other side."

Brenda squatted next to Joceri, picked up an extension, and pulled it hard. "Girl, what is the matter with you?"

Joceri winced, pulled the braid out of Brenda's hand, and kept talking. "Thanks, Rene, but I am taking out my braids, as you can see, enjoying the sun, and in another hour will be taking a short swim, reading my book, and then sleeping the day away in utter bliss. My afternoon is set."

"Set in the Dark Ages," snapped Brenda.

Rene sat next to the two women. "Brenda, you go along. Ted brought some potato salad and chicken, make you want to open up a restaurant. I can help Joceri take out these extensions."

Brenda stood up, laughing. "I bet you can."

Joceri turned her head and looked at Rene. She realized

that every time he came close she caught her breath. That's why she kept her distance. She really wasn't ready, not ready to get and definitely not ready to lose, but that was the pattern of her life. As often as not the men she settled with were attached to someone else, or else to themselves in a way that didn't give room for much real to happen that wasn't happening between the sheets. She wasn't like Brenda, able to just be inside the moment and take the pleasure of the surface, never going much farther. That's why she had decided to leave all of it alone for a while, a long while. "I really don't like a whole lot of people up in my hair. Thanks though."

"Last time I looked I wasn't a whole lot of people, just one. And anyway I've got plenty of experience, girl. Five sisters, Joceri. Three older, two younger. I've taken out a whole lot of braids. And it looks like you've got a whole lot to do in the back. I'm not going to mess with you."

"Somebody needs to," said Brenda under her breath. "Which way to the barbecue, Rene?" He pointed up the beach toward the parking lot. "See you later, Jo," Brenda laughed, full hips swaying from side to side as she eased down the beach.

Joceri sighed. "I should have known Brenda was plotting when she was so insistent I come out. She just wouldn't let me stay home. I swear I'm going to get her back for this. And don't try to tell me it's just a coincidence you and your posse showed up at the same time on the same piece of beach."

"My plot, Joceri. My plan. I know you've been under a deadline getting that last project out, and I thought, well, now that it's passed maybe you'd have room for a little more me."

He picked up a braid and was fingering the strands loose. The edge of his palm rubbed the back of her neck. After a couple of minutes he reached the edges of her real hair and was deftly separating out the strands without pulling or tearing the ends. As the false hair came out he gently rubbed her scalp and then picked up another braid. This time he slid his hand across her shoulder. She could feel his breath at her back.

Joceri didn't say anything. She liked his smell. Soap and salt, she thought. Rene readjusted his legs, sitting full in back of her with her hips in between his outspread thighs. He had been careful not to touch her back or hips, but she could feel his heat and was self-conscious. She adjusted herself nervously, moving forward a few inches. Rene said nothing; just kept unbraiding. As each braid came out Rene became more forward with his touch. At one point Joceri hunched her shoulders, which were beginning to cramp in her efforts to keep them from touching his chest. She wanted to lean back and rest her lower back, but didn't dare. It was too close.

"Hard to keep sitting up, huh. Do you mind?" Rene dropped the braid he had been holding and placed his hand on the side of her neck. He found the precise place in her shoulder that was cramping and softly rubbed out the strain, his fingers pressing into the muscle firmly but without gripping, pushing the crick out from the back of the ear where it started, around her shoulders, and then smooth down her back.

Joceri tried not to sigh at his touch. It was soothing. The two of them worked out the braids, rarely talking. After a time all the braids were out. Joceri was about to pull away when she felt Rene's fingers weaving through the remaining thick brush. He began to gently rub her scalp, calming the itches that had been rising. "My oldest sister, Melanie, used to make me take a comb and scratch her head after we got all the rows out. She said the itch would drive her crazy." He rubbed her scalp and then gently ran his arms down her neck, smoothing its long lines. Joceri dropped her head forward and enjoyed his touch. She knew it was time to run, time to jolt. She knew she needed to find a way to get away, but he was so calming and so quiet she just sat there. Her breath was becoming too heavy. She tried to hold it and then let it out hoping he wouldn't notice. Wouldn't notice that her nipples had begun to harden. She pulled her knees tighter into her chest.

"Do you know this beach?" Rene asked.

"I come out here a lot every summer and fall. You know. Mostly this end. Sometimes we drive a couple of miles farther down."

"No, I mean there are some caves around the way. You have to wade through some water, but the view is beautiful. There are rock formations in one of the coves and a little isle where the otters come and rest. It's the funniest thing you ever saw. They lie all over each other and just belch and honk and snort. And then after an afternoon nap, they slip back into the sea and swim down the coast. Come on, let's walk."

Joceri jumped up. "Good idea. Let me grab my bag. We don't have any beer here. Just some sodas and water. You want to go get your friends and . . ."

"Let's take a couple of pops and let it go at that. We can get some food later, I mean unless you're hungry."

"No, I'm fine."

They began to walk down the stretch of beach. Three children were having a race down the beach, and one of them almost tripped Joceri. Rene caught her.

"Dangerous out here," he laughed.

"Maybe too dangerous," said Joceri.

"Hey, I'll keep you safe." Farther down Rene stopped and helped a little boy build a part of a sand castle. He showed him the right mix of water to sand so that he could use the small pail as a mold for the buildings. Joceri watched his hands pat the flat top of the corner barricade, his fingertips softly clearing a ledge and making a place for armaments to go. "Take it easy, boy, and you'll have a fine castle."

Joceri had to admit he was a nice man. Didn't impose himself exactly, just knew how to make a place for himself. Find the gaps and fit on in. She sighed as they walked.

The beach became emptier and emptier as they got farther from the entrance. By the time they reached the caves he had spoken of almost no one was around. They had to climb over two ledges, up, down, and around, and then up, down, and around again. Joceri's sarong kept getting caught under her feet and knees, but she would not take it off.

After going past two coves they had to wade through the water to get to the place Rene had talked about. Joceri lifted the sarong as she walked until she was holding most of it midthigh.

"I thought you said wade. Wade usually means the ankles, not chest." She smiled at Rene's back. He was a few steps in front. "How high is this water going to get?"

"Just to your waist. Doesn't reach the shoulders when the tide is all the way in. I've swum out a few times. But it's just a little farther." He glanced over his shoulder. "You might want to take that skirt all the way off before it gets wet."

"I'm all right," Joceri answered.

"Suit yourself." Rene laughed. "It'll dry fast enough in the sun anyway."

Joceri realized he was right. She took a deep breath and stopped to take off the sarong. She was relieved that Rene did not look back immediately. Even if he had looked back, she reasoned, he would only have seen part of the scars. Maybe he wouldn't have seen any of them. He seemed to always be looking at her face or at the sky or at the water. And if he did see some, maybe he really wouldn't care, a least not that much.

Maybe Brenda was right. Maybe Joceri did trip about her legs too much.

They walked around a bend that gave the illusion of leading only to more water when a small beach appeared nestled in a hilly recess. When you sat in it you couldn't see the rest of the beach, only the ocean sparkling against the sky. Two otters were resting on a small rock rising out of the sea about fifty yards away. Past them was a pinnacle of rocks that had been smoothed by ocean waves. They were thick, shiny, and twisted and seemed to point at the sun.

"Do you swim?" Rene asked, stepping onto the shore.

"Yes, but I'm not interested in meeting any otters today, thank you."

"I thought you might like to see God's Fingertip up close."

"What?"

"That's what I named that formation. Doesn't it look like a finger reaching upward? Like it's just telling the sun to shine brighter, and the moon to hang low in the sky. Wait until you see the way the moon looks . . ."

"I'm not going to be here that long," Joceri said, starting to loosely wrap her cloth around her waist and sinking down to the ground.

"Joceri. The sand is kinda hot. Can we use your skirt to sit on?"

"I just put it back on."

"Why?"

"I really don't like to show my legs." As she spoke she realized that the cloth was split open right at the lightning bolt that ran from her hip down toward her knee. She started to cover it up.

He lifted her hand. "Why not? You have lovely legs. I noticed when you came up on the beach. Real pretty." Joceri did not move. "Both legs. Real nice." He was smiling at her and everything seemed far away. She could hear a distant echo of children's voices. She could hear gulls singing as they swooped at the top of the cliff. She could hear the waves softly licking the edge of the shore. Joceri smiled back. "I guess it'd be okay." She untied the cloth and spread it over a patch of sand and left a space where Rene could sit.

Rene moved next to her and rubbed his shoulders against hers. They sat that way for a long time. Finally Joceri spoke. "What do you want, Rene? Why do you keep trying to pass through this way?"

"I'm not trying to pass through, woman. I'm trying to get in."

"I know you're trying to get *in*," said Joceri lightly, turning it to a joke, unconsciously licking the edge of her lip as she spoke.

"Yeah, that, too. What fool wouldn't want to get close to something as fine as you? But I mean into your life, not just in between your legs. Into your mind, into your spirit. I'm trying to find the road in and you just keep putting up stop signs."

"Under-construction signs," Joceri said so softly he almost missed it.

"We're all ongoing projects, Joceri. You can't, I mean you can, but you shouldn't just shut out everyone until you decide you're done. We're never done."

"I have a lot of repair work to do."

"Not so it shows."

Joceri didn't answer. She stared out at the water. She began to count the waves to see how many were coming in at the same time. Rene moved in front of her, blocked her view. He lifted one of her legs and examined the crooked lines. One ran like a vine on the outside of her ankle, another a cross-stitch across her knees, and a third from under the edge of her bathing suit to the middle of her thigh, thick, black, smooth, and inflexible.

"They're so soft," he said almost to himself.

"My legs are not smooth and soft."

"Not the legs, the designs on them. The scars, they're actually quite soft." He ran his fingers around her ankles, drawing the tip of the index finger across the raised welt. "You know you have some pretty feet, too." His fingers softly ran down the arch of her feet, his thumb gently covering and then revealing the scar.

"Yeah, if you don't look above them," snorted Joceri.

"And yeah if you do." He ran his hands up the calves and into her thick thighs. Joceri looked at the fingers as they moved. Wide, flat, sure. She looked at the sand, almost the same color as her, large grains, some of them seeming to shine. She looked straight into the sun.

She did not look at Rene.

He kept stroking her legs. Massaging them softly. Teasing her inner thigh, which was becoming hot. "You want me to stop?"

"I don't know what I want." Joceri was barely able to get the words out.

"How 'bout what you need. Do you know that?"

"I know what I don't need."

"And what's that?" He had moved one hand to her face and was cradling it softly. The other rested on the outside of her bare hip. Joceri looked at his eyes, which were so close to hers. She could barely breathe. She didn't want to run, but she needed to go. Maybe they should swim, but she didn't move.

"What, Joceri? What don't you need?"

"I don't need to get hurt. I don't need any more B.S. I don't need—"

Rene cut her off. "I assure you I have no intentions of hurting you. Not in the least. I'm not into pain myself."

His hand slid down her face, across her shoulder, close to her breast, and then around her back. "That's not what I meant." Joceri turned her side to him.

Rene moved in front of her. "I'm not into hurting, in any way." One of Joceri's legs was stretched out in front of her. The other one was bent up to her chest, preventing him from getting any closer. He sat facing her and stretched that leg to the right side of him, smoothing the skin.

"That's my good leg," Joceri said, trying to keep any kind of words inside her head. Trying not to get any more caught up in the rhythm of the surf and the softness of his voice. "Only one hip broke. That one just had a simple fracture."

"They're both good legs," he said and brushed the sand from between the toes. "Really nice legs. I've been wanting to see what you kept hidden under all those pantsuits for a long time."

Joceri pulled her foot out of his hand and tried to move in front of Rene. He adjusted himself and squatted in back of her. She looked hard into the water. He ran his tongue around the rim of her ear, down her neck, onto her shoulder, pushing down the suit's thin straps.

"It really is beautiful here. It's like we're in a secret world. You'd never know there was a beach full of people just around a couple of bends," Joceri jabbered. "Really, just like you said, beautiful."

Rene didn't say anything, just laughed softly. "And it's beautiful here." His tongue was running down her spine. She gasped lightly. "And here." The front of her swimsuit fell and her breasts slipped out of the bra cups.

If Joceri was going to stop this, it had to be now. They

should talk. What about a condom? How many women had he been with? Safe. She wanted to be safe. She watched Rene's hands travel across her chest. He cupped one breast on each hand. They were small, only slightly overfilling his hands. She had once thought about getting them enlarged but decided the risk was not worth it. He softly turned the nipples between his fingertips. They were hard and almost quivered beneath his touch.

He put his lips next to her ear. "You know, Joceri, I'm a one-woman man. One at a time. For as long as we can make it work. It's been five months since I had anyone . . . waiting on you and just didn't feel like messing around. Longest time in my life, woman. Celibate, I mean. So if this isn't what you want, now's the time to say so. Because I plan on being around for a while."

Joceri was breathing hard. She needed to feel him. She leaned back into his chest arching back just a little. "What about . . . ?"

"Everything you need, Joceri." His lips were on her shoulder, he was turning her to face him, her back to the sea, his mouth filling with one breast as he gently sucked it. And then pulled away. "I swear baby, everything you need."

She pushed him back. "Does that include condoms?"

"Hell, woman, that's what *I* need. Of course. I mean I got everything else. Condoms, that's just the mechanics." He looked at her and saw that her bottom lip was lightly trembling. He leaned forward and gently nipped on it. Pulled it softly with the edges of his teeth and then settled his lips around hers, waiting for her to open her mouth and invite him to move forward. She sighed again and began to kiss him back. This time he pulled away. "Everything you need . . . and nothing you don't."

Her damp suit clung to her hips as he pulled it down past her knees and to the side. He left his own on, just taking the time to look at her. Smiling and looking. "You one pretty mama." He laughed and lay down next to her. "I'm going to enjoy getting to know you." Rene's hands moved slowly, as if he was measuring every inch of her. And then his fingers would stop at the elbow crevice, at the wrist bump, at the shoulder hollow, and each time they stopped they were replaced by his lips, which smoothed, tasted, breathed hot, then cooling air around her. There was nothing then except the surf, quiet at first, barely there at the edge of her mind, and the gulls above, calling out to each other, and his lips and fingertips discovering the round of her abdomen, grazing around the backs of her thighs, separating the hairs between her legs, licking the salt and syrup that were trickling out from between her legs.

It had been so long that she wanted to hurry, to feel him inside her now that she had decided to let this happen, but he wasn't going to let her rush it. When he finally entered her he stayed on top for only a moment before rolling over and letting her sit high above him, holding on to her hips, which circled in wide, dark arcs, echoing the eddies of water that circled the rocks in the cove. As Joceri rocked the waves seemed to get higher and higher; she heard her own moans and could not separate them from the ocean's foam, sizzling as it melted into the sand. He went deeper inside her and she gripped his hips and was inside the water's currents swirling and turning until the tight rope that bound her ankles and thighs fell away and she was inside herself and swallowed in his touch and gasping for air that poured through her skin, every pore open and alive. Finally damp and sticky, laughing she collapsed on his chest just as she felt him tremble and heard him call out her name across the ocean's expanse.

"That was nice," Joceri sighed, nuzzling his neck.

"Just a beginning, woman. We got a lot of places to go and things to see."

"For example?" Joceri teased.

"Wait till you see the moonrise. I tell you it's a beautiful sight. A beautiful sight."

"I'll bet." Joceri closed her eyes and listened as the otters began to bray, and the water washed against the shore.

The Princess and the Cop

by Kathleen Morris

Kim moved through the mass of elegantly dressed wimmin talking in well-educated, modulated tones. She stopped at an occasional clique to chat, then moved on, heading for the double French doors which opened on to the terrace. The cool air pushed its way through her mauve-colored chiffon cocktail dress. She stopped for a moment to enjoy the pleasant sensation on her skin and then continued over to the stone wall that separated the house from the sculptured gardens beyond, with a sigh.

She was bored. The same wimmin gathered at every event she'd been to this summer. Boat rides and barbecues, brunches and golf outings—and now this fund-raiser for some wimmin's arts foundation. The same wimmin. She'd been through the interesting ones already, none intriguing enough to continue with beyond a week or two.

It was a dark and clear out, the constellations of stars lush and bright in the country sky. She imagined herself walking down the flagstone path that wound through the gardens on the arm of her partner, a gentlewomyn in tailored linen. She was athletic, smart, funny, and successful. And of course, she adored Kim.

"Is this a private party?"

The soft music playing in the house floated out to Kim,

and she turned from the phantom lovers reluctantly to face her friend and host, Lynn. Following just behind Lynn was a womyn Kim had never seen before. Kim's eyebrows raised in question, and Lynn smiled playfully as she began introductions.

"Kimberly Somers, I'd like you to meet Tracy Landon. Tracy is a deputy sheriff up here." Lynn's voice lowered slyly as she said the last.

Kim quickly assessed Tracy. She was a handsome womyn, tall—and that was saying a lot for the five-foot, ten-inch Kim. Her hair was locked. The salt-and-pepper serpents were impeccably groomed and showered over her shoulders. Tracy's body was lean and hard beneath her clothes, and Kim trembled inside as she sensed the rippling strength in Tracy's broad, swimmer's shoulders. Her face was slightly square; a friendly smile revealed charmingly crooked teeth.

But she was wearing a crumpled blend jacket over black khaki trousers. And boots. Boots! Kim sighed. Too bad.

Still, she smiled politely as she allowed Tracy to shake her hand.

"Pleasure. Are you our security for the evening?"

Tracy's jaw tightened slightly, but her voice was even as she replied, "No, ma'am. I'm off duty. Tonight I am just a supporter of the arts, like you."

"Hmmm. How nice." Kim looked down at her glass. "Empty. Anyone want a refill? I sure do."

Tracy took the glass. "Why don't I get us all fresh ones?" She nodded her head at the ladies and then disappeared into the house.

"Utilize the butch." Lynn smiled as she watched Tracy stroll back inside and make her way to the bar. She turned to Kim. "So, what do you think? Not bad, huh? She's a local, but nice enough. And she's been watching you all evening. Huh? Huh?"

Kim looked back toward the house and then, lowering her voice, said, "You have got to be kidding. Look how she showed up for this event. Hello? This is a cocktail party, not hoedown at the corral. And boots?" Kim rolled her eyes. "She's probably wearing tube socks."

"She isn't that bad, Kim. And I'm not talking about marriage. I'm talking about a little fun till the end of the season, for pity's sake."

"Right. Then why don't you take her? You're much more interested in soaking up the local flavor than I am anyway."

"Don't think I wouldn't if I didn't come up here every year. But, oh my God, what a disaster if she tried to attach herself to me next year. Can you imagine? And you're just here for a few more weeks. She does seem kinda nice—and she's got a great bod."

"Forget it, Lynn, okay? I can't even imagine how you'd think it. Me—with a yokel cop who says *ma'am*? Where could we go together? The local crab and beer joint? Because you know I couldn't be caught de—" Kim looked up just in time to see Tracy place the drinks angrily on the stone ledge, turn, and stalk, back rigid with anger, through the party and out the door.

Lynn's eyes widened in horror. "Oh m'God, that was horrible. She had to have heard us."

Kim rolled her eyes. "Yeah, well, you got her fifty-buck minimum contribution, didn't you? So? I doubt we'll die if we don't get that invite to the crab and beer fest."

Lynn gasped, and then doubled over with laughter. "You are awful!" She covered her mouth to stifle the giggles. "And she did only give fifty dollars." A second later Kim was laughing, too.

Finally, Kim dabbed her tears and said, "All right. So the evening won't be a total wash, let's go back in and have another look at the B list."

Lynn smiled as they linked arms and went back to the party.

⚙

The party had wound down hours before with no interesting developments. Kim lay in bed staring at the ceiling. She was too wired—and too hot—to sleep.

It was not quite one o'clock in the morning. She sat up, deciding that a long drive might relax her. She smiled to herself. Maybe she'd take a long drive—back to the city. She was getting sick of all this damned bucolic beauty anyway. She picked her discarded cocktail dress from the chair beside her bed and slipped it on. Running her fingers through her hair, she picked up her shoes and headed out.

Once she cleared the tree-lined drive of the property, Kim turned on the radio and opened the windows. As she suspected, she felt herself relaxing as she sped down the dark, narrow roads. A familiar song came on and Kim turned up the volume, singing along.

Lights flashed in her rearview mirror. Turning down the music, she heard the sirens as the flashing lights grew closer. She put her foot on the brake, watching the speedometer drop from eight-five to seventy . . . sixty-five . . . sixty . . .

"Please, please let it be an ambulance racing to some emergency up ahead," she prayed. But as the lights drew closer, the car slowed. A police car.

"Pull over and turn off the engine," the bullhorn ordered.

"Shit, shit, *shit*," Kim cursed as she pulled onto the gravel, stopped the car, and cut the motor. The police cruiser pulled off a few feet behind her, the siren dying with a whine.

She heard a door slam, boots crunch on the gravel toward her. A gun belt, khaki uniform, leather glove on the driver's door. "May I see your license and registration please?" A womyn's voice.

Handing her papers over, Kim tried to keep her voice steady. "How fast was I going, Officer?" she asked, knowing full well the answer. The officer didn't answer. She just continued studying the license, her flashlight shining into Kim's face, hurting her eyes.

"Is there a problem?" Kim shielded her eyes and tried to look up into the face of the officer.

"Step out of the car please." The voice was curt, no nonsense.

Damn female cops, Kim thought as she unbuckled her seat belt. *Always have to be tough, gotta prove they have balls or something.* Kim realized charm might not get her off this time. Well, one more try. As she stepped from the car, she asked in as innocent a voice as she could muster, "Is there a problem, Officer?"

"Three. You were going fifty miles over the speed limit, your right taillight is out, and you . . . are a snotty, rude bitch."

Kim squinted her eyes at the face beneath the cap's visor. "Tracy? Oh God. Is this about earlier? Look, I didn't mean what I . . . I mean, I'm sorry about earlier this evening. My behavior was completely out of line. I was just blowing off steam—I'm not really like that."

Tracy just stared at her, her mouth tightly pressed.

Kim thought quickly. Maybe she could work this out . . . maybe. She tried again. "Listen, let me make it up to you. I'm really very nice, once you get to know me. Why don't you come by the house and have breakfast with me tomorrow? We'll start over, make believe it's our first meeting, and forget this whole evening happened. What do you say?" She smiled hopefully.

Tracy adjusted her cap before she answered. "Well, that might make up for your earlier rudeness. It might even get you off on these tickets." She paused for a moment, as if considering, then continued, "But I think I've already met the real you. And she is snotty bitch to the bone. So . . . I think not."

Kim was shocked, then insulted, and then angry. "How dare you?" Kim's hand flew up to slap Tracy's face, but Tracy was faster. She caught Kim's wrist, spun her around, and pushed her up against the car.

"Oh really. Now you're attempting assault on an officer? Very stupid. And common. Is that the way you play?"

Tracy's voice was low and menacing. "Put your hands on the hood and spread your legs." When Kim hesitated, Tracy grabbed a handful of her hair and jerked her head back, hissing in Kim's ear, "*Do it*. I won't ask so nicely again. I'll just cuff you."

Kim assumed the position quickly. She was furious, but she didn't say another word. She knew Tracy would make good her threat. Handcuffs. Kim shivered. She could hear Tracy moving behind her but didn't dare turn around.

Tracy stopped just behind her. Kim could hear Tracy breathing shallowly and then, a moment later, felt Tracy's hand softly stroke her neck. Kim's breath caught at the sudden sensual act. She felt a confused mixture of fear and longing.

When Tracy spoke again, her voice was soft and thoughtful, but still slightly tinged with anger. "Not so high and mighty now, are you . . . princess?"

Kim felt the fear rising. Her eyes raced across the landscape as she realized her predicament. It was dark, deserted. While driving down the narrow road she hadn't seen a single car. No one knew she'd left the house. There were no lights, no houses, no one anywhere in view.

Tracy removed her hand from Kim's neck and knelt behind her. A moment later she started stroking Kim's bare calves. Kim fought to hold on to the fear and anger that were beginning to dissolve into heated desire. Tracy's leather-clad hands were moving slowly up Kim's bare legs, squeezing and stroking as they moved upward.

"Not so mouthy away from your high-flying friends, are you?" Tracy breathed huskily as she inhaled Kim's reluctantly rising arousal. "Well, I'm not one of your friends or—colleagues who lap up all that princess shit you fling around."

Her hands gripped the hem of Kim's skirt and lifted it as she continued making her way up Kim's thighs . . . until Kim's silk-clad ass was revealed to both Tracy and the night sky. Hiking the skirt around Kim's waist, Tracy squeezed and then smacked Kim's ass, smiling as Kim groaned deep in her throat. Tracy reached between Kim's legs, fingering the creamy wetness now staining her expensive panties. She slapped Kim's ass again, harder. Kim gasped and arched her back.

"Just as I thought. An ass in need of a good spanking. And you know you deserve it. Don't you? You know you want it." She slapped the right cheek harder. "Don't you? You want me to spank that spoiled ass of yours." Tracy's voice was pitched to a seductive growl as she pulled Kim's panties roughly down, forcing Kim to stumble as Tracy lifted one of Kim's heeled feet, leaving the silken rag around the other ankle.

Tracy parted Kim's cheeks and then slipped a black kid-covered finger into the crevice, rubbing the soft hide over Kim's drenched pussy and slipping a digit inside Kim's pulsing hole.

Kim struggled to keep her knees locked as Tracy's knuckles teased her swollen flesh. She pumped backward, tightening her inner muscles as she tried to take Tracy in deeper, but Tracy withdrew her finger.

"Are you sure you want this? Sure you want this local trash to fuck your proper ass?"

Tracy's hands slid along Kim's trembling inner thighs. "Yeah, you want it, don't you? You want it right now, don't you?"

Tracy pushed a finger into Kim and pumped her slowly while her other hand continued to softly massage Kim's ass. "Answer me, Kimberly. You want it, don't you?" She pushed a second and then a third finger inside Kim's pussy and said harshly, "Don't you?"

It felt as if Tracy's entire hand was inside of her, filling her, feeling her aching want. An orgasm was rising in Kim. *Please don't stop,* Kim begged silently, as she nodded furiously and gasped aloud, "Yes . . . yes!" Kim thought she'd explode as she rocked into Tracy's rhythm, her insides clenching and unclenching spasmodically.

Suddenly, Tracy smacked Kim's ass again, hard. Again, harder. All the while she continued a slow manipulation of Kim's insides. "You don't cum until I tell you to—understand?" She slapped her again, smiling with satisfaction as she felt the heat rise on Kim's fleshy flank.

Tracy twisted her hand until her leathered thumb, lubricated with Kim's cream, rubbed against Kim's swollen, throbbing clit. She began pumping her harder, deeper, raining spanks on one cheek and then the other with her free hand, the weight of her body keeping Kim's thrashing, bucking body pinned against the car.

Tracy pulled her hand almost out of Kim and then slammed it back in. Again. And again.

"Please . . . please . . . ah . . . please," Kim chanted over and over as Tracy spanked her, pumped her, played with her clit. Tracy pressed hard circles on Kim's hood and then held it, flicking the head back and forth until Kim let out a long keen, her knees buckling beneath her. Tracy pulled her body away from Kim, and Kim reeled and then collapsed against the car, a powerful orgasm sweeping over her.

Tracy stilled her hand as Kim's hot cunt pulsed around it. She rested her cheek against Kim's flamed flank and carefully withdrew her fingers, tracing a slick digit through Kim's tangled pubic hair and cupping the source of Kim's heat in her palm until the throbbing stopped. Then she stood. She turned Kim to her, smiling slightly as she watched Kim regain some measure of composure. The haughty tilt of her head was gone, her eyes were soft, a little bewildered, her lips wet and parted slightly as she pulled in small gasps of breath.

Tracy took several steps backward, moving from the gravel to the grass, her eyes never leaving Kim's. She stopped, legs planted firmly, and removed her gun belt. Kim watched as Tracy unzipped her pants and then motioned for her to kneel in front of her. Kim didn't hesitate. She knew what Tracy wanted.

Kim knelt on the soft grass, her face level with Tracy's crotch. She rubbed her hands along the khaki trousers, kissing Tracy's mons as she worked the pants down. Tracy's engorged clit extended beyond the plump outer lips, peeking through the thick, curling wet hair that usually protected it.

Tracy placed her hands on Kim's head, her fingers digging in to the scalp as she led Kim's mouth to her. Kim licked and sucked hungrily, moving in rhythm with Tracy, increasing speed, pressure, as Tracy's hands dictated. She felt Tracy's body tense, her clit pulsing on Kim's tongue. And when Tracy pressed Kim's face hard into her and held it there, cumming silently, Kim felt the intensity of Tracy's release and her own body responding in kind.

After a moment Tracy pushed Kim away. Kim sank back on the grass, watching Tracy pull up her pants, reattach her holster and belt. Tracy looked down at Kim, a strange smile on her face, but she said nothing. Kim stood and brushed her dress, then moved toward Tracy.

"That was incredible. I . . . I have never . . ."

Tracy's smile widened. "I know . . . I guess I will forget the ticket and just issue a warning this time."

Kim laughed. "Thank you. I'm glad you're going to give me another chance." She leaned forward to kiss Tracy, but Tracy sidestepped the gesture, turned, and headed for the cruiser.

"Where are you going?" Kim's voice rose in confusion as she watched Tracy's retreating form.

"I'm on duty. Back to my post."

"So, will I see you tomorrow at breakfast?" Kim came around and stood beside the car as Tracy climbed in and turned on the motor.

"I don't think so, Kimberly. This was nice, but I think you're a little rich for my blood." And with that she pulled away, scattering gravel, made a U-turn, and drove away, leaving Kim standing by the side of the road in the dark.

Popsicles, Donuts, and Reefah

by Bruce Morrow

When Roy Williams sticks his head in his father's bedroom, the day nurse is feeding Clarence while watching *Regis and Kathie Lee*. The room looks and smells like a hospital room, and Roy has to rub his eyes and clear his throat before speaking. He asks, "How's he doing this morning, Fami?"

"Just fine," Fami mutters through a genuine smile. Although she moved to the United States from Haiti more than twenty years ago, she's still not sure of her English; she smiles a lot and mumbles to cover any chance of mispronunciation. She has a heart-shaped face and thick features, with a hairline that seems to grow too close to her eyebrows. She reminds Roy of a Hershey's Kiss wrapped in a brightly colored flowered dress instead of silver foil. "Come on. One more," she says holding a spoon to Clarence's slack mouth. After each spoonful of oatmeal, she wipes his mouth with a small yellow towel. "That good for you. One more. Come on." It's been two months since Roy's mother's death and the hiring of Fami, and Roy has never seen Fami lose her patience. But he does sense she's overburdened. Sometimes on weekends she brings her teenage son, who studies at the kitchen table while his mother works. He's the only person Roy's ever met who actually has sickle cell anemia, which might explain the boy's delicate nature, his careful way of looking away from you without seeming impolite. He's the stillest person Roy's ever met—except for his father, who waits and needs to be waited on constantly. Roy tries not to look at his father, the simple look on his face, his gray complexion, his diminishing stature. How could this man who doesn't look like he could climb out of his bed without assistance have ever scaled up and down bridges, checking suspension wires, fist-size bolts, beams as wide as most buildings are high? Roy could never understand how a bunch of wires could hold up a bridge.

"Fami, I'm running to the store. Need anything?"

"No, I'm okay. Mr. Williams?"

"Roy. Call me Roy." Mr. Williams is right there, he wanted to add, you just changed his diaper and are now feeding him. Roy wants no part of taking on his father's identity.

She hesitates. "Okay." After more than two months of looking after Clarence she still doesn't want to use Roy's first name, so she skips over it, doesn't call him anything. "I was hoping to leave early today. About twelve—noon—instead of three, if that's all right with you."

"I guess. It's a holiday. You going shopping?" Roy has a bad habit of trying to speak in as few words as possible to Fami, as if she won't understand complete sentences. It makes it sound like he's being condescending, which makes him think he's having a tougher time dealing with being served than she is with being a servant. "Nothing crazier than shopping on the day after Thanksgiving."

"Yes. Maurice is at home. I didn't want to bring him today. He's hurting a little. Not much."

"Oh. I hope he's all right, Fami. I can take care of everything. Just let me run to the store for a few things and you can go as soon as you want."

In the gilded mirror in the front hall, he checks his face; his reflection becomes a part of a gameboard of bright yellow light and purple shadow squiggling around the living room of his family's brownstone in Brooklyn. "I'll be right back," he yells up the stairs after putting his jacket on.

It's a lot colder than he'd imagined. The crystal-clear sky had tricked him but he doesn't turn around, go back inside, and put on another layer of something warm. With only one or two leaves still miraculously hanging on, even the trees look underdressed for this cold snap, especially the little maples that were recently planted to replace all the diseased elms. Crisp and cold, the thought of another tragedy, his mother's passing away, his father's failing health, and the cutting of all those beautiful old trees chills him to the bone, crystallizing, crumbling like the brown leaves under his feet. He picks up his pace, lifts his shoulders to protect his neck from the cold, and watches his breath freeze into streams of mist.

On Flatbush the bustle of shoppers seem to respond to him and he to the forgotten smell of his mother's favorite perfume, White Shoulders, mixed with the smell of her soft black leather gloves holding his small mittened hand—blown away by a cold wind laced with laughter and candy wrappers. Even though he wants to turn back, he realizes the truth: There's no need to run, no need to race the wind; nothing will ever be the same. Taste it now. Unwrap life. Lick it, bite it, suck on it like a Popsicle because in the end all that will be left is the stick and the wrapper. Litter if you don't make it in the can. Garbage if you do.

Even though his hands are cold, he pulls out the little date-book that he keeps in his back pocket and writes down his idea of life being like a Popsicle, sweet, colorful, but always melting away, a mess waiting to happen. He writes furiously. His face disappears in a cloud of frozen breath. Excited and inspired.

He walks past the grocery store and heads for his favorite donut shop. *Bowties all around*, he wants to announce when he enters the door, but he's silenced by the familiar sweet smell of powdered sugar, vanilla, yeast, and something else. Oregano? His mouth waters too much to talk. Though the little old mustached Italian guy behind the counter immediately recognizes Roy, Roy tries not to make a big deal of his return and quickly orders his usual two bowties and one jelly donut for his father. The old man doesn't press Roy for news of his family or school. He's busy with other customers steadily coming and going, for one thing and, for another, he's being respectful of Roy's privacy; everybody in the neighborhood must know that his mother, one of their best-loved customers, just died. Roy and the old man stand on opposite sides of the counter with shelves of donuts on display between them. Rows of glazed donuts, chocolate donuts, honey dipped, jelly stuffed, and cream filled with red and blue sprinkles on top. The old man is waiting for a fresh batch of bowties to be brought out for Roy. He tells Roy that his mother was such a lovely lady, a woman with a sense of humor, always suggesting that he make his crullers longer and sell them by the inch. The bakers laughs too much at this, which makes Roy think there's something else going on, a little sexual innuendo. "Ten cents an inch. Lovely woman," the donut maker laughs. Roy nods and smiles. She would say something like that, test the edge of decency to make sure she got that extra donut slipped into her bag each and every time. With his mother's good graces, maybe an extra bowtie will be slipped in his bag, too.

"Ah, and what can I get for the little Reefah today? Two chocolate-dipped crullers, coming up." The old baker oozes with sweet stickiness. "For you, Reefah, anything."

Roy expects to see his old friend Luna's little girl in braids and knee-high socks standing behind him. But what he finds is a very beautiful young woman with shiny black hair that matches her shiny black eyes, dressed in a black down jacket and black mini skirt, with, sure enough, black above-the-knee socks that leave exposed a thick band of tanned thigh, just enough to make Roy imagine he's seeing the rest.

"Hey, what's up?" he says.

She nods and quickly steps back and to the side to let him by.

"You might not remember me," he starts but decides to change tack after looking at that tan band of thigh again; in a situation like this, it's not going to help to mention a girl's father. "Wish they had this donut shop back at college. I could use a jolt of fresh bowties to help me pull an all-nighter." Awkward, but it got the right information across.

"College boy. I guess I'm getting impressed. Is that what you wanted?"

A stab in his left side. "No. Well, yes. Make a good first impression, always helps. Roy. Roy Williams."

"So what's up with you? I guess you're back home for turkey and stuffing."

He hesitates, not wanting to talk about his mother's recent death and funeral. "Yeah. Thanksgiving break," he says, bending the truth. She'll be impressed with his college credentials and keep talking to him. It's only a short leave of absence from school. He'll be back next semester, he thinks, even though he doesn't know for sure. How old could Luna's little girl be? Fifteen. Sixteen. Doesn't fucking matter when she's got it going on like that. Big time. Some Asian-Latina fried rice and plantains. Her father's Rican eyebrows and cheekbones and her mom's tight little Japanese body. He'd run into Luna and his wife over the years, always rushing off to some important appointment or event—sans daughter.

Roy's fresh hot right-from-the-oven bowties are bagged and ready to go now, and he feels the other customers behind him pushing forward for their orders. "Take it easy," he says casually, almost under his breath—suggestively, he hopes—to Reefah and maneuvers through the crowd and out the door.

The first bite melts into sweet vanilla pudding in his mouth. Standing in the middle of the sun-soaked sidewalk, he closes his eyes for more than a blink and sways. Swoons. The sun has finally melted away the morning chill and is now slipping behind the cornices of buildings. But for now the street is soaked in vanilla custard sun. In shop windows Christmas decorations glitter silver and gold, cherry red and pine green. Bursts of white light bounce off the windshields of passing cars, blinding Roy for brief moments, hiding him in sunshine. He closes his eyes again for more than a blink. Again. And again. Passersby step around him. In the broad stripes of sun, a steady stream of life rolls by, on leash, on foot, on bicycles, in rusted Chevys and new BMWs with tinted windows and chrome mag wheels—funny-looking dogs and grouchy old women, but mostly groups of bouncing boys wearing baseball caps and down jackets that look like quilted balloons. Standing in the middle of the sidewalk, he trembles in the sunlight that seems to be shining from within.

Reefah, who's been watching him with a knowing smile, laughs; a flash of silver disappears in her mouth. "Sure beats Dunkin' Donuts."

"That's for fucking sure." After licking his fingers, he pulls out a pen and his datebook and quickly writes down his response to his first taste of the donut, the bright sunlight of midday, and the urgent need to remember. He's overwhelmed with remembrances. "There's this joke my dad always told about this woman who bites into a donut and, somehow, jelly shoots up both her nostrils. Don't ask me how she did it, Pop probably exaggerated the whole thing, but that guy, that same old fart in the donut shop, tried to revive her, give her CPR or something, he was in such a panic, and a slug of jelly flew right out of her nose and into his mouth and all he could do was swallow it."

She grimaces. "That's gross."

"Isn't it? My father used to tell stories like that all the time. Over and over again. And I'd be down on the ground laughing every time."

"When'd your dad die?"

"He's not dead. It's just—" he starts, but doesn't know how to continue. He doesn't want to talk about his father losing his mind. Dementia. Some unknown form of senility. Not Alzheimer's but something like it, he thinks to himself. He doesn't want to explain. He doesn't want to talk about his mother's death or having to leave school to take care of everything. He doesn't want to feel like his world has fallen apart anymore. Right now he wants to experience some new things, to find some new raw material to replace all the old memories. Hesitantly, he continues his story. "I'd be on the ground rolling, thinking about some guy swallowing jelly shot out of a lady's nostril."

"All that from a donut."

"Oh yeah. I've probably been going to this donut shop longer than you've been living." Roy's sugar high has peaked and he's trying to make his thoughts slow down; he wants to take his story back and keep his father to himself. "I'm sorry. I sound like one of those old heads that's always talking about how everything used to be so much better, like, back in the day and shit, as if that weren't a couple of months ago. I'm sorry. Roy," he says and extends his hand.

She takes his hand in both of hers. "Nice to meet you. Again. No more sugar for you, okay?" A flash of silver white light disappears in her mouth again when she laughs.

"What's that? What's that in your mouth?"

"Oh, I got my tongue pierced this summer. It's fun," she says, and flicks her thin pointy tongue at him.

"Ouch," he says, even though it bumps his sugar high to a different level, his crotch.

"Doesn't hurt. Anymore. You just play with it. Oral gratification. Helped me quit smoking. It's like attached worry beads."

"Yeah, back at school, my friend Rupa has one. Pierced tongue, pierced nose and eyebrow, and earrings all around her ear. Her face looks like a constellation, like it's stuck full of silver shrapnel."

It's as if by frowning she's saying, *Too much detail, too much sugar.* They start walking in the direction of Roy's street, but they're really not headed anywhere in particular. "So what were you writing in that little book?"

"Things. I just write down little things. Notes to myself. If I'm thinking of something, I write it down. I usually can't read my own writing afterward, but then I remember what it was I was thinking. Things I hear people say. Things I read. Whatever."

"Like?"

"Poems. Pieces of stories. Ideas. Good quotes. Things I want to remember. I write these things that are like somewhere between a poem and a story and a novel. Like Bataille."

"Like a good song that tells a story but if you read it, it doesn't make sense."

Even though her guess isn't what he was thinking about, Roy wasn't expecting her to be so smart, but he should have, considering who her parents are. He was thinking more like sex as art. "I guess. Bataille wrote these little nasty stories. *The Story of the Eye.* It's all about sex but's all about everything. Ecstasy. Obsession. The way people have to live. It's not a novel, really, but it's more than a story."

"I saw a movie like that." Roy doesn't see any need to compare books to movies but, out of politeness, he lets her continue. "Did you see that movie, *The Lover?* I love that movie."

"Uh-uh."

"The book's better than the movie. For some reason my teacher told me I should read this book about growing up in China. No, Vietnam. That's right. So I rented the movie first. It's about this French girl who has a Chinese lover and they fuck like crazy but her family has to leave and go back to France."

"Girls always read. I wish I was reading all that time when I was watching TV and playing Nintendo. Where you go to school?"

"The Academy for Social Change. In Williamsburg. I skipped ahead a few grades." He knows she's trying to impress him now; and he is impressed. "It's sort of alternative. We, like, study our community and how it relates to things like oppression, colonialism, and revolution. We read things like *All Quiet on the Western Front. The Wretched of the Earth.* The Declaration of Independence. Articles about Haiti's revolt against the French. *Survival in Auschwitz.* We watched the Million Man March on TV. Did you go? It's about ending oppression right now, right here. In Brooklyn. In the city." Her genuine way of saying this excites him even more. A baby activist. She adds, "It's more than a school, it's like a community center. People from the neighborhood come in and stuff."

She smiles, then quickly looks away, across the street, biting on her lower lip.

Was that a signal? Is there something there? Someone over there? He wants to tell her his left side's aching, his heart's palpitating, he wants her, he wants to say anything so they can stop wasting time and already know each other. Teasing takes too long. He always wants to be honest with girls but he gets afraid, doesn't know what they'll do. What if he scares them off? But right now, all he knows now is this: Like a plant leaning toward the sun, every muscle in his body is stretching toward her, pulling his joints, organs, all the electrons in his body, tugged by some kind of energy coming from somewhere inside of her, pulling him to her and her to him. "Cool. I've got to check this out. They didn't have schools like that back in the day." He can't help but try to make himself sound older than her, impress her, even though they're maybe four years apart. *What's four, five years?* he asks himself as he looks down at that band of exposed thigh—honey in a leg-shaped bottle, with black knee-high socks and ruby-red combat boots.

He can't get over how there's hardly any whites in her eyes, the irises are so big, like blossoms. "Want to hang out for a while?" He buys a newspaper at the corner store.

"Oh, I don't know." She squints and looks into his eyes.

"Come on. We can watch a movie or something. And I have to go look after my dad, he sort of has something like Alzheimer's but it's not. It's different. And the nurse is getting off soon."

She doesn't say no and she doesn't say yes. So, with his newspaper under his arm and his bag of donuts in his hand and the cute girl beside him, he pushes forward toward home.

Inside, it takes a while for his eyes to adjust. The checkerboard of morning light in the living room has faded and it looks as if Fami has straightened up a bit and gone home. He takes Reefah's coat and hangs it up, offers her something to drink, a glass of milk to go with her donuts. They settle down on the couch and watch TV. The reception's bad. Meteor showers of interference race across the screen; he tries to fix it first with the remote and then by playing with the cable box and jiggling the wires in the back. When he sits back down he's a little closer to Reefah. Nothing harmful in that. It's going to take a while to close the gap between them. Like a planet, moon, or satellite in orbit, he feels as if he's set on a predetermined course. To reach for the remote. To show her the photo albums he's been looking at night after night, black-and-white pictures of old Harlem streets and distant relatives from his mother's side of the family. He tells her about his mother's death and his father's slow deterioration and then decides talk like that's not going to turn anyone on but doesn't know what else to say.

Then he becomes aware of something that was already there, as soft and warm as his favorite comforter. Is her thigh rubbing against his? Has she leaned against him too long? Too hard? Her hand drifts down his stomach then hesitates and settles on his belt. He doesn't know if he likes it, the pressure of her hand near his crotch. Can he wait? Is she going too fast? His pants are too tight and unyielding. He needs to shift everything to one side instead of letting his hard-on point down and rub against his thigh; it feels too good, too soft touching his own skin, too hot and sweaty. Can he move? Should he take control? As she places her hand right there, right on target, she looks him directly in the eye and sighs. It looks as if her eyes are filled with shining black oil that spills down her cheeks. Is she crying? Is he forcing her? Roy opens himself, his arms and his legs and his lungs to make sure he's still breathing, and with a quick turn and strategic pivot, she pours herself into the space he's created; she straddles him, hip to hip, face to face, his whole body now filled with her. He pushes his hands up under her shirt and rubs her hard nipples, spreads his fingers to touch more of her, cover more of her, feel more of her, know more of her, be in control of her. She's got to slow down. He squirms. Her skin is too hot.

Her hands tug and pull his belt open, his fly open. Because he doesn't have underwear on, his hard-on leaps out of his pants. She takes his cock in her hand and, as if in approval, as if in response to hold him, her mouth becomes a black-filled O. Her hands move fast and assured, tugging his pants down, feeling what she can't see. What's she doing down there, measuring his cock with her fingers? She giggles and sighs as she rubs the head to the base of his hard cock, and then guides him inside her. He begins anew, to stretch, up his spine, his neck, to the top of his head and down his pelvis, his legs, to the tips of his toes, lifting him up off the couch, pushing his face into her covered breast. They kiss for the first time with such force that their teeth click. Or was it her pierced tongue? It hurts. "You okay?" he asks but her answer is to bite his lower lip, which forces him to open his eyes—he remembered that he could open his eyes—and he sees her as if for the first time, not the pretty girl, not his friend Luna's daughter, but he sees in her shining black eyes nothing less than the endless sky filled with radiant stars.

It feels really good. Fucking good. The silver bead on her tongue leaving trails, from his ear to neck, chin, and nose. He leans back on the couch and slides his hands up her thighs to where her legs join her torso. He really wants to see her, her pubic hair, her tight pussy, her tender clit and folded lips; he wants to make sure that this is true, that this is really happening, and he's fucking her the way she wants to be fucked. He tries to pull her skirt up but she pushes her weight down on him harder, keeping him in check. With his thumbs, he searches for her clit and rubs, hardly touching the head, until she begins to shudder and quake, and her sighs turn to low moans that she doesn't want to let out, it seems. "Oh yeah," he responds and rubs faster. He's there but he's not ready, not yet, he's got to hold on, but he can't. Constellations contract. Stars implode. And the rocket, man, doesn't wait for the countdown to reach zero.

"Okay? You okay?" he asks after a few moments, not expecting an answer.

"No."

He's alarmed. He's hurt her. "What's wrong?"

"Pull out. Take it out. Now."

It's awkward and takes all the strength he has to scootch back on the couch and sit up with Reefah sitting on his lap. With both hands he pulls his cock out of her and is surprised to feel plastic, a condom. "Hey, when'd that happen?"

"What?"

"The condom."

"What?"

"When'd you put the rubber on?"

"Who cares? It was on, wasn't it? What do you think I am?"

He's scared by her sarcasm but feels relieved about something he hadn't even thought about: safe sex. "You're amazing. Really."

"None of that. Okay?" she says, silencing him.

Behind him, he hears a cough and clearing of the throat. Then, "Mr. Williams. I'm ready to go now."

It's Fami.

"Shit," he says under his breath, but doesn't look back to

see Fami standing on the stairs, trying not to look at him and that girl. He's back on earth. "Okay." He wants to make an excuse, to say, I thought you were gone, really; but, with a girl straddling him on the couch, he doesn't want to start a conversation, and he hears Fami go back upstairs.

"I better go," Reefah says, swinging herself off of him and back on the couch. "An old head like you has a lot of things to do." Does an orgasm bring out all the sarcasm in this girl? She pulls her panties on and stands up; the elastic pop feels like a gunshot in his left side. She tugs and twists everything back into place, smoothing down her skirt and blouse with measured strokes, carefully, the same way she must have rolled the condom on him.

"So why don't I give you a call later." Roy carefully pulls the condom off so as not to spill its contents, stands, and buttons his pants. He doesn't know what to do with the used condom and Reefah doesn't answer. "Let me give you my number . . . I'm just going to be hanging out here. If you want. You can stay too. We can polish off the rest of those donuts."

"Thanks. But I've got to get home, and I'm going to a show tonight."

"Oh, really." He puts the soppy condom in his pants pocket. "Maybe I can get a ticket."

"With my parents. My mom and dad. You know my dad, don't you? Luna? Luis Rodriguez?"

"Well, ummmm."

"He's cool, as far as dads are concerned. They're cool. They're like into the here and now, being in every moment and shit. So, thanks, Roy. It was great. Really hot. I'll call you tomorrow or something and we can get together for some cream-filled donuts." She walks over to the front door, puts on her coat, and checks herself out in the mirror, never once glancing back at Roy standing behind her dumbfounded. " 'Bye."

Standing, hands in pockets, he feels something wet, cold and wet. A spilled drink. A melted Popsicle. Wet, thick, and gooey. Jelly that's oozed out of a donut. And then he remembers where he put the condom.

Even with the sarcasm he might have chased after her if she hadn't thrown in his face the fact that she knew she was fucking her father's friend all along. How old was she anyway? He doesn't want to calculate. What was she really doing? Retaliating? Rebelling? Going through a phase? What the hell was he thinking, bringing her back her to his house while his father waited, motionless, for nothing in particular? All his fears and anxieties had disappeared for just a little while. Or had his anxieties completely taken over? He'd fallen for her as soon as he saw her in the donut shop. Reefah. The girl's no joke, putting her panties on and leaving without even a kiss or a handshake, while upstairs, Roy imagines, sweet old Fami waiting in his father's room, trying not to listen to what's going on downstairs.

The Blue Globes

by Thomas Glave

But first beginning with their secret. That of the blue globes.
    Which are always blue, as
they always were. In the beginning. When he was thirteen
years old. When I was twelve
years old. When we were

                        sixteen
years old
:

But yes. Beginning with their secret. That of the blue globes,
their secret, and his secret, which was also mine. The secret of
"Smell," he said, smiling down. "I want you to—" "Smell," I
said. Smiling up. My jaw feeling the (but yes). My face moving
toward what he wanted me to smell. Toward what was his,
and his alone, until I made it mine. Until I breathed it in.
About which I said I would never tell. "I'll never tell," I said.
Said to him. To his face. His laughing, smiling face. His face
that smiled as (in darkness, in light) the blue globes descended,
came closer and closer and "Smell it," he said. "Just like that.
Now. That way," he said. And laughed. Both of us laughing,
laughing now, as no one will ever know.

I breathed in. Am breathing in. But he has not yet danced. Danced over my "Face," he will say. "So that you can look up, even in the darkness, and see them. The globes. As I dance. Dance over your face. The globes, that will be blue, as you look up and call my name. My name," he will say, reaching down to pull that part of me closer to his (yes).

I am calling

his name. I am looking up and calling

his name. I am calling his name as he looks down at me and
then

"Oh, Jesus!" I say. Yes. *As he pulls that part of me closer to
his (yes) and I am O I am and*

I

am and O.

❧

He wants me to breathe. To inhale. He always wanted me to breathe, to inhale. To take in all of it and carry it "to your dreams," he would always say. "I want you to smell me in your dreams." But yes.

❧

If they had ever known—any of them, the ones who were never there when we, the ones who never heard when we in that time or this one—if any of them had ever known, "They would have laughed," I said. "They would have said—" "Uh-huh," he said. "They would have thought—" "Of course," I said. "They would have—" "Exactly," you said. "And we wouldn't be—" "No," I said.

And so they who were we
will never tell. I will never. You will not. And no.

Years later, they will look back. Both of them. They will see
  themselves holding
each other. See themselves smelling
each other (yes, and laughing). See themselves
doing those things that require a little assistance
with each other. Moving groceries, starting a car, or "Do that
  to me," he said. You said.
"Like that." Dusting off furniture in the secret place they
  kept, the place no one ever knew
about except themselves. Where they could go sometimes
  and "Underneath?" I said.
"Between the—" "No," he said (you said), "right there, next
  to my—yes, yes, that's it.
That's it," you said. Between the groceries, moving the hand
  to pull the clutch.

Looking back. But so much ahead.

৯৫

All right, then. And so the globes. That began when I was in
(summer) camp. When we were in camp. When there was
nobody around. Nobody because "They're all swimming," he
whispered. "In the pool down by the—"

"Getting wet," I said, pulling at the—

"Yes," he whispered (you whispered). And laughed.

৯৫

In camp. Where I was. Right there. Just there. Lying on my
"Back," he said, quietly. "On your back. Stay there." "Why?"
I asked. "Because," he said (you said), smiling. But I didn't
have to ask. Because that would be the first O yes the first yes

time that he would ask me to do that, to do just that, to put my face there in that way, near the blue globes.

❧

He liked the color blue, he said. His mother bought it for him to wear when he was in water, he said. Which was often. He liked the water. He liked the blue thing his mother bought him. He liked the way it fit so nice and tight around his (yes, me too). He liked the way it slid so slowly off his (but of course. And I did too). He liked the way the blue shone in the sunlight and the way it glistened when he dove into the water. When he parted the water. When his form streaked through the water and he moved his legs and there was no smell, no sense of smell, only his open mouth and his legs, arms, moving. Stroking. Only watermovement and darkness there. His belly flat between the strokes. His open mouth moving through the water. His open mouth tasting it. Between strokes. His mouth moving above his legs, above the water's mouth, in darkness, yes, and light.

Smell it, you said
Why, I asked
Because you like it, you said
Because you like it, I said
Yes. Yes, I really like it, you said
You want me to smell it. You want me to breathe in, I said
Jesus, yes, you said. You groaned. Jesus yes. Yes yes yes yes
    yes. As I did, and you did,
and no one ever knew. Because we can't ever tell. O no.

❧

And so a dance. A dance of the afternoon. A two o'clock
dance, a move out of dusty corners, a move of hips. Moves
when all the others were away. Away swimming, getting wet.
Wetting their mouths, soaking their thighs. A dance that began
when we were thirteen and fourteen years old—began not
quite with the blue globes, though they were there, but with
"A skirt!" I almost shouted. Lying on my back, on that small
camp bed that fit only one. "Where did you get that?" A skirt
that you had stolen from—from her? The one whom you
would later kiss while I watched? From her? "Do you like it?"
you said. "Jesus Christ," I said. A skirt. The blue globes
(though I didn't know it then) beneath. Shining. Beckoning.

࿇

Yes, I liked it. Just that way. The way the blue thing your
mother bought you fit so slyly, ever so slightly, around your
hips. They way it breezed, ever so slightly, when you did what
you always did. "Wear it," I said, quietly, very quietly, as you
watched me holding myself. Lying on my back. "Wear it," I
whispered, as you climbed above me, stood above me, dancing
over my "Face," you said. "Over your face. Look up," you
said, "and tell me what you see."

"I see everything," I said.

࿇

*He was dancing over my face. They were all away, away at two
o'clock in the afternoon. Wetting themselves. Splashing each
other's back parts, each other's chests. Away as he danced over
me, as the skirt swished around his hips. As I saw everything.
The blue globes beneath. Beneath the skirt. And everything
pressing beneath them. I could see his ankles, his thick-to-thin
ankles, on the bed on either side of me. His feet, at that time*

without shoes. Without the high heels that, while again dancing over my face, he would wear years later, in that secret place we kept, where groceries crackled in paper bags and the furniture sprouted dust. I could see his ankles as I would see them years later, when, on those nights that were still to come, long after camp and the bed that fit only one, long after hidden afternoons when they all were away wetting themselves with their shouts and splashes, long after the rings we would eventually place upon fingers in pledges to other people who would never know, long after the children we would each beget who also would never know, he would come to that place, that secret place that had begun long ago with a dance whispered out of dusty corners at two o'clock in the afternoon, and once more dance over my face with a skirt that swished about his hips, that swished to reveal—only now and then—the blue globes, and all that pressed behind them, beneath them. He would dance years later, as he danced only yesterday (but I will never tell), with those black patent-leather high heels wrapped tightly about his ankles. Those shining high heels close enough to lick. He would dance, and still, when the desire came, he would command me to "Smell it," he would say, and I would. Clutching myself. Smell it, O my God, smelling it as my face disappeared behind the blue globes and they, yes, they, became all and everything. Became my face.

⊹

No, we can never tell. He can never tell how much he enjoys when I "Smell it," he said, and "I'm smelling it," I whispered, and "I know," he groaned, holding my head there. Keeping my head there. He can never tell. Not ever tell the one who now delights in the rings about their fingers that both share, nor the many others who share merge reports and analyses, spreadsheets, of his days—the days when he thinks of me, I know, and of how, on some night soon to come, far away from the children he begat and the she who bears the ring that matches the one he wears, far away from the children I begat and the she who loves my smile as I delight in her face, I will smell him I will smell him I will "But just kiss it," he will say some night, "just this one, or twice, or three times." "What would any of them say if they knew?" I ask one night as he dances over me, trying to aim everything for right there, just there. "If they—"

"But they'll never know," he says—and though I cannot see him entirely, for the darkness of that place that is this one, I know that he is smiling, that he will soon laugh—yes, laugh the way he always does when he comes down over me, when the skirt billows over my face, when he knows that I am closing my eyes as he closes his and smelling it, taking it all in, about which we will never tell "anyone," I say. Say to the darkness. To the globes, that will become (but not for the first time) my mouth. Open my mouth.

The first time, you wanted me to touch them. You put them in
  my face.
They were wet. And I
Yes. Was thirteen
years old. Was fourteen
years old. You were fifteen (sixteen?)
years old. You were
"swimming," you said,
"swimming. That's why they're wet."
"They're blue," I said. "Front and back. I like the color. Blue
  like—"
"Don't say it," you said. "Just put your face there, and—"
"Smell it?" I asked.
"Yes," you said. "There. Right there!"

❧

That was camp. When we were twelve or thirteen or fourteen years old. By the time I was seventeen and you were

"Eighteen!"

I thought with purest secret pleasure as you danced over me and I thought about doing so much more—yes, so much more than merely kissing it. You were eighteen and had graduated from lifting first one leg, then the other. From laughing so uproariously when you did what you did, and I breathed in. From sticking it out so that the blue globes, especially when it was time for you to do what you did, touched my face. From balancing over me just that way, gently, ever so gently, so that, when it was time, when you next wanted me to, I would inhale all of it and reach up just that way—yes, still lying on my back—to kiss the blue globes that would be "wet," you whispered, "yes. For you, always wet. Like the first time when I came in from swimming and they were—"

"Soaked," I say, remembering.

❧

No one else ever inhaled. Ever smelled. You promised me that they wouldn't. You promised me that you wouldn't do that with "Her," you said, "no, of course not. Are you crazy? How could I? She would think that I'm the ultimate—"

"Pervert," I said. "Yes."

"Yes," you said, blowing out the candle next to the place where we stretched, fully prepared. And then it happened, you did it, did it without lifting a thigh or arching your back (yes, even while lying on your back), it was one of your most reckless, and you commanded me to "Smell it," you said. And I did, O yes, but of course, as you pressed down upon me and kept me there. Covering my face. Covering. Allowing me to breathe in. Ensuring that I thought only of you and what your she or mine or any of the children we had begotten would say if they could "see us," I thought, closing my eyes. Sucking silent air.

❀

But don't worry, I said years later. When I was forty-one years old. When you were forty-two years old. When we were
"in secret again," I said. "Yes," you whispered, taking that part of me in your hands and smelling it. "Yes."
Don't worry, I said, squeezing that part. You don't need to worry, I said, for (but how powerful it felt in my hands!) there will never come a time when the globes are not blue and there. When you do not wear that thing that makes them blue, as you did when you
were
fourteen
years old. There will never come a time when I will not want to smell their secretmost things, those things shared only with me, about which I will never tell. You will never tell your her, I whispered into one of your parts last night, and I will never tell mine. I will take my finger that bears the ring that pledges my self to my her and put that finger in your secretmost place that is only for me, and never (but no. How could I?) tell her that I did so. You will take your hand that bears the ring that pledges your self to your her and do that to me as severely as you can, yes, please, once more and again, just like that, with those circles, those spirals, all of those circlings around the secret part—you will do that, I will command you the way you command me when I smell you and open myself up to (uh-huh), but you will never tell her, her whom you never ask to smell anything as you ask me to and have asked me to since the two o'clock dance of that first afternoon. Don't worry, I

said, because you are—of course—deep, deep down inside my lungs. You've been there deep down there for every year of all these years. The way I've been in your dreams and you've been inside my (yes) and we in all the secret places for all of these years. The way no one will ever know about it. No one knows about it. The way your ring shines when you move it around me that way and I can still smell you because the blue globes are only inches over my face. The way the globes move when you dance, the way they shudder when you want me to breathe in. The way the children you begat laugh when you come home. "Daddy," they say. "Daddy, Daddy!" The way she smiles at you when you're tired. Smiles, not knowing not ever knowing how you have been smelled for years, and how another face that smiles at her ("How are things, baby? Looking good, baby!") has disappeared within your secret-most parts for more than (fill in the years). The way you dance over my face, wearing that skirt (last week it was a Scottish kilt with pleats) and those shiny high heels prance close enough to lick. The way I inhale you—

❧

No. No one will ever know. Will ever see. Will ever hear. Nor smell. Smell that smell that is for me. Me only. Only mine. In darkness, yes, and in light. The globes in blue.

Close to my face. As you do that. Yes, please do that. And
    that and. About which we will
never tell. Never tell as I am smelling you. As I am fifty-one
years old. As you are fifty-two
years old. As you are

❧

Above me. Dancing, yes. And the globes. Shining, always in
  blue, full and round.
Shining, before they descend. Descend to cover my face and I
  inhale and

❦

Laughing. We who are laughing. We who are—

A Different Drummer

by Cheo Tyehimba

Cam was late for rehearsal. The door to the Caribee was swung open and strong gusts of wind were violently slamming it back and forth against the wall. He grabbed the door, ducked inside, and latched it shut. Then dashed upstairs.

Sekou's djun-djun was vibrating the wooden steps beneath his feet: BOOM-boom-boom! BOOM-boom-boom! Ba-ba-boom-boom/Ba-ba-boom-boom! At the break the djembe player rolled in: KRAK! Kri-kri-kri-KRAK-KRAK! . . . then the hollow, jostling sound of beads shaking against the thin calabash shell skin: Shi-Shi-Shika! Shi-Shi-Shika! Shi-Shi-Shika! . . . the cowbells' jingling music kept time and completed the orchestration.

The second company was going through warm-up steps, moving across the floor in successive waves as the drummers played. Three drummers, Tunde, Randy, and Sekou, were assembled down in front, by the stage. Sekou, the elder of the group, shot Cam a look of disapproval as Cam unwrapped his drum and began to set up. When they finished playing, Cam approached him.

"Peace," Cam said, extending his hand. Then he greeted the others. "Sorry I'm late, I had an appointment that went overtime."

"Okay, we've got to tighten this up," said Sekou, stepping out from behind his djun-djun. "I agree with Grace, we're lagging behind her dancers on both '*Lindjian* and *Sedeba*.' We've got to pick it up, play, play, play . . . *together!*" he said, glancing at Cam.

"Well, I'm ready," Cam said, tightening his drum strap over his hip.

"Now that's what I want to hear," said a female voice. Cam turned around and saw her beaming, hands on her hips. It was Grace.

"Greetings, sista, sorry about holding you up."

"No apologies," she said with a quick wave. "Sekou, y'all ready?" With a quick nod between them, the short, yam-colored woman spun on her heels and walked out to the center of the floor.

"All right, now." She surveyed the dozen or so women standing in front of her. "Now I want to go over '*Lindjian* and *Sedeba*' again until we're moving on spirit. Spirit alone. Remember, this is an initiation dance, it has to be on this plane," she said as she spread her long arms wide, letting her elbows dangle high at about ear level.

They were playing the rhythm light, at slow tempo, while she demonstrated. She sprang, rising slowly, came down and kick-stepped, kick-stepped, turned, sprang again and spread her arms up higher in top flight, then fanned them down across her heart as she descended. She gathered a personal mist between her arms and seemed to move with the sway of its tide. Grace broke the dance down into parts and moved very slowly, dancing in and out of a solitary square of light on the floor from a nearby window. She dipped her head forward in a delicate bobbing motion with each fluid swoop of her arms, a black swan lifting off in the hot light.

Cam looked over at Nyema. Grace's moves mesmerized her; she swayed her own arms slowly in imitation.

"This is the dance of the bird!" shouted Grace, swirling to a stop. "And I want y'all to fly! We've got two weeks before we take this out on the road, so let's do it!" The light from the window filled the room as the women began dancing upstage in rows of four. The drummers picked up the tempo. A pulsation of plum-, chocolate-, caramel-, and honey-colored limbs flew and flailed forward beneath a jungle of brilliant sarongs and head wraps. They moved confidently, smiling and dancing up to the feet of the drummers. Black women, all, full of creative longing and tangible fire.

Then they spun around and hurried back to try the move again. Tunde was picking up the pace, slapping his djembe harder and harder. The BOOM-BOOM from Sekou's bass drum began to come quicker. Everything was rising. After a few passes, Cam could see steam vapor just above the heads of the dancers, seeping up into the wooden-beamed ceiling.

As twilight filled the room, the dancers flew through the routine. Cam's arms were burning and beginning to sag but he sucked down a deep breath and bore down. He straightened his back and slapped out his part. Then he played a break and Tunde quickly rolled from his drum part into a solo. Tunde lit out like he was on fire! Cam nodded and smiled at him to show his admiration, but the brother was already gone. His eyes were closed. He tossed his head to the right, as if listening for some faint note.

Tunde was a tall master drummer from Mali. He'd been teaching Cam and a small coterie of drummers for several years. He stood, half crouched, and feverishly pushed beats out of his drum like it was a sonic washboard. Spikes of sweat shot off his locks as he tossed his head in a fever. Slapping his hands against his drum with the speed of a humming bird, Tunde rapped out a succession of fire-crack beats: KRAK-kri-kri-kri-kri-KRAK! Then a machine-gun solo:

PING-PING-PA-TA! PING-PING-PA-TA! PA-TA-PaTaPa-TaPaTaPaTaPaTaPaTaPaTa-PATOW-PATOW!!PATOW-PA-TOW!!DOW!! He spun in the direction of approaching dancers, shooting his rhythms directly to them. Supernatural foods rolled and popped and riffed from the skin covering his drum. The lines of dancers moved across the floor like high-kicking, soft-sailing birds of paradise on some high-speed assembly line. They were flying!

As they moved on in a trance to Tunde's energy, Cam watched Nyema swirl to a stop in front of him and felt a thin tingle in his middle. He held his rhythm tight. She was lovely, and with each pass she gave a little more of herself to him. As spirit rose, all of the dancers began to move on feeling, on the love that they already possessed. Tunde played on, in some preternatural zone, and soon even Grace had to jump out of her skin. Her long black braids spilled out of her white head wrap and as she tossed it aside, she hopped in front of his drum and received his offering.

Cam yearned to play like Tunde. Knew he would one day. He was drenched in sweat and began to feel himself lag behind and even play over Tunde's parts at times. But he avoided Sekou's piercing eyes. He just shook his head clear, grimaced, and tried to level his breathing. He moved to the edge of his chair and got ready for his solo.

A red sweat burned in the crease of his eyelids and his stomach blazed but he had to play! Had to play! Cam brought his part to its crest, playing a quick combination of slap, tone, and bass notes with a rapid succession. Tunde had sat back down and was back to playing his minor part. He nodded for Cam to go for it. Cam glanced at Sekou. He was solid and cadence-sure on the djun-djun. Four sistas simultaneously dipped their wing-like arms low as they knelt in front of Cam, then shot up in a turning kick-spin. Their soft, buoyant forms swelled beneath the thin multicolored fabric covering their bodies.

Nyema was dance-stepping forward in a line about two rows back. She was smiling at Cam, reassuring him. He heard Tunde's break and lit into it. His heartbeat popped in his throat and he bit down on his lip, pounding the drum as fast as he could. Suddenly it seemed the dancers were flying directly into his face, flashing madly forward like a spray of fluttering pigeons rising quickly beneath the feet of running children. Cam tried to match their movements with each roll and finger pop but found himself outpaced. He felt his knees tightening around his drum like a vise. He tried to concentrate.

Nyema's line was now dancing in front of him. He stood up. Just play, man. Relax and play, he told himself. Nyema leaped out in front of him, just as she'd done so many times before. Beads of sweat spiraled off her and splashed the teak hardwood floor as she spun and dipped and successively stretched forth her arms, seemingly beckoning him to play faster. The dance danced her. Cam felt a surge of strength coil and radiate behind his navel and invigorate his sinews. It simmered up through his sweaty skin and found his fingertips. Once again she'd saved him. Buoyed his failing energy and made him proud to love her.

But after she turned and the next line danced forward his power waned. Cam shook his head, trying to play above the furnace raging in his lats and deltoids. He felt Sekou's eyes on his back. He knew he was supposed to play longer but he couldn't. He'd strained himself to maintain the energy level and he only hoped he wouldn't be peeing blood later. So he lapsed back into his familiar drum part, hoping no one would notice.

Almost immediately, Tunde stood up again and brought the energy back up, rapping out another lightning-crack solo.

Simultaneously Cam felt a rush of relief and a stab of shame. Tunde saved the dying rhythm and the dancers flew on, unaware, but Cam hadn't been able to sustain his solo. They were coming to the end of rehearsal. Tunde's solo rose in a crescendo and when he gave the nod to bring it all home, Cam was thankful.

Sweaty footprints from the dancers dappled the floor in front of the drums. The dancers bowed and touched the floor in front of the drummers and then danced off. Grace made a few announcements about the next rehearsal and Sekou told the drummers he wanted them to stay longer to practice and listen to a new drum tape from Guinea he'd just bought. As the dancers left the room, Nyema nodded to Cam. She mouthed the words "see you tonight." He managed a half smile, then grimaced as Sekou lightly slapped him on his right shoulder.

"Don't worry about your man," Sekou smiled. "Yes, *I know*—you can heal him. But he must learn the drum. It will heal him tonight."

❀

After midnight Cam reached Nyema's place and dragged himself up to her second-story flat. Before he could key the lock, she was at the door, letting him in. The room was dark, except for flickering candlelight from the nearby bathroom. She lifted a finger to her lips, then quietly took his drum from his shoulder and sat it in the corner. Cam slipped off his boots and put them next to his drum. Then she led him to her bedroom.

"Will you let me, baby?" whispered Nyema. "This time?" She knew his resistance, understood his constant struggle with his own vulnerability. He nodded, and she saw something in his expression then. Something like a low-tone blues out of his brown eyes, placid, sweet, and completely resolved. Nyema returned his smile and kissed him lightly on the lips.

"They really worked my baby, huh?" said Nyema, taking off his shirt. "Let me see . . ." She looked at his hands. They were still throbbing as if he were still pounding out mad rhythms on his drum, hot skin on skin. As usual, they were slightly swollen, callused, and still warm. Nyema softly kissed each finger then finished undressing him.

"What you need after these brutal rehearsals is a helper," she smiled. "Let me help."

He watched her as she hovered over him, saw the glossy brown pools of her shoulders glisten in the small light. Sweet spices hung about her, and she draped them over his body with her touch.

"Okay, now let's get you in the tub."

"Hold up, baby," he insisted. "I can, you know, take one after, um . . ." He was supposed to be letting go, letting her run things, but damn, he couldn't help himself.

"Camden," she said, and shot him *that* look. It silenced him.

It was a deep, old-fashioned bear-claw tub and the water was hot and low, maybe three inches. Through the steam, he could see a plastic pitcher on the sink. An incense stick and a candle burned nearby; on the floor next to the tub, a silver tray was stacked with a few items: sunflower oil, a carton of comfrey leaves, a bowl containing a greenish, creamy mixture, and a glass of water. As Cam stepped into the tub, he playfully tried to pull her in with him. She laughed and resisted, then sat down beside the tub. From there, she began to wash him with a soapy body sponge. Soon he was awash in a glistening white lather from head to toe and standing before her, hard in the orange light. She sat him back down. Then with her pinkie finger she drew a heart over the lather on his chest.

"There, I made it. It's mine," she said.

"Uh-huh," he intoned as he caught her hand and pulled it down into the water, between his thighs. She stroked him gently, peering hard into his eyes. His look was serious, necessary. She would have to slow things down a bit. After all, she wanted only to replenish and nurture her man—at least that's what she told herself.

"You know what?" Cam asked. "Suddenly, I'm not tired anymore. Come on in."

"Shh," she whispered. "I want you to close your eyes and see our fantasy, remember it?"

"You mean . . . ?" He knew it well but wanted to try to tease her, too.

"Mmmm-hmmm," she hummed. "You're already in water."

She rested her fingertips upon his temples, then his eyelids, closing them gently. He sighed heavy and sank back into the tub. She slowly poured the pitcher of water over his chest and body. Then she rubbed oil into her hands and began to massage it in to his shoulders and chest. Her slender hands made circular motions as she gently stroked his muscles back and forth and toward his heart. Next, one by one, she laid the cool comfrey leaves on his shoulders and arms.

As she worked over him, he felt her dark breath on his skin and the wisp of her long, black dreadlocks. But he was having trouble visualizing their imaginary love-dream. So for inspiration, he cheated and peeked up at her. He could see her firm brown nipples sway in little circles beneath the worn, almost transparent fabric of her fading batik wrap. He squinted and saw a high forehead flash, her laughing eyes, both shiny and bright. Then he pressed his eyes shut and revisited their silvery tropical fantasy over again in his mind. When she finally finished preparing him, she instructed him to go into the bedroom and wait for her.

Cam sat alone on the edge of the bed. The night released a muted, heavy drone, which he initially though was her refrigerator or some other electric appliance. But it wasn't. It was the night, alone. Then he heard the pull of a freight train clicking into the nearby West Oakland scrap yard. The train's distant whistle came to him softly, stirring something deep within. "How odd," he thought, as he lay back onto the satin sheets and tried to be patient. His hand slid down his slick body and found a familiar hardness.

"I see you have your energy back," said Nyema, suddenly at the foot of the bed.

"What? Naw . . ." muttered Cam. "What took you so long?"

"Don't worry about that. I'm trying to hook you up," she said, handing him a cup of tea. "Come."

"Your famous tea?" he said, sipping the steaming roots-and-bee-pollen elixir.

"Uh-huh."

"Girl, you my juju queen."

"Uh-huh," she said. "Okay, lay back now."

Nyema laid a long beach towel on the sheet next to Cam and told him to lie on it. Next she picked up the bowl of greenish cream, which was really an avocado-mango-almond-oil balm, and massaged small amounts into his palms. The sensation of the cream, first cool upon his skin, then like ice melting beneath her hot hands, was immensely intoxicating. He wanted to ravage her right then but for some reason, he gave in to her pace, allowed her to tease him. Soon she'd worked the luxuriant deep into his arms, elbows, biceps, shoulders, chest, stomach, and thighs. She was moving down to his pelvis when her wrap fell off. Naked and shimmering, she tossed it to the floor and continued her love chore.

Nyema held Cam firmly in her hand and slathered the cool cream on his dark shaft. She massaged it between his thighs and lightly rolled it onto his balls. He tried to sit up but she pushed him onto his back, told him, "Relax." Next she slowly kneaded her way down to his knees, past his cream-covered lance, which quivered and twitched from side to side. But a heat, an electromagnetic compulsion, drew her back to his center. She knelt over him and let her breasts sway lightly upon the hard candy she found there. Soon her chest was frothy with the cream.

Now Nyema was on her back and Cam was over her, stiff and plunging, teasing her lips. Her hands caressed his buttocks and invited him deeper.

"You did it, baby," he whispered. "Now I want to do something for you."

"What?" she said, licking the sweet-smelling cream from her lips.

"Stay just as you are. I'll be right back."

Now it was Nyema who heard noises in the night and anxiously awaited her lover's return. Soon he was back with a smile and a steaming coffee cup in hand. He sat it down and took her hand and led her to the bedroom wall. Cam instructed her to close her eyes and to stand with her naked back to the wall. Nyema eagerly played along. Her naked body flinched against the cool, cool wall but Cam made sure she remained there, pressed lightly.

He stood back briefly and admired her anxiously trembling form. He believed her sloping dancer's body carried ancient memories; each curve, crevice, and muscle revealed a story. Her sista hips and her high, round ass teetered back and forth, kissing the chilly wall. Cam spread her legs slightly and told her to try to remain still. Then he began his experiment. He took the coffee cup and dipped his finger into it. A string of hot honey ran off his finger and onto Nyema's left nipple.

"Ooohh, ahhhh . . ." she moaned. "That's hot."

"Too hot?" he said, as he dripped more onto her other breast.

"No, uh, it's okay," she muttered. "Aaahh . . . baby, what are you doing to me?"

With his finger, Cam painted a line of honey across her full, plum lips, down the slope of her neck, and into the tiny reservoirs at the top of her shoulders. Warm amber dripped from her swollen breasts. She quivered against the wall.

"Don't move, baby," Cam begged. He couldn't help himself. He leaned in and began hungrily sucking and caressing her fig-colored nipples. Then he regained his composure and continued his sweet plan.

He dripped the viscid liquid over her navel and between her thighs. The combined effect of the cool wall and the hot honey gave Nyema the sensation of floating downstream and being showered with tantalizing, warm raindrops. Coils in her skin tingled from the soles of her feet and shot waves of frenzied, vibrating signals to her disparate parts: her nipples, her ears, her scalp, her stomach, her thighs, and her clitoris, which now dripped with her own honey. Cam licked the honey from her lips and tongued his way to her navel.

Cam turned her around so that the palms of her hands were raised over her head and flat against the wall. He spread her legs, starting by sliding his hands up under her buns and letting them glide down her thighs on the thick, slippery, hot tide he found there. Honey dripped down the small of her back and seeped into the pearlike crease of her magnificent ass. Then quickly, without notice, he turned and dipped down between her legs, catching the streaming honey in his mouth before it hit the ground. He lapped and sucked his way up to her sweet center and used his hands to further part her round, dark rift.

The effect he was having on her was unprecedented. He'd put the honey down in favor of her nectar—then suddenly another idea grabbed his imagination. He seized a small wooden stool, draped a towel over it, positioned his back over the top, and slid under her. It was a perfect fit. As Nyema readjusted her spread legs, his face and mouth slipped into place and he held onto her soft, abundant ass cheeks with both hands. From his upside-down position, he glanced up and saw her face. Caught in a grimace of pleasure, she looked down at him and their eyes locked. He glided his tongue lengthwise along the sugary valley of her vulva. Nyema moaned and clung to the wall, her back dancing fervently. He remained there for a while, licking and sucking, until her collapsing weight upon his face was too much to bear.

He slid off the stool and madly tossed it aside. She was bent halfway over, still holding fast to the wall for support. Suddenly he had an unexplainable ache to bestow her with his sight of her; she deserved to be drenched in her own light. The dimples on the small of her back, the slinky valley between her shoulder blades, the ellipse of her navel; all were divine movements. He kissed his way back up the backs of her calves, to her inner thighs. Then Cam stood behind her and slid his shaft up and down between her ass cheeks.

When their pleasure became too immense to bear, he sank inside of her. Just the tip at first. The tip teasing like a sticky tongue. Then delicious, direct, long, slow strokes. Stroking in and in. Deep. He was up against her back and she was pressed hard to the cold wall. Slowly, Cam began to churn her in small in-an-out circles, his hips on a 360-degree swivel. His hands found her breast, his tongue her neck and hot ears. They blazed on.

Nyema clenched him tightly, then the small of her back fluttered like a blanket, sending quiver shots out to all points north and south. She inhaled and the sound of rivers and streams rushed past his ears. Camden held on, neither thrusting nor remaining motionless; they were drifting, swamped in each other. They collapsed, still united.

The near lightness of outdoors spread shallow whiteness through a bare window. A morning bird singing on the ledge sounded like a small child teasing a tune through a toy whistle. Nyema's head rested on his chest, her brown leg securely clamped across his. They were in bed; their warm breath heavy, brown bodies coiled. He awoke. Strength surged within him and he held her close, feeling the waves of her body rise to meet his. He drank her kisses and replenished her with his own. Her fingers found his spine. Cam yearned to give this woman his breath, whatever it was he had. He was empty with her in almost the way he yearned to be with his drum. She *was* his drum.

They inhaled and as their bodies sank deeper down, below, into that unknowable nearness of man-woman, a sly, crushing feeling rose to meet the night music lingering into the room. The present moment evaded. Nothing. Everything. Eyes, spirit, merged. Their kisses and fervent declarations multiplied to the sway of their drenched arched forms and made even vulnerability a sweet remainder. Her femininity had nurtured him, enveloped him, and commanded a power worthy of worship.

For the first time in his life Cam felt a oneness with another human being that belied definition. It soothed him and he found himself floating, a white cast of light upon an ebullient blue tide.

He inhaled, felt a shudder, a gentle tapping of delicate white birds. They lit him up and took him away.

Maya

by Jennifer Jazz

It was Yvette who hipped me to Starchild—of all people, Yvette, the witch, but I was desperate.

"Ask her!" I prodded Shytiq when I overheard him chatting with her on the phone and Shytiq, sadistic sunnuvabitch that he was, blew me off, pretending not to hear. Gay and horny as the best of them, homeboy could be such a straitlaced prude when it came to me getting my groove on.

"What do you need to go to a dyke bar for?" he groaned after he'd hung up.

"That's fucked up, Shy," I complained with more attitude than usual. Shy and I were not the kind of roommates who lived according to rules and schedules. We did our laundry together, shared soap, and, when we had nothing to do, would lounge side by side in bed and watch TV. He knew what he had to do to keep his best friend.

A few days later he called Yvette and passed me the phone, and even though I'd heard through the grapevine that Yvette considered me a "flake," I overlooked my mutual distaste for her and suggested she take me with her to a woman's club some night. There was some hemming and hawing. After all, Yvette was a career lesbian and arrogant as hell about it and I was just single and bored with the men I'd met. Still, acting like the gatekeeper to a world too real for a flake like me,

Yvette halfheartedly agreed to an outing with me the next night.

Being that I lived in Harlem, it was a long trip via the subway to the street in Brooklyn where we met, but I would've traveled to Timbuktu, I was in such heat. Yvette had driven, and when she stepped out of her car she was wearing the usual smirk on her face. With the same condescension, she led me into a storefront with blacked-out windows past a monster-size doorwoman who stamped our hands with fluorescent stars as we entered a crowded room of throbbing black and Latin women. I might as well have landed on another planet, I was so awestruck. Unfortunately, Yvette kept me cornered at the bar over my Scotch and soda and her beer, interrogating me about whether I was coming out or not. Nothing I said seemed to satisfy her. It was only out of courtesy that I didn't drift off to explore the red-lit hallways and rooms of the club. I felt like a child in an amusement park. Checking out every woman who passed, I barely paid attention to Yvette's bitter tips on how to pick one up and didn't notice that in her own frigid way, the witch was flirting with me.

I returned to Starchild a couple of weeks later by myself. It was a relief to be alone. I started at the bar, got myself a drink, and found a wall to lean on by the dance floor. There was a constant stream of couples holding hands as they made their way into the center of the action. Occasionally a woman would make eye contact with me, and I'd realize the part of myself I considered odd or ugly was now my most electric asset. It was as if I'd found a home I'd been lost from my entire life. After a few drinks the novelty wore off a little or at least enough for me to dance. There was no one I was attracted to enough to leave my shadow, but it felt sexy just being in the midst of so many out-of-control, sweaty sisters.

Starchild became my regular spot. I'd head there after work almost every Friday, making the acquaintance of one of the bartenders and a friendly enough sister who'd check my shoulder bag, but that was the extent to which I socialized when I was there—then enter Maya.

She was the dirty fantasy in my head so suddenly real I thought someone had slipped some drug in my drink. Let me describe the moment: I was soaked with sweat, stomping my heels to an insane rhythm around two A.M. The DJ was deep inside the acid-house trance funk thing. I don't know what it was, but it felt sublime. The ladies were bouncing, howling, grinding themselves into oblivion. The club was a big, sapphic orgy; then a set of such haunting eyes surfaced out of the fog, I did a double take, but there she was, studying me, something in her stare that signified sensitivity, kindness, compassion. Acting coy, but not too coy to tug me out of hiding into the heart of the action, Maya teased me up close with her perfect tits and tiny waist that swerved into hips she gyrated to maximum effect.

"Can we go somewhere? I feel light-headed," I gasped, really, truly dizzy.

Without hesitating, she took my hand and walked me to a windowsill, where we sat arm in arm. Whenever she'd put her lips to my ear, the heat of her breath would send shivers through me; her voice had a breathless quality as if she were talking while coming.

"God, you're beautiful."

"No, you."

"No, you."

There was little we could think of to say. I couldn't look her full in the face. It was all so much, her creamy gaze, the softness of her body next to mine. Then as suddenly as she appeared, she asked for my number and said she had to go.

In the morning I woke up euphoric, fearing that my memory of the night before was just a good dream when the phone rang. I picked up on the first ring. It was Maya. Then the rush began again, the dizziness, accelerating heart, and wet panties. My voice was trapped in my chest, but I managed to make a date to meet her the next afternoon. She said she wanted to take me to a movie.

Sitting in a dark theater beside Maya was an exercise in self-restraint. She was wearing a smooth sweater that clung to her tits. The girl emoted a feline charm that turned me on and up. I couldn't concentrate on the screen in front of us. Nothing mattered but her. Crossing Times Square, she informed me that she had to rush home. Something to do with her eight-year-old. I couldn't focus on what she was saying, she was too gorgeous. It was blinding.

"Come home with me. Please or I'll go crazy."

"Shhh," she warned. "You don't want a million guys sweating us." As was now her habit, Maya tugged me like her naive puppy into an empty subway stairwell. There, I couldn't take it anymore and pushed her into a wall and began kissing her, the smoky flavor of her tongue rushing like some high-powered medicine to my head, her lips tasting of Newports or spearmint gum or some exotic spice that seemed to ooze from her pores. I was so aroused, I was in pain.

"Please," I begged as she eased me away.

I walked her to the downtown train platform in defeat. At least she agreed to meet me again.

When we met the following Saturday she was wearing a pair of white leather pants and sling-back heels that seemed too dressy for the occasion; her hair was twisted into corkscrews that didn't fit her face. She wavered between being distant and nervously silly. Loitering randomly through

Greenwich Village, we did some window-shopping and had lunch. We wound up at my place in the early evening. Shy wasn't around. It was perfect for my plans, but Maya didn't seem to want me. I tried to undress her, but she laughed it off, keeping her seat in a chair that felt a million miles away from me and humming along with a song wafting from my stereo. All I could do was accept that I was with her. That's how it was with Maya.

Then one Sunday afternoon as Shytiq and four of his Jersey City buddies were drinking Knotty Head and arguing over the best way to prepare collard greens, she called.

"Hi, it's me. I guess I'm sad. I don't know. I need to see you," she stammered after I finally heard the phone ring over all the commotion. She wasn't far away, she said. In half an hour she'd stop by. I went back to the kitchen to sit with Shy and his friends, sure I wouldn't see her that day, but Maya showed up about an hour later, as social as she needed to be, helping dice some condiments for a meal the guys were surely now too drunk to make.

After a while we went to my room and closed the door. A cool autumn chill was sneaking through the window at the same time that the first heat of the season was hissing from the radiator. Maya pulled off her sweater, watching me intently. I sat on my bed and pulled her to me.

"I'm so glad to see you," I said, expecting her to laugh at how serious I could be, but instead she buried her face in my neck, lightly biting me and moaning. Maya worked out religiously. She was strong, and when her teeth and tongue began to tickle me and I began to resist her, she sucked harder, holding my hands so I couldn't move while I writhed deliriously beneath her. When I was fully whipped by the hickey she had so expertly placed on my neck, she wriggled out of her pants then panties, but before she unclasped her bra, her eyes filled up with tears and her lips got poutier than ususal.

"I have stretch marks. After my son was born . . . this is how I look . . ." she apologized, her tongue darting in and out of my ear. It was hard to separate Maya's tits from the rest of her. They were flat, yet full like two ripe mangoes, but bouncy like mangoes aren't. So this was what all her hesitation was about!

Taking one in my mouth and then the other, I told her, "You're crazy."

"No, you," she said.

"No, you," I said, wrestling Maya down beneath me, her cunt rising to my hunger like a tray.

The Warm and Quiet Storm

by Andrew Oyefesobi

I locked the front door, hoping to lock out the pouring rain with the day's frustration. It was day three of my wife's vacation with her girlfriend, so again, I was returning to an empty house, another microwave dinner, and another sleepless night.

We promised one another we wouldn't call. She deserved this vacation away from all the responsibilities waiting for her in Chicago, which included me. I didn't deserve the loneliness I felt, but I wouldn't have been able to contain myself if I had heard her voice. I would have begged her to return home to fill the empty house, fill my stomach starving for a home-cooked meal, and fill our bed with the other warm body I needed to sleep through the night.

We were newlyweds of six months. We were sickeningly in love. We missed each other if one of us simply left the room. Our sex life was magical. That's why we promised we wouldn't call.

I removed my cashmere trenchcoat, flipped on the jazz station, and sat at my computer. I wanted to check my e-mail to see if my best friend, Victor, had responded to my invitation to hit the racquetball court the following day. At that point, I needed anything that would take my mind off Delia.

My electronic mailbox contained an apology from Victor for having to forgo our racquetball appointment in favor of an art opening at the college with his new armpiece, Nicolette, and a reminder from my supervisor about the deal-breaking lunch meeting with a client the next day.

The sigh I released was worthy of a reaction to losing my treasured Thelonius Monk record, but it was really a response to feeling thoroughly detached from any sense of fun or pleasure. I missed Delia like a desert rose misses rain.

I went over to the bay window and gazed out onto the wet world. The rain was quiet, and since summer lurked around the corner, it was warm. The storm—its wetness, its warmth—made me think of Delia. Her presence always had a way of doing that, appearing in everyday things, keeping her with me when she wasn't in arm's reach. Then it hit me. She was thousands of miles away, and my satisfaction was with her.

I dragged myself to the kitchen to stick a frozen meal-in-a-box in the microwave.

"You've got mail."

The computerized voice startled me, since I'd convinced myself that I was completely alone in the world. I dashed over to my computer, hoping the new message was from Victor, saying Nicolette called off their date, or from my boss, saying the client canceled the lunch meeting. No luck . . . but the new message intrigued me even more.

I was glued to the screen as I read:

Hey, Sugar. I miss you dearly. I know we said we wouldn't call, but I would go insane if I couldn't communicate with you in some way for the length of my trip. I can't say much, because I slipped away from the group to drop you this message, and Sonya and Karen would kill me if they caught me. *Essence* magazine organized a really great event for book lovers called Passion in the Pages. Anyway, just thought I'd let you know that I was enjoying myself, but every night I climb into that unfamiliar hotel bed, and I turn and you're not there . . . my goodness, all I can say is my body is calling for you. The passion in the pages of these books has nothing on the passion we share. I can't write much more, otherwise I'll be on the next plane out of here and into your arms to pick up where we left off. I'll be home tomorrow, so save a place for me in your dreams. Aching without you, hugs 'n' kisses, Delia.

My mouth hung open. I was lost in her written words, wishing she was in my ear whispering them in that honeyed voice I fell in love with. I was so distracted I didn't hear the firecrackerlike pops alerting me that my Lean Cuisine was burning in the microwave.

Delia had done it. She had violated our no-communication stipulation. There was no way she would escape my mind that night. I needed my precious lover with me. I needed my new wife to make me feel that old feeling. Outside, the rain came down harder, feeling my pain as well.

I walked upstairs to our bedroom, stripping my corporate costume along the way. I dropped my silk tie on the stairs, my starched shirt at the bedroom door, my pressed slacks at the foot of the bed. I flopped onto the king-size waterbed, but my journey from the computer to the comforter didn't relieve a drop of my frustration.

The rain didn't wash away Delia's warm words, which I could hear echoing quietly in my ears. I was dying to pick up where we had left off, too. Alas, my queen was missing from the king-size bed we shared. There was an empty space where she used to rest, an empty pillow where she used to dream.

I approached her vanity, looking for her perfume. The one she loved so much. The one I loved so much because it reminded me of the contours of her coffee-colored skin. Realizing she had packed it with her on her trip, I pouted like a child who's lost his toy.

Suddenly a single streak of lightning split the sky and zapped a flash of light into our dark bedroom. I saw the reflection of silver wrapping paper on my oak chest. I had purchased a six-month-anniversary gift. I was going to surprise Delia with a new bottle of the precious fragrance when she returned from St. Lucia.

It was *her* present, but I needed her near me. Selfishly, I figured this could be her gift to *me*—a way to make up for leaving me in the rain while she romped in the fun and sun of Jamaica. With guilt running through me, I ripped open the perfect packaging and sprayed the scent all over our bed. I inhaled the perfume and became intoxicated.

I climbed under the comforter and let my dreams bring her to me. I held myself like I thought she would if she had been there. I massaged the part of my body that longed to connect with her body. Working it with gentle friction, I prayed my imagination would make my efforts feel like the real thing. Her real thing. Her rain.

I let visions of her pleasuring me fill the moments between missing her and liking the feeling. I let the tranquil sound of the storm playing outside stand in for her sweet sounds of lovemaking. I handled my pulsing love limb until I psychically reconnected with her supreme love grip.

Her mist coated my root with the affection it needed to

grow and expand, and rise and resist. Drenching my dreams with desire, lubricating my loins with lust, her rain rose like a typhoon. With the force a turbulent system passing through a balmy night, she bathed me in passion like an adult baptism.

She took me into the wetness of her garden, raining pure satisfaction on my desert rose. My palms felt her saturating the soil of my soul, flooding the fertile ground of my fantasies. The overwhelming sensual sensations—the perfume, the rain, the warmth—rolled like thunder.

I rode the waves of our waterbed as the storm raged.

With the mental rhapsody and physical gratification swirling with the intensity of a hurricane, I bloomed with ecstasy, releasing hot nectar on her side of our private flowerbed.

Dripping wet with sweat, I lay exhausted on the soaked satin sheets, dreaming I was sinking into the soft earth beneath me. Eventually my excitement subsided with the rain. I slept the night away in the calm after the storm.

The next day weak sunlight peaked through the transparent curtains over our picture window. It announced itself, as it always did after a rain shower, coming to replenish the love that makes the earth's flowers blossom. The dew on the windowpane was Mother Nature's quaint reminder of the pleasure the night had created.

Delia arrived while I was still acquainting myself with the sun and the new day.

She was still beautiful. Her radiance provided the extra light the room needed.

"Sugar, I'm glad to see you," she beamed, dropping her travel case. "But I didn't expect this kind of homecoming. I was welcomed home by the computer left on, jazz blaring from the stereo system, a burned mess in the microwave, clothes strewn about the house, and urgent phone messages from your boss saying you missed the lunch meeting your job depended on."

"Get over here, baby," I replied, grabbing her and pulling her onto our bed. "Happy anniversary, sweetheart." I kissed her passionately and handed her an opened bottle of perfume.

"Well, I'm a little upset that you got started without me," she said, slipping out of her clothes. "But let's finish together."

She joined me under the sheets. The sun suddenly disappeared, leaving us alone in our intimacy . . . until a quiet Chicago rain joined us in the moment.

Sausage Boy

by Robin Coste Lewis

She tells her that her fingers feel like sausages. They've only known each other for five days and already they're fucking. They are having an affair. It is both horrible and delicious. Everything is a secret, a whisper.

The younger woman is wettest when she has her two stubby fingers worming loverly into the older woman's caverns. It is the perfect drama. It gives the sausage-fingered girl exactly what she needs: an older woman with breasts forever warm to have and sidle next to all for herself. And what the older woman needs right now, more than anything else, is a large round mind to put her words into. So she concedes and lets Sausage Fingers call her "Mama," just as long as they can talk the whole way through.

Sausage Fingers pretends the older woman's breast is a plank of wood and her own mouth a course sheet of sandpaper. "Mama," the girl says, smothering the older woman's nipple with her tongue. Mother. Mamere. Mamon. Sweet Pussy.

The older woman, Mrs. Sweet Pussy, loves all of these names, but she wants them to be worse than all that. She wants to hear words no one would ever imagine calling her in any other position. Words like: *bitch, my bitch, my sweet little whore, cunt, rotting cunt, don't move, don't you fucking move.* She wants to come slower, harder, faster, in no time. She wants to be turned over, tied down, beaten like a ferret, spanked with a stingray. She wants to try to come while tied to a chair, in a straitjacket, in a room, by herself, using only words. *Mamon* is just the first little dirty letter. *Mother* is the beginning of her alphabet.

They fuck in the car driving along the turnpike. Their fingers are hungry blue crabs burrowing into each other's panties. They fuck upright in the library between the stacks with half-eaten apples green and sour and browning in their hands. Sausage Finger's breath smells like sweet corn tortillas. Mrs. Sweet Pussy's skin like slowly warmed milk.

They've only known each other for one week and already have invented their own private language.

"Mother," Sausage Fingers says. "*M* is for Mother." Sausage Fingers puts Mrs. Sweet Pussy across her lap and demands, "Repeat after me." Mrs. Sweet Pussy arches her back into the air and waits for Sausage Finger's next command.

Sausage Finger's other hand is beneath Mrs. Sweet Pussy's mound, diving like a sandpiper's fluted beak for a runaway crab. Mrs. Sweet Pussy opens her legs without Sausage Finger's permission. The sausage-fingered girl slaps her hand down into Mrs. Sweet Pussy's ass and whispers, "*F* is for French Angelfish."

She traces her fingers from Sweet Pussy's crotch, up toward her anus, but teases and stops just when her Sweet Pussy starts to sigh.

Mrs. Sweet Pussy is a rare yellow sea horse hiding in a thick bed of grass. She camouflages herself, wrapping her tail around her single flowing blade, changing her color to fit the occasion. If the night is blue, her skin jets teal. When it is raining, she is gray and speckled. She flickers her dorsal fin and anchors herself to the nearest sponge

"*P*" she says, "*P* is for Peacock Flounder. *S* is for Stinging Sea Cauliflower. *T* is for Throbbing Pink Moon Jellies. *A* is for the Atlantic Spotted Dolphin. *D* is for Farming Damsel Fish."

They drown in each other's language. Their play is a nautical loveland and they are worthy navigators reveling in each other's wakes. They tickle each other's bellies with their own little pectoral fins. They spin around that single blade of grass like ripe young maidens around a maypole.

Mrs. Sweet Pussy is coming like an old well-traveled estuary: a little fresh water, a little salt, a little oyster, and a little mother-of-pearl.

"Are you my little one?" she asks. "Are you my Sausage Boy?"

Sausage Boy is too somewhere else to answer. For the first time in her life she is wishing she had a penis, a dick, a hard stiff stick. She is having what Mrs. Sweet Pussy calls a phantom. She is like an amputee who still feels the thick throbbing limb years after it's been removed.

They don't know each other at all, yet they know each other very well. Sausage Boy already knows how much Mrs. Sweet Pussy likes to be fucked up her ass, and Mrs. Sweet Pussy knows that what Sausage Boy needs most, more than an apprenticeship and more than a Ph.D, is a mouthful of mammary glands rammed into every crevice of her throat.

So late one night in the kitchen Mrs. Sweet Pussy hoists herself onto the counter and opens her blouse as a treat. She takes out a breast and offers Sausage Boy a feeding. Sweet Pussy teases Sausage Boy, passing the hard raised mound too quickly through his lips. He clamps down, but Mrs. Sweet Pussy pulls it away, then spanks his cheeks with the tight, tiny sand dune masquerading as a nipple at the edge of her breast. Sausage Boy lifts her by her ass and spins her like a sea cucumber down onto the warm wooden floor.

He's trying to put his knee in her, and Mrs. Sweet Pussy doesn't mind at all. She can take a knee, she thinks, a knee, a foot, a leg, an elbow, an anything. Every part of her wraps around his torso, as if she is a giant monstrous squid. Mrs. Sausage Pussy Sweet Boy Boy Sausage Sausage Fingers Fingers Pussy, the older woman thinks, sweating, disoriented. Mother Bitch Cunt My Little Whore Filth Sin Devil in a Brown Body, he answers.

Sausage Boy is all apuddle. He feels his phantom. Mrs. Sweet Pussy throbs on her own accord. She's pulling every spare molecule of oxygen deep into her own wet cavern. Her thick purple ink syrups their entire world.

The best part about the affair is that they are pretending they know each other better than this. They are not ready to admit that what is actually happening is that they have never fucked anybody's body this way before. They have never let anyone in this way. And the joy of it all, the unleashed boredom finally taking its authoritative way, is a greater pleasure far exceeding any salty word or properly seasoned whip. Better than coming. Coming would be incomplete without the confession of each other's private little historical dissatisfactions.

This is the Game of Life, but Sausage Boy thinks it's called Love. This is a Trick of the Wrists, but Sausage Fingers thinks it's called Happily Ever After. He wants to believe in something more than a warm wet slightly sugared strawberry. But Mrs. Sweet Pussy is only willing to believe the game is called How We Get Through the Night.

Mrs. Sweet Pussy is bored and likes her Sausage Boy because he is honest about his needs. He comes to her office one a week and gladly writes a check for her services because he is getting what he really came for: not a better understanding of his issues, but the actual thing he has wanted all along: a Mother, a Mamere, a Mamon to fuck. All Mrs. Sweet Pussy has to do is open her legs, and he falls right back in.

They pretend they are faggots meeting in the woods. She drops her skirt, wraps her arms around their imaginary tree, ass exposed, puckered and beaming for the world, and he's in, way in. So in that Mrs. Sweet Pussy can feel him coming in, up, through her mouth.

He's the best client she's ever had. He learns more about his issues in one session than ten years of psychoanalysis could ever teach him.

But Sausage Boy only thinks about Mrs. Sweet Pussy in relation to himself. My Pussy. My own. Sweet Pussy is just what he needs to help him forget that vast howling canyon in the middle of his body. She is exactly what he doesn't know he desires: an elaborate fantasy to fill his gaping motherless wound. Sausage Boy only wants to see Mrs. Sweet Pussy as his own personal convenience store. She is a microwave turned to its highest setting. Opened twenty-four hours a day. A place to stop for uncomplicated coffee, condoms, and high-octane fuel.

Meanwhile, Mrs. Sweet Pussy has her own Monument Valley to contend with. She's ignored herself for so long, so busy milking herself for the world, that she's developed an art, a career, of not listening to her own voice. She doesn't know the word *no*. She doesn't even know the letter *n*. Her yes is automatic, something she can't help. Her breasts leak milk at the very first glance of a mouth.

Mother. Mamere. Mamon. Sweet Pussy.

Until Sausage Boy, Mrs. Sweet Pussy has never told any- one that she wants to be tied up and left there. She has never been able to admit to all of those safe professional women with whom she has traveled, taken home, and purchased property that what she wants is rough and simple. Cell to cell. Southern, or not at all.

Mrs. Sweet Pussy is trying to admit that she is dying to be fucked properly, serviced regularly, lubricated on a ritual basis. She is trying to work her way up to telling her perfect, old-school, lefty girlfriend that what she needs right now—more than safety, more than feminist rhetoric, more than a progressive presidential candidate and a long-term monogamous relationship—is someone, anyone, with a tightly packed fist who does not want to get to know her.

Sausage Boy has never known a mother. Mrs. Sweet Pussy has never been a child. Sausage Fingers is trying to remember. Mrs. Sweet Pussy sees immeasurable value in forgetting. Sausage Fingers is a little boy trapped inside a young woman's body. Mrs. Sweet Pussy is an older woman trying for one last time to get the animal in her right.

Three months later and their fucking gets ruined by their discovery of lovemaking. They slow down, having remembered how to think. Their gestures become complex. Intellectual engagement and elaborate calisthenics are not enough to keep them afloat.

Their boat is only one solitary plank of wood. And they have splinters and mother-of-pearl chafed into their asses. They are sinking like two large volcanic stones, and all they know how to do well together is fuck like young randy dolphins playing Grown Up beneath an ancient coral reef. Six moons later, when Sausage Boy's apprenticeship is over, they see each other on the street, but they do not speak. Only their bodies know that brackish and salty language.

Mrs. Sweet Pussy is walking with her wife and grandkids. One of the children pretends he is playing volleyball with a purple balloon. Sausage Boy sees the balloon and remembers her thick dark ink. Sausage Boy is with her partner. They are carrying signs on their way to a rally. The girlfriend has no idea that the graying, older woman walking toward them, dripping in coral and freshwater pearls, has fucked her partner on several occasions in positions she herself is too landlocked to imagine.

They all pass each other like two friendly schools of fishes, the air around them mingling like warm currents in a small tide pool. Mrs. Sweet Pussy nods, Hello, and thinks that both women combined are younger than her own daughter. Sausage Boy nods back, like a dolphin pecking with his snout. Mamere. Mamon. My Pussy.

They don't know each other at all. They fuck each other very well. Their bodies have a secret language, a private little alphabet. *Mother* is the first letter. *Father* is a dead language they laugh about no longer speaking. *Pussy* is a letter like an *s* or a *t*. They use it all the time.

The young woman's mouth smells like warm tortillas and her fingers feel like tightly packed blood sausage. The older woman's breasts are like a million mothers. She is a walking ocean of sweet warm milk.

 Orca.
Pectoral Fin.
Throbbing Pink Moon Jelly.
Hawk's Beak Turtle.
Sargasm Weed.
Stinging Sea Cauliflower.
Damsel Fish.
Peacock Flounder.
 Stingray.
A jellyfish.

If Only

by Krystal G. Williams

It's Wednesday, six-thirty A.M. Summer solstice—the longest day of the year. The sun has only been up for an hour or so, but already the dreaded Houston humidity has kicked in. I don't mind. Not really. I hardly notice the slick cool trickles of sweat making random tracks down my back. Perspiration beads across my forehead, settles in little droplets underneath my nose and across my top lip. If I stay here much longer, I'll melt. But I don't intend to be here long. No, not long at all. I'm on a mission, with no time for mistakes or delays.

Sounds of summer are all around me, chirping, buzzing, leaves rustling at the barest hint of a breeze. I can tell that it's going to be another beautiful day in Memorial Park. I sit at the far edge of the parking lot—car windows tinted as dark as the law allows are partially lowered to give me a good view of the area. From where I sit, I can see the die-hard athletes preparing for their morning run. The savvy ones go in pairs, with either a partner or a faithful, if not willing, pet. If I listen really closely, I can hear the *snap-snap* of a leather leash to make the less willing more so, or the crunch of a well-deserved doggie treat given after a drag around the park.

The not-so-smart single runners stretch to make them-selves limber. These joggers will be moving faster than the ones who've paired up. They're racing as much against the probability that they'll be singled out for mugging as they are racing against the rising sun with its heat-sapping strength.

"Looks like it's gonna be another scorcher."

A bike patrol officer coasts by. The sounds of gears changing, chain rattling, draw my eye. He gives me a half nod. I nod back, then fan my face with my hand. Three months' worth of recognition in that nod. He's seen me here before. It only took a couple of times of me stepping out of the car, going through the motions of the runner-style stretches and warm-up exercises, before duty-honed suspicion turned to pleasant surprise at seeing me here every Wednesday so diligently.

What am I doing here? What is my mission? Certainly not to run. Diligence, yes. But not for the benefit of my own body. It's another body that I'm waiting and watching for. It's a body that I've come to know and love just as dearly as my own. *Stalking* is such an ugly word. And I'm sure Mr. Bike Patrol Officer wouldn't nod so kindly to me if he thought that's what I was doing. I prefer not to use that word. *Diligent admiration* sounds so much better.

I check my watch. 6:42 A.M. Three more minutes and, yes . . . finally. Here he comes. Right on schedule. I get back into my car and slide farther into the comfort of cloth seats trimmed in vinyl. A popular newsstand rag raised as my shield. My ears, so accustomed to the sounds of the park, pick up the one sound I've been waiting for.

Day-Glo orange shoestrings, leather uppers with carefully crafted rubber soles slap against the pavement in an oh-so-familiar rhythm. I've been listening to that sound every Wednesday for that past three months. Steady. Strong. Purposeful.

Bronze skin streaked in sweat, white tank top, navy spandex leggings and gray, boxer-style shorts worn over them flash by. His stride is long and controlled. Biceps sculpted by hours of Soloflex pump in sync with the contractions of rock-hard thighs and ultracut calves. Power. Endurance. Commitment. Ten long strides and he disappears around a bend in the path. One hour's wait for one minute of watching. I should be disappointed, but I'm not. Not really. It's a trade-off that I've come to accept after all this time. But I can't help thinking, *If only I had the power to manipulate time.* What would I do if I could make time bend to my will? If I had such power, would I end world hunger? Would I command world peace? My wants are simple, but all-consuming. All I want to do is sit and watch him, over and over, until time itself gets sick of watching the same scene and changes the channel.

6:49 A.M. Still on schedule. I back out of the parking space and onto the feeder road. A U-turn under the freeway, three lights, a side street, then another parking lot. This time I'm in for a longer wait. I've got to give him time to stretch out the kinks, chat with his frat, and saunter back to his car.

7:20 A.M. and the flow coming out of the coffeehouse is measurably more frantic than the flow going in. Caffeine-induced energy. Get the morning started with a jolt of mocha motivation. Out of the corner of my eye I see him. Full, firm lips are clamped to a white, lidded Styrofoam cup. Enough care taken in that first sip to keep from singeing his tongue. Oh, lucky coffee cup! Flecks of sugar foam are perfectly camouflaged by a salt-and-pepper mustache. He's got his Wednesday-morning usual—one large coffee, one small bag with a bran muffin. That will be his breakfast. Got to be good for the doctor. Got to get that cholesterol level down. Only he and I know about the extra raspberry jelly-filled donut that he'll pinch on from about noon until the end of the day. A steady stolen supply of saturated fat and complex carbohydrates, like a glucose drip, will get him through the rest of the day with just the right edge. Only he and I know.

Secrets within secrets. He doesn't know that I know. I keep that to myself, even as I keep my diligent admiration to myself. If only I had as much power over him as that jelly donut. If only I could be the one to feed him, to give him his sustenance. Why can't I be the one he longs to taste? I could go down as smooth as raspberry jam. I could make him smack his lips, long for another.

8:15 A.M. and I've got to go if I want to get back in time for lunch. We've got a standing lunch date on Wednesdays—he at his table and me at mine. At the sandwich shop, a sea of green-and-white-striped umbrellas stands between us. But that has never stopped me from enjoying my meal. Neither does the lack of conversation. In my head we've talked for hours. I know him so well. On Wednesdays past, I imagined that I knew what he was thinking. Nibble. Nibble. Munch. Munch. Wishing there was something more appetizing than tuna on wheat for lunch. No mustard. No mayo. Only a little pepper to kill the bland, fish taste. If only he knew he could make a meal of me. Spread me, smear me with any condiment he wishes. I wouldn't complain. I would be better than that stale jelly donut that he's always got stashed in his bottom desk drawer. I could be there for him. And I wouldn't even attract the ants.

8:20 A.M. The freeway is packed by now. Inch by inch, I crawl. For the first time today, I'm starting to feel a little anxious. This traffic has put a serious crimp in my plans. I've got a 9:30 in the Fifth Ward to touch up my roots. If I'm a minute late, I know I'm going to be six deep in the waiting room. Chantalliqua doesn't play. When she says be there, you be there. So I get there, passing two blue-and-white squad cars—

one in the process of giving someone a ticket for trying to pass up traffic in the breakdown lane and the other simply stuck between an eighteen-wheeler and an overturned cattle car.

When I arrive at the beauty shop, Chantalliqua is as chatty as ever—cussing and fussing at the high price of hair rinses, and the worsening quality of wigs and weaves, and at Erica Kane because she wouldn't know a good man if he came long and bit her. I laugh appreciatively, but my mind isn't on shoptalk. I can't work up the energy to talk about some soap opera sad case that's hours away from taking up my TV airtime. I need to figure out how I can make time with my own man.

12:05 P.M. and Chantalliqua's got my hair looking tight and oh-so-right. I haven't had this much body and bounce since my great aunt Bobby-Lynn used a pressing comb and big pink, foam rollers slept in overnight with a scarf, more holy than righteous, tied around my head to keep me from sweating out the straightness.

I pay Chantalliqua for her time and add a little just to keep her happy. Because everybody knows, if Chantalliqua ain't happy, nobody's happy. The last time she was in a snit, there were more hats and wigs coming out of her shop than you cared to count. That was known as the Great Wig-Out of Ninety-eight—a dark, dark time in the history of hair.

As I pass her the extra twenty-dollar bill, she grabs my hands and starts to inspect my nails. She clucks her tongue loudly, shaking her head. At her denouncement of the condition of my nails, you can feel the wind whip through the shop as everyone moves to hide their own hands from Chantalliqua's field of vision. She nods her head in the direction of the chair. Oh no! I know my face is showing my dismay. Not *The Chair!*

It's one thing to be trapped under a hooded hair dryer, trying to maintain conversation when it feels as though your ears are being seared and every time you try to shift positions, you wind up knocking the gooosenecked dryer onto your forehead with a *thunk*. It's quite another thing to sit face to face with someone who can't stop talking while she's filing your nails down to nubs. Even with huge box fans blowing, the smell of nail polish is so thick in your nostrils that you want to gag. But you can't because if you open your mouth to try to breathe, Chantalliqua will take that as a sign that you're trying to get a word in edgewise and will talk faster and longer to get in her point of view. The faster she talks, the slower she files. The slower she files, the longer you suffocate. No. Anything but *The Chair*.

I try to beg off. I've got to run. I may not make my lunch date with him, but I've got other errands to run. I've got other tasks I need to accomplish before tonight. For you see, tonight I will wait and watch no more.

On second thought, I take another look at my hands. I weigh how they look now against how they're bound to look later. I imagine them raking themselves across his broad, bronzed back and give a shudder of disgust. Not because of him! Heaven knows, that man is way too fine to give a woman a response like that. I tremble because these chipped, cracked ends would splinter before he could utter his first moans of pleasure.

I sigh. Chantalliqua is right. She always is. Well, almost always. There was that time last summer when she convinced me to go cherry red. If only I hadn't let her convince me that that color would be good for my dusky skin tones. I looked like an inside-out cherry cordial. After a few wisecracks from my friends and what I'm sure was one offhand, chance disapproving glance from him, you could best believe that my disposition was far from sweet. Just in case, I give Chantalliqua the go-ahead to set me up for a pedicure, too. Nothing kills the romantic mood faster than when you're playing footsie with some doggish-looking feet.

I don't get out of her shop until 1:45 P.M., looking good from head to toe. There's still a few more stops to make, a few more items to get before I make this the most memorable night of his life. If only those stops were on the same side of town. Instead, he's got me so turned around, I'm driving all over the place. He'd better appreciate all this trouble I'm going through. From the Galleria area, to the Fifth Ward, back across town to a shop in the Village. My best girl, Jolene, told me that there is a woman who sells one-of-a-kind perfumes and body oils. Jolene warned me that they were pricey but worth their weight in gold. Her man took a whiff of her new perfume and couldn't leave her alone for the rest of the night. Personally, I can't see how "smell my neck" would be thought of as a turn-on. But Jolene has always told it to me straight. I have to take her at her word.

I walk into the shop, completely overwhelmed. There are so many scents, my head starts to spin. How can I find the one unique scent that will drive him wild? If only I'd known that it would be this difficult to choose, I would have asked Jolene to join me.

As I wander, my eyes (not my nose) are drawn to a shelf lined with plain brown vials covered with black tops. They're sitting in long wooden trays. A small, gold numbered sticker is placed in front of each bottle. I'm not sure if the stickers are meant to count the number of bottles or to identify each unique scent by number. My hand reaches instinctively toward a vial. Number seven. Lucky number seven. If I'm not lucky, I want to *get* lucky. I want to get him.

I lift the vial from its casing and unscrew the cap. Knowing how potent these perfumes are rumored to be, I wave it cautiously under my nose. Too little care, too late. I'm not prepared for this experience. All at once, all senses fire—and I'm sure, some senses spring to life that I invented right on the spot. I've never experienced anything like it, and certainly never from any of the bargain-basement designer knockoff scents that I've been known to pick up when money's a little tight.

My heart races ahead of my breath as my head reels back. I see visions of pleasures to come, or perhaps they are memories of lives past. I can't be sure. I'm awed by images of verdant gardens. Paradise lost and longed for. Explosions of flora and fauna of every hue swim before my eyes—crimson and cream, azure and amethyst. Colors so dazzling, they hurt my eyes to look at them. Luscious fruits so heavy with ripeness that hints of evening breezes send them plummeting to the ground. My mouth waters. I want to gather the fruits, to clutch them greedily to my chest before the lion and the lamb lying by the stream can gobble them up.

Suddenly, I see him. He is as naked as the day he is born and unashamed—unfettered by man's modern notion of modesty. He beckons me with a crooked finger and an even more crooked smile. My mouth goes dry. He sees me. After all this time, he finally sees me!

He pours a droplet or two of the oil into the palm of his hands, warms the scent briefly between clasped hands before touching me. Pressing me back into the hollow of the earth, he works the oil, a small swipe across my forehead. An anointing. The balls of his thumbs press gently on my cheeks before trailing downward. His ebony eyes reflect total understanding as he traces the tracks of tears shed long ago. They are tears of frustration and denial. Tears of hurt and want. He wipes the traces away. Now they are tears of hope and healing. Melancholia moves from me as swiftly as the stream we lie beside.

Skilled hands continue to smooth over me, kneading the oil deeper than flesh, all the way into my soul. I become as liquid as the oil, flowing freely. He cups my breasts, then lowers his lips to them. His warm breath flows across my skin. And despite his warmth, raises gooseflesh. I tremble because I'm afraid. I'm afraid that my body won't do justice to the tribute he pays. If only I'd used that health club membership. If only I'd passed up those second helpings of anything, everything.

Permanents and colorants, polished nails, potent perfumes—almost two hundred dollars' worth of artificial beauty. In our private garden, all is stripped away and it's only me . . . me with the too-wide hips and the too-full lips and the less-than-trim tummy. He doesn't seem to notice. Or maybe he does? Maybe the me he's looking at is the real me, the woman I could be for him if he would let me—if I would let myself.

"That'll be thirty-two ninety. Would you like to pay for that with cash, check, or charge?" A sales clerk with a face too young and eyes too old touches my shoulder and jerks me back from the precipice before I can experience total free flight. I can almost read her thoughts. You break. You buy. With her cruel interruption, more devastating than coitus interruptus, she doesn't break the spell of the scent—only postpones it.

My hand trembles as I try to replace the vial, but I've already unleashed the genie. Unlike Pandora, I'm proud of what I've done. I have to have it. I have to have *him!*

3:30 P.M. By the time I make it home, it'll be almost five o'clock. For him, it's quitting time. For me, the real work begins. As I set my packages by the door, I weigh the pros and cons of a quick shower against a long, lingering bath. A shower would quickly rinse away the heat and grime of the day. But the moisture in the air would destroy my ninety-dollar 'do. After all of the effort Chantalliqua put into it, I would never be able to set foot into her shop again. I'd be shunned as an outcast, forever known as the woman who killed Chantalliqua's curls.

A bath would relax me. But I don't want to relax. If I soak in that tub, I would melt away my backbone. This is no time to back out now. I'm on a mission. So I fill my tub with cool water. I place a few drops of the body oil into the water, swirl it around and around until I see a million tiny droplets floating on top. Slowly I lower myself into the water and clench my teeth in mild protest. It's liquid ice. Not unlike I imagined the stream in our private garden to be. Cupping my hands, I gather water inside them, raise them toward the ceiling, and let the water trickle down again. A silent libation. This is for the brother who isn't here.

5:15 P.M. I smooth the emulsified water over my shoulders, down my arms, and over my belly. I massage in a circle, imagining this is how I'd do it if only I could be with his child. Over, under, and between my thighs, down the shins and under the instep of my pedicured feet. I've got every inch covered. A little longer to soak. 5:21 and I've got to go to him. I've got to go for him. I step out of the tub, forgoing a towel to let the artificial breeze generated by air conditioner and ceiling fan dry me. They can't cool me. I'm on fire. They can't compare to the breezes of our private garden. But for now, they'll have to do. I've run out of time.

I enter the bedroom where I've spent weeks, days, and hours scheming and dreaming. And now, it all comes down to this moment. A quick flick of a butane lighter and candles by my bedside send their scent wafting on the air. I lie across my bed and close my eyes—waiting.

Six-fifteen P.M. An engine purrs, then falls silent. A car door slams. Size fourteen Stacey Adams clomp across the cobbled pavement of the drive, then disappear in a whishing hiss as they cross the grass on the way to the front door. Keys jingle. Door squeaks. *Thud-thud.* It's not the beating of my frightened, faithful heart, but the sound of a briefcase falling to the floor.

6:20 P.M. Sun sets on the longest day of my life. The last rays of day slide across the floor.

"Happy anniversary, sweetheart." Words whispered, soft, sweet and low. I tremble, because I know they are meant for my ears only.

In the Rain

by Travis Hunter

Guy Sparks was driving north on I-85 in his convertible Porsche, which could only be driven in half-decent weather because of its broken top. Since it was such a pretty day, he decided to drive to his mother's fifty-fifth birthday party. He was halfway to his mother's house when his car stalled, and just as he pulled off the side of the road into a construction zone, the rain came. First there was a light drizzle, then an all-out storm. Rather than sit in the ever-so-quickly flooding car, Guy popped the face off the CD player and began to hop out.

He couldn't have found a worse place for his car to stop. As he opened the door, he stepped into a puddle of mud. Guy slammed the car door, cursed under his breath, and trotted toward the red-and-white QT gas sign that hovered above the exit about half a mile away.

As his soaked gray linen pants and white silk shirt clung to his body, making him miserable, his luck changed. Through the pouring rain Guy noticed the lights of a white sports car pull over onto the shoulder of the road up in front of him. As he approached the car, the passenger window rolled down.

"Is everything all right?" a soft Caribbean voice asked.

"Nah, my car broke down and I—"

"Would you like a ride?"

"If you don't mind, I'm—"

"Get in before you catch a cold," the soft voice stated in a motherly tone.

Once inside the car, Guy glanced over at the driver and thought, *I must be dreaming.* Her pleasant smile immediately changed his mood. Without her saying another word, he felt something for the sista sitting behind the wheel. He appreciated her caring side already, but he found it a bit hard to put his mack down with a broken car and soggy feet.

"If you could give me a ride to this QT up here, I'd appreciate it."

"It's no problem."

"What's your name?" he asked, trying not to shiver as his body adjusted to the air-conditioned car.

"Terri, and yours?" she said as she slid into drive, never second-guessing her decision to pick up this strange man.

"Guy Sparks, but everyone calls me G. I'll be happy to have your car cleaned for you. I'm making a mess," he said, looking down at the orange Georgia clay mud dripping from his black Nautica sandals onto her navy floor mats.

"That's fine, don't worry about that," Terri said, waving him off. "You have a nice name."

"Ya think so?"

"Yeah . . . I do."

"Well, thanks."

"I take it that you are having car problems."

"Yeah, I guess she's seen better days."

"Aren't you going to put your top up?"

"It's broken," he said, not even trying to make up a lie. "Where are you from?" Guy asked, pondering her accent.

"Born in Jamaica, raised in Canada." She smiled and pulled off the exit ramp and into the QT parking lot.

"Thanks a lot. How much do I owe you?"

"Nothing. You didn't ask; I offered. Glad I could help."

"It's kind of dangerous picking up strange people on the side of the highway. You shouldn't do that," Guy said seriously.

"Nothing is going to happen to me. I'm protected by the essence of God. Plus I have my girlfriend with me," Terri said as she opened her thick thighs and stroked the top of a .22 Derringer handgun that rested near her love nest. Looking at her toned legs, it was obvious that she frequented her neighborhood gym.

Guy chuckled. "That lil'-ass gun ain't gonna do nothing but piss somebody off."

Terri smiled back at him with her pearly whites. Her complexion was a flawless dark chocolate. Her hair was cut close in a Nubian sista kind of way, no perm, all naturaaal. She had thick lips and Guy noticed that she bit the bottom one on and off, out of habit or nervousness. Guy wasn't sure which one it was, but either way when she did that, he had to turn away to keep from getting too excited.

"I'm not in the business of hurting anyone. Just keep enough to make 'em say ouch," Terri said as she gave Guy a friendly wink.

"Well, thanks for the ride. Can I give you my number? Maybe you'll reconsider my offer once you try to clean this mess that I made," Guy said casting his line.

"Sure! Just as long as I don't have to explain to anyone why I'm calling." He sensed that was her way of asking if he lived alone or if he was seeing someone.

"Now that might be a problem."

"Oh, really?" Terri asked, eyebrows raised.

"My son is four years old, and he likes to screen my calls."

"Does his mother help him out from time to time?" Terri asked, eyebrows arched, lips twisted.

"Nah, he handles that on his own."

"Are you married?" Terri asked, pulling her ink pen back toward her B cups.

"No! Now, would I offer you my home number if I were married?"

"It's happened before."

"Nah, it's just me and my little man."

A skeptical look came across her face, and then her eyes brightened again as if a small voice inside her said, *Take the tall, brown-skinned brother's number.*

"Okay," Terri said as she handed him the ink pen and two business cards for Nubian Town Bookstore. "So you're a single daddy raising your child alone?"

"Yes, and no. I have a lot of help from my mom. That's where I was headed. Today's her birthday and the family is giving her a party."

"Oh, how sweet. What's your son's name?"

"Jordan."

"Like Mike?"

"Yeah, and he thinks he has a lil' game, too."

"Too cute," Terri said as her eyes drifted off to another time and place. "What are you going to do here at the QT?" she asked as her mind snapped back to the here and now.

"I was going to call someone to come and get me."

"Where does your mom live?"

"Gwinnett County, off Beaver Ruin."

"I'll take you."

"Nah, you've done enough. I don't want to take you all out of your way. I'm cool. Just give me a call," Guy said as he opened the door to get out.

"It's not out of my way, I live one exit past that on Pleasanthill. Now close the door. You're letting the rain in.

And I know you wanna make it to your mother's party on time, don't you?"

Guy glanced over at her gas needle, which was just below a quarter of a tank. "All right. Pull over to the pump. I have to do something for you. I'll fill you up, and run and call a tow truck."

Terri nodded and pulled up to the pump. Guy filled her car and called the towing service; they jumped back on the freeway headed north on I-85. On a normal day the trip would take fifteen minutes, but Atlantans always lost their damned minds when it started raining and drove at a snail's pace. During the forty-five-minute drive, Guy and Terri found they had a few things in common. They were both Pisceans, born two years and three days apart. Terri was the older one, she was twenty-nine; Guy was twenty-seven. They shared the same philosophy on being self-sufficient and not depending on someone else to take care of their individual needs. They both enjoyed reading African American fiction. She owned a bookstore but was thinking of selling.

"So you know my status. What's yours?" Guy asked.

"Single. Been that way for the last year and a half. Don't have any kids yet, but I love 'em. Proud owner of a chocolate Labrador retriever named Sable," Terri rattled off.

"So why are you thinking of selling your store?"

"Competition's too strong. I can't discount like the chains and still keep the lights on."

"Sure you can; we just have to get creative."

She smiled, looked at the brown-skinned brother with the short twisted braids and perfect teeth and shook her head. She knew he was a total stranger, but when he mentioned the word *we* it made her feel like she wasn't fighting this thing called life, alone!

"I'm going to give it another year. If nothing changes, then I'm out. Add it to the long list of other things that didn't pan out."

"So what are your other options?" he asked.

"Pray! And hope for the best."

"I hear you."

"So, Guy. What do you do for a living?"

"Well, right now I'm looking," he said, but immediately noticed that not-another-broke-brother look on her face. "No, no, no, it's not what you think. I play pro basketball over in Europe, but I'm tired of being away from my son. I have enough change put away to start my own business, so I'm looking for a second career of sorts."

"Okay!" She dragged that word out like she had before when he tried to give her his number. "You know I can't stand a lazy brother who won't live his life."

"The feeling is mutual. I like a sister who does her thing. Can't take a sister sitting around waiting with her hand out. Those are the ones that get nada."

"Nada?"

"Not a damned thing!" They shared a brief laugh.

"Okay!" Terri said, giving him a high five. "Hard as I work, I'd be damned if I let someone sit around and live off me."

"I feel ya!"

"You seem to be a pretty cool guy."

"And you're way too nice, plus you're cute. Yo, you wanna come to my mom's party?"

"Do you see how I'm dressed?" Terri asked with horror as she opened her arms to show her jean shorts and a white spaghetti-strapped halter with DELTA SIGMA THETA stitched across the front. "I just ran up to the store because the alarm was set off. I'm not prepared for a party."

"You said you didn't live far. How long could it take you to get dressed?"

Terri briefly contemplated his offer, biting her bottom lip the whole time. "Nah, I better pass. Maybe another time. Thanks for the offer, though," she said as she playfully slapped his leg. With the exception of their quick little handshake, that was their first touch. Guy felt something, a connection. He wanted to see more of this sista. He believed in fate: his car breaking down, Terri just riding by. As far as he was concerned, this meeting was no coincidence.

"There is not going to be another time. My mom will only turn fifty-five once. Plus, I know she'll wanna meet the woman that saved her only child from catching pneumonia."

"Only child! Spoiled!"

"Only child, yeah! Spoiled, a little."

"So you're used to getting what you want?"

"No! I want you to come to this party with me, but it doesn't look like that's happening. Here, get off on this exit," Guy said as he pointed to the Beaver Ruin sign.

After a few more turns they were pulling into Guy's mother's driveway. They sat in the car a few minutes and enjoyed the sound of the rain pounding against the windshield and the wipers slapping back and forth.

"So . . . will I hear from you soon?"

"Yeah, I'll call you. You better get out of those wet clothes before you get sick."

"Do you wanna come in for just a second and meet everyone?"

Terri opened up her arms again to show how inappropriately she was dressed and twisted her lips.

"All right, you can slide this time. Thanks for the ride."

Funny how one minute you can be total strangers with someone and feel so close to them the next, Guy thought as they made serious eye contact.

Terri shifted in her seat and said, " 'Bye, G."

"Okay, Terri. Call me."

Guy let himself out, jogged to the side door, and disappeared. Terri sat for a few minutes and tried to gather herself. It had been a long time since she had that I-like-that-boy feeling. After a few minutes of sitting there smiling, she shook it off, put her car in reverse, and drove home.

҈

Guy and all his relatives were laughing and talking loud when Terri walked in. The CD blasted something by Carl Thomas. There were a few older people playing cards at the kitchen table, and a few of the younger ones were playing dominoes on the island that separated the dining room from the great room.

Guy didn't notice her but Terri spotted him right away. He was straddling the arm of a love seat with a handsome little almond-colored boy standing between his legs.

That has to be Jordan, she thought. *He looks just like his father.*

Terri was standing in the doorway when Uncle Willie pounced on her.

"Come on, gurl. Lemme see whatcha got," Uncle Willie said as he did his version of the George Jefferson dance. The one where he frowns up and acts as if he is about to fight, arms flailing all around and feet sliding every which way.

"No, thank you," Terri said, never bothering to move.

The younger kids who were playing dominoes at the island

stopped what they were doing and shouted in unison, "She ain't ready, she ain't ready, she ain't ready . . ."

Guy turned around to see what the commotion was all about. He chuckled at the sight of a confused-looking Terri. He decided he'd try to rescue his new friend. He made his way over to Terri and smiled. Uncle Willie was still dancing. Guy tapped him on the shoulder and asked if he could cut in.

"What?" Uncle Willie turned around as if he was really about to fight. "Boy, don't get knocked out on my sista's birthday. I ain't know who you was grabbin' all up on me." Uncle Willie cracked a smile, exposing about five missing teeth.

"I see that you met Uncle Willie," Guy said to Terri.

"G-man, this you?"

"Yeah, she's with me, Uncle Willie."

"Got damn, boy. You got taste like your uncle. Ya auntie use to have an ass—I mean—look like that. I don't usually like women with all they hair cut off but . . . give me ya number," Uncle Willie said as he extended his hand.

"Watch out, man," Guy said as he playfully pushed his uncle to the side.

"Boy, don't make me pull it out," Uncle Willie said as he placed his hand over his pocket for the same elusive knife he had been pulling out for the last ten years.

"Ima take you to the barber shop and cut that mess out of your head," Guy said, referring to Uncle Willie's Jheri curl, which wrapped around his bald top.

"Oh no, that's my love jones," Uncle Willie said as he walked off, no longer smiling, and patting the side of his greasy hair.

"Well, all right then. Uncle Willie is something else," Terri said as she followed Guy back toward the sitting area.

"Tell me about it."

"Are you surprised to see me?"

"Yeah, I didn't expect to see you. You look nice," Guy said as he glanced down at Terri's yellow strapless sundress, which exposed her coffee-brown shoulders.

"You don't look bad yourself," Terri said as she reached up and pulled a black thread from Guy's shirt.

"Thank you. What made you change your mind?"

"I got home and decided not to have another boring Saturday night."

Since he wasn't able to tell how tall she was in the car, Guy was surprised at how short Terri was. He was six foot five inches tall, she was maybe five foot even. But her beauty was not to be denied; whoever made up that saying that good things come in small packages must have been thinking about Terri.

"Well, I'm glad you did," Guy said with a big grin.

"I can tell. Stop cheesing."

"Whatever. Come on over here and meet my mom and my son."

Terri followed. She was not nervous like she was every time she met one of her previous boyfriends' parents. Maybe it was because Guy wasn't her boyfriend.

"Mom, this is Terri, the young lady who rescued me today."

"Hi, I'm Thelma. Thank you for picking up my baby. I told him to get rid of that piece of junk."

"It's a classic," Guy stated flatly.

"A classic piece of junk," Thelma whispered to Terri as they shared a laugh. "Did you eat?"

"Not yet. What do you have?"

"Oh, Boney, I like this girl. Ain't too cute to eat. Fix her a plate."

"Boney? I thought you said everyone calls you G."

"Whatever! And this fellow here is Jordan," Guy said as he reached down and picked up his son. Jordan didn't speak, he just laid his head on his father's shoulder.

"Hi, handsome."

Jordan lifted his head and waved.

"He's sleepy. Give him here," Thelma said as she took her grandson. "Terri, I saw my brother dancing with you. Don't pay him any mind. He snuck out of the mental hospital about a week ago. Go on and get yourself something to eat. I'm going to put this lil' rascal to bed."

"It was nice meeting you," Terri said.

"Yeah, girl. We'll talk," Thelma said as she walked off.

"Okay. 'Bye, Jordan," Terri said, waving at the sleepy child.

Guy led her into the kitchen, where Terri instinctively took over. She fixed both of them a plate, and they headed for the quietness of the sunroom, which was adjacent to the kitchen.

Before they knew it two hours had passed and all the guests were gone. Guy walked Terri out to her car, and they hugged; he stole a kiss on the cheek. She promised she would call when she arrived home. He headed back into the house, and turned on the television in the sunroom, and soaked up the scent that she left behind. After Terri called to say all was well, he drifted off to sleep.

❧

The rain was coming down hard. Guy heard a knock on the window of the sunroom. He stood up to answer, wearing nothing but his silk boxers. Terri's yellow sundress was soaked. Her hair dripped little drops of rain into her chocolate face. She was breathing hard as she motioned for him to come out onto the deck. He followed her outside as the thunder exploded and the trees cracked. As the moon illuminated the night, Guy found himself standing on the deck in only his white silk boxers, which the rain had made practically see-through. Terri pulled a lawn chair from beneath the table and motioned for him to sit down. He was a little confused but decided to let her take the lead. Terri's nipples clearly showed through the sundress, and the rain made the thin fabric cling to her body. She lifted her dress as she straddled Guy and stuck her tongue into his mouth. With the rain rolling off their lips and sliding into their mouths, her breathing became heavy. He rubbed his hands down her back, over her ass, and felt her heat as his fingers grazed across her love nest.

It was raining hard but the wetness he felt was different. It was thicker, warmer, juicier. Terri rolled her hips slowly back and forth on his lap as she ran her tongue across the wide of his face. She ripped the top of her dress apart, tearing the buttons off as she pushed his head down toward her firm breasts. As he sucked on her nipples, she moaned and ran her fingers through her hair. Her hands found their way down to his already growing manhood. She stroked her fingers up and down until his moans matched hers. Guy pushed her dress up around her waist and lifted her enough to enter her. She gasped, held on tighter as she felt her emptiness being filled with his rocklike manhood. Guy closed his eyes and moved with her. One arm was still around her waist, the other stroking her ass. Terri's moans became louder as she buried her head into his shoulder. The rain was coming down harder as Guy stood up with Terri still in his arms and laid her down on the glass table. He stood between her legs, grinding a long, slow grind. She wrapped her legs around his waist and slowly ran her fingernails down his rippled chest. Terri reached up and pulled Guy's head down so that they were eye to eye and began speaking in French, "*Faites-l'amour moi,*" then she let out a soft scream and held him tighter. Guy let out a moan and the thunder rocked the night.

"Boney . . . Boney . . . Boney . . ." Thelma called out to her son.

"Yeah, Ma!"

"Wake up. Telephone. It's Terri."

Guy grabbed the phone and heard that familiar accent. "Hello, lady. I was just dreaming about you."

"I dreamed about you last night, too."

"Was it raining in your dream?"

"Don't remember, but I did feel some thunder."

She Cums Every Night . . .

by Jacqueline Powell

Monday/10:57 P.M.

She comes every night except Wednesday. I feel her voice vibrating through the wall. Her moans rise like the sun at dawn. Slow and inevitable. I don't know what he does to her . . . but I'd like to.

※

I sat in bed, sipped on a white wine, and let my mind wander. The battery in my laptop was quickly running out, and the only words I could amass were the ones I'd written. They had nothing to do with the story and everything to do with the moment.

My neighbor, Rod, was entertaining as he does almost every night. We've only spoken briefly in the hall and know very little about one another, but there are some things you learn when the walls actually begin to talk.

Almost every night this mystery woman shows up at precisely nine o'clock, knocks at his door, greets him with silence, and stays till morning. This ritual-like behavior caught my attention three weeks ago when I was leaving on a late-night run to the convenience store. I was walking toward the elevator on my floor when a woman dressed in a powder-blue business suit and heels, with her long sandy brown hair cascading around her shoulders, sashayed past me with a swiftness that made every thing else in the corridor seem irrelevant. She appeared preoccupied only with making it to her destination. Didn't speak and neither did I.

When I returned home I heard her voice, though she wasn't speaking to me. Her dirty pillow talk seeped beyond the beams in the walls. I heard her call out Rod's name in ecstasy, beg him for mercy. And secretly wondered exactly what it was she wished he'd stop doing.

After that week, I began to wait as impatiently as I assumed Rod did. I would dress in one of my satin pieces, grab my laptop, get settled under my cranberry-and-cream comforter, and lightly press my back against the wall in my bedroom. Plugged myself into the moment, their moment. And when it ended I usually disconnected my sexually aroused imagination only to find that my screen was blank.

But tonight was different. I had to work on meeting a deadline. She'd been over there for almost two hours and I'd heard only a little D'Angelo, Maxwell, and Gerald Levert setting the mood. I got out of bed, wrapped myself up in a matching peach satin robe, and walked out onto the balcony. The night air was warm with just enough breeze to send my auburn bobbed hairdo blowing across my caramel skin. I sat down at the small glass table with white wrought-iron chairs and prepared to get back into my story. There were only thirty-six minutes left on the battery and seven hours before she was scheduled to leave.

Monday/11:27 P.M.

What appears to be even more baffling is her inability to make him yell fervently. Or maybe she's simply leaving him speechless.

My glass was almost empty and my imagination, plentiful. They began several minutes ago. The intoxicating sounds of gratification drifted outside and took a seat in the empty chair across from me. My concentration had gone from slight to nonexistent. The wind then ruffled the leaves and drowned out the little I could hear. Shifted my attention toward the sky. The dark blue, silent sky. I assumed it could relate to me with its seemingly anticlimactic nights. I closed my eyes and leaned my head back when a noise came from the balcony next to mine—Rod's balcony. I abruptly looked to the right as he pulled the glass door aside and walked out wrapped in a hunter-green bath towel. Beads of water trickled down his robust, chestnut-brown back as he leaned over the railing. Rob rubbed his bald head toward his face and then ran his fingers along his jet-black goatee. The smell of sex caught a ride over on the wind and shook its shimmy under my nose. Rod continued to focus straight ahead as I sat quietly waiting for her to join him.

Then without looking in my direction he asked, "You always sit out here like this, Clev?"

I sipped my wine and answered, "I'm working."

"What do you write about?" he asked, turning only his head.

"Self-help."

He nodded and then looked back out into the night sky. "Do you believe in an ability to help yourself?"

"You say that as though you don't."

"I'll take that as a yes."

"So what do you believe in?" I asked.

"Happiness, complete happiness."

Having said that, he turned and looked back into his apartment. Adjusted the towel around his waist and wiped the excess water that hadn't escaped the barely coiled hair on his massive chest.

"Don't work too late," he told me.

I glanced down at the slight bulge in the front of his towel, smiled, and whispered, "You either."

Tuesday/10:03 P.M.

He appears to have trained or hypnotized her in some sort of way. How does he get a woman to show this level of dedication to a relationship that travels no farther than his walls—and mine?

I had gone from eavesdropping on his nights to wondering about his days. Whether or not they met at some café for lunch and discussed the evening's events. Whether nine o'clock on the dot was only minutes after she'd left the office or the earliest she was allowed to arrive. Whether or not it was the same voice I heard every night maneuvering its way into my psyche. And then, just as it had become apparent that he had begun to touch her, I wondered if just maybe, one night, that voice could be mine.

I moved my work space out onto the balcony for the second night in a row. And to tell the truth, I did so with hopes that Rod would join me when he was done. When he had washed away all evidence of her presence. I decided to leave the robe that went with the black satin negligee I was wearing at the foot of my bed, walked into the kitchen to fill a glass with white wine, and took a seat on the balcony.

As if he had expected that I would be waiting, forty-nine minutes into my story Rod stepped outside wearing boxers and rested himself in a charcoal-gray chair that sat next to the door. I stopped typing and sighed aloud but apparently I had already grasped his attention.

"So tell me a little more about helping oneself," he said, folding his hands atop his treasure trail of hair below his navel.

"Well, first you have to want to help yourself. You have any habits you're trying to break?"

I looked toward his door, attempting to point out one I'd noticed.

He laughed and answered, "That's what I meant by happiness."

"I don't understand."

"If I'm happy with what I'm doing, there should be no habits to break."

I sipped my wine and licked around the rim of the glass before setting it down. "Did you know there's a difference between happiness and satisfaction?"

Rod lifted his brow and placed his feet upon the railing. "So what is that you've got over there?"

"I've got a little happiness over here, but you were asking about the wine, right?"

"Not anymore."

"I've got a question."

"Shoot."

"She comes every night except Wednesday. Why?"

He turned to look back into his apartment and then smiled at me. "I think six nights is enough for satisfaction. I'm saving my Wednesdays for a little happiness."

I became moist between my legs as my nipples stood on end like pencil erasers. Noticed he had moved his hands from his stomach to his lap. Noticed how stimulating the thought of those large hands gripping my sweaty hips from behind was. Noticed the following night was Wednesday.

"What do you do on Wednesday nights?" he inquired.

"Imagine that I can still hear you."

"Who says you can't?" he asked, laying his full erection against his stomach in his boxers.

I didn't respond. Just let the night air blow by me with hopes of cooling my body. I sat longing for penetration as he went back inside and caused her to climax one more time before the clock struck midnight. Before a day strictly designated for happiness began. I think he made her scream like that because he knew I was listening, he knew I was still dripping wet, and he knew I'd be ready to cum on Wednesday.

Wednesday/8:47 P.M.

I was just about to undress and slide into a lavender bath when I heard a knock at the front door. I stepped back into my slippers and turned down Donnel Jones's sultry CD as I passed through the living room.

"Who is it?"

There was silence. I put the chain on the door and opened it as far as I needed to see. Rod stood there holding a medium-sized black box with a gold-and-white ribbon tied around it. He didn't speak. Simply handed me the box and walked back over to his apartment. I slowly closed the door and sat down on the edge of my couch. I pulled out a black silk robe with a belt and a white rose. Under the tissue paper were a pair of red edible panties and a note that read: "Clev, try them on for size and I'll eat them off for dinner."

By the time I'd dried off from my bath, I was all wet again. I oiled my caramel skin and secured my hair behind my ears with diamond-studded hair clips. Applied a little perfume behind each ear and a dab on the small of my back. Slid into the playful panties that Rod brought me and wrapped myself up in the black silk robe. Grabbed two wineglasses, a bottle of wine, and a bag of scented candles that I'd picked up earlier. Then headed out the door with all of the nerves I could gather to stand in the hall dressed that way.

I tapped on Rod's door three times but it was right before the fourth that he appeared with a bare chest, wearing nothing but a pair of black silk boxers. He took my bags and kissed me lightly on the forehead. Made way for me to enter his domain, the very one I'd stayed up late imagining losing control in. All of the lights were out but I could hear D'Angelo's soulful sounds pouring out of a distant speaker. Rod shut the door behind me and disappeared into another room for a minute. He returned smiling devilishly and took my hand. Led me out onto his balcony, where he had lined the two black metal chairs on each side and left the table centered. He stopped in the threshold and held me from behind. We swayed to the music as his hands traveled to sacred places. I did figure eights with my hips until he groaned with anticipation. Making him hold me tighter, press my body into his.

I turned to face him and said, "Just do what you would normally do at this time."

He smiled and pulled a chair over to me.

"Is this what you would be doing, sitting out on your balcony?" I asked.

"Not when I'm looking for satisfaction. That doesn't go any farther than my bedroom—but you would know that already, wouldn't you?"

"How could I not?"

"Does it bother you?"

I quickly changed the subject with, "Could you fill one of those glasses for me?"

Rod stared at me with a blank expression and then raised his finger to beckon for me.

"C'mere," he told me, "I want to show you something."

I stood to my feet and walked up close enough to feel his breath on my cheeks. He untied my belt and let my robe fall to the ground. I covered my 36Cs as he kissed me from the top of my head to where my hands were planted. Slowly removed them and then kissed the inside of my palms as if to bring validity to my touch.

At that moment it became clear to me that he had an agenda. Rod was aware of how the sensory deprivation had affected me. I wanted to see and touch, not just hear and smell. He placed my hands upon his chiseled stomach. I stepped closer. Let them travel along his arms and up to the back of his neck. Found those hairs that stand on end when the sweet scent of warm lubrication is in the air.

He whispered, "I want you to touch me every way you've thought about when you were on the other side of that wall."

"And I want you to touch me every way I've ever thought about when I was on the other side of that wall."

Just as I turned my back to him and buried myself in his chest, Rod took his right hand, grabbed the inside of my thigh, and maneuvered his fingers inside my honey hole. When he felt the abundant moisture, he moaned in disbelief. I massaged his fingers with my wet walls and did pelvic thrusts that made him gasp for breath. He kissed along my neckline. Took his free hand and swept me away to his bedroom where he had lit the candles I brought and placed them around his bed.

I pressed my hand against his chest and pushed away. "Not in here, Rod."

"Why?"

"She's been in here. This is my night. It's not about satisfaction anymore."

"Where do you want to be?" he asked.

"Where we always meet."

He looked puzzled.

"The balcony," I answered, reaching into his boxers and
massaging his head.

He gave a grin that could be considered almost criminal.
"You're freaky like that, huh? You want to be seen."

I laughed and shoved his boxers to the floor. "And you're
freaky enough to want to be heard."

"I guess that makes us good together."

I kissed his full, soft lips and invited his tongue inside.

He took that short stroll back outside and stationed the
table in a corner that was blocked by a few trees but not
enough to cause voyeurs to mistake my curvaceous ass, which
I'd gotten on all fours and audaciously pointed toward the
east, for anything else. Rod's tongue moved with the precision
of a surgeon, bringing me to almost fatal climaxes and then
easing back in time for me to regain composure. Caressed my
breasts from behind as he challenged himself to lose his tongue
inside of me.

A sound grew from deep down in my soul and as my taut
caramel legs quivered on that table and the night wind blew
over my ass, I recognized it. They were the expressions of
ecstasy that I'd long awaited. That I'd heard her make. That
I'd come to find.

As my screams heightened, Rod pulled away with red saturated lips and an erection that demanded immediate attention. He stood to his feet as I held position and listened to him
fill a condom with a chocolate pleasurable. Rod placed his

hand on the small of my back and slid himself inside. At first, slow and steady. Then as the slurping sounds of him swimming in bountiful liquids increased, so did his movements. He began to thrust harder, causing his hand to slip in my sweaty back. I noticed how his conversation seemed to diminish by then. Almost as though he were in a trance. The sounds, the wind, the sweat. It all combined to make the sudden knock at his door even more inopportune.

I stopped moving, but Rod grabbed my hips like a guard seizing stolen property.

"Please, Clev, don't stop."

I looked back into his dimly lit apartment in time to be startled by a second knock.

I asked him, "Are you expecting company?"

"It's her."

"But she doesn't come on Wednesday."

"Then let her hear that tonight is your night to cum."

Rod pulled out and flipped me over on my back with such a swiftness that he sent one of his chairs falling over the railing. I lay on my back with sweat rolling down my legs when he opened them and planted himself even farther into my cave. Applied just enough pressure with his pelvic region to make my lips flutter and flood him with more juices.

"Ooo, Clev," he whined, "I need this."

I moved with him. Began wavelike motions as I wiggled my hips and licked his nipples. Then came another knock.

"Clev, she can't year you," he uttered through his exhaustion.

I looked him in the eye as a bead of sweat fell and ran along my shoulder blade. "Then let her hear you."

I placed both my hands on his ass, gave myself a little

leverage and brought the honey to him. The slurping of my black box became louder, my grip got tighter, and in a matter of seconds she not only knew that Wednesday belonged to someone else but knew my name, too.

Specialgrl Meets Gntlwmn

by Darris

We're walking on the warm, white beach feeling the soft grains of sand between our toes, under an unbelievably clear sky, talking about small things—how pretty you look in that sundress, how healthy my hair looks. *placing my hands into yours* . . . Look at the sunset, isn't it beautiful?

For seven months they were cyberfriends—they shared cyberwalks on beaches in both California and in Maine, each describing her own beach and its beauty to the other. They shared cyberpicnics, bringing their favorite foods, often feeding each other, taking little nibbles on each other's fingers, arms, necks, cheeks. Sometimes they boiled fresh Maine lobster on a fire outside of a cozy cabin at an inland camp. Sometimes they went for a drive up the California coast from North L.A. to San Francisco, stopping at their favorite spots, enjoying picnics with freshly picked fruit and champagne. And always, lately, they find themselves in each other's virtual arms, holding, hugging, loving, kissing, making sweet, passionate, but gentle love tailored to each one's fantasy.

Dana has envisioned what Janell's voice will sound like—sweet, womynly, articulate, and oh, so sensual. It would have to be. She could tell by the way she "talked" on line. She knew that the only voices in her head were her own, but Dana had a collection of voices in her head for people she had never met yet whose words were familiar through cyberspace or through letters. Janell was assigned the one that reminded Dana of a sophisticated and intelligent womyn she'd met long ago, who was from California, but lived at the time in New York. And she had the pictures that Janell had scanned into her computer during the seven months they had been communicating.

She knew Janell's stats, that she was five foot seven, weighed 175 pounds, and had a 36B bust. She knew she had deep brown eyes, jet-black hair; that she wore it long; and that her skin was chocolate brown. So Dana had a relationship with these images, this imagined voice, and the words—wonderful, intelligent, sensual words—on her screen.

❧

I can't believe I'm really doing this, Janell thought, interrupting the flow of memories of her cyber-relationship, while looking out of the airplane window down on the Northeast landscape. *Maybe we should have met in Cali, in my territory, or even somewhere in between, but then again . . . Maine, I hear, is beautiful, "vacationland" they call it, especially in the summer, so if nothing else, it's a chance to see Maine.*

While they were meeting in Dana's territory, they were very careful to plan their union so that neither would feel disadvantaged. They reserved two rooms in a lesbian-owned bed-and-breakfast in Belfast that was a couple of hours' drive from Bar Harbor and three hours from Dana's home. They'd planned their weekend with plenty of distractions, just in case their 3D experience was different from their cyber experience.

Plus, they'd assuage the awkwardness of their first meeting.

> I'm kissing you, on your mouth, then your neck, your
> shoulder, stopping to gently bite your shoulder, right
> here. Yes. Now I'm moving down to your breast. I see
> that your nipples are erect for me, mmmmm. Now I'm
> kissing each one, your left one first, then your right. I
> am holding your right breast in my left hand, and I
> have your left breast in my mouth, licking and sucking
> your nipple.

❦

Dana has finally reached Route 95 after an hour and a half of
back roads. The pleasure of some of her favorite fantasies,
coupled with the anxiety of meeting Janell, made the ride seem
quicker than she remembered. After a few months of sharing
each other's sensual and sexual fantasies, each knows what the
other enjoys and would like to explore. Dana knows that
Janell loves massages, especially foot massages. She knows that
she likes it when Dana gives her sweet, sensual kisses all over
her body, from head to toe, nibbling on certain favorite spots
along the way. And she knows that Janell likes baths scented
with aromatherapy oils, rose and lilac petals in the water, and
candles around the tub.

Dana even remembers their shared Jacuzzi fantasies with
the jets massaging their bodies, enhancing the pleasure, while
making passionate love. *It's too bad the bed-and-breakfast
doesn't have a Jacuzzi,* she thinks as she looks at the picture of
Janell she has in the memo clip on her dashboard. *She says she
really looks like her picture. God, I hope so.* "I don't," she
remembers replying. "I don't have any pictures of myself, but I
can try to get one for you before you come out to Maine.
There was this newspaper article . . ."

I am on my knees, in front of you, my arms are wrapped around you, holding your butt, and I'm kissing your navel, rimming your belly button with my tongue. Now I'm moving lower, mmmmm, you smell so good; I'm kissing you now, your lips protrude to me, I kiss them, they kiss me back, I open them and taste your juices, mmmmm, you taste good, too.

Janell could hardly contain herself as she smiled at her gentlewomyn's consistent and thorough kisses all up and down her body, including her toes. She wondered if Dana would really kiss her toes, or if it will remain a fantasy. She got a fresh manicure and pedicure just in case. Just in case Dana really wanted to suck all of her digits, as she told her on the screen.

▢

Dana remembered their first date. They had been chatting for a while in chat groups, but both claimed that they ignored those little IMs that flashed across the screen by someone's wanting to fulfill their cyberfantasies. Until one day, when Janell asked her on a date.

Come on, it will be sweet, safe, just a date, okay? And if you're uncomfortable, we can stop.

I'm shy, Dana responded, and I am not into cybersex.

Me neither, but I'd like to take you on a date.*s*;)

blushing okay . . .

Here, I'll pour you some champagne.

Great! That's my favorite too. Okay, *pouring each of us a glass of champagne*

Dana remembered the champagne, she remembered the fresh fruit, she remembered the roses and lilacs—all ordered and waiting at the bed-and-breakfast. She turned off the Portland exit, heading toward the airport. Janell's plane would be landing in just a few minutes—her anxiety intensified. She manicured her own fingernails, something she had never done, but she remembered Janell's comment about long nails being a sure sign of a lack of sex. So she gave a little extra attention to brushing under them and buffing them to look pearly. She smiled as she thought about the humor they shared, even in their fantasies.

⚙

I'm putting my hands into you, gently, sweetly, I feel your softness . . .

How are your nails? *LOL*

Janell chuckled out loud at the thought, then turned to see if the womyn sitting next to her noticed. Her heart jumped as she heard the pilot welcoming them to Maine. She took another look at the black-and-white picture she found on the Net herself after Dana told her about an article that a Maine newspaper had run on her. Janell figured that they might have a Web site, and that if there was an article on her with a picture, she might be able to find it. She was quite excited when she did, and found that Dana was a very intelligent-looking, attractive womyn. She held on to the image of the face in the picture, imagining the way she must look in person, envisioning the hue of her skin, the texture of her hair, the thickness of her lips, the whiteness of her teeth, all in relation to the black-and-white picture. *She does look like a gentlewomyn,* she thought. *A gentlewomyn and a scholar.* She chuckled at Dana's self-description. She was anxious to see her in person.

And now, specialgrl would meet gntlwmn and their fantasies would hopefully become realities, their voices would exist outside of their imaginations. Their faces would be three-dimensional, not Janell's scanned, polished image or Dana's black-and-white newspaper photo. Their blemishes would be uncovered, their words unedited.

※

Dana hops up as the announcement is made that flight number 2318, arriving from California with connections through Chicago, will be disembarking at gate number three on the upper deck. She stands. She sits. She pulls out the picture again, takes another long stare, and stands again . . . She brushes her pants, pulls down her shirt. She runs her hand over her hair. *She's here,* she thinks, then she pulls out the placard she had made for Janell.

Janell walks out with the crowd, anxious to meet Dana yet worried that she will not recognize her. But Dana assured her, humorously, that there wouldn't be very many wimmin who looked like her in Maine. Janell walks into the terminal and sees a beautiful, full-figured dyke smiling pleasantly and holding a sign that says SPECIALGRL ;) in bold, purple letters. At the same time a voice on the airport speaker says, "Welcome to Maine, the way life should be."

He Makes Love Like a Woman

by Carl Weber

When I was eighteen, I was working in a strip club and I ran into this nigga named Black who I really cared about. He was real smooth and told me everything I wanted to hear. Like most young sisters, I confused good sex with love and I ended up giving him my money. I didn't mind giving Black my money, though. Especially since he kept tellin' me how much he loved me and that he planned on marrying me when we had enough money. But after a while he started beating on me and when the beatings got real bad, I had to cut his ass loose.

I'd tried guys and that didn't work so I looked to chicks. I'd been attracted to females ever since I was a kid and experimented so chicks weren't a real problem. There's nothin' in the world like a sexy sister. Don't get me wrong, I like guys, too, but the way women make love is so completely different from the gruffness of a man. There is nothing in the world like the gentle touch of a woman when she kisses your breasts, or the expertise she has when she goes down on you. Try as hard as you want, some things you just can't teach a man. Or so I thought.

By the time I was twenty, my older sister had joined me in the strip club. I don't know why she didn't wanna learn from my mistakes, but six months later she'd hooked up with a brother just like Black and ended up pregnant. After she had her baby, I left the streets and came on home permanently. I wasn't stripping as much. For some reason my heart just wasn't in it anymore, plus Black was back in town and I was sick of fucking niggas just to protect me from him. He'd been popping up talking a lot of shit lately and although I don't wanna admit it, I was more than a little scared.

When I got home, my mom was on that crack shit so bad I felt obligated to take care of my brother and nephew. My sister was straight up out of there and the truth is, I was more of a mother to her child than she was. I guess inside I really wanted a baby of my own—someone I could care for and be that family I'd always wanted.

At that point in my life, the only thing I really had besides my little brother and my nephew was my singing. I loved to sing more than anything in the world. Shit, I was good at it. I could sing my ass off and that's what I did every chance I had. I belonged to two churches and was a member of both their choirs. I know it sounds fucked up, a stripper going to church, but God knows the deal. I was doing what I had to do.

My life wasn't great but it wasn't that terrible either. These things were the best I had. That is, until I ran into him. He wasn't all that—short, dark skinned, with dreads and a beard. Truth is, I really don't know why I stopped to talk to him in the first place. Let me stop lying, it was his eyes. From the second he laid his eyes on me that nigga thought he knew me. I remember him asking me for my phone number. I smiled right in his face and gave him some bogus shit. Then I started to walk away but something inside made me go back and get his number.

That's when he handed me some poetry he was writing

and it was real good. So I told him about my singing. He was the first person I'd ever met who was really interested. That's when he asked me for a kiss. Would you believe I almost gave it to him, too. There was something about that brother. I don't know what it was but I kept thinking about him when I got home that night. I didn't even know what kind of car he drove. The nigga could have been a broke ass but it didn't matter. He'd got to me that quick.

I called him at work the next day and set up a date. I knew he wasn't gonna be anything more than a slam-bam-thank-you-ma'am but that was okay. I figured if I wanted to be truly intimate, I woulda called a girl. Truth is I was horny as hell. When he picked me up, I didn't invite him inside. I was too embarrassed. My moms was home and she was high as shit. He asked me if I wanted to go to the movies and I just told him to take me to a hotel.

When we got inside the hotel, Homeboy took off his clothes and got into bed. He propped up a pillow behind him as he watched me undress. He was smiling like he was really looking forward to getting some. When I got all my clothes off it was cold and I couldn't wait to get under the covers. The sex was gonna have to wait till I warmed up a bit. To my surprise the bed was real warm and when he wrapped his arms 'round me so was he. He stared at me with those eyes and I didn't know whether to laugh or cry. He was making me feel like they do on the stories when they make love.

He began to gently kiss my neck the way I like it. I closed my eyes and it was almost as if I was with a woman. I rolled my neck around so he could kiss the on the side and he did. I couldn't help myself, I let out a few moans. He took his time switching between my ears and my neck but not once did he touch any other part of my body. I was getting moist and my nipples were begging to be touched. He must have read my mind because his fingers oh so gently began to rub up against them. I was in heaven and when we made eye contact, I tried to let him know how good it felt.

His lips moved down to my breasts and the way he licked them made my womanhood gush. The way he wrapped those sexy lips around my nipple was driving me crazy and I slowly began to grind my hips. He was moving back and forth between my titties like it was the last time he'd ever see them. I'd never been with a man who was so attentive. Hell, I'd only been with a few women who were that attentive. After he'd given both my titties proper attention he surprised me by kissing his way down to my womanhood. He didn't just shove his tongue inside me or take his hand and open me up like most men. No, he knew exactly what he was doing.

His tongue ran down my pubic hair and found its way right to my clit. When he touched it, I tensed up it felt so good. I looked down at him again, and he smiled before licking me again. My toes curled that shit felt so good. I glanced down at him and he was into it, I mean really into it. I just prayed he wasn't gonna stop and if he had I would have begged him to continue. I was so close to coming it scared me and the pleasure was beginning to become too much. He wrapped his lips around my clit sucking on it gently as his tongue danced on the tip. I couldn't take it anymore and tried to get away but he held on and when I moved he went right with me. Tears of pleasure were falling from my eyes and I felt like I was gonna pass the fuck out.

He eased up, smiling. He knew exactly what he was doing to me. I wanted to say something but I couldn't. I was confused by what he had done to me. He made his way up my body until his face was directly over mine. He didn't say a word, just kissed me, and I liked the taste of myself on his lips.

I slid down between his legs and looked at his thing. It wasn't huge but it wasn't little either. What I did like about it was that it was smooth and didn't have a lot of bumps like some brothers I'd been with. I wasn't really into giving head but I know men like it so I licked him, hoping to return the favor. He jumped when the ball from my pierced tongue touched him. I did it again and he moaned. He was a real gentleman about it. He wasn't like most guys who tried to shove their thing down my throat and hold my head. He let me do what I had to do. I liked that and I could tell he was enjoying himself. After a few minutes he stopped me. Pulling me up, he whispered, "Ride me."

I looked down at him in amazement. How could he know that was my favorite position? I gently took his thing and slid down on it. Damn, that shit felt good. He was the perfect fit for me. As I rode him, he began to suck on my breasts and I have to admit I was wetter than I can ever remember being. I felt the urge to move faster on him and the faster I went the closer I was. He was doing a masterful job on my titties and when I closed my eyes things started to happen. My upper body went rigid and my lower half exploded, sending me to a place I'd never been before. I collapsed on his chest with a smile and surprised myself by kissing him. Then I looked him in those eyes and said, "I love you."

He smiled, almost laughed, then rolled me over on my back. I didn't know what he was thinking but I didn't care. I was feeling something, maybe it wasn't love but it was something. When I was with Black and them I had to say, "I love you." It was just part of that game. But with this brother, I just wanted to say it. I pulled back the covers and looked at his body. It wasn't anything special but it had done special things to me.

"I love you," I told him, again.

"Sure you do." He smiled again, wrapping his arms around me. "Sure you do."

He kissed me and the only thing I could think was that I wanted to give him the same pleasure he'd given me. I began to massage his muscles as his hips began to move him deeper inside of me. As he moved faster, a wave of pleasure hit me and it was hard to concentrate on his pleasure when mine was so great. He was doing it to me again and this time I was going to be ready. This time I was going to savor the moment. When the time had come, our lips were wrapped around each other and my body let loose again but this time was different because his body did also. When he looked at me with those eyes, I could feel the warmth he was splashing into my womb and at that moment I knew I was in love.

We left the hotel that night a couple. He may not have known we were a couple, but we were. When he pulled in front of my house, I refused to get out. No way was I letting to of what had just happened to me. I needed to know he was mine.

"You got a girl?" I asked.

"No."

"You got a wife?" I checked his finger for a mark or wedding ring.

"No."

"What you got?"

"I got you," he smiled.

Then I smiled. I never smiled like that before in my life. He made me feel so good with just a few words. I got out of his car that night but the next day he picked me up and took me home to his moms's. She was a churchwoman and took me in right away like I was her own daughter. Me and him, we're married now and we got three kids counting my nephew. Well, I guess that old cliché about women in the life is wrong in my case. You *can* make a whore into a housewife; you just have to make love like a woman.

Mojo Lover

by Donna Hill

Hot, muggy, the kind of heat that coats the skin, pushes the wetness through the tiny pores of the flesh, covers the body in a thin sheen of dewy dampness. A Bayou heat. Summer heat in Louisiana.

The hot, demanding hands of it fanned across my bare back, eased me toward the porch door and out into the clingy night seeking what I could not see. But I knew it was out there, just beyond the mist hanging over the lazy, lapping river. Hanging like warm breath puffed into the frigid air—waiting, changing.

Frigid, ha, yeah, that's what they call me. At least that's what the men in the dim saloons and sweaty cafés, where I work, call me. Call me Frigid, instead of Chantel when they can't get their grubby, gumbo-stained fingers around the swell of my breasts, their lips locked on to the hard nipples that poke out to taunt them, or their thick, knobby cocks into that damp darkness between my brown thighs. Brown-sugar thighs, I've been told. Frigid. Ha. They know nothing about my heat, my secret, my mojo.

"Cher, what you got so good under them skirts we can't have?" they'd taunt, between long, dribbling swallows of ice-cold tap beer and hurricanes that would have them speaking in tongues before the night was over. I could never tell them.

They wouldn't understand. Neither did I, didn't want to make sense of it no how. Just didn't want it to ever stop being what it was.

So I just stroll by their tables, slinking slow, like the hypnotic drip drip of a faucet, letting their eyes measure every strut, dip, every jiggle, smiling a pussycat smile. If I turned just right at the precise moment, the one hanging lightbulb would cut straight through my thin gauzy dress, give them an eyeful of lush tits, firm high ass, and that dark space between my sugar-brown thighs they couldn't get up in.

Those boys would holler and squeal like tortured pigs, banging the tables and tossing dollar bills at my feet, just to get me to bend over. Look, look down. I never took no money, though. I'd just toss my head back, smile my pussycat smile, and go about my work—wetting the tables and wiping them down.

Sometimes, when it was getting close, close to the time when I knew it wouldn't be much longer—like tonight—and my body hummed and vibrated with electricity, my nipples turned a deep purple, and my swollen clit poked out from between my lips I'd let them touch me—just a quick feel—cool the burn, muffle the humming.

I'd walk even slower between the tables, stopping a moment longer to rub the rag across the chipped and scarred wood. Sway my hips back and forth to the tune of the blues, blowing in time to the stroke of fingers that played on the globes of my behind, squeeze out a note before letting go. Take that quick dip down the valley of my damp blouse, pinching the purple nipples, knowing the flow would come—squeeze out over my puffy clit, between my sugar-brown thighs, wet and sticky in the heat. It would be soon—tonight.

And I'd laugh, laugh at my secret, knowing what awaited

me beneath the overhanging willows, on the bed of the cool waters, in the wake of wet mist. Tonight.

♋

Fresh from the shower with those urging hands at my back, I crossed the creaking threshold, finding my space on the top step of the porch, enough room on the two below to stretch my legs, loosen my thighs, and catch a little breeze. Catch something.

Elbows found their resting place behind me, neck arched back as a single line of sweat trickled down the deep cleft of my naked breasts—eyes closed, waiting.

Behind my lids I could see. Tall, sleek as polished wood. Dark as ebony. Solid as a shadow. A whisper, no more than a ruffle across the flesh. Hairs stand on end. Tonight is now.

Like silk, beaded with satin, long and wet, the tongue licks away the soft, sweet cream from my cunt in slow up-and-down strokes. Tease the clit. Suck it gently. Mojo hears me. No need to speak.

Yes, tonight. Elbows brace my weight. Hard purple nipples jut toward the stars. Hips rise, rotate around the tongue of silk and satin—draw it in with two, three quick pulls of my well-trained cunt.

Hot breath rushes up the dark, wet hole, spreads out, fills me. Fingers, long and hard, caress my flesh with a tenderness that squeezes tears from my closed eyes. Lips on mine, the taste of me on my tongue. The scent of him is everywhere; in the trees, the moist earth, the planks of wood that brace my elbows, cradle my hips.

Stars rain down on us, sear our flesh, making the steam rise from the river as we undulate on the rhythmic crest of its ripples. Glide over and then under the lazy current, submerged in wanton abandon—limbs light as air, mouth open, gulping down the sweet shots of release.

Tremors, beginning deep in my womb, spread like a mad flock of doves, clenching my toes, curling my fingertips. The power of it lifting us to the bed of grass and moss beneath the willows.

Wrapped in the dark embrace, the willow's vines encircle my wrists, ankles, securing them wide and willing. The silk and satin-beaded tongue licks my lashes, traces the bridge of my nose, dips deep into my mouth, circling, dancing, quivering.

My pussycat smile opens and closes begging to be filled. It cries its own river of white tears that soak my gaping thighs. The flesh there trembles.

I cannot cry out, plead, or implore. The bulging thickness fills the hollow of my mouth, stretching my cheeks, teasing the back of my throat. Ribbons of hard muscled thighs clamp the sides of my face, fighting for control, losing the battle on the downstroke—suckled and teased with the tip of tempting tongue. One drop, two, I savor the bittersweet nectar.

An almost animal howl, heavy, deep, inflamed, pierces the night sky, tumbling over and over, scattering the birds, rising the tide of the river, stirring our bed of mint-green grass and moss.

The eager, skillful mouth that moments ago held captive the cock upon which all time and man began was suddenly empty, gaping, needy like a babe hungry for its mother's tit.

I felt then hard and sleek, wet with the pleasure of my mouth—felt it slide down my chin, probing, looking. Swallowed now in the warm valley of my breasts, dripping a dewdrop path of eternity in its wake. Across my belly into the circular hole of my navel—hovering there, taunting me.

Round hips arch, ready, as the vines tighten—stretch wider, the loose thighs higher, legs spread east and west.

Clit, like a pink pearl, slick, pulsing and hard—my tiny cock—needing someone, something to fuck. Tonight.

The weight of his rich, shadowy blackness bears down on my spread-eagle form, light as air, heavy as night.

The head, full, round like the polished knob of an African walking staff, probes against the wet walls of my smile. Wide. Wide. Inch by inch. Creamy flow smooths the entry, pulses like my own heartbeat growing.

Hip-length dreadlocks descend around us in a blanket of black velvet, shutting out the world. Only us now—pumping, grinding.

No words, just sounds tear from my throat. White light dances behind my closed lids. Farther, deeper, the mahogany staff plunges, pries—wider, slower. Maddening.

Shuddering waves of lust electrify, send my body jerking toward the heavens, bound to earth only by the tender vines and the pulsing, pumping shaft that remains locked deep in my pussycat smile.

Hips above me move in a hypnotic, rotating rhythm. Teeth nip the purple nipples—snapping my well-trained cunt open and closed. Silk tongue with satin beads is everywhere at once, even as the African staff swells, beats, meets my heart. My skin sings to its song. Bodies tremble, rising from the bed of grass. Wanting it. Wanting more. Tonight.

"Cher. Cher," croons deep in my ear, hot as a desert wind. Large hands cup the perfect globes of my ass, squeezing the cheeks, kneading. Faster. Pulling me closer.

Vibrations consume me, stiffen my limbs as the cock reaches that hidden place deep within the walls that suck and tease—touches it. The perfectly carved head rubs it, bumps it, strokes it. Delirious now with pleasure, time and space merge as the eruption of eternity splashes within, the promise of forever fills me, and I weep in joyous response.

Tender lips, tinted with honey, kiss away my tears, join my mouth in silent song. Bodies locked into the hereafter begin to beat again, insatiable, eager. Again and again. Over and over.

"Cher," he cries now, the only word in my ear. All I ever need to know or hear.

Night moves toward dawn. The scorching orange sun rises above the horizon, hangs above us, darkening our blacker-than-black skin.

More. Again. All through the day we love, fuck, screw, come again and again. On the waves of the rivers, the bed of moss, the planks of porch wood. Even as the world moves around us, without us. And night returns, then dawn, still we are bound—pushing, pumping, crying, coming—over and again.

A cool breeze slowly sneaks through the willows, ruffles the blades of grass, and we know that our time is near.

My eyes drift open in time to see the shadow and hip-length dreads move in a blink beyond the threshold of my bedroom door.

The scent of him lingers in the air, clings to my skin, crawls through my hair, creeps up between my brown-sugar thighs to whisper good-bye to my smile. "*Au revoir,* Cher."

And I sleep.

When daylight streaks through my window, slowly I rise from the dream that held me captive for three days and nights. My reflection mirrors my mind. Blades of grass cling to the backs of my thighs. Prints from the vines outline my wrists and ankles. My cunt throbs and beats to the tune I sung with him in my head. Clit, still swollen and hard, peeks out from between wet lips. The taste of honey still clings to my mouth. The deep-throated groan of "Cher" burns my ears.

Yet I am alone in my room in the light of day.

I smile. Mojo lover.

❧

Washing down the tables at the saloon, dress clinging to my damp curves, body humming to my Mojo's tune, I smile.

"Where you been, Frigid?" one of my regulars asks as I dip out of the way of groping, gumbo-stained fingers. "Lemme see what you got under those skirts."

I laugh. My pussycat laughs, too, just as I catch a fleeting glimpse in the dulled saloon mirror of a shadow draped in locks of black velvet.

I arch my neck as the single thread of sweat dips between the swell of my breasts. White tears slide down my brown-sugar thighs. The heat is near. I feel it fanning against my back, pushing me out into the night.

About the Contributors

Anne Atall is a scholar of American and Caribbean literature. She enjoys reading modern fairy tales—erotic and otherwise. She lives in America's heartland.

Breena Clarke grew up in Washington, D.C., and was educated at Webster College and Howard University. She is the author of the national best-seller *River, Cross My Heart*, which was an Oprah's Book Club selection. Her writings have appeared in the anthologies *Contemporary Plays by Women of Color* and *Streetlights: Illuminating Tales of the Urban Black Experience*.

Darris is an essayist, book reviewer, fiction writer, lecturer, and public speaker who also works as a college administrator in Washington, D.C., as well as teaching women's studies courses at local colleges. She lives with her partner and mothers two children.

Eric Jerome Dickey is the *New York Times* best-selling author of the novels *Liar's Game*, *Cheaters*, *Milk in My Coffee*, *Sister, Sister*, and *Between Lovers*. He is also a contributor to the photography book *Mothers and Sons* and was one of four contributors included in *To Be Real: Four Original Love Stories*.

Carolyn Ferrell is the author of the short-story collection *Don't Erase Me* and winner of the *Los Angeles Times* Book

Award along with the QPB New Voices Award; she was a finalist for the Barnes and Noble Discover Award. She is also the author of the novel *The Big Book of Fairy Tales*. Her work has been anthologized in *Streetlights, Giant Steps: The New Generation of African American Writers, Children of the Night: The Best Short Stories by Black Writers, 1967 to the Present,* and *The Best American Short Stories.* She has been a Fulbright fellow and currently teaches writing at Sarah Lawrence College.

Lolita Files is the best-selling author of three novels: *Scenes from a Sistah;* its follow-up, *Getting to the Good Part;* and *Blind Ambitions.* Her novels have appeared on a number of best-seller lists, including those of Blackboard and Barnes and Noble, and Ingram's Top 50. Lolita, a native of South Florida and current resident of Los Angeles and South Florida, is a student of pop culture well versed in literature, film, television, and music.

Thomas Glave was the first black gay male writer to win the O'Henry Award since James Baldwin. He is the author of the short-story collection *Whose Song?*—a finalist for the Violet Quill Award.

Reginald Harris is the editor of *Kuumba: Poetry Journal for Black People in the Life.* His work has appeared in online and paper journals such as *Blithe House Quarterly* and *Obsidian II* and anthologies such as *Men on Men 7* and *His3.* A recipient of an Individual Artist Award in Fiction from the Maryland State Arts Council for fiction, he lives in Baltimore.

Donna Hill has penned more than twenty books, *Temptation, Masquerade, Spirit,* and *A Private Affair* among them. Three of her romance novels have been made into movies for BET. Dubbed "the queen of black romance," Hill is also the author of the novel *If I Could*.

Margaret Johnson-Hodge is the author of five novels: *The Real Deal, A New Day, Warm Hands, Butterscotch Blues*, and *Some Sunday*.

Travis Hunter, a native South Carolinian, is a novelist, songwriter, and father. He is the author of the novel *Hearts of Men*. He lives in Stone Mountain, Georgia, with his son, Rashad.

Jennifer Jazz blends narrative and visual art in *Bronx Brazil*, a book funded by the Bronx Council on the Arts. It can be found in the Dia Center for the Arts' Printed Matter Collection in New York.

Robin Coste Lewis teaches fiction writing at Hampshire College. Her writing has appeared in *The Massachusetts Review, The Harvard Gay and Lesbian Review*, and *GCN: A Queer Progressive Quarterly*. Her academic work explores the probable impact of censorship on African-American women writing about sex in the United States during the twenties. She is currently completing a collection of short stories, *Telling the Truth About My Experiences as a Body*. The story included here, "Sausage Boy," was written specifically for an OUTWRITE conference panel. Her goal was to write something lewd and lyrical while making as much mischief as possible.

devorah major works in the Poets-in-the-Schools program in California. She is the author of the novel *An Open Weave* along with *Street Smarts: Poems,* which won a PEN/Oakland Josephine Miles Award for excellence in literature.

Janet McDonald is the author of the memoir *Project Girl*—a finalist for the New Visions Award. A Brooklyn girl who works as an international corporate lawyer in France, she is also the author of the young-adult novel *Spellbound* and currently at work on a sequel to her memoir, to be titled *Paris Girl.*

Bernice L. McFadden is the author of the Blackboard best-seller *Sugar* and the critically acclaimed sophomore effort *The Warmest December.* Toni Morrison has described her work as "riveting." McFadden lives in Brooklyn, where she was also born and raised.

Kim McLarin is the author of the novels *Taming It Down* and *Meeting of the Waters.*

Kathleen Morris is the author of *Speaking in Whispers: Lesbian African-American Erotica.* A follow-up collection is forthcoming. Morris's writing has also appeared in *Best Lesbian Erotica* and several magazines, including *Venus, Women in the Life,* and *Mosaic.* Morris, a native of Mount Vernon, New York, now living in Maryland also facilitates the Erotica Pen, a national workshop series designed to encourage women to discover their creative and sensual powers through the art of writing.

Bruce Morrow is coeditor of the anthology *Shade* (Avon Books) and an associate editor of *Callaloo: A Journal of African American, African and African Diaspora Arts and Letters.* A recipient of a Frederick Douglass Creative Arts Center Fellowship for Young African-American Fiction Writers, his work has appeared in numerous publications, including the *New York Times, Speak My Name: Black Masculinity and the American Dream, Men on Men 2000,* and *Step into a World: A Global Anthology of the New Black Literature.* He lives in New York City and is at work on a novel.

Andrew Oyefesobi, a native of Daytona Beach by way of Nigerian parents, was voted Prom King and Most Likely to Succeed in high school. He discovered the power and sex appeal of writing while interning at a Beverly Hills talent agency and has been writing ever since. He holds a master's degree in journalism from Stanford; his work has appeared in *Vibe.* Oyefesobi is the founder of Urban Prince Publishing and the author of the spicy novel *Sin in Soul's Kitchen.*

Elissa G. Perry's short fiction has appeared in the anthologies Girlfriend Number One and Beyond Definition: New Writing from Gay and Lesbian San Francisco. Her story "Revelation" is excerpted from Ephermeris, a novel in progress. She lives in Santa Monica, California.

Jacqueline Powell is the author of *Someone to Catch My Drift.* She currently resides in St. Louis, Missouri, where she is working on her second novel.

Kiini Ibura Salaam is a writer, painter, and world traveler from New Orleans. Her short stories and essays have been anthologized in *Dark Eros, Dark Matter,* and *Men We Cherish,* and included in *African American Review, Essence,* and other national publications. She is currently writing a novel, *Bloodlines,* and a collection of erotica entitled *Lust Heals.* She lives in Brooklyn.

s smith is a recipient of a Serpent Source Foundation grant, awarded to outstanding artists who are women of color. She has twice participated in the Zora Neale Hurston/Richard Wright Foundation Writer's Week. s smith currently resides in Oakland, California, where she is working on a collection of poetry.

Camika Spencer is a native of Dallas, Texas, who was a bookseller at Black Images before she became a writer. After writing two novels that went unpublished by traditional venues, she wrote a third and published it herself. akimac publishing made such an impression in Dallas that *When All Hell Breaks Loose* was picked up by a major publishing house and became a Blackboard best-seller.

TaRessa Stovall coauthored *A Love Supreme: Real-Life Stories of Black Love*. TaRessa, a native of Seattle, has been a writer since age seven. Her poetry has won awards and appeared in national magazines. Her plays have been produced throughout the Pacific Northwest and in Chicago. TaRessa is coauthor of *Catching Good Health: An Introduction to Homeopathic Medicine* and author of the young-adult book *The Buffalo Soldiers*.

Cheo Tyehimba is an award-winning journalist and former senior editor and staff reporter of *Code* and *Entertainment Weekly* magazines, respectively. He has written for the *Washington Post*, *Writer's Digest*, *Vibe*, *People*, and *George*, among other publications. He is working on *Carving from the Rock*, a novel excerpted here.

Carl Weber wears the two hats of bookseller and writer. Shortly after he was awarded the Blackboard Bookseller of the

Year Award in 2000, he published his first novel, *Lookin' for Luv*. He is also the author of the novel *Married Men*.

Krystal G. Williams was born in Jackson, Mississippi, in 1965. She received her undergraduate degree from Rice University in Houston, Texas, where she double-majored in English and legal studies. She is currently a full-time technical writer and mother of two. Her motto—"Too many words, not enough paper"—has helped her publish several romance novels, a play for her alma mater, and a planning guide for family reunions. She currently makes her home in Texas.

Jacqueline Woodson is the award-winning author of many novels and picture books for young readers, including the Maizon trilogy, *The Other Side, Lena, I Hadn't Meant to Tell You This* (a Coretta Scott King Honor Book), *The House You Pass on the Way, From the Notebooks of Melanin Sun, If You Come Softly,* and *Miracle's Boys* (also an Honor Book). Among her other titles are *Autobiography of a Family Photo: A Novel* and the anthology *A Way Out of No Way: Writings about Growing Up Black in America*.

Bil Wright, recipient of a Millay Fellowship, is a fiction writer, playwright, and poet. His debut novel, *Sunday You Learn How to Box*, was published to much acclaim. His fiction and poetry have appeared in *Men on Men 3, The Road Before Us, Shade*, and many other anthologies. His plays have been produced in the United States and Germany and published in the anthology *Tough Acts to Follow*. He lives in New York City.

About the Editor

Retha Powers is a writer and editor whose journalism and essays have appeared in national publications such as *USA Today, Essence, Glamour, Ms.,* and the anthology *Skin Deep: Black Women and White Women Write About Race.* She serves as executive editor of Quality Paperback Book Club, a division of Bookspan, and lives in New York City.

Acknowledgments

The editor wishes to express gratitude to the writers herein who conjured up passionate and thoughtful tales told through the lens of the erotic. She also wishes to thank her agent, Neeti Madan, for her tremendous support and friendship, and her editors Amy Einhorn and Sandra Bark. Kathleen Morris's referrals to many fine writers and the creative input of Christopher Nickelson were also invaluable.

Made in the USA
Las Vegas, NV
20 December 2022